This special signed edition is limited to 1000 numbered copies.

This is copy __720__.

THE BIG CRUSH

THE BIG CRUSH

David J. Schow

Subterranean Press 2019

By David J. Schow

new

3/19

The Big Crush
Copyright © David J. Schow, 2019.
All rights reserved.

Dust jacket illustration by Timothy R. Bradstreet.
Copyright © Timothy R. Bradstreet, 2019.
All rights reserved.

Interior design by Desert Isle Design, LLC.
Copyright © Desert Isle Design, LLC, 2019.
All rights reserved.

First Edition

ISBN
978-1-59606-902-2

Subterranean Press
PO Box 190106
Burton, MI 48519

subterraneanpress.com

Black Leather Required: **davidjschow.com**
https://www.facebook.com/david.j.schow

Manufactured in the United States of America

Dave

There's a reason why they call it a "crush."

If you were ever a high-school level student, your first pangs of unrequited love were probably suffered during a severe hormonal onslaught that generally occurs when you are most powerless; no longer a child, not quite an adult. Statistics vary. The damage is universally known across all cultures and brackets. But stop kidding yourself; you know what is meant here: the one you carry in a special, private pocket of your heart for the rest of your life.

That one. *The* one.

Wistful recollect of it is sometimes obscured, but not displaced, by equally potent statistics—such as the memory of whomever captured your virginity, or the first time you saw your own blood. Car wrecks. Hasty marriage.

Nevertheless, you have a name or a face in your mind right now.

The person who escaped your grasp, or never noticed you. The person who seemed so far above you that you could never aspire to them, or muster the courage to try. The one unattained...and unattainable. Maybe they moved, slipped away, or metamorphosed into something less desirable. Other similar grail-people happen along later in life, but all they do is remind you of the first one.

Youth is loud, and the world goes on. If your formative years were spent trying to figure out the latter half of the 20th Century, you witnessed the awakening of a sleeping dragon called the Internet, and if you courted this technology, you might find yourself on the brink of middle age, perhaps as a parent or divorcee or the unwilling incubator of some baffling new medical condition. You learned to drink, to drive, and some learned to drink *and* drive. Bills. Errands. Responsibilities. If you're lucky, you've only seen the inside of a courtroom in passing. If unlucky, you've seen the inside of a jail cell or worse. An "ordinary" life, not even counting battles or wars or holocausts. Getting by. Making it to the next day. Being a grownup.

When your life-clock turns irrevocably to double digits, at age ten, all you have behind you is childhood. At twenty, all you have behind you is an additional decade mostly squandered in being a teenager. At thirty, you have another decade to account for, one during which you were supposed to have made something of yourself. That's why thirty hits some people so hard.

It's no coincidence that one possible fate of the entire universe is called the Big Crunch. Because the Big Crush can destroy your world… what there is of it, especially when you're a teenager.

And it's the micro-universe of DNA that causes you to feel the need to kill yourself, like *immediately,* seeing as how it's *the absolute end* as you know it.

We gussy it up with all sorts of civilized dressage, but at the core we are all viruses hardwired to eat, excrete, and make more viruses.

And kill, not to put too fine a point on it.

While the pubescent flashflood of biochemicals brings on unlovely acne, menstrual periods and distressing weight and growth shifts, it is also responsible for a panoply of *urges.*

Create or procreate. Eat and excrete. Destroy.

Kill.

Die if you cannot.

In the mainstream heterosexual gridlock of things, once the available females sprout breasts, it's basically all over for the males. Men should look women in the eyes when speaking to them, at least once in awhile for propriety's sake, but women should also acknowledge that men are doomed by their genetics, persistent goblins who constantly scream *you must fuck that* inside their heads.

The living hell of high school—prime time for the Big Crush—is usually when the tits emerge and the boys turn into slavering hounds. Hormonally, they're all drug addicts via positive reinforcement, like the rat pressing the cheese button until it dies.

It has nothing to do with personality and everything to do with those fizzing brain compounds that command you to reproduce. Beauty and love are just some of the lies with which civilized humans complicate this biological mandate. Just observe Mr. Cheese Rat, above, when given the opportunity to copulate with a female until she dies. Or watch dolphins rape a wounded shark until *it* dies.

Watch high schoolers get impregnated and then blame it on recreational drugs. We are a culture self-immolated by handy excuses. Without all our excuses and rituals, the idea of seduction would still be stuck at *bash 'em in the head and take what you want.* Bash 'em with a club, or money, or trinkets, or pheromones, but get in there and start bashing, young amoeba.

The Big Crush is a biochemical train wreck of all these loopy imperatives and more. That hollow ache in your chest is not love. It's hunger.

Just watch what happens when the governors are deactivated, when the human mind boils away to fight-flight-or-fuck. It becomes pure survival. Today, we call many examples psychotics or sociopaths. Tomorrow we'll call them something new, but the chemistry is always the same.

Sometimes the Big Crush yields headliners and miscreants in fast-forward. More often, it settles into a back lobe of the brain to fester for a lifetime. Think gangrene versus amputation; eventually the rot drops off either way to leave in its place a phantom pain from something that no longer physically exists.

David J. Schow

Being civilized, most of us tamp down the Neanderthal to lock in his or her proper cage the moment maturity looms. This leaves us free to fantasize about the ones who "got away" or never were. One manageable heartstring, trailing away into the distant fog of past young adulthood. Or several. But you dip into that memory well more often than you'd care to freely admit.

The next thing you have to worry about is how a quarter of a century could have passed so *fast*.

And let's face it: Once you've been rejected or discarded, betrayed or fucked over, doesn't the caveperson within you really wish that the people from your past would just do the decent thing and die once they were finished with you? Flush the flotsam, cleanse the slate, move on. You don't want them to "have a nice life." You want them to suffer for underestimating you. To resurge, all damaged, to beg for your help so you can refuse them.

Still, how did this one or that one have the ungodly power to make your heart speed up, twenty-five years after the non-fact?

That's how it was for me with Dalia Villareal, "Daisy" to her circle.

She said maybe eight complete sentences to me in her entire high school career. I was completely gunshy, inexperienced, fearful and clueless. Crushed, was I, back then.

I had no fucking idea how bad it could get.

So now you have become an adult, full of missed opportunities and accelerating years, and you have become reasonably adept at surfing the tides of what is called social media, it might occur to you to see if you could ferret out the tiniest sliver of updated intel on one of your long-losts. Family sites, genealogy sites, and reunion sites all beckon.

You linger there, knowing your time could be wasted better.

You let that urge take control. *I wonder whatever happened to...?*

But eventually, you click on a name.

Word of advice: *Don't.*

It could cost you your life.

If you'd like to lose all hope for the survival of humanity as a species, check out any Internet chat-comments section. There you will witness what are presumed to be fellow bipeds, spewing forth their true rancid natures under the delusion they are electronically anonymous, out of reach and beyond meaningful retaliation. You don't need an opposable thumb to log a comment on anything; perhaps that is why so many of them are all rendered in lower-case letters.

Know this: You have left a digital footprint anywhere and everywhere you have ever been on the web. Encryption helps but is only a stopgap. For most regular folks, leaving a comment online is like thumbtacking a note to a phone pole at a busy intersection—you have no control over who reads it. It doesn't take a Mensa superstar to suss out a spoor-track of numerals. Worse, most people are so besotted by the temptations of the information superhighway that they don't bother to learn concealment, or are too lazy-stupid to figure it out. Just look at how many of them post pictures of themselves with their lamentable shithole apartments clearly visible behind them, or their tragic peasant bathrooms.

There are whole second, third, and fourth-tier users out there smarter than you, more cautious than you, and more deeply determined than your casual addiction to entertainment or distraction, or your shallow need to feel that some stranger might give an honest crap about little ole you.

And that's not even counting government hellhound watchdogs, spies, secret agents, stolen identity brokers, or homicidal maniacs with a flair for the digital.

For most people with a clutch of functioning neurons left, social media had metastasized into a shrieking imposition that made the old-fashioned telephone ring seem quaint and benign. Constant contact with everybody you've ever met? It seemed too close to the brain implants everybody feared half a century ago. So you turn off the phone or ignore it, and promptly get several million text messages, the over-riding concern of which is *why didn't you hit me back?*

Everybody is five again, on the playground, shoving.

If I really wanted you to catch my point, I would have limited this to fewer than 140 characters. Not less than. Fewer than. But the people who might benefit from such news are already incapable of reading it.

Because reading is *sooo* 20th Century.

You had to admit, though, that just as fax machines displaced snail mail and "mobile devices" displaced everything two weeks older, email pretty much put paid to the antique idea of correspondence.

Nostalgia is a trap, and everyone thinks their nostalgia beats every-one else's. Nostalgia should come with a Surgeon General's warning sticker. Too many people default to *better then, worse now,* and let it bottleneck their lives.

Daisy Villareal's 1987 yearbook photo was nothing special. You'd never look twice at it. I found it on the Internet.

Through a haze of improper scanning blur and the tweed effect of inadequate pixelization, the tiny photo depicted a dark-haired girl in a graduation collar (because it was a senior class picture), bangs, high cheekbones, wide, winning smile, gaze not offsides but directly facing down the camera, eyes a bottomless, sparkling black.

The first time I saw her was two years earlier, sophomore class homeroom. Her hair was indescribably thick and she smelled like fresh laundry that had dried in the sunlight. The brown stains of dental fluorosis that mottled her teeth were due to the metal content of the available water during her childhood in Pueblo Nuevo, Mexico. Because of this, Daisy rarely smiled, and took pains to conceal her mouth from anyone who might look at it.

A year later, she was wearing braces, and the brown streaks were gone. Her smile was worth the wait.

Her voice was mellifluous, not the birdy chatter of many of her cohorts.

One of the rare times she spoke to me directly was during a career quiz in homeroom. Some government genius had concocted a book-let library that was supposed to guide you toward your most likely calling, based on a 100-question test, yes or no, from *strongly agree* to *strongly disagree*. Your tallied score related to a series of numbered booklets outlining jobs for which you were most likely suited, accord-ing to the test.

For the test, and for this test only, my class was redistributed so that I wound up sitting right behind her.

Mid-high school, I thought I wanted to be a writer. I sneaked a look at the booklet titled WRITER. It might as well have read PICK ANOTHER BOOKLET.

The two runners-up were JOURNALISM and LIBRARIAN.

Thanks a buttload, Students Assets Corporation of Galveston, Texas, Smasher of Dreams, Reiver of Aspirations, Big Brother to the Lock-Step. Make sure everybody works in the proper widget factory, you Nazi pods, you Orwellian non-people...

At which point Daisy said to me: "You should be a librarian, I mean, you like books and all of that stuff."

Then she turned her back on me. She was wearing a bra now; I could see the topography against her floral blouse.

That was one of the Eight Official Sentences, apart from conversa-tional nods and grunts, hallway murmurings that might acknowledge your existence, but granted you no status.

A *librarian*. What I should be. Not the sex fantasy of a foxy-booklady photo-spread, but a dusty academic filed away in a room where every-body has to keep quiet.

Dismissed, all at once, is what I was.

My then-latest stepmother was no help, either. She once tried to box me into that conversation parents force on their offspring, the *what-do-you-want-to-do-when-you're-grown-up?* trick question that asserts (a) you are far from grown up, and (b) you'd better have a job when we kick you out of the house.

I said, "I think I'd really like to be a writer."

She said, "No, seriously."

I left home at age seventeen, after quitting school and taking my equivalency. I miraculously aced the English section of the ACT tests, which won me several semesters at a university before I got bored with that.

But you want to know more about Dalia. Daisy.

A Tri-Hi-Club photo on page 47 showed her legs. Mesmerizing even then, in flat, sensible loafers.

Goddamn the Internet; this was worse than porn.

Daisy was in the photograph, but not in the Tri-Hi's. She had accidentally wandered across the background of the shot, taken by one of those erstwhile newshounds on the Yearbook Committee. She appeared nowhere else in the yearbook files online; evidently, she had not been a joiner.

After our freshman snapshots came out so dark we looked like zoo specimens shocked tharn by a sudden bright light, I and a fellow named Andrew Kopelanski made sure we never sullied the yearbook again.

Plus, my formerly even café-au-lait complexion fomented a sebaceous revolution, and I determined to keep my rampant acne off the public record. All at once, I knew how self-conscious Daisy had felt about her teeth.

Self-doubt in a high-school student? Alert the media!

There was one more junior-year photo of Daisy to be thieved, her mouth pressed into an enigmatic smile to conceal the braces. And that was it. Three pictures and an ungainly, embarrassing flood of memory.

Short story shorter: There were all sorts of contact and marry-up options on the available Locator dot-coms.

There were a hundred and sixty Dalia Villareals currently living in the United States, which rattled my notion of what I thought was a unique name. In my youthful ardor I had neglected to record a middle name or initial, or any of the stalker-y specific intel most obsessives normally amass by reflex. I had a name and a tiny New Mexico town from over twenty-five years ago.

Worse, Dalia had probably gotten married. Was graying by now. Weighed nine thousand pounds and had fourteen kids.

Are you the Dalia ("Daisy") Villareal who attended San Andres High School in Las Cruces (Mesilla) 1985–87? Forgotten classmate (Derek) David Vollmand here, checking in from the mists of time via the unblinking eye of the Internet. I never did pick that "Librarian" booklet and came out much better for it. I hope you are as beautiful as always and that your life has gone spectacularly. Cheers, DDV.

That was the message. Innocent enough, except for that completely gratuitous "beautiful." Signing off "love" just would have been too repulsive. Now all that remained was to hit SUBMIT. Like "crush," "submit" also has more than one meaning.

About two years ago, out of the clear blue, a guy I knew shortly after I had fled the homestead tried to ping me on Facebook. Rex Tolacheck had been the son of a Mormon Treasury agent when I met him. Good source for dope. His contact had a federal kickback number attached to it and I realized Rex was doing hard time. Worse, thanks to the contact, the government was probably reviewing drug references in my past eight bazillion emails, right now.

I never friended Rex.

But if you don't drop the line in the water, you'll never hook anything. In olden days, that meant you got to starve.

SUBMIT. I did.

In four days flat I got a response from the real girl herself.

Every computer in the world should have a button marked TAKE IT BACK. A convenient time-travel option that permits the withdrawal of bad choices, or the elimination of the wrong keystroke for the fumble-fingered.

TAKE IT BACK. Be careful what you wish for.

My driver's license says my name is Derek David Vollmand, but now I'm not so sure. My passport says the same thing. If somebody said, "prove it," what would you do? Assemble witnesses, drag out paperwork? Witnesses can be bought and documents faked. Otherwise, WitSec—the Federal Witness Protection Program—would never work, and they've vanished thousands of people successfully, and legally, since they fired up in 1971.

And if you know how to protect, relocate, and give new identities to that many people, successfully and legally, doesn't it stand to reason that you could shave points for yourself? Amass a wallet-load of utterly vaporous credit cards, say, or pull Social Security checks under ten different names? Be five people, have thirty bank accounts, and skim multiple lucrative tax refunds?

And that's just *one* legitimate way. Many more people can utilize "dirt" methods, as in down-and-dirty. All you really need to do is hijack some dead person's Social Security number, or easily process a brand-new one for as many other people as you'd like to be, census be damned.

The whole idea is to get you to think hard about the people you think you know. Most people don't bother. Constant terrorist and fiscal panic keep their attention on subsistence, not diversion. Narcotics and entertainment reel up the slack left by consumer urges. Everybody crawls along in the same gutter, not stopping to wonder whether the person next to them is who he or she says they are.

Like me: Derek David Vollmand, Dave to my intimates, these days. I used to be David Kemp. Because of assorted scams against that name, I had it legally changed to a different family name. The Derek was short for Darius, which I retired because it struck people as pretentious. It's easier to change your name than you might think, unless you, too, have done it. I knew several past people who did so in order to clean up their credit, or blindside stalking exes, or simply to reset their personality. Half the people in the country who get married change their names, and therefore their identities, and no one bats an eyelid.

Not so long ago I would have told you that Dave Vollmand was what you got. That he had never committed a crime worth mentioning, had never sought to alter or obscure his identity for criminal reasons, and had never lied or misrepresented the facts to authorities in a destructive way, except for trying to con a meter maid into letting his parking violation slide (it didn't work).

When Dave Vollmand told people his job was watching movies for a living, they tended to disbelieve it, but never asked if his name was real. Curious, that.

Are you really you? How do you know?

I'll skip the part about how intrepid wannabe writer Me wound up staring at flatscreens for a living wage, at a place called Starburst Post.

The second thing most people say when they hear about this gig is, "Oh, that must be sooo fun." Actually, it requires a grueling amount of concentration and an almost mandarin focus.

(The first thing they say is always, "No, I mean, what's your *real* job?")

If I want to drive my interrogators away, I unleash a dazzling spiel about bi-directional inter-frame macroblocking, artifacting, digital noise, edge enhancement, hue halos, upsampling, bit budgets, region coding, lossless compression, luminance versus chrominance, rotational latency, interlacing, psychoacoustic theory, and by now your eyelids are getting heavy...you are getting *sleeeeeepy...*

David J. Schow

The job goes like this: I sit in a very comfortable, soundproofed room with several large state-of-the-art flatscreens to technically vet the DVDs you rent, buy or download—the official versions, the commercial releases. The last thing I want to do is pay any attention whatsoever to plot, character, camerawork or cutting. I'm there to acid-test the presentation, and frequently, I have to do it in two or more passes. I'm looking for everything from substandard picture and sound to glitches and manufacturing defects, and judging if and how these should be redressed by logging copious notes.

Now, try to *not* pay attention to a movie while you're watching it, and I don't mean by eating your fingernails or texting someone. Not allowed. It is very much like trying to shift your critical eye to seek things ordinary humans would never perceive.

I become the walking avatar of human error, very much like those Internal Affairs officers that all policemen are supposed to despise. If your DVD passes muster, nobody catches hell. But there's generally something wrong with every disc ever pressed or burned. Premise, conclusion, simple math.

What's strangest of all is that in order to "watch a movie" I have to do it at home or a cinema, even though I may already have "seen" it five times. Movie theaters are better since they immerse you in darkness—or used to—but that experience is quickly waning into the boutique realm of opera or ballet. Loading up a disc at home quickly feels too much like going back to work. You say you love movies? Think twice.

Hanging out at some dismal bar and courting shop talk is an even more depressing idea. You can't find a watering hole any more that doesn't have giant screens screaming at you all the time. Then you go home to indulge the Internet, if you haven't caught up already on your mobile device. More screens. To paraphrase a great musician, the outdoors is what I go through to get from a lobby to a parking lot. I came to think the worst thing that could ever happen to me was a power outage.

My roomie for the past year was named Kingi, pronounced "King G," as in Godzilla. He used to be somebody else's dog. Full-blown German Shepherd short-hair, classic saddle, beautiful casket-shaped head almost entirely black. We met one evening when I was returning from a short stroll to pick up mail. I never receive mail at my home address; only a fool would. A drop-box place presented itself a comfortable fifteen-minute walk from my current roost, a cluttered, too-small Studio City apartment I had somehow avoided vacating for the better part of the past decade. Bills needed someplace else to land. Someplace secure; I used to get mail stolen a lot. The crew there was amiable and pleasant, recent high school graduates all bound for better lives. They handled packages and cured many shipping headaches by giving me a house account; they dutifully notified me if anything interesting showed up. Walking there was a good excuse to air myself out, particularly after spending an entire day peering owlishly into one screen or another.

After the rest of the world got done boozing and fucking off for New Year's, 2010, I walked to my mailbox to see what the first cull of the fresh year had brought, kind of like when you wake up, check messages, and the first message of the day sets the tone for the rest of that day. The previous few days had been a dead zone of no calls, no messages, no mail. Everyone else on the outside had spent that time fiercely pretending too hard to have too much fun before their next Back to Work Monday in order to soldier fatalistically onward to Wednesday—Hump Day—and grind toward the rewards of a Finally Friday, whereupon they proceeded to get and stay shitfaced and comatose on their drug of choice, the whole catalogue from liquor to Ecstasy, from sex to—you guessed it—emptying their minds into a screen. Later they could boast about what they had done when they were like, *sooo* fucked up. Great when you're in your twenties and can still process the damage; not so great when you can see forty from here. You either fight to remain a post-teenager or you grow the hell up. I didn't know many of the former any more; they had become too tiresome as clubs got louder and music got stupider. I didn't know many of the latter, either, because they tended to bitch too much about how they were no longer the former. You know—the ones who peaked in high school, and are still talking about it, ignoring the fact that your eyelids have lumbered to the point where you have to choose between killing yourself to get free, or killing them to make them shut the hell up.

Two blocks from my place there was a dead dog who had been unceremoniously dumped on the shoulder of Laurel Canyon, mostly hidden from view in the debris that piles up in the spillways near the overpass at the stone canal called the L.A. River, even though, I mean *look* at it—it's a canal. Man-made; always was.

Sad. I paused just for a moment, to wonder what kind of person would run down a dog and then just abandon their crime to one side of the road like rainwash flotsam. Somebody distracted by their yowling offspring or texting while driving; somebody who quickly reevaluated their crushing schedule, thought *cripes, I don't need THIS shit*, quickly looked around for witnesses, and then just as quickly disposed of this uninvited speedbump in their busy day.

And then I heard an ephemeral little whine.

The dog's eyes were dull, but open, glassy-brown and looking at me, wondering what I was doing there, a pedestrian in a city where nobody walks anywhere. That tiny sound he made sounded like a last gasp, for sure, as though this creature was asking, *You're the only other lifeform I see around here, do you give a damn?*

I had never actually saved anything before in my life.

This guy's left side was bloody and broken, which meant he had most likely been centerpunched while crossing the span of northbound lanes and had not even made it halfway. His left front leg looked snapped, guaranteed, and his shallow breathing meant a couple of ribs had been sundered, too. He had taken the hit mostly on his left shoulder, and lost a couple of teeth in the process. Maybe he had not been dumped. Maybe he had flown here via vehicular propulsion, or crawled this far to find a place to give up.

There was a veterinarian's office on Ventura Boulevard. I'd passed it a million times on my way to and from Starburst Post. I ran the rest of the way back to my apartment, gunned my Infiniti, and slewed it to block the outmost lane right at the overpass. I didn't ever want to feel again the way I felt when the dog first saw me run away. I lifted him and he came up like an eighty-pound bag of wet rice, unprotesting, even though he had to be in a lot of pain. I laid him down as gently as I could across the junk dump of papers and DVDs in my backseat. His blood got all over everything. Didn't matter.

He had a jangle of tags and numbers attached to a chain collar, but nothing with a name. No license. There was a mutilated tine of metal that suggested one or more tags might have blown off on impact. Later I searched for evidence in the street and found none. One of the remaining tags was cryptically stamped *King of the Monster Fighters*, nothing else. Maybe this guy's name was King, typical for a German Shepherd moniker, but he did not seem to respond to that name when spoken.

A very nice animal doctor named Marion Fuller scrambled all systems to high alert when I came in the door at the pet clinic, scaring the other two customers there with my blood and bluster, and especially freaking out a fluffy Persian in a pet carrier that had been aimed right at the door. Pet clinics always smell like medicine and hint at imminent death. You can always hear a critter or two somewhere in the back, invisibly, yelping to be set free, or mewling because they know they are on Death Row.

I told Dr. Fuller my amateur speculations while she rushed us into an exam room so the Dog with No Name could be assessed. She hollered for an assistant and a portly young woman rushed to help, clad, I guess, as a candy-striper version of a real vet. I filled out forms with shaking hands. I knew the gaze these people were giving me, even the citizens in the waiting area. They all thought I had done the ugly damage myself, and was now making up a story like a contrite wife-beater.

The candy-striper girl, Beatrice, was assigned to notify the contacts that remained on the dog's tags. Before Dr. Fuller emerged from the back, Beatrice informed me that the phone number stamped on one badge was no longer in service. There was an email contact there, too. I was told we would just have to wait and see. Responsibility had already flown out of my hands. There was nothing else for me to do here. I had been dismissed.

By morning, all I could think about was how the drama might have climaxed. I called the vet's before they could call me. A different assistant told me Mr. No-Name was going to live, but that he was also running up a huge bill and needed certain decisions made before more progress could be enacted. The standout detail was that none of the information on any of the tags was any good. No response, no messages. A lot of scenarios were in play, foremost of which was the notion of vacationing owners. The dog had not been micro-chipped and there were no ear tattoos or other ID.

"This happens a lot, actually," the girl on the phone said with grim finality.

I burned rubber back to the hospital with the dog's blood now dry on my backseat. One credit card swipe later, I got to visit what I had rescued.

Cleaned of dry blood, the dog looked fifty percent better. His leg was in a cast, his ribs were bound up, and there were several huge, suppurating dressings dotting his hindquarters. An IV had him dopey and unresponsive, except for his breathing—slow and steady, with a periodic snort through his big black nose, as though he was sighing, tired of this circus already—and his eyes, which tried to keep track of things a couple of beats behind the curve. When I put my hand on his head, his tail rose and fell in a single leaden thump.

"Marion—that's Doc Fuller—she was with this guy until three A.M.," said the daytime duty doctor, who was named Ernest DiFalco, and was the man who had the most framed certificates strewn around the office. "You were right. He was either hit by a car or dropped from a great height. I'm thinking the bumper of one of those steroidal pickup trucks, from the impact elevation. He's got a little internal bleeding but he was very lucky, all things considered. He's going to need a canine dentist to extract the shattered teeth; that's a surgery we don't do here. Thing is, we can't find an owner. We have no idea who he belongs to, or whether he's far from home. He actually looks like a K9 to me, or a service-trained dog."

"How can you tell?" I said.

He peeled back the dog's lips to expose the gums. "Look at that. I think there was a tattoo there—but it's been lasered. Marion missed it because of all the blood."

He didn't need to explain. It had been frantic. I had been there to watch Marion Fuller battle to save the dog's life.

"Now look here."

DiFalco gently probed the space between the dog's shoulder blades. "See that scar? That's where a microchip *would* have been. Everything about this guy screams service dog."

The scar was miniscule. "How big is the chip?" I said. I had no idea.

"About the size of a grain of rice. It's injected via syringe—'inject to protect,' and all that. But it would have to be cut out—that's why the scar."

"Almost like somebody erased his identity."

DiFalco smiled. "Well, good Samaritan that you are, you can give him a new one, yes?"

This anonymous canine had become incredibly important to me in record time, and I couldn't explain why, exactly. It just happened. I said, "Can you chip him again?"

"Sure. It's not traumatic. Costs about thirty bucks, and he's in our database forever."

"Then do it. Whatever it takes."

"I'm glad to hear you say that. Because here's the part everyone hates." DiFalco handed over a clipboard fat with forms. "Everybody starts with a name. We've got to call Mr. Dog Doe something. Any ideas?"

I recalled the tag that said *King of the Monster Fighters*. One of the DVDs I had vetted for domestic release was the vintage 2-in-1 of the original Japanese 1954 *Gojira*, the first-ever movie about that big, atomic firebreathing dinosaur, resurrected now into a co-issue with *Godzilla, King of the Monsters*—the American recut featuring insert scenes with a very young-looking Raymond Burr. Forget the sniggering slacker disdain for all the subsequent juvenile sequels toplining the Big G as some dude in a floppy cartoon monster suit, pulling wrestling moves on an army of other dudes in suits even more ridiculous; the original was a fairly somber parable about Japan's legacy of nuclear destruction. King G. I wrote it down as Kingi.

Later, I pondered the whole Monster Fighter thing long enough to figure it out. Shepherds were always the first line of defense against the living dead, mummies, aliens, in dozens of movies. Always a GSD, walking point for humankind's protection. Once you see the pattern it's impossible to ignore.

To this day, Kingi will lend a warning bark if he sees a monster approaching on my flatscreen. That was his covenant, his side of our deal. His job was to stay on the lookout for monsters.

He was mine from that day forward, convalescence and all.

My nominal best human friend is a fellow named Hayden Mathis, who—surprise—designs DVD snapcase art for the great consuming masses. Ex-publicity, fellow divorcé, comfortably bipolar, as concerned as I am that the trend toward direct download of entertainment fodder might somehow jeopardize our employment jacket. Hayden has wild, bleached surfer hair, intense little gold glasses, and some internal gyro utterly in sync with the Earth's gravity; the kind of guy who might stumble but never falls down to shatter his bones, and if he were to take a tumble, he knows how to instinctively slap the ground to absorb the impact, the way stuntmen do. Some people stub a toe and their whole week is gone. Hayden could take the hit, duck the pain, and keep marching. He has a grip like an industrial vise, so when he shakes your hand, he is intentionally gentle. His hands got veiny and blocky from bucking boxes for Fed Ex over two years, then he segued into the confabulation of images, which left him staring at a screen most of the time, too. I've known him for going on four years.

I asked him about the whole high school-heartthrob syndrome over label-less bottles of a pretty good craft brew from Junkyard Duck in Seattle. We were idly glancing at an aircheck disc of an action shoot-'em-up called *Short Fuse 2: Flashfire* in the stacked clutter of my too-small apartment—the one I kept talking about moving out of. I had successfully forestalled the willful labor of relocating with the narco-tizing slouch that comes from staying put. Kingi was newly-walked and now parked near the sofa. Action movies were a bore to him.

"Oh, god," Hayden said. "Lola Wiseman. She was the daughter of my eighth grade health teacher." Hayden was able to call up the memory in a fingersnap, just like most people if they were honest about them-selves. No hem, no haw, there it was and always had been.

"Some genius linked up the boys' and girls' Phys Ed classes to learn square-dancing for two weeks," Hayden said. "It busted up all the little cliques because the instructors were guest-stars from another school, and they got to randomly pick who danced with whom. I got to dance with Lola, who was one of those rah-rah future student body president-and-valedictorian types, right? Polite and cheery to everyone but with a clear sense of caste, because she was at the top? Here she is, all blond and long-legged with skin like velvet—"

"And there you are," I said, "trying to figure out how to ditch this stupid dance class so you could go mourn Kurt Cobain some more."

"Basically. I heard fiddle music and nearly had an aneurysm. So we're dancing—and it's just as uncomfortable as you can imagine, awk-ward, plus I know I can't dance worth a shit—and our faces are *this* far apart and my hand is on her back and I can feel her bra strap, and she smells like money and success and unlimited horizons—"

"And you convulsively vomited all over her."

"Damned near." He took a long swig of his Duck Junk (our appella-tion) to settle into the memory. "She knew right away I was fumbling the step, so she whispers in my ear and says, 'Let me lead,' and then she says, 'Do what my feet do right after I do it.' Now square dancing is arranged into pretty rigid groups of steps and movements so nearly anybody can do it; it's kind of mathematically pure. It's further arranged around gender but it's pretty easy for girls to dance the 'boy parts' and vice-versa. And pretty soon, in minutes, we're reeling around and half the hardasses in the school are getting ready to sign up for Western Swing, because it offered actual *girl contact* in a school-approved context."

We silently toasted this concept. Kingi snorted. In his world, courting was a simple butt-sniff.

"She saved my ass from public humiliation. Me, a total stranger. After that we always said hi in the hallways but that was the limit of my blazing crush. I think she married some guy who ran for the Senate. But if I had an ideal, it was Lola. Did I mentioned the bra-strap thing?"

"You realize, of course, that you are talking lust about a thirteen or fourteen-year-old girl."

"Yeah, but when *you're* thirteen or fourteen too, isn't that okay?"

"Yeah, but you're thirty-seven now, and you're still thinking about undoing that fourteen-year-old girl's bra."

"Point," Hayden said. "It cannot be denied. Better lock me up. Kids are banging each other at what, ten, twelve, now, anyway? I'm talking about the remnants of my fourteen-year-old self that survive within this worn-out thirty-seven-year-old shell, and no, I do not slow down in elementary school zones. Besides, teenagers now are all twits."

"All teenagers are twits, you included, at fourteen. When I stop to think how far my head was up my own ass when I was twenty-one...cripes."

"Check your ass, Dave," he said. "It's still up there." He squinted his eyes at the TV screen. "Can you really outrun a fireball? Technically speaking, I mean."

The hero of *Short Fuse 2* was outrunning a fireball. I freeze-framed the shot.

"No," I said. "Normal human walking pace is about three miles an hour. Running, about twelve. Sprinting, maybe fifteen. That's about twenty-two feet per second. Explosions are basically expanding gas and heat, which equals pressure—instantaneously."

"How fast does the explosion go?" said Hayden.

"In fireball terms, over 26,000 feet per second, like I said, practically instantaneous. So in a shot like we're looking at here, at detonation, our guy would be thirty or forty feet away at top speed, and he'd still be a crispy critter."

"Is that why the running-away-from-a-fireball shots are always in slow motion? To buy more time for the hero not to get his ass burned off?"

"Well, there are other factors, number one being that this is a Mason Stone movie, and Mason Stone's butt cheeks are certified fireproof; I think it's in his contract. What concerns me more is the white balance on the explosion. At 1080p resolution, it's gonna flare out."

Given a good disc, most of the presentational problems presented by high-definition were fixable on the TV itself...not that most owners would know that. And not many of them would lay out hard cash for things like an optical comparator to establish what is called a "light reference." Scratch that "not many;" *none* of them would.

Hence, my job.

I unfroze the shot. Dash McChance, action hero, a.k.a. Mason Stone, action star, survived the fireball. Even better, his thirty-round machine gun clip still had bullets left after about eight hundred shots fired on full-auto.

Not my job.

My job had nothing to do with continuity, realism, or plot resilience, but concentrated instead on technical finesse. Release schedules most often forced a rough compromise, and discs with sub-par specs slid through all the time, because most consumers wanted it *big* and *loud* and they wanted it *now*. Complaints and nit-picking were admirably incarcerated by online bulletin boards and chat threads, where the choosy deluded themselves they enjoyed some freedom of speech, content to insult each other and play an endless, winless game of trivial one-upsmanship, whining sheep in a barnyard about which no one cared. Even if they hated the product, they'd still buy it in order to secure bitching rights.

None of this mattered in the screening bay, where I did my job and was well-paid, even occasionally appreciated. The folks who sniffed around Best Buy or Wal-Mart for the cheapest price on some animated turdball to keep their children stunned for a few hours had no idea that I spent many more hours sitting in a small, secret room, working quality control. It really was an invisible job.

"Do you really have to know all that shit about fireballs?" Hayden said.

"For my job? No. It's just homework. I got curious."

Kingi had turned around and aimed his hindquarters at the screen just in time to unleash a truly toxic dog fart, by way of review. We couldn't outrun that, either.

Alma

Alma enjoyed killing strangers. Less muss, zero fuss. It was the way contract assassination should always go, in a perfect world. Your target never knew you, or did not see you until it was too late. Wrong place, right time, a couple of seconds of intersection, then out, clean.

Morgan Deane had pissed off someone by winning a lawsuit against them. From what Alma had gathered, the legal action was a complete insider fix whose monetary reward was eclipsed only by its humiliation factor. *Nobody fucks with Morgan Deane.* Deane did not need a huge punitive court judgment to amass wealth because he was rich already, thanks to nepotism and a family fortune founded in several very popular and venerable brands of household cleaning products—the kind of stuff his underpaid and possibly illegal maintenance staff used to polish the Etruscan marble, buff the stained glass windows, and shine the abundance of too-tacky brasswork that littered Deane's home.

Deane lived in a palatial estate in Mount Olympus, a sort of wannabe-Bel Air enclave of midlist celebutards and monied Russians. He had scored the six-bedroom, five-bath Greek Revival spread three years ago from some bottomed-out panflash of hip-hop; yesterday's superstar. From this base of operations, Deane currently put up with his fourth wife (thirty-six years his junior, a failed actress), supported seven assorted lackluster children (both in-house and via remote apron string), and comped two mistresses on the side (whenever he traveled). Morgan Deane had a cadre of legal bond-slaves on speed dial and was known as a pitbull for any kind of litigation.

In due time, that special anonymous someone, his back bristled by Deane's abuse, had calmly decided to *fuck Morgan Deane up*, like, forever. He had solicited a legitimate hit through reliable channels, putting in escrow the standard rate for a simple murder-by-contract.

Mount Olympus, with its gated arch and suggested status, wasn't even a real mountain. It sat in the Laurel Canyon foothills far below the elevation required by cartographers. It was just another development in the maze of "planned communities" that loved to burden the county assessor's office with the demands of a busybody homeowner's tribunal. It was defined by dead ends and restricted entrances. At least the streets were well-maintained.

Primarily because of the residents' obsession with security patrols, Mount Olympus was a great place to slip in, target, and slip out.

Standing in shadow near the patio to the east wing of Deane's manse, Alma knew certain details about the man, but only those facts that might contour the job in some way. She knew, for example, that somebody had tried to have Deane killed once before, about a year ago, and had failed. That fumble had caused Deane to upgun his security systems, like most Los Angeles paranoids. That was a wrinkle of which Alma absolutely needed to be aware.

The beauty of the whole scheme was that the hit was not traceable to Alma. She and others in her profession had initiated a trade-off system, very much suggested by Hitchcock's *Strangers on a Train*. You take my hot job, and I'll take yours. No trail, no motive, no connection to the contractor.

Alma and her peers jokingly called themselves the Handi-Wipers. They were professionals. They were durable and resourceful, holding in contempt the hacks—the government-backed killers or the corporatized hit men who needed black vans and dirty tricks and huge mobile teams. The mercenaries, the politicians, the people who engineered the worst crimes and enjoyed the best deniability. Alma had a single job caveat, and that was she would accept no pact to kill, say, an artist or writer—somebody creative. There were already too many paracreative human termites out there with their sleazy little gameplans and bail-outs, practically begging to be killed.

Whom no one would miss, not really.

Alma had come to Deane's home through a complicated trade-off with an associate named Bryan Silver, who had in return agreed to pick up one of Alma's pending assignments. This time, it had been strictly a matter of more efficient scheduling. Silver was boxed into a New York trip and Alma had wanted to come back to Los Angeles. Rather than rush things, they simply swapped.

Alma watched an ADT patrol car swish past on the damp pavement. The nationwide watchdog company had been founded in 1874 and still used the acronym derived from its original name, American District Telegraph, although Xuna Ochoa, a pal of Alma's, claimed the initials really stood for Attention-Deficit Tools. They advertised "armed response" mostly because it made their signs look imposing. Their response time in a violent confrontation was more likely to result in what Xuna called HEPD—house empty, people dead. Home video had captured similar bastions of home security helping themselves to loose items in a burgled home, even sampling stuff from the fridge. Workers at this pay grade were better at fire alarms, heart attacks and pet emergencies, and who could blame them?

Xuna was one of Alma's "otherworld" friends who had no clue as to Alma's primary vocation. Xuna did desk-work for an accounting firm lost up in some Culver City high-rise; as far as she knew, Alma was a financial planner with a lot of frequent flyer miles—a job Alma had actually logged as an office assistant, in order to get the patter correct, for cover. Xuna and Alma always hooked up during the latter's L.A. jaunts, to get tipsy and trade sexual misadventures (real or confected) and maybe catch a movie at one of the few cinemas still capable of presenting films properly.

Bryan Silver, on the other hand, had hit on Alma more than once, in apparent defiance of the don't-mate-where-you-eat ground rule. He had always been politely rebuffed with just a hint of flirtatiousness—*you'll never know what you're missing*—because Alma preferred to keep her sexual encounters anonymous and controlled, compartmentalized into other cities.

Virtually every heterosexual male who encountered Alma got that lean and hungry look; quite a few women, too. She was tall, lithe as a panther, admirably shaped, not a couture stick-insect but curvy for her height, with a lush mane of hair so black it seemed Asian in its fullness, and frank, penetrating eyes of double espresso, shading toward crème with amber flecks depending on her mood. Bold, natural brows. Her gaze was consciously enhanced, because she had learned it could be used to mesmerize, the way a cobra is said to spellbind its prey.

Even her victims checked her out, if they got the time, and this was frequently their undoing.

Alma unsleeved the Colt .22 longbarrel from its snug nest against her left armpit. The holster was supple boot leather, softened to silence, black-on-black against the rest of her stalking ensemble, down to the crepe soles on her boots. The plantation rubber add-ons utterly lacked a footprint signature and tended to shuck dirt, rather than track it. The custom chamois boots themselves featured several straps—Alma liked her legs to feel tight when she worked—and a vertical scabbard for a special double-edged blade of pattern-welded steel with a tanto point.

The .22 was also matte-black for nonreflection, with a ten-shot cylinder to forestall the need to reload. The cartridges alternated between lead heads and steel jackets, five each. The lead bullets had been carefully dum-dummed. Steel to penetrate and lead to mutilate. Alma had adapted the tool to close-quarters surgical application, sure shots with no doubts. A government hack would have loaded himself up like a SWAT berserker with eighty pounds of gear: radios, too many extra clips, goggles, armor, and tac toys behind a gun so overdosed on caliber and railed up with suppressors and laser sights that it resembled a mad midget robot. Hacks were all about sponsored flamboyance. Alma, like most freelancers, had learned how to budget.

She zeroed Morgan Deane in his home office—a lot of Macassar ebony on the walls, dotted with brag plaques and framed keepsake photos in which no one looked particularly happy. Most of his antique collaborator's desk was littered with gear and packaging from a recent overall computer upgrade to wireless. Deane—bulky, gray, jowly, with slightly protuberant, iron colored eyes and a rubescent complexion— was seated in an old leather exec chair, mousing around what appeared to be a soft porn site; amateur candids. Alma could see the reflection of the monitor in the balcony window glass behind him. She was already posted in the room. The outdated copper-strip alarm trips on the windows had proven laughable.

Before Deane had entered, Alma had paced out the circumference of the big room to determine perimeter and reveal any squeaky floorboards. Muted wall sconces provided murky pools of jaundiced light. The only other lights were on the desk: a dim Tiffany clone on one corner, and a halogen lamp on a swing arm closer to the monitor. For someone sitting at the desk, the oncoming diffusion and bounce-back from the monitor would render most of the rest of the room imperceptible.

Deane paused to fire up a spicy Cohiba with a electric butane lighter that probably cost as much as the box of ten Maduro Five Magicos cigars. The smoke quickly formed a hanging inversion layer in the still air that would betray any sudden movement. But Alma was behind him now, breathing thoracically.

More positive ID was not necessary.

She put a single lead round through the back of his head. The flat crack of the shot went unnoticed, no louder than a dry stick snapping in two.

The deformed slug stayed inside Deane's skull vault to bounce around and puree his brain to baby food. There was almost no blood leakage.

He slumped forward, already brain-dead. His innards would shut down at their own pace. Alma moved the dropped cigar back to a big crystal ashtray so it would not burn the place down. The website that had been the last thing Morgan Deane had seen while alive was called *Just Past Jailbait.*

She had prepared the Arcadia doors in advance for a fast exit, not wanting to retrace her egress pattern. She dropped down from the balcony and went prone behind a sculpted row of English boxwood shrubs. Her departure plan would take her around to the backside of the house, outfoxing the sensors that would trip exterior hazard lights, then in a zigzag around the formal pool (already lit up), to bounce up and over the wallwork there.

"Omigod!" said a startled male voice. "Are you okay?"

Alma looked up into the pale face of an ADT private security guard.

CHASE

Rolf Dettrick's cover identity was as field technician for IBM. He was not in danger of anyone saying, "No, I mean, what's your *real* job?"

Rolf's real job was as a troubleshooter for an organization called CHASE, which was supposedly an acronym for Coalition to Hamper, Alibi, Sequester or Execute, a designation about which no one in the organization could say for real, since their founder had been a piece of Fifties boomer-generation fallout named Henry Hawker Seligson, a Vietnam vet known to be into James Bond-isms on a geek level. Rolf's handle was Chase Delta. The current Chase Alpha, their gang-boss, was a total black-bag hardass named, no kidding, James Smith. For real, Smith being America's most common surname, and James at number one for males.

One private joke shared among Rolf and his fellow CHASE operatives was to repurpose the definition. Like: Cheesy Hambone Asswipes Squandering Expenses, or Chiseled Hunky Aryans Suckling Executives. It was the sort of gag one never brought up in the presence of James Smith, who, rumor had it, had never actually smiled in his life, except to mimic human behavior as a distraction. And if James Smith deployed distraction protocols in your direction, best to make sure your estate was in order and your funeral arrangements were set up, because you'd never have time to feel the kill.

Not that anyone would ever find your body.

David J. Schow

CHASE was a bureaucratic neutron star composed of several collapsed subterranean organizations and bottomlessly funded by American tax dollars, which had been rerouted through enough laundering shells to drive the Watson supercomputer bonkers if it ever attempted to track cash flow. Originally an unacknowledged tentacle of the Fed, CHASE had diversified into private contracting, exploiting a decade's worth of blackmail bugs ported over from its initial incarnation to keep certain elected officials from getting all self-righteous about the covert. The government would occasionally utilize CHASE—begrudgingly—but never move against it. CHASE's correlation to the bank of the same name was nonexistent and strictly coincidental...but the confusion sometimes made for unintended hilarity, as when one state senator thought he had been targeted for termination by his credit card company. The man had died less ignorant.

The Chase financial octopus was well known. CHASE, the shadow company, did not waste a single dime on public relations.

During his tenure with CHASE, Rolf Dettrick had overseen, coordinated, or directly caused the deaths of sixty-seven irritants similar to that late senator. The last decade or so had been a tightly-wired succession of painstakingly-organized missions, one result being that Rolf had become a workout junkie (keep the machine optimum) with a very (*very*) mild methedrine habit (insert booster fuel into machine when needed).

But in that decade, Rolf had also seen his temples go gray, and caved in to the reality that he now required low-power reading glasses for fine print. Drills revealed slight erosion in his reaction/response matrix, tiny drawbacks that only he could see or feel, for now. Handicaps could be dodged or compensated, but buried worry could cause cancer if left unaddressed. Only pro athletes had a more restricted window when it came to their period of "prime." At thirty-five, Rolf desired at least one more decade as Chase Delta—or better—if for no other reason than to outperform the next crop of young killer turks, and prove that experience brought advantages unsuspected by the piranha swarms of white-hot twenty-somethings nipping at his legacy.

In nearly every other industry, you were finished at thirty-five, remanded to the realm of jokey old-age birthday cards and expected to drink the Kool-Aid of mid-life crisis. When memory itself was considered a symptom of your own obsolescence, it was time to change the game.

Rolf frequently argued with his mirror, upon rising. Chase Bravo, James Smith's second, was preparing to opt out for the bounty of the private sector, and both Rolf and a woman named Mindy Zayden (Chase Foxtrot) were angling for an intramural promotion. Basically a female analogue to Rolf, Mindy had fewer field kills but more hours logged in disposal and coverup. The unfair assumption was that wet workers—death specialists—were glorified muscleheads with no panache for backstory, deep intel, or spin control if the orbit of an op began to decay.

As deeper minds had observed, "no fair" was the complaint of a child.

It was something Rolf's last target had said, before he died.

Rolf's previous field gig had been a month ago. A bailout banker named Charles Wainwright had gotten his firm in deep shit with the government, for laundering drug cartel money from Colombia. Wainwright was preparing to take a very long "vacation" in an non-extradition country. Rolf considered the difficulty of a moving car strike and decided to compromise Wainwright's limo driver instead. When he dropped the privacy screen and dead-centered Wainwright with a silenced Sig Sauer SP2022, the banker had gone all weepy, saying, "This just isn't *fair,*" drawing out the vowels of his protest like a whiny little kid. Rolf shot him three times, chest-chest-head. The gun was fitted with a passive transponder that could store usage data valuable to a debriefing. The transponders had been Rolf's idea: A low-frequency, on-demand packet-based protocol that could be used in high security areas where Bluetooth, Zigbee, RFID and WiFi were banned, a magnetic system nondependent on radio waves, which featured a crystal to track elapsed time, a battery, and a static memory. They could also be used as transceivers in a pinch.

The suppressor, a Hartcoat anodized Impuls II-A, was rated at 32 dB. Rolf had not even had to use earplugs.

Today, Rolf's secure cellphone gave him a single message: *Call Home.* That left him an hour to shit, shower, shave, caffeinate, and launch.

The phone itself was a minor marvel. No brand name. They were individually manufactured within CHASE. Maximum encryption, no polling, no roaming loopholes through which spyware might creep, and anti-cloning software with tumbling protection. The whole unit could be immersed in water to wipe it right down to the chip, in case the phone had to be discarded in a hurry.

In today's CHASE docket was a dossier on a woman who needed killing named Theresa Brewster. She turned out to be just another political whore who had begun to make noises about going viral with the kind of evidence children should really not see on the Internet. As a job it was strictly bread-and-butter makework, but Rolf took it anyway in order to buttress his rank as a team player. One did not always get the fancy assignments. What Rolf really craved was a challenge, a worthy adversary that could showcase his skills for an upgrade in rank.

He took Theresa Brewster in her own Manhattan townhouse, late at night, while she was in the midst of swilling Pinot Grigio from a balloon glass and uploading incriminata. She offered to fuck him, mistaking this for a negotiation. He declined. There were so many pill vials in her shoulder bag and bathroom that enacting a suicide-by-overdose was easy. Then Rolf degaussed her hard drives and overloaded her plug-strips, to make the computers appear to be collaterally damaged by a power surge, after ducting her data onto a thumb drive to be delivered back to CHASE. For good measure and investigative continuity, Rolf also electronically futzed other obvious items in the townhouse, like the satellite TV and her iPhone (by burning out the charger). Using lamp-cord, he fried the hard line by sending 120 volts back through equipment built for six volts.

In and out in less than an hour; no gun work.

Afterward, he met Mindy Zayden at a Village bar called Steerage, a basement dive with a so-called art gallery in the rear, low-ceilinged, threaded with painted pipework overhead. She drank shooters of Sambuca and Bailey's, commonly known as a Slippery Nipple. Rolf charily stuck to black-and-tans, which were less complicated but a small pleasure when done correctly.

He had never considered Mindy Zayden in a social context. But here she was, after-hours, mildly tipsy, winking and touching his arm to make little private points, just between them, about the goings-on at Chase—all the language appropriately disguised, of course.

He had never considered Mindy Zayden in a sexual context, either, but here she was, coming on to him, just like Theresa Brewster had a few hours earlier.

That last part wasn't entirely true. Mindy was a strawberry blonde who used expensive heels to adventitiously present her short legs. Her mouth was gamin and generous; one of those smiles that always appear to house too many teeth. Her nose had a sloping uptick that lent her an interesting profile. She had a good beach body, the sort that goes unremarked while clothed, but whose curves could drive entire fraternities sperm-blind if displayed. Rolf had noticed all these things the very first time he had seen her, but had dismissed his own primal read. This was not, could not be an *attraction.*

Because Mindy was a viper who begged constant caution.

"I don't want Smith's job, you know," she said, conspiratorially. She tended to stress certain words in a breathy way, in an elaborate pantomime of punctuation for emphasis. "I don't want *your* job. I don't want your job to be compromised at *all.* But we are *next*, you and I. We'll be *running* the joint in two years. Your jacket plus mine? What better team could there be?" She crossed her legs, one heel wedged against the crossbar of a high leather stool.

Rolf loved that sound, the hiss of nylons whispering past each other. It was too loud inside Steerage to hear it, but he imagined it. It was a potent sense memory whose origin was obscured by too many clouds of the past.

"You're jumping ahead too fast," he told her. "We have no idea what Smith is going to do."

"Smith is *fifty*," she said. "He's practically a *mummy*." She signaled for another Nip Slip.

"Don't underestimate him. That's Rule One; that's CHASE Prime. That's reckless talk."

"Nobody can eavesdrop us in *here*," she said, furrowing her brow to indicate why she had chosen this rendez. "Don't you feel the least bit *insulted* by that last job, whatshername, Miss Fuckypants? A mugger could have cleared her."

"You know and I know that's not what the contractors pay for." He sipped his black-and-tan, winning a foam mustache. How the hell could British people drink this shit at room temperature?

"Got milk?" She smiled and reached to dab his lip with a cocktail square.

"Listen, the Brewster thing. It was just a matter of rotation. You might have gotten it instead of me; what would you have done?"

"I would have marched into Smith's office and said *what the fuck?*"

"Well, we don't know that, do we?"

"Damned *straight* I would have." She worked up a pout that was almost cute. "Point is, Smith could have handed that off to a beginner, a virgin, even. You're too *valuable* to piss away in entry-level wet work."

"You seem overly concerned with my career outlook."

"Oh, Rolf, you get so *funny* when you slap on that stony face. All tough guy, like your *privacy* has been raped." She tossed her shooter back like a pro.

"What privacy?" He imitated her tone and rolled his eyes.

"See, that's better. I'm just saying that there's a wakeup wave coming in. The winds of change are gonna blow harsh and fierce. You and me, we're not obsolete *equipment*; we're seasoned *pros*. Do you want to wait for a guy like Smith to retire you, or step up, is all I'm saying."

"While you hold back and watch to see which way the empire falls?"

"It's not a *plot*, doofus. I'm in the same boat."

It was a plot, all right. Mindy was not interested in the number two slot. She wanted to elbow Smith out of the way to gain Chase Alpha status. Rolf was beginning to ache for a fast, cleansing workout. An Epsom soak to liberate toxins. Free-weight burnouts. Anything but this guarded fencing, which was turning out to be a regrettable choice. Mindy was running the stealth agenda playbook line for line—the chatty familiarity, the veiled seduction, the implied blood-brother promise. She was probably acting more inebriated than she really was. What the hell did she really want from him?

"Why this little colloquy?" he said. "You working up a jacket on me?"

"Baby, I've already *got* a jacket on you." Her expression narrowed. "All the way back to the Airborne Rangers and that little coverup in Istanbul. That place was like the Alamo for you guys. You were outnumbered twenty to one, and that's *after* the car bomb blew it to shit and gone. The only mystery is how you managed to walk out alive."

Was this her chaser? A hot shot of buddy-speak, followed by a punch line of implied leverage?

"I wasn't the only one who survived," he said.

"Mm-hm. There were three others. One died on the way back here—funny, because his shrapnel wounds weren't critical. One disappeared; fancy *that*. And the other supposedly committed suicide. Leaving you to get recruited straight into CHASE as soon as you got your boots on American pavement."

She was angling back toward Theresa Brewster, deliberately citing the suicide profile Rolf had just used. She was getting ready to ambush him with some vital secret no one was supposed to know about him, or so she thought.

Rolf was sure his slate was pristine. But not sure enough. His instructions in Istanbul had been gruesomely succinct: *Ensure no op survivors.* He had done as ordered, like a good soldier, and been vetted directly into CHASE.

"Is there a point to this?" he said. He was exactly halfway through his pint. During that journey he had watched Mindy bolt at least five Nips, alternating with seltzer.

She gave him a sly grin. "Just sayin. Cards on the table and all that. I'm not trying to *antagonize* you, lover. I *like* you."

They decided to go back to her place at about three in the morning. By then she had taken hold of his arm and begun nuzzling and snuggling. She draped one of her fine legs over his in the cab uptown.

Rolf was pretty sure that Mindy would try to kill him before dawn.

Dave

Four days later—surprise. More like shock. I actually received a message from my long-lost high school crush, Dalia Villareal. *The* Daisy.

It was not precisely what I expected.

omg derek for real? 4col! that's me, aas...wayn? la? wtgp? ?^. d.

Maybe Daisy was still fifteen, as I'd last seen her. Maybe it was some Internet shark pretending to be her just to goon me.

Roughly translated, the gist was:

Omigod, Derek for real? For crying out loud! That's me, alive and smiling...where are you now? Los Angeles? Want to go to private (messaging)? Want to hook up? Daisy.

One abbreviation this maybe-Daisy did not need was TYCLO, for Turn Your Caps Lock Off, because all-capitals, in IM and textspeak, was *SHOUTING* as far as millennials were concerned. That is, those people who by birthdate or ignorance were incapable of remembering a time when emphasis in electronic communication was prohibited by its own primordial limitations, which did not allow <u>underlining</u> or *italicization*. Underscores were monomanically reserved for URL destinations—web addresses—so for a while, whenever a title had to be cited (say, for a movie like *Short Fuse 2: Flashfire*), some users defaulted to all-caps, while perverting the completely inadequate asterisk (or its nearby companion symbols) to the purpose of emphasis: "This is what *I* think." Many veterans of the Second World War would disagree; all-caps had once been their generational custom for submitting typed forms. Ordinary modern people, thrust into unaccustomed keyboard usage by their new need to communicate online, were unsurprisingly innocent of typesetting protocol even though there were shelves of stylebooks to guide them with chapter-and-verse. Books were, like, *sooo* 20th Century.

Daisy, if this really was her, had adapted to the Age of Text wholeheartedly. It made me feel weirdly old, or painfully out of touch.

I had six email accounts on ascending levels of exclusivity. Nobody I knew except for Hayden had the third deepest one, which spared me a lot of spam. I had very few constant contacts as it was—no family members, few co-workers at Starburst Post, and zero old friends from other pasts. Like I said, I had to stare at screens enough already, and so-called social media held no enticements for me.

It's really anti-social media, when you think about it.

I gave maybe-Daisy my virtually unused e-ddress, in effect granting her Hayden-level clearance. Again, the hesitation came to my fingers; that reluctance to shoot this news off into the ether. Every contact was a unilateral invitation to some kind of trouble, like leaving your door unlocked or your wallet lying around on the street. There were people out there in tiny rooms, concocting yet-unsuspected new ways of shoplifting your credit, your data, your very identity, and you would never see them but you knew they were there, tirelessly inventive and biliously unconcerned about who you really were. What mattered was the use that could be made of you, or any other blundering techno-naif. People like the rape victim of whom investigators say, *well, it's HER fault, look how she's dressed.* Online, everybody's ass is hanging out.

Pause now, for the part of the story where I outline how unforgivable I am.

Pause now, for the revolting male game of enumerating sex partners. (We presumed women did it too, but one pastime upon which
the average heterosexual male does not want to eavesdrop is the klatch
conversation of females—it's just too earthy and specific. Anyone with
gay friends already knows how catty *that* gossip can get. As far as trans-
gendered contestants, I was NMI: *Need More Info*.)

One of the things that bonded Hayden and me was the fact that we
had divorced about the same time. His second wife, my first and only.
We exploited an obvious cliché by leaning on each other like battlefield
survivors. He just appeared in my current life as a willing ear, and I
returned the courtesy. Sometimes we sucked it all up—the waistline,
the depleted courage, the bankrupt ego and woeful self-image—and
made combat sorties into the present-day Otherworld of dating, with
the fatalistic view that in too short a time, we'd be sitting around, alone
again, recounting post-mortems. At almost the same time, we both
realized we had reached the stage where we could no longer recount, by
name, every single woman with whom we had slept. My brag was that
I had only ever had a single one-nighter. For the rest, I either hung on
too long or willfully ignored the stop signs. You do that, sometimes, to
delude yourself that you are giving and human.

Neither of us, Hayden or me, wanted to become one of those tiresome shut-ins, porting their imaginary sexual existence into some free
porn site. The universe of adult entertainment was in jeopardy, too. It
was hard to get people to pay for dirty pictures and video when so many
amateurs were giving it away for free. There was a site called Industrial
Gothic Hott for which Hayden sometimes wrote code when his finances
needed bumping. Every Hott—every eccentric, delectable offering on
view, male, female, or other—was a complete fake, a persona manufactured in order to make money.

Bar crawling, as I have said, had its own problems. Too many people want to win the lottery, thinking they'll trip over their soul mate
in some pub, and winding up as solitary alcoholics instead, wondering

why life kicked their ass. Hence the term SINBAD: *Single income, no boy-friend, absolutely desperate.*

Honestly, I met more women thanks to Kingi, now, during our constitutionals. Everybody wants to caress his doggie head. *He won't bite, will he?*

Plus, people always cheat when they sum up their sex lives. You tick off the list of partners, then stop to congratulate yourself that you've forgotten a few key names. *Wow, there's so many I can't keep track of 'em!* And no matter how many there are, you cheat again by augmenting the list of dates and lovers and fuck-friends with the names of those you *wished* you could have gotten naked with...but didn't.

The ones you wanted, but who wouldn't have you.

The ones who wanted you, but you were too self-involved to see it, or worse, you had your eyes on a better target.

Naomi. Rebecca. Victoria. Jennifer. Deb, Deborah, and Debbie. Suzanne. Susan. Suze. Margaret and Maggie. Tiffany, whose real name was Caroline. Amber. April. AnneMarie. Althea, Alea, Anna and on to the B's: Brenda, Barbara, Boots (the one-nighter), Bronwyn...

If I ever met a Zelda, a Queenie or an Ursula, I'd have the whole goddamned alphabet. On the surface, this was understandably vile. The way normal people excuse this is by professing a willingness to *get back on the horse*, no matter how many times they've been shot down, dumped, or replaced. And—be honest—after a time, don't you want to put some of your pain back out into the world? Exact emotional payback? Break someone's heart for no other reason than your own damage?

It doesn't work. You feel shitty no matter what.

At rock-bottom on the list, A#1, the main root from which all others branched, was Dalia Villareal. The unrequited template for my entire love life. The woman who had—apparently—tossed back a scrap of code that got me far too excited all over again, and caused me to ignore hard life lessons about sticking out my neck one more time. It was exposure I should not have risked. But having risked first contact, I had made it through unwounded, and perhaps gained a bright spark from my distant past to cherish anew. Or put in a grave once and for all. I liked the clarity of that.

Want to hook up?

Please.

There's no way to describe what she looked like, but I'll try.

East of the downside end of Hollywood Boulevard, past where the sidewalk stars end at Gower, there's a coffee dive called Espresso mi Historia, run by a pleasant fellow named Jesus who will tell you more than you ever thought possible about the precise temperature at which beans need to be nurtured before grinding. It has a high ceiling and the interior is splashed in bold serape colors, the walls adorned in an ever-cycling parade of local art, which quietly insists that you purchase it. They have open-mic and poetry slams, hopeful yet lamentable. Most often the joint is cluttered with earnest LOLs—Losers on Laptops, cadging the free wireless in pursuit of their perfect screenplay. One seemingly homeless dude has staked out the northwest corner of a recess in the back, making a single Americano last half a day and hoping someone will pay him to read a tarot throw. He reads the free papers at great length, with monkish concentration, eyes always apprising the talent of the room above the paper's edge. Pretty soon he's going to have to get a laptop or mobile device, if he wants to stay current.

This seemed to be good, noncommittal, neutral ground.

Best of all, and in open defiance of local regulations, Espresso mi Historia welcomed my dog to sit inside with me, so long as Kingi observed proper dog etiquette. Jesus was a dog person who kept peanut butter biscuits in reserve for his well-behaved, four-footed visitors.

And once again, I thought: *Somebody had trained Kingi. Trained him expertly. Then lost him.*

David J. Schow

Daisy turned every head in the room when she entered, in a flash of harsh mid-summer sunlight that rebounded off the heavy glass door. She had matured to about five-nine, plus three inches for the heels on the calfskin boots that hugged her legs almost to the knee. Tight, distressed denim jeans that made her stride a thing to behold. Too many people slouched along, throwing their legs in front of them to keep from falling down. She strode, instead of walked, powerful and declarative. Loose, flowing black top with cuffed sleeves. Her hair was richer than my memory of it, tied back now in a horsetail in deference to the heat outside. A bold silver ring or two on her fingers, and sterling drop earrings that accentuated her thoroughbred length of neck. She scanned the room through chunky dark glasses and immediately nailed me. I was already half-standing, broadcasting naked hostility at anyone else who dared consider her. Mine. She's here for me and I want you all to writhe.

And there we go again, off down the slide of unreality where women were chattelized into the reductive categories of bitch, nag, whore or goddess. This last, a perfect porcelain siren who existed only to be worshipped, desired and rescued, never had stinky feet, a heavy period, B.O., zits, or mood swings. As long as she was an unclaimed conquest, she enjoyed immunity from the mileage of crying jags, hyper-acute self-centeredness or imagined victimization. The magnetic pull of the untasted is that you don't yet know the grisly details of ingrown hairs, relationship psychosis, emotional flatulence, spotty personal hygiene, or apocalyptic sloppiness...and the same goes for you, too, buddy. *No matter how gorgeous she is, somebody somewhere is tired of putting up with her shit.* Satan said that, I think, frustrated by some ladyfriend who probably turned out to have swamp crotch. And the same goes for you. It's the eternal difference between the real and the idealized.

None of it mattered when Daisy strolled into the room. Victims— aren't we all?

"Derek—?" She didn't care who overheard. The others here did not exist. Wide, genuine smile of matte lipstick. Her teeth were perfect now.

I shrugged. Yeah, this is me, more or less. I guiltily spot-checked her ring finger for a wedding band and was relieved to see none.

"I'm going by Dave, now," I said, not able to keep my own smile in check. "So what about you? Is it Dalia or Daisy?"

"Daisy, for you. C'mere."

She wrapped me up in a hug while we were standing. Eat your hearts out, LOLs. Just like that, her body was pressed against me, and she smelled like freedom and joy with a nice, spicy afterburn. No bra, below. The world seemed to tilt. *There lye dragons; beware, foolish mortal.*

Kingi was at full attention. "Who's this?" she said.

"That's my squire, Kingi."

She ruffled his head. As soon as she sat down he planted his nose right into her crotch. "Aha," she said, amused. "One of those."

Kingi backed off before I could order him to, the sneak.

"What's up with your name?" she said. "You're not Kemp anymore, but—?"

"Vollmand. I had to legally change it. Long story."

"I still totally cannot believe you found me," she said. "But it's awesome that you did. Made the effort, I mean. Holy shit! It's really you! I'd know you in an instant. You're looking good. Healthy. Still got your hair; wow, sit down and let me really *look* at you."

This was already going slightly better than anticipated.

She took her latte strong, with three shots of espresso, which I appreciated.

"My god," I said. "You look like a model or a movie star or something."

"This?" She gave a vague hand-wave to indicate the whole package that was her. "Please. Not in this town. Not with this nose."

There was a microscopic bump right on the bridge.

"And look at my eyes. They're off. The left one is a teensy bit lazy. It's more obvious when I've been sleeping."

David J. Schow

One of her dark eyes seemed a little bit wider open than its partner, but the effect was anything but a detriment. I quickly decided to stop complimenting her like a gushing fool.

We time-traveled. All the way back to San Andres High School. All the remember-whens. I told her my story about her eight sentences and she scoffed. Surely she had said more.

Then we traded other stories. She had married—once, like me— gotten pregnant, miscarried, gotten divorced. She had jettisoned domestic bliss in favor of work-related travel. I told her about sitting in little rooms watching big movies, just grinding away on the day-to-day, and that I had recently gotten mildly drunk with a pal named Hayden, whereupon he and I recounted our lifetimes of sexual misconduct. She seemed amused enough by this confession to offer up a few of her own ups and downs, like we were instantly best buddies and confidants. It was that easy.

"You remember Quentin Farrier?" she said.

"Big jock, student body vice president," I said. "No. I hated him so much I've tried to blank him out."

"He was my dream date, back when I was short and had bad teeth and was surrounded by corn-fed blondes," Daisy said. "Fucking *cheerleaders*. All that school spirit rah-rah-rah." Sports still held the alpha-dominant role in high schools across the Midwest. They were the perfection models of student aspiration, especially for administrative minds still trying to preserve and embalm an idealized 1950s mindset, a world before Crips and Bloods and nationally despised kiddie porn, an alternate dimension that did not admit of publicized serial killers, gay marriage or the Internet.

"I passed Quentin a note in civics class. Mr. Brandeston. Remember when people passed notes to each other? I know; we're old. And in big girly handwriting I decided to go for broke and profess my love for this boy. I watched him peek at the note when Brandeston's back was turned. My heart was hammering. I was sure I was going to pass out. Quentin wrote on the note and passed it back. I could have died right then and all would have been right with the world."

The thought of Daisy throwing herself at this footballer's feet was mildly nauseating, even now. The dairy and sugar in my own cappuccino kept my indigestion from broadcasting itself with unseemly noises.

"I got the note back, and you know what he wrote on it? He wrote it right across the face of what I had written. He didn't even use the blank space below, where I'd put my name. He wrote: *No Mexicans*."

"Oh...boy."

"Yeah." She drew a deep breath and let it out slowly. "But you know what? I went all suicidal and lovelorn, got over it, graduated."

"That would have been after I left," I said. "I was never in one place, at one school, for very long."

"Then I checked up on good ole Quentin, like five years ago. He died in prison, up at Roswell Correctional. He never made it more than two hundred miles from where he went to high school."

"What did he do?"

"Put his wife in the hospital. Glenda Subiron. She lost an eye. They drank a lot."

"Glenda Subiron was like..." I tried to scare up the memory. "The one who wore the really short skirts and nylons, so short she got sent to the principal's office? Big campus booster chick?"

"The same. Blond, blue-eyed, leggy, cliquey. He impregnated her. She gained nearly two hundred pounds and grew a mustache. Most of his hair fell out by the time he turned twenty-five. His dad's car dealership failed and he hooked up with some bikers and a meth lab—there's more of those in the desert now than there are cactus."

"Just another American success story," I said. "Rah-rah-rah."

She raised her cup. "Here's to him."

"I don't want to toast that asshole," I said. "He did dirty on you."

"No, here's to him dying, like he deserved," she said with an impish glint in her eyes. "Fuck that *puto*, he got what he'd earned."

It had turned into a challenge, and I did not want to defy her so soon. We clinked cups.

"He *was* kind of a dick," I said. "How about everybody else? Did you keep in touch with any of them?"

"Not really. I sorta cut them loose, you know. After high school is really the time to reinvent yourself. Get out in the world where nobody knows your baggage, be more like your best version of yourself."

"Amen to that. What about your husband?"

"Not from the school. Not from Las Cruces at all. That was what made him attractive. He was from somewhere else. He represented the notion that you could get *out*, get free. And I was twenty-one, already starting to feel like a spinster. It was what you'd call a hasty love affair. Marcus wasn't a bad guy. We were just so hormonal and urgent, you know?"

"You get to the point where you say, 'I'll go with this one,' instead of waiting around any more."

"Yeah, exactly. That how it was for you?"

"Pretty much. I wanted the feeling of someone who had my back. Another heartbeat in the house. Somebody who could speak your secret language, that you didn't have to *explain* every single goddamned thing to."

She shot me that look again. "Was she pretty?"

"Good looking but not gorgeous."

"Ah. *Suitable.*" Now her smile was truly evil. "Who dumped who?"

"That's the crazy thing, Daisy. Nobody dumped anybody. It just sort of...ran out of gas on its own. Death by disinterest."

"You still haven't said her name."

"Tracey. Prosaic, huh?"

Daisy just smiled, almost privately. I had just given her a piece of personal intel I didn't share with just anybody.

First Daisy had hugged me, which nearly made my skull explode. Now she was touching my arm every so often. Facing me with her legs slightly apart, not defensively crossed. Her posture was not rigid or on alert. She looked at me more than she looked away in reverie. She leaned in from time to time. She had arranged herself to block intrusion by other eyes, in a way, shielding me. Cops used this grammar of body language all the time to sniff what people were really saying when they lied. At the same time, Daisy had a complete awareness of the room around her, sort of a radar about who was moving where. But she did not do that side-to-side flicker of the eyes, indicating that she wanted to escape.

We went on this way until the sun started ebbing, changing the light. I took her saying that she was going to be in Los Angeles for a few more days in the open spirit she offered the information.

"How about this," she said. "Day after tomorrow, dinner, for real. But you need to give me your vital stats, since you're the local."

I had already written this stuff down, hoping for such an opportunity. But to make it look more honest I wrote it down again, fresh. We were supposed to meet up, like today, but she had already offered to pick me up if needed. I made sure she had my street address, which I normally don't give to anyone, just in case something—anything—went askew. A solar flare that knocked out all communications. A tsunami or earthquake that might hamper the rendezvous.

She embraced me again when we parted. She left a chaste kiss on my cheek, and I one on hers. I felt thunderstruck, almost teenaged.

Remember the TAKE IT BACK button? I wish I'd had one on my goddamned pen.

Alma & Rolf

About the time Alma had nonlethally put away the ADT rent-a-cop on the front lawn of the late Morgan Deane's home in Mount Olympus, Deane's youngest live-at-home stepson, Kyle, seventeen, was dipping his finger into the blood of his newest surrogate dad's corpse upstairs. Then Kyle put the finger into his mouth, almost absentmindedly.

"Aww, *dude*," Kyle said to no one in particular.

Later, long-distance from New York, Bryan Silver asked, "What happened to the flop-cop?" His face shone on Alma's iPhone as high-contrast sodium murk, as though he was someplace with incandescent lighting behind him.

Alma, freshly showered, was wandering barefoot around her Echo Park apartment, one lush towel draped around her hair, another loosely strung around her hipbones. Her curtains, closed as always, would permit no one to see her topless. She kept the angle on her return video feed tight, just to her face. It was amusing to tease Bryan, who was always too quick to rise to the bait.

"Elbow pivot to the forehead," she said. "*Bam*, out, done."

Actually, once the ADT man had figured out that Alma was not a victim, but a perp (about one and a half seconds), Alma arrested his arm and pulled him downward, redirecting his energy toward his own leg and using his momentum to set him up for her elbow strike (five tenths of a second), right between his eyes. He wound up in the hospital with two black eyes, a mild concussion, a frontal sinus fracture and a whip-lash injury to his neck.

She saw Bryan chuckle as he pictured it. "Otherwise okay?" he said.

"It's solid," she said, meaning several things: The job had been executed. No spoor, clean exit. The payments had cleared and been disbursed.

"So I owe you one, now," he said.

"No hurries, no worries. Deal with it when you get back."

"Tell me over dinner?"

"Not a chance, Bryan. But thanks for asking."

"You're beautiful when you're angry."

"Fuck you. Hit me when you're local."

"Will do."

Neither one of them said "goodbye" or signed off. It was the way most of their casual communications went. Stick to job-speak. Don't get personal.

Especially when they yielded trouble-free success, gigs generally left Alma in one of two moods. Either she could sleep for fourteen hours straight, or she felt the itch to indulge in some vigorous sexual steam-venting. Tonight was one of the latter. She had already made arrangements to meet an escort named Court—probably a working name—at the Beverly Wilshire. No wining, dining or cocktail chatter, just straight to the king-sized bed, where Court would follow her instructions to the dime. She would probably leave the hotel before Court did, leaving no trace of herself.

Alma would never bring one of these cocksmen into her own apartment. This was her space—her West Coast way station—too private for such hijinks. She didn't want these overblown Ken dolls checking out the shoes in her closet, or investigating the contents of her fridge, or maybe spying on her computer.

Court was the type Alma usually rented. Bright-eyed, square-jawed, fit. The former varsity letterman made good. One genetic step shy of an

Aryan ideal. Non-chemically-enhanced endurance. Staying power, so she could finish up on top. Foreskin a plus. She counted it a small win if she could make them lapse into sleep when she was finished. Even less natter that way; she could shower and scoot and be back in her sanctuary in a few hours.

She got home in time to watch a movie—*Cold Barrel Zero*, an utterly unrealistic espionage thriller—then check up on the various Internet personas she had established. She had no time for or interest in watching some moron do a moronic thing on YouTube, although she understood there were people who could waste whole days doing just that.

Alma had very few Internet contacts that were non-work related. The important ones got directed to secure accounts. One hangnail message looked like the usual spam, but there was just enough doubt to cause her to open it anyway.

Red flag. Like, instantly.

Alma dug out a very old and well-thumbed address book. Listed inside, in alphabetical order, were a series of names, about half of them crossed out in scarlet marker. She quickly scanned the names and compared them to the data in the mystery email. She was completely awake now.

Every time she thought she had laced enough new rabbitholes and dead ends into the Skinner box maze of her past, some new/old detail would jump forth to bite her ass, and thus threaten her security, and all that she had built. It happened every so often, and she did not berate herself for dealing with the inevitable. You got a leak, you either plugged it, fixed it, or moved to a different place that didn't leak. What you didn't do was ignore it, because a dribble could easily wax into a flood.

Then she remembered: Bryan owes me a hit. I can hand this job off to him, and everybody will stay innocent.

This kind of crap, residual fallout from the old Alma, had not occurred for a while, and after the sticker-shock moment, Alma realized the difficulty was containable, controllable. Even as she reviewed the information on her screen, she had already begun to formulate a plan. No hurries, no worries.

By the time she put her head down, she was able to sleep well and deeply, undisturbed.

Rolf Dettrick's last-minute summons had come at exactly 1:01 A.M. *Call Home.* He walked into the office of James Smith, head honcho of CHASE, at 2:00 AM, exactly. This kind of thing was not for a hurried telephonic conversation.

En route to the meet, Rolf treated himself to a hit of benzedrine to streamline his perceptions. Smith never called after-hours on a whim. The accelerant sizzled through Rolf's metabolism. He was proud that he had been able to wean off the meth for the most part—that shit stayed in your system too long; detectable in your piss for a couple of days and your hair for, well, until your next trim. Nobody wanted to "drop dirty" on a urine test, though many had tried to beat it by doing everything from overhydrating, to gobbling creatine, to taping a condom full of clean pee to one leg (which didn't work because the temperature would not register). Bennies and dexies were an adequate form of stand-in methadone.

Smith did not appear agitated, but then, Smith rarely leaked any of the more demonstrative emotions. He was ensconced behind a broad, glass-topped desk with nothing on it. The glass was lit from within and Rolf knew it to function as a giant flat monitor with touch navigation. Smith himself could have been made of glass. The man seemed smooth and featureless, almost sterile, yet like the desk, teeming with information. His eyes were the color of brushed aluminum, his hair like backswept ice, boldly corrugated. His lips were thin and bloodless, like cold metal.

No palaver. Right to biz. Rolf felt high-tuned and ready.

"One of our West Coast enablers just got his brains scrambled by a point-blank subsonic round," Smith said. "Morgan Deane. It has the earmarks of a freelance job, a much better job than the first try, which means it was farmed out to an expert, and our first impression is that the shooter might have been your girl, Alma. She does L.A. stuff, correct?"

So that's why the dead-of-night call. Smith was probing by fire, and Rolf was still liable for past depreciation.

In 2005, Rolf had recruited the woman currently IDed as Alma Acevedo to CHASE under the name Lily Tamario; she had graduated the program as Chase Lima. The corporatized nature of CHASE had caused her to splinter in 2008. Smith still blamed Rolf for losing an asset who had performed exceptionally in the field, irrespective of her views on the political temperature of some CHASE assignments. Alma had balked at killing some pop-culture loudmouth whom certain good old boys wanted dead. Chase Foxtrot had tried to pick up the slack, but the target simply vanished...probably with Alma's help. Instead of being rudely judged and demoted—in CHASE you needed a convincing reason to turn down a contract, one that could survive Smith's unforgiving scrutiny—Alma had chosen to part ways. Good help was always hard to come by, and difficult to lose, but damned near insulting when it turned out one of your brightest fireballs was now working for a lower-rent group, a loose co-op that was practically a fucking commune, patchouli and all, in comparison to the glossy Swiss movement that was CHASE.

"What makes you think it's...her?" Rolf didn't know whether to call her Alma, Lily, or Lima.

"Soft-nosed lead .22 round, one shot to the back of the head, all amplified security neutralized, no traces except for a flop-cop in the hospital with the kind of damage *you* used to instruct so well."

"That's really light."

"Security guy positively identified a long-barreled .22—same as Alma's specialty gun—before his lights went out."

"Observant fellow."

Smith seemed to be looking around a basically empty room for better evidence. "I acknowledge it's thin, Rolf, but you must acknowledge that we're accustomed to looking for patterns, even vague ones. The bigger issue is this: whoever destroyed Deane has to be erased, for the well-being of CHASE. We have to step up to protect our own interests. Whether it's your girl or not, CHASE must respond quickly and surely. Doubt must not be incurred by any of our other enablers. If it's not her, we're still looking after our own. If it is her, we've scotched a potentially dangerous wild card that *could* in theory do us more similar harm in the future. I'm not merely asking you to ferret out who it was; that would be a waste of your talent. I'm asking you that if you do flush the hitter, and it turns out to be her, do you feel any sort of residual obligation to her?"

"No, sir," Rolf said. "That ended when she left CHASE. Abandoned CHASE, rather."

Smith looked at Rolf for perhaps the first significant time that night, and let his gaze linger. "As you say. You have your assignment. Report to me as soon as you know more, because our satellites in L.A. are sometimes unreliable when it comes to full disclosure. And I don't trust these maverick operatives at all, these...freelancers." The momentary upward curl of Smith's lip was calculated to broadcast his opinion of non-sponsored regulars—anger, annoyance, mild distaste for competitors, but not so much as to lend them more than perpetual nuisance status, like household pests needing repeated extermination. "They're the Wal-Mart of the profession, when we need to maintain a standard closer to DeBeers."

"Copy that," Rolf said. "If I find anything flammable, I'll need authority to bring in a CHASE team, my picks."

"You have carte blanche. Your jet leaves in an hour. One more thing."

Rolf was already on his way out the door. He stopped.

"What happened to Mindy?"

James Smith, Chase Alpha, had never been an advocate of the psychic program phased into CHASE during the 1970s by his predecessor, Henry Hawker Seligman. Most black-bag clubs back then had pursued similar enquiries in the manner of a subterranean fad, hoping for a jackpot in the form of telekinetic soldiers for some future cyberwar. Mind control. Hypnosis. It all seemed quaint today, a withered branch of weaponization. True mind control over ordinary citizens had already been established by media and advertising; there was no need to scan their brains from afar because they had all been rendered so predictable. The masses spied on each other, with a bloodhound enthusiasm for tattling. Their passions were easily directed. Fake terrorism and manufactured recessions did the rest of the dirty work.

During the glory days of disco, the hot-button idea of cultivating psychic warriors had been as vital and exciting as the coming wave of laptop computers, which in as little as ten years might store an astonishing three hundred megabytes of memory. Nobody used a PowerBook 100 today. And very few bothered with high-maintenance sensitives, anymore.

The CHASE psychics were relegated to the dormant status of an infirm relative who is trotted out during the holiday season, then quickly tucked back into bed in front of never-ending television before he can embarrass anyone. Smith wanted to permanently unplug them, but the program lingered like furniture left behind by your dead parents, kept in a corner out of misplaced respect. *But this was Mom's favorite chair.*

Like Bumblebee.

Carlotta Elsinore had been code-named Bumblebee by Seligman, who had seconded her to CHASE when she was fifty-seven. Today she was ninety-six, and according to some forgiving accounts could still be rating as "living." Lesser talents had burned out or worn out long ago— by suicide, madness, decay, or decommission—but the Bee was still part of CHASE, one that Smith was reluctant to release into the afterlife.

David J. Schow

This meant that Smith, ironclad and steely-eyed, ruthless and specific, without mercy or hesitation, was also just a teensy bit superstitious about his own future.

The drawback with Bumblebee was that the woman could not scan other people's thoughts, predict the future, or move objects with the power of her mind. Rather, she caught information the way a randomly-cast net might snare passing fish. She was unaware of the hierarchy of the data she trapped; strange thoughts and impressions lodged in her mesh and strangers came along to take them away as though pulling cash out of an ATM.

Imagine your most beloved granny with all her blood sucked out, sunk into a therapeutic bed that has become a template for her featherlight frame, subsisting under muggy, hydroponic lamps like a night-blooming weedstalk, vampire machines pumping fluid in and waste out through twelve different hoses. Bumblebee weighed about as much as a bottle of sports water and her flesh had gone translucent, cobwebbed with the deep purple of varicosity. Teeth gone, gums receded, she required a prosthetic to eat or speak. The last time she had been out of the bed had been in 2002.

"Take out my brain," she said, her voice an arid whisper that retained a chilling squeak of her lost femininity. "Put it in an aquarium. Hook it up to a computer. Then you'll see, you fucking prick."

Smith stood near the left side of the complicated bed, wearing the eye protection necessary for this ultraviolet hothouse.

"Carlotta," he said. "No need to get uppity."

"You still want to fuck me, don't you? I'd burst apart into bones and rags. Might be worth it." In a horror movie, she might have smiled hideously, but her mouth merely twitched up on one side. She might have raised one skeletal claw, the fingernails long gone, to point like an avenging ghost, but only a finger spasmed upward, then down, like the second hand on a clock managing only a single tick of time, then relapsing as the battery died.

"You said you needed to see me," said Smith.

"Take out your cock." Her dental bite-wing was moist with cloudy saliva.

"No," he said in a bad-dog tone.

"Can you sit on your own balls yet?" she croaked. "You're really getting old, Johnnie." She always called him Johnnie; nobody knew why. "You taking those blue pills to make your weeny stiff? Pretty soon those won't work, either. Your knees will dissolve and you'll be face-down on the floor, trying to beat off."

"This is really enjoyable, Carlotta, but if you don't—"

She overrode him. "Shut up and listen. Alma. Some last name begins with an A, too, but that doesn't matter because she's got two dozen fucking names anyway."

"Acevedo. She used to be Chase Lima." There was no earthly reason that Carlotta should remember who-was-who in the doublespeak of the CHASE role-call.

"And she quit because you tried to *fuck* her."

This had been Carlotta's pattern for the past fifteen years or so—the fantasy that Smith was an old lover who cheated on her. She had once accused him off sucking off a horse that had come second in the Kentucky Derby. She had once tried to murder Isabella Rossellini, that man-stealing bitch, with mind-crisping death rays. It hadn't worked.

"You *still* want to fuck her; Alma. Well, don't."

"I promise," Smith said, already looking at the door.

"No, I mean don't track her. Do *not*. You want to put paid to her. Don't pursue it. Do *not*."

"Why?"

"Because it will be the end of you. And if you're gone, who's going to pay for all this lovely equipment to keep my cunny ready to trim your twig?"

"You'll be taken care of." Sometimes he indulged her by pretending to care. Carlotta had lost almost everything, but she was not senile or deranged, and even now after all this time Smith still feared her mind.

The fear was atavistic and unaccountable, but there nonetheless, even though he would never admit this to anyone. Every so often, that mind, imprisoned in the torture dungeon of Carlotta's useless body, would snare something scary.

"Your ex-honey patched one of your sugar daddies, you big fag."

"What do you mean?"

"Morgan Deane, that baby raper. That Alma, she took him out slicker than jism."

This was news. Carlotta had no interest in current affairs or breaking reports; there was no TV in her room. She had no access to the brokered goings-on of the kill-for-hire subculture. Her handlers would have no knowledge of Morgan Deane's connection to CHASE. In Carlotta's situation, there was no crack through which gossip could seep.

"And she's just getting started. She wants to erase her past. So you have to watch your ass, or you won't get to eat me out any more."

This parsed with the shreds of intel trickling eastward from Los Angeles. The style and method of the Deane assassination were reminiscent of Alma Acevedo's old CHASE jacket. It was a paper-thin coincidence…but now Carlotta had just spliced Alma's name to Deane, with no way of knowing the facts except for the supernatural ability that had married her to CHASE in the good old days. Her pings from the megaflow of the collective subconscious (or whatever it was) were frequently meaningless, spotty, or irrelevant. But every so often, the Bee could still deliver a stinger.

"Bring me a double martini," she said. "Pour it on me and lick it off."

This was how the world ended, with a code name and an adult diaper. It was why people demanded sex, to bathe in the meat-bone-gristle of humanity to keep from fading away like a depleted ghost or an obsolete component for which there was no longer any demand. It was why you needed to get real blood on your real hands from time to time. It was the ancient yin-yang of lust and murder, sex and killing, love and death.

"Sure thing, Carlotta," Smith said. It was time to go turn Rolf Dettrick, Chase Delta, loose on the City of Angels.

Rolf had gone willingly to the uptown apartment of Mindy Zayden, a.k.a. Chase Foxtrot, fully knowing she was intent on killing him in order to clean the chute for a little career advancement. In a backhanded way, Rolf admired her drive. Mindy would not target him, another CHASE operative, unless she felt he was a bona fide threat.

Her own work file had betrayed her method. She had used seduction to mouse-trap two-thirds of her assignments, earning her the nickname of "preying Mintis." She favored needles over gun work; Etorphine for paralysis, followed by an extract of the fruit of the Pong-pong tree, *Cerbera odollam*, also known in India and Asia as the "Suicide Tree," for a fast finish that could admirably confound autopsy. If this more exotic poison was unavailable, Mindy might use a simple distillate of nicotine sulfate, which you could make yourself, practically anywhere, with a few good cigars and an espresso machine.

She had poured some cold, clear, crisp wine. "It refreshes and keeps the body fire up," she said, before shucking her top and adding, "I've got something to show you."

With her clothes off she was pretty scrumptious, Rolf had to admit. She was randy and humid, eyelids hooded, ready to party.

But Rolf had already found the hypodermic secreted near the bed. He rolled her face-down and jammed her in the right-side carotid artery. She was, at once, totally aware and utterly immobile. Since she had het him up so much, he made use of her body before he killed her. The act reminded him a lot of his college days, and all those drunken, sloppy Lit majors and sorority airheads, who were little better than flumpy rag-doll fucks, anyway.

David J. Schow

Smith had asked about Chase Foxtrot's fate, and Rolf did not lie.

"It was her or me, sir," Rolf told James Smith, honestly. "She called you a mummy."

Rolf thought he caught a flicker of pique as it zapped through Smith's metallic eyes. Smith exhaled nasally.

"I have been aware of Mindy Zayden's designs on the Alpha position for some time," he said, not entirely truthfully. "You did what you had to do and reported it to me, directly, just now, with no prevarication. But this adds to your own task. Now you must find a suitable new candidate for the Chase Foxtrot position that has just been vacated. Perhaps one of the team members you select could be that, or mature into that, with your guidance."

"Will do."

"That is another reason I chose you over her for this excursion," said Smith. "Please do not disappoint me. Go to L.A. Utilize the data pull we have on local contract hits. Use a stalking horse to infiltrate them if you want. Our earliest skim indicates Morgan Deane might have been a completely random kill, a vendetta thing, one dissatisfied customer erasing a personal complaint. But if it is not..."

"I've got this, sir," said Rolf. His promotion was practically assured.

Bryan's Night Out

The Fourth of July, in Los Angeles, is an excellent night for shooting people you do not like. Same as New Year's. For whole days before and after, the residual pop-pop-pop becomes just another melody line of the urban symphony. You hear Black Cats and firecracker strings banging away while $100-a-shot skyrockets and pyro stars light up the sky from Long Beach to the Hollywood Bowl, sparkling explosions of faux warfare all across the basin. Little dandelion puffballs of chemical light blooming out near San Pedro, muted by the marine layer. Giant galactic starbursts blasting straight upward from Dodger Stadium. Then, in the midst of the cacophony, right when you're thinking this is what Beirut must look and sound like on an average business day, you hear a *wham* that has to be a shotgun going off, or the measured one-through-six reports of some wily troublemaker emptying a revolver. He or she could be firing into the ground just for general noisemaking. Worse, he or she could be blasting lead skyward, to rain down wherever. Or he or she could be squelching another him or her by blowing holes in them, because, hey, the time is right and the night is made to party.

Everybody is staring up at the skyline, disqualifying themselves as witnesses. This made it easier for Bryan Silver to do a hot prowl on the address Alma had given him to process in return for her picking up his tab on the Morgan Deane job.

Bryan was fresh off a return flight from JFK, his accounts squared during his absence with Alma's able assistance. He slept well on jets.

Bryan soared his vehicle off the northbound 101 at Laurel Canyon. The Buick LaCrosse, rented blind, was a good work car for anonymity, just another sliding box in whatever-blue. Bryan had recently admitted his tendency to acquire job cars in silver, in deference to his own name, and that was a pattern, and patterns were traceable and therefore discouraged. He hung a right on Moorpark—famously known as "Kraproom" locally for obvious reasons, although for Bryan the entire San Fernando Valley was one big crapper of urban sprawl. Parking options quickly reached migraine level.

At least it wasn't Burbank.

He was still getting accustomed to his iPhone. When he called Alma, one button tap brought her image, live, talking back at him, which was a bit strange. It was Dick Tracy's old wrist-radio video-phone brought to life in an unexpected form. It was still mildly marvelous, like science fiction come to pass. At least as marvelous as the notion that Alma had been naked the last time they conferenced. Fucking tease. One of these days...

It was eminently possible that Bryan could curry her favor by making quick, clean work of the gig she had tossed him, to "scratch the subject" at least as well as she had eliminated Morgan Deane on Bryan's behalf.

He parked a block and a half away from target, on the east side of Vantage Avenue so the car would be aimed north, back toward the freeway. The objective address was halfway down the next block on Bellingham. It was the usual dump of two-story hellhole crackerbox found in these parts, with a bald smudge of yard beyond a loose gate, and exterior breezeways. Number 107 was in the back.

Nobody home yet.

The rear kitchen door, put there only because the law required apartments such as these to have more than one exit, turned out to be a repurposed interior door. No core, no solidity; it barely classified as a barrier.

There turned out to be a dog inside, a big, honking German Shepherd who started barking the moment Bryan began to breach the door. Bryan unclipped his Taser.

Tasering a dog was almost the opposite of hitting a standing human target and putting him fetal. For one thing, Tasers were necessarily designed to work best when striking center mass, which meant that to take down an animal, the gun had to be held sideways, gangsta-style, to achieve the optimum probe spread of six inches on a canine torso. Too much distance and one of the barbs would miss. Thick fur could be worse than clothing.

Bryan let the beast charge, which it did. *Bzzt*. The barbs were propelled by liquid nitrogen at 180 feet per second with less energy than a BB gun, but had boosted stopping power—50,000 volts at 26 amps—because Bryan had packed the military derivative, the Advanced Model M26-C. He minded the wires as the big dog was arrested in mid-jump and went down hard, twitching. The live leads could still shock. It was a misnomer that you could electrocute yourself with a Taser. Idiots in movies shot them into pools of water and incapacitated whole cadres of bad guys. Never happen.

Bryan placed the Taser pistol unit on the arm of a ratty sofa. If the dog stirred, he could trigger a fresh dose.

Shep's owner was due back within the half-hour. The man's schedule was dunningly predictable, therefore Bryan could use the pattern to his advantage. The only wiggle would be if the target decided to work late. Alma had mentioned being privy to some inside news that suggested this would not be the case, today. If so, then Bryan would fall back and kill time. His main concern was finding some decent Chinese in this neck of the flats—afterward—because his stomach was starting to rumble. Bryan never did lunch. Maybe some black pepper chicken would be good, or some sesame lo mein.

David J. Schow

The joint read as a typical bachelor cave: unmade bed, bigscreen TV, second-hand furniture, boxes still collecting dust in every room, rust-stained kitchen sink (an old-school, tub-style probably original to the building), too much ancient paint on the door hinges, grout ditches, forty-year-old wood paneling starting to lever itself away from the wall, cobwebs on the ceiling lights, lamentable carpeting, and the general transient air that oppresses most similar digs. Nothing had been hung on the wall. This was not a living space. It was a way station from one calling to a better one in a hopeful future that would never happen, now.

The apartment read prime for that old standby story, the Drug Deal Gone Bad. Bryan had brought along a packet of heroin, vendor weight, for just that purpose, amused to think that no one ever heard about a Drug Deal Gone Good.

Say, this cocaine is excellent root-canal quality, friend! You constantly deliver value and stand behind your product. Here, please take some more money for your trouble.

The Bad was a venerable but reliable fiction that made policemen's jobs easier, in the normal world where cops conveniently cleaned up after you without knowing it. In less than an hour, Bryan would have recycled the old story again and be making tracks for the Blazing Wok, over on Ventura.

The apartment's occupant bustled in on time, calling for someone named King Gee, probably the Shepherd. What a fucking stupid name for a dog; some butt-plug rapper handle, yo-yo-yo. The dude matched the photos Alma had shown Bryan.

The dude saw his doggie sprawled out on the floor, where Bryan had intentionally left it to misdirect attention. It could not be seen unless one was already inside the apartment.

The dude's mouth dropped slightly. That was the beat Bryan had waited for—the surprise, followed by the shock, then the hesitation, then the fear, all in a big Dagwood sandwich pile-up.

74

That's when Bryan stepped out from the kitchen (over the dog, minding the Taser wires). Per test range specs, he had fitted his Glock 19 with a Lone Wolf threaded barrel to take a GemTech silencer. Out in the world he carried the Glock unsilenced in a Crye precision gun clip because the GemTech can was longer than the pistol itself. Now he raised the assembly to aim one-handed, at chin height.

The guy started to protest.

"No," said Bryan. "Sit. Now."

A hostage ramped up on fight-or-flight will hurry to comply with the business end of a weapon in order to buy more standing time, in order to stammer excuses. It is a kind of forced speed-politeness, talking more to the weapon than to the assailant, trying to talk the gun out of firing. That half-beat of stopped time was what Bryan would use to put him down.

That didn't happen.

Quite without warning, the guy was suddenly two feet to the left as Bryan fired a double tap that made twin plaster puffs vomit from the wall.

Even more unexpectedly, the guy executed a hellbent, face-first dive over the kitchen table, landing in a scatter of flying junk to seesaw the whole table up as a shield that stopped Bryan's next two rounds as Bryan tried to center him on the move.

A total surprise was the giant flatscreen blazing to hellacious life, really loud, with an image of some actor trying to out-run a fireball. It turned Bryan's gaze for a crucial microsecond, and the noise startled him.

Most unexpectedly of all, when the dude came up he had a god-damned *pistol* in one hand. No load or rack, no precious, effete handling, just an instant *bang*.

Now where the hell had the gun been hidden? Bryan had scoped the room and found no obvious stash-points.

A heavy-caliber slug grabbed Bryan by the shoulder and pitched him backward into the kitchen. His gun arm had been hit. He squeezed off two useless shots—they hurt—as he tripped and fell over the prone dog. He bashed the back of his skull on the counter edge as he plummeted, sending a dish there airborne like a big earthenware tiddly-wink.

His Glock was three feet from his grasp. Before he could roll, another shot punched all the sound out of the room and his right thigh lit up in a volcano of molten lava pain. Despite all his training, he contracted—*away* from his gun.

Now he was the one who was fetal on the floor.

Things were not going as Bryan had planned, and he had a feeling he was never going to make his rendezvous with the black pepper chicken. All he could hear was the white wash of five-channel noise as the hero in the movie ducked explosions. No Blazing Wok, for Bryan. Just the 5.1 Dolby digital thunder of things blowing up and falling apart.

Dave's Independence Day

In about twenty-four hours, I was going to have my dream date with Daisy Villareal. It had only been time-delayed about a quarter of a century. From her manner at the coffee shop, sex seemed a not-unreasonable bet, and having seen her with her clothes on, now I couldn't stop thinking about her with them off.

It was the Fourth of July, whoopee-shit. Fireworks going off for two days now. The reek of grilled meat everywhere. Reenacted warfare from over two centuries ago, but with "safe-and-sane" detonations in the sky, to make the local tribes ooh and ahh. Maybe Burbank would call up and surrender. I was already old enough that bright sparkly things had lost some of their primal allure. Besides, I already had better fireworks of my own, going off inside my head.

I must have looked at the old yearbook photos of Daisy two thousand times, when I wasn't trying to hurriedly straighten up my rathole (would we wind up at her place or mine?) or slow down my runaway-train heartbeat.

(Or even more excruciatingly delicious, was the possibility we might tease the whole incipient lovemaking thing for one more encounter, so eventually our shared bodily fluids would evaporate as instantaneous steam.)

I polished off the reference disc of a movie called *Ripdown*, which had severe authoring problems unrelated to the director's fanboy lust for energy-drink-infused shaky-cam shots obliterated by lens flare. The combination was headache-inducing, not helped by the render-down from 3-D (for theaters) to 2-D (for everybody else). This waste of time co-starred Teagan Conner, widely blogged and tweeted as the sexpot of the moment, famous not for thespic ability so much as for her bedroom smile, her saucy candids and heroic implants (part of the rationale for the 3-D). The digital bump-up revealed her complexion to be as rough as particle board. Frankly, she struck me as dogmeat next to the likes of Daisy.

Man oh man, did I have it bad now. Pity me.

I dropped off my eleven-page stat sheet on *Ripdown*'s problems at the Starburst Post front desk, having logged extra hours in order to take off early the next day, D-Day. I even bought extra grooming products on the way home. Scented soap. Lanolin-infused shaving gel that would be extra-kind to my skin. No cologne. She would not like men who wore artificial scent. I just knew this.

I flashed back to Step-Mom, the one who had disdained my inclination to write. My dad's second wife, after my real mother died. One Christmas when I was about twelve, we found ourselves jostled along in that ninth circle of hell known as the 1980s shopping mall experience. The whole place was noisy and overcrowded with grimly determined holiday consumers; joy everywhere for sale, and scant happiness on view. Step-Mom actually grabbed my head to aim it toward a perfume counter at some Macy's. Then, pushing me by the head, she walked me closer to the counter to point out a bottle of Opium Eau de Toilette. She pressed some moist cash into my hand. "Buy that," she said. "That will be your Christmas present to me."

At least the woman knew what she wanted. But to this day the sight of a perfume counter can still trigger that old unease, the feeling that I was completely out of control, impotent and useless except as a tool for the desires of others. Men's scent displays prompted the same old fear, so eventually I trained my eye not to mark them. To willfully break character and tart myself up in smelly-spoo for Daisy would ring falsely...unless I could get information out of her on how she liked her men to smell; then I'd be back at that counter faster than birdshot.

Tonight's order of business would be to make sense of the chaos in my apartment—just in case. Scrub out the rusty drips in the kitchen sink, which were chronic. Make sure the bathroom wasn't an abattoir of rushed maleness and was suitable for feminine use. Try to reconfigure all the piles of DVDs and junk so they seemed somehow aesthetic. Maybe get around to hanging that framed Alphonse Mucha print of his justly-famous *The Four Seasons*. It might divert a critical eye. It had been a housewarming gift from Hayden Mathis, what...two years ago? Three?

On second thought, it would be a major victory just to get the stray socks off the floor and make sure the bedroom was cleared of its gym locker funk. Who was I kidding? No matter what I did, the place would look like a teenager's shit pit. I still had end tables made out of thieved milk crates, for god's sake.

I butted the Infiniti into a barely adequate spot on Bellingham, the front bumper clearing a driveway by about two inches. A front dent from a parking garage mishap made up the difference. I really needed to get that fixed. Pounded out and cleansed of the white sideswipe skidmarks.

I had my remote for the flatscreen with me. I had taken it to work to disassemble it and clean the touch-pads. Those things get grimy and uncooperative when you use them as much as I do, and I disliked the "dirty feel" of buttons blackened by skin oil. At Sunburst, a tech rat named Rocky had micro-tools and a magnifying bench lamp, plus silicon cleaner for the circuit boards.

The routine Kingi had laid out for me went as follows: He knew my footsteps. He would immediately begin barking like a lunatic at my approach. The sound of the key in the door would not fool him; he had to see my face before he stood down.

I had my key in the upper deadbolt and Kingi still had not made a sound.

My first thought was that he had figured out the back door. It was a piece of Masonite garbage with a knob lock I'd already seen the dog try to open with his teeth, several times, like a willful adolescent pissed off at not getting his own set of keys. A sneeze would blow it down. Whatever gremlin kept me from repairing my scuffed car had also infinitely delayed the project of reinforcing the back door. I spackled over the whole issue by deluding myself that I had nothing worth stealing, anyway. No burglar was going to heist away my flatscreen without helpers and a truck. I didn't possess jewelry or cherished family photos. I had some beer in the fridge.

"Kingi, you scurrilous mutt, what are you up to?"

I had one foot inside when I saw Kingi lying on the floor with Taser filigree dangling from his ribs. The ugly pistol unit was perched on the arm of my sofa. Someone was in here. I could feel the displaced air and intruder vibe. My thumb clicked on the TV almost unconsciously. Distraction.

The man who stepped out from the kitchen over Kingi's prone form was about five-ten and looked like a slumming car stereo dealer. Sandy hair and a PR face. He was wearing a very light black windbreaker that was still absurd in today's balmy heat, which always hits the Valley harder. If it's 90 degrees in Hollywood, it's a hundred-plus in the Valley. That's why this whole spread used to be nothing but orange groves. Plus, the Santa Ana winds were taking the day off, making the climate hot and oppressive. Only homeless people wore jackets in this kind of basting heat...

And people who needed to conceal a Taser in a holster, and perhaps other items best not glimpsed by neighborhood dog walkers or sweaty joggers...

Like the Glock he was pointing at my sweet spot. He stepped over my dog as though Kingi was a trash bag, and I already wanted to kill him just for that.

"No," the man said. "Sit. Now."

He would expect me to freeze up and then try to tell him this was all some bizarre error. To lull me so he could place his shots. That was the only moment inside of which I could move, and I side-stepped.

He fired twice. The game was on.

I hurled myself at the dinette table and it collapsed, as I expected it to. My nearest gun hide was a spring-clip inside the kitchen cabinet. There were seven firearms total concealed in easy access hot spots around the apartment. Maybe that was why I never got around to fixing the back door. The kitchen gun was a decocked Sig P226 with a .40 caliber wadcutter already chambered. With the table up as a temporary shield, the pistol came instantly in my hand. Two more shots flew at me. The shooter would glance to see if they had hit.

That's when the flatscreen popped on, resuming play on the warmed-up DVD of *Short Fuse 2*, with Mason Stone's fireball sprint. The gunman could not help but look at it.

Sight, squeeze, and the intruder toppled.

Time window for neighbors to call the cops: about thirty seconds if there was another shot. Lag time for the police: maybe half an hour unless they were cruising by, which they never were.

Fireworks ignited the evening sky outside. The other people in the building had their doors open or were watching from tiny so-called sundecks. My own front door was still open.

The guy reached for his dropped Glock and I centered him in time to put another round in his leg, to dissuade him. That was my second shot. Now people would be looking toward my apartment instead of the bright diversions in the sky.

Kingi stirred with a tiny whimper. Apart from the EMD— electro-muscular disruption—those probes hurt, and drew blood.

Sometimes you luck out and score a parking spot. Or get a second chance to meet up with the dream girl of your past. Sometimes the police are right in the neighborhood. Already there were sirens and lights, dammit.

It appeared that my cover identity as Derek David Vollmand had been well and truly blown.

Agent Collins

Special Agent Collins flashed his FBI credentials at the duty guard outside room #302 on the third floor of St. Joseph's Hospital, in Burbank. The sprawl of the medical facility and its attendant outbuildings was easily perplexing to non-natives, who in searching for doctors or an ER might just as easily find themselves facing a structure held up by the Seven Dwarves, in the equally-sprawling Disney complex right on the other side of Buena Vista Street. The dichotomy summed up all of L.A. County for outsiders and tourists. *Paging Dr. Sneezy...*

The sentry, an LAPD regular, nodded and admitted Agent Collins to the private room, trying for something like sympathetic camaraderie, since Collins was a GS-15, Level 5 man dispatched by the local field office—a Bureau climber near the apex of the pyramid, not to be dealt with lightly.

"Sorry about your man," the officer said, knowing that this government suit probably raked in ten times his cop salary.

"It happens. Thanks, officer. Okay if I close the door?"

"Your show."

"Thanks again." For Agent Collins, the officer immediately ceased to exist.

Bryan Silver, incarcerated by hoses, dressings and an elevated leg brace in his adjustable bed, hissed out a deep sigh as though the last thing he wanted to do was just lay there, helpless, and answer more stupid questions. Collins allowed Bryan to read his Bureau particulars.

"Thomas Collins?" said Bryan. "That's pretty adorable."

"No more so than Les Buttram," said Collins, taking back the bifold wallet. He had cited the pseudonym under which Bryan was checked into the hospital, also as a presumed FBI agent.

"I see you outrank me."

"Why not? Maybe we should both be working for the government."

"Nahh," said Bryan. "Too socially limiting. Who are you really?"

"CHASE."

"Oh, *no*," Bryan groaned. It was the sound of a man way past bedtime, watching his toilet overflow. "Why?"

Rolf Dettrick pocketed his superb false ID. "Because I want you to tell me every single little thing you know about Alma Acevedo, also known as Lily Tamario. She's ex-CHASE. She's tied up in that little boutique kaffesklatsch you also work jobs for. And it appears she just killed a benefactor of CHASE. I want to know who called the assignment, who paid for it, and where Alma is now."

"And I should help you because...?"

"Because we don't want maverick hitters thinking they can blithely assassinate people like Morgan Deane, for whatever reason. People who benefit CHASE are entitled to feel protected by CHASE. The efficacy of CHASE cannot be put into doubt."

"Can you say 'CHASE' one or two more times, like it impresses me?"

"This might impress you." Rolf pulled out a latex glove affixed to an IV needle. He blew in the glove to inflate it like a cartoon udder. Then he attached it to Bryan's IV port. "One squeeze and you're gone by pulmonary embolism, which is entirely predictable in your condition. Two .40 caliber slugs, your heart rate is spiking right now, you tried to self-medicate and blew it."

"Okay, all right. Jesus, you guys are such drama queens." Bryan secreted panic sweat. The goddamned monitors would betray every metabolic jump. It was worse than being hooked up to a polygraph.

Now this man will test the waters, thought Rolf. See how far he can lie.

"I don't know anything about that job," Bryan lied. "Don't you think if CHASE had bothered to let anyone know that Morgan Deane was off limits—?"

"You're saying that the hit was outside of CHASE's interests?"

"Yeah. All I heard was that some guy Deane sued wanted payback, and had the bank to get it. We had no flags on Deane. Maybe you guys should be a little more sharing with your do-not-knock lists."

Bryan fought not to fidget. The Deane score had been *his* job and he'd traded it to Alma. Why? Because the first Morgan Deane hit—the failed one—had been Bryan's failure, and you never get personal about a repeater, and Bryan needed to bury old mishaps. It was a professional embarrassment he did not want out in the open air. What was a good way to skate around this? "I heard it from Alma. Nothing more specific."

"Seems like you 'heard' a lot about a job you had nothing to do with." Bryan had said "heard" twice now, as though he operated via rumor. "Why did Alma tell you?"

"Shop talk."

"Bullshit." Rolf's hand enclosed the inflated glove.

"Okay, wait! Christ." Bryan groped for his empty water cup. Rolf filled it halfway from a plastic carafe. "Okay...you know Alma. You've seen her."

Rolf nodded. "I recruited her into CHASE before she quit."

"Okayokay then, I mean, you know what she looks like. We were just *talking*, for god's sake."

Rolf's expression pinched as though from a minor gas pain. "You mean you were trying to chat her up?"

"*Yes*," Bryan said, trying to make his exhalation sound as annoyed as possible. "Look, I know you guys like to overplot, to find the agenda behind the cover story that masks the lie. But this is simple because it's true. Yes, I wanted her attention. Yes, we talked about some things very peripherally, and one of those things was that single fact about the Deane job."

"So you would potentially compromise an op to get into her pants? That's not very professional."

"Call a lawyer," said Bryan. "File a lawsuit. I don't expect anybody from CHASE to understand why one human being might want to sleep with another human being."

This was going well, Bryan thought. He was settled into his role now. Hadn't this asshole ever slept with a co-worker? The sex angle was a terrific diversion. He might get to leave this room alive.

"Clarify something for me," said Rolf. "The Morgan Deane hit was definitely Alma's work."

"Yes, as far as I know."

Now Rolf could tell Chase Alpha, James Smith, that his refrigerated psychic, code-name Bumblebee, had been right on the nosey. Maybe that was why Smith kept that crumbling, cackling old bitch around. An ex-CHASE had killed a CHASE asset, confirmed. That was all the permission Rolf needed to retire old business currently at large, and clip a hangnail using the name Alma. Rolf was still suffering demerits for bringing her into CHASE, then losing her. A decisive and corrective action on his part would impress James Smith and wipe out the lingering debt. Maybe he could bring Smith Alma's head in a bag; *that* would certainly be a statement.

"Where is Alma now?"

"All I've got is a number," said Bryan. He and this guy, this fake Tom Collins, were bonding now. Just two men in similar professions, sharing intel instead of blackmailing each other at gunpoint.

"If there's a number, there's a phone," said Rolf. "And if there's a phone, she can be vectored, right?"

"Standard operating procedure." Bryan was beginning to breathe easier, lulled calm.

"You wouldn't be shining me on, would you, Bryan?"

How had this fucking guy gotten his real name? Oh, man, thought Bryan, I've got to be more careful. Not that "Bryan" was his authentic, actual childhood name. It was merely his latest identity. But it was supposed to be hermetic enough that this CHASE dickhead shouldn't know it. Bryan should also have known about Morgan Deane's connection to CHASE; perhaps that was why Bryan had to call an abort on the first planned hit—incomplete intel. Getting the window to hand the job off to Alma had seemed like a godsend. Done deal, *twice*, even, and still nobody had mentioned CHASE...that was how deeply Deane's association had been buried.

"Tell me everything you know about the man who shot you."

Praise Jeebus—an escape hatch.

"Uh, bread and butter. A blind contract. I fly in, do the job, and fly out. Except this guy wasn't the grunt he was supposed to be, either."

"Obviously," Rolf said with a hint of disdain. "He took *you* out and escaped."

"He knew evasion and cover. Distraction and stress-firing. He had at least one stash gun. He didn't hesitate. He wasn't who he was supposed to be."

"And you didn't think, 'setup'?"

"Yeah, I'm thinking it *now*," Bryan said with just the right touch of irritation. "An attempted and *failed* hit lends credibility to somebody else's cover story. But I'm not in on the story. Maybe that's why the contractors hired freelance, instead of going to somebody like *your* fine organization."

"Disposable hit men," said Rolf.

"Exactly. I want to know what's really going on as much as you do."

"No." Judicial finality, from Rolf. "If you're as big a tool as I think you are, you'll run around on your own vendetta and muddy up the pond to clear your own ego. On the other hand, that might have harassment value. Do it well, or come up with an interesting plan, something outside the box, and there might even be a place for you in CHASE."

Rolf was James Smith's avatar in this deal. He had to make command decisions. He was akin to a captain on a far war front who could not wait for approval from headquarters.

"I wouldn't mind that," said Bryan, lying again.

Rolf chewed on the inside of his cheek, thinking it over, weighing the variables. "No. Can't risk it."

He squeezed the rubber glove and clicked off the monitor alarms. Then he quickly went through Bryan Silver's effects before departing.

There was no phone.

After trying Dave Vollmand's cell for the tenth time and still getting fobbed off to voicemail after nearly a day, Hayden Mathis visited his pal's apartment and found it sealed in cop security tape and no-entry notices. He rang a few hospitals and got nothing. The police were looking for Dave Vollmand.

He rang Starburst Post and Conchita—gatekeeper and guardian of the front-desk switchboard—told him that if he had any idea where Dave had gone, could he please tell Dave to get in touch, for crap's sake?

Hayden's second suspicion was predictable: a crime, a mugging, something brutal and abrupt with the force to knock a person out of the societal loop in an instant. His *first* suspicion was a shade darker, and had to do with the information Dave had shared about hooking up with the high school honey, that Daisy chick.

Hayden had excellent knowledge of his friend's emotional ups and downs. Lesser beings had succumbed to weaker myths before. In marriage, the traditional warning benchmark was the seven-year itch. In divorce, the parallel delusion went that your spouse dumped you or your partner abandoned you as part of a larger karmic scheme, to make you available for a latecomer you really should have been paired with in the first place. Stuck at the statistical midpoint of their predicted lifespan, many people could only look downhill at the rest of their lives, lament their choices, and spend the years suffering in silence. You know these people—the resigned ones, the cheated, whose quiet battle-whimper is that *the world fucked me, waahhh.* If you don't recognize the syndrome, you might be one yourself.

Some people in the midstream of their existence took the pat shackles of routine to be a sign that they needed to do something, well, crazy. Stir up the life-silt in an unexpected way to see what floats. Get back on the horse, as Dave had once said.

Maybe that was what had happened with Daisy.

If so, Dave might resurface in due time, either squashed anew or so happy that nobody would want to be around him. If not...

The whole police thing cast a much darker pall.

Hayden found out that Kingi was boarded at the vet's on Ventura. While not privy to client information, he was able to charm a heavy-set young assistant named Beatrice into divulging that that dog had been Tasered. Hayden whiffed Beatrice's life story in an instant. She was one of the resigned ones, the ones whose mothers called from afar to chide them about not being married or not reproducing. She might have been pretty, but she had long ago eschewed cosmetic artifice and taken herself out of the mating game, justifying this course through her commitment to animals who would not judge her so shallowly. Beatrice was a walking embodiment of the mercy fuck, and easy to manipulate.

Hayden made a few more calls. No flags. Until a new development surged forth, there was not much to do except go back to his own place and try to dope out how to configure a DVD cover for a movie called *My Best Senior Prom* without resorting to the usual collage of big actor faces, all a-grin with idiotic expressions designed to signal the illiterate that this was, in fact, a bouncy comedy romp about how life was much simpler, and more vital, in those wacky high school days. The back-flap synopsis revealed the film as another spineless feel-good wallow, the kind that always ends with a wedding.

Social programming was everywhere. Poor Beatrice.

Hayden's apartment was on Columbus Avenue in Sherman Oaks, near the interchange of the 101 with the San Diego Freeway, the dreaded

405. For assorted reasons the location had been a good pick for its proximity to the Van Nuys airport, with LAX as a southward fallback. It was close enough to Dave's place that Hayden could be considered "local" within the vast, flat, depressing autoshop dealership that was the Valley.

His apartment was airless and beige—similar to Dave's—and Hayden wondered when the more soul-deprived, yet efficient Japanese housing model would swoop in to displace the chockablock human file cabinets here, all sagging structures still unrecovered from the last big quake over a decade ago. His door key still stuck in the grime of the elderly lock and had to be jiggled just so. The door, crooked in its frame to begin with, required the choreography of a light kick to the lower right side to open properly.

Inside this sanctuary was another sofa, just like Dave's. Another recliner, ditto (it no longer reclined). Flatscreen TV, check. Piles of junk, check. Every day, Hayden opened the door expecting to see something new, the way you constantly revisit your refrigerator, lowering your standards each time until you can finally compromise on something to eat.

Today there was something new waiting in Hayden's crib. His TV was on, and there was a man sitting in his kitchen, holding a gun.

David Kemp's truncated writing career, and the reason he had to change his last name, had to do with a lower-tier Florida power broker named Aristede Wilsoni, whose legitimate business fronts were diversified across everything from slot machine manufacture to vote-counting computer software. Invisible to the surface world, Wilsoni thrived as a behind-the-scenes player of intrigues high and low...until a nosy buttinski named David Kemp exposed him.

The creatures of the pit do not like having light shined on them.

David Kemp broke into journalism during the 2000 presidential election, when reporters could not illuminate the mysteries of hanging chads fast enough. Every new dawn brought another layer of corruption and back-room fast-buckery to investigate, and every ring of the tree led to another, more hidden ring. It wasn't the makers of the voting machines at fault, for example, but the wraithlike conspirators far behind them, concealed by siege walls of false identity, shell corporations, and deeply strategized deniability. The kind of war-chamber brain trust that could cheese an entire election while outraged citizens scurried around and placed blame on easy targets that were merely symptoms. It was the damned computers, known to be vulnerable and inaccurate since the early 1970s. It was the lack of audit trails. It was lax security. It was the Vote-O-Matic disenfranchisement of hundreds of thousands of lawful ballot-casters. It was the ATM approach to voting brought by the Direct Recording Electronic (DRE) system—a brilliant cups-and-balls setup that did absolutely nothing to ensure that the onscreen voting data was actually recorded on its memory cartridge, or that the same data would appear on a printout from that same cartridge. It was the staggeringly handicapped tabulation system. It was the software. It was useless, shiny equipment that practically invited fraud. By god, it was the very election system itself, all the way back to 1776.

Aristede Wilsoni was the sort of fellow whose specialty was slipping through cracks, like all those mentioned above. He was not one of the reptilian control freaks, the high plotters, the beings who depended on him as a functionary. Aristede Wilsoni was content to enable the machinations of those whose purpose he neither comprehended nor cared about, so long as his percentage held firm. He was, in short, the perfect employee.

Until David Kemp shined the light on his name.

It started with a freelance op-ed piece titled "I Know You Are, But What Am I?" about the media circus generated by the underhanded 2000 Florida elections, published in a Miami free paper called *GladesBeat*, which up until then had been content to print flashfire pieces with titles like "Genocide Against Teen Drunk Drivers." Kemp's

David J. Schow

informed rant was contentious enough to grab the notice of the wire services, with observations such as:

> *It is child's play to cite the needs of the many over the few, which keeps those needs diffused and spread out too thinly to ever snap into critical focus. The solution starts not with biased quantities, "many" versus "few," but with individuals, one at a time, each judged on his or her own merits.*

One of the individuals Kemp chose to exemplify this was the man behind shipping and maintenance of the voting devices themselves, who turned out to be Aristede Wilsoni...who ignored callbacks, refused interviews, and embarked on a closed-door campaign to discredit anyone who sought to sully his reputation as anything other than a rock-honest Miami businessman and community booster.

Despite Wilsoni's disinformation—a rancid Swiss cheese of half-truths and coverups that only got more naked as each update went viral—Kemp quickly gained the ear of various government watchdogs, who were happy to have a busybody so willing to throw himself on the pyre. The government was not paying him. He was another misguided idealist who thought the truth would see him through to fulfillment in a kind of ultimate rightness. He was the best kind of sacrificial lamb.

The sentences that killed Kemp's career as a muckraker were:

> *Until working moms like Kathleen Morris and blue collar bread-winners like Moe Brannigan know the names of people like Aristede Wilsoni, the real puppet masters of your government will remain anonymous and invulnerable, and the USA will remain an ignorant, knee-jerk ideal instead of a thinking reality. To cite the famous quotation attributed to everyone from Shakespeare to Jefferson to Hunter S. Thompson, people—as in "We, the People"— will get pretty much the government they deserve.*

David Kemp's Miami apartment filled up with bullets on the evening of November 10th, 2000. It was written up in *GladesBeat* as "a drug deal gone bad."

Uzis spewing nine-mil hardball destroyed all the front windows, then everything behind those windows in an extravagant display the police estimated as consuming five hundred rounds or more. It took fewer than ten seconds.

Dave Kemp was hunkered down in his kitchenette, covered in glass fragments and the spaghetti sauce he had been warming up for a snack. When the responding officers first saw him, they thought he had been hacked with a machete in the manner of Colombian book-keeping (hence the drug deal angle that percolated through to print in *GladesBeat*; nobody had bothered to double check).

Kemp armed up with an old, unpapered Beretta nine from an almost-forgotten, dusty shoebox waiting in the rear of his closet, just in time for the second organized attempt on his life. On this occasion, he returned fire in a manner not dissimilar to his writing style. Unfortunately, the event transpired in a much more public place—the lobby of the New Neon Palms Hotel, where he had retreated after his apartment had been destroyed. One gunman went down (out of three), two bystanders were wounded, and Dave caught a slug in his right calf. He had stung Wilsoni and Wilsoni had stung back, but that was not the end of the matter.

After a third pass—a genuine drive-by in broad daylight, machine guns and gangsters straight out of a Thirties shoot 'em up that obliterated a lot of storefront windows, patched several pedestrians and won Dave another bullet (this one in his upper right back)—the FBI and ATF begrudgingly allowed that David Kemp might be in residual danger. So they placed a team around his hospital room, which was a good thing since it deflected the five-man squad sent to kill him again, two days later. As soon as David Kemp was coherent, an FBI field agent named Stanton Weeks offered him a witness-relocation deal on the condition

David J. Schow

Kemp turn over all his research into Aristede Wilsoni. It was a bare-bones pact, no frills, but good enough for government work.

As soon as Derek David Vollmand had been established in California, the Wilsoni files disappeared into the nearest shredder. As long as he did not require any exclusive, costly monitoring or support, and as long as the newly-minted Vollmand was paying for his own upkeep, the Bureau saw no reason to reopen his jacket. The management flipovers of the next decade helped cloud the issue, and the Vollmand file went dormant as just another satisfied client of WitSec. The "retcon"—retroactive continuity—provided by Agent Weeks convinced Aristede Wilsoni that David Kemp had died in an automobile accident on the Don Schula Expressway. Video was provided to prove this. Agent Weeks was killed in the line of duty in 2002, and Wilsoni was assassinated by malefactors unknown in mid-2004.

The criminals who replaced Aristede Wilsoni had scant interest in the exposés of journalists, and even less interest in the written word itself. The first decade of the 2000s demonstrated that the power of the press counted for squat when Internet grazers rarely read past the first paragraph, if they could read at all. So many people bellowing so many points of view online, constantly, diminished the import of any single news item, which could be handily buried amidst the breaking headlines of cute pet videos and the fashion faux pas of celebrities. The needs of the "many" had won out on the brave new Web frontier. The cliché of the crusading reporter had shaded to sepia, to be benched alongside the cassette tape and the rotary land line. It wasn't that bad things no longer happened or that good people failed to care. It was that the nebulous "system," the City Hall your parents warned you against fighting, had rolled an entire population over into submission and despair. Good people still cared, but *most* people cared more about paying their bills, feeding their children, and cowering against the boogeyman of terrorism. The brokers of modern fear were the real terrorists, keeping the citizenry in a high, humming state of fatalistic compliance.

Even better for the high plotters, no one could remember the lessons of history, or apply such fragmented information as they might have retained. Such dangers as rational thought were easily blotted up by the calculatedly deployed hysteria of manufactured crises that were only intermittently necessary, since very few people could remember a world before 1995, anyway.

The revised version of Dave studied "body awareness," which made him slightly more graceful and taught him how to absorb impact without disorientation—a thing his friend Hayden Mathis knew by instinct; how to fall down without killing yourself. It was also a bit like the Zen of parking your car in a space you cannot fully see; an enhanced sense of balance, dimensions and micromovement. Be prepared, just in case. Have it and not need it as opposed to the deadly opposite.

The revised version of Dave slowly amassed a collection of handguns, at first to see if his new identity could withstand a DROS background check from a federally-licensed weapons dealer. The ten-day wait from the Dealer's Record of Sale started the clock on your own lawfulness. In California you also had to prove residency, acquire a Handgun Safety Certificate (via written test) and perform a twelve-point handling demonstration. If you passed, you got to purchase one handgun per month in the Golden State; the regs on rifles and long guns were much looser. Only two out of seven of Dave's weapons stood registered and legitimate. The problem was that if any of them were used in the commission of a crime, all of them became hot, interconnected, and open to investigation by people who already knew how many registered firearms you had. Guns shows and cash deals came later, simply as a matter of backup. When strangers could know your armament at the touch of a button, it was valuable to acquire unpapered firearms. Dave still had his old Beretta. The authorities had very kindly overlooked it, back during the Florida debacle.

The ten years since David Kemp's journalistic mistake had been a sweet, sweet era for the manipulation of the ignorant. Derek David

Vollmand no longer cared whether people knew the truth. He cared about keeping his own skin on. A name was just a label. The threat of Wilsoni's blood oath gradually faded along with Dave's old label. The looming eventuality of an incautious slip still had the power to refuel that diminishing hazard, and if ever a mistake was to be made, Dave wanted to be prepared for the consequences.

Years passed.

The video playing on Hayden's flatscreen was bottomlessly stupid and undeniably funny. It was one of those old-skool "'hos by the pool" presentations featuring a three-hundred-pound hiphop dude named Black Victoriuz and his posse. When the screen wasn't filled with signifying faces in distorted, 80-millimeter lens close-ups, it was wall-to-wall with truly awesome buttocks.

> *Righteous man*
> *A righteous man*
> *Hero*
> *A hero man*
> *Righteous Hero Man*
> *Weird Dude*
> *Righteous Weird Hero Dude*
> *Son of a shut 'yo mouth*
> *Smeggo*
> *Nudist*
> *Nudist Nazi*
> *Wow*
> *Righteous Nude Nazi Smeggo Man*
> *Who's righteous?*
> *He is*

The Weird Nude Smeggo Nazi Man
Righteous
Weird...

This was not a channel to which Hayden would have left his satellite tuned. Onscreen, Victoriuz drove his vintage cherry-red Coupe De Ville into the pool, scattering the hos, with the help of generously seamless greenscreen effects.

The man sitting in partial shadow in Hayden's kitchen had a gun aimed almost casually at Hayden's midsection. The long black tube on the business end of the muzzle was a silencer. It looked as though the pistol had a hard-on.

"Close the door," said the man. "Bolt it."

"Well, I'll be goddamned and gone to hell," said Hayden.

"Most likely," said the man.

Daisy & Alma

Daisy examined herself from three angles on a vanity mirror. This was the Daisy that Dave Vollmand not only expected, but wanted. He fell into the goofy puppy category, so lovesick from the first moment he'd laid eyes on her, live, that it would be a minor tragedy to tell him that this first date would be the *only* date, regardless of how entertaining it might become.

Therefore it came as a complete surprise when Dave Vollmand called up to *cancel* their planned liaison tomorrow night. With regrets.

What?

Was one of her best resources failing her? She'd cranked the charm on full blast at the coffeehouse, enough to faze a whole firing line of mere mortal men, and David had hung on her every word.

Now the duel began. She called David's cell. Voicemail. Repeatedly. She had no message to leave, but on the third try decided to feed some bait.

"Hey," she said. "Daisy. Let me know what's going on, okay?"

She tried to match Dave Vollmand-Kemp to the online high school venue he had used in the first place. David Vollmand, it seemed, was one of those people with next to no presence on the Internet. The few hits on David Kemp were all a decade old. He had told her he'd changed his name. Why?

Because David Kemp had apparently died in 2001, the victim of a vehicular collision on the Don Schula Expressway. Faulty fuel feed. The car had become a blast furnace.

"Burned beyond recognition" was one of those alarm phrases that tripped the "coverup" switch.

Was Daisy being played? She could interpret the possible objective only one way: if this was a work, it was designed to draw her out into the open.

This was confirmed when David finally rang her back.

"Daisy?"

"David? *Omigod!* Are you okay?"

"Stressful day. Daisy, I need you to answer a question for me, and please think hard."

She sensed the hammer, coming for her.

"Daisy...why am I looking at your picture on this iPhone?"

Mounting dread. "What iPhone?"

"The iPhone of the guy who just tried to kill me."

Alma Acevedo was difficult to reach on demand. Problematic. Because Alma usually called the shots, set the ground rules, said when, where and for how long. Daisy did not know whether she could catch Alma's ear on such short notice. One had to leave cryptically banal messages, then wait. And wait.

If romance had been involved, Daisy always knew she would be the bottom. Whenever Alma summoned her, Daisy had to drop everything and direct her attention, and the system did not work two ways because of the debt.

Daisy owed Alma. Repeatedly, expensively. Alma had helped Daisy clean up her entire life. There was no price you could put on it. In return, Daisy bowed to Alma's monomaniacal need for privacy and security.

Daisy had emerged from high school as one of those people who believed honesty and fairness would come back to them, if dispensed. People were basically—sometimes unexpectedly—kind at their core, even if the bad old world abused them, or made them cynical. If you held the market door for the lady hampered by using a walker, some stranger might pick up the five-dollar bill you accidentally dropped in the vegetable section and hand it back to you with a smile. Someone you would never see again might remind you that you left your cellphone on a table while leaving a restaurant, with no string of obligation. For many men, a polite ogle was enough, and Daisy accepted that she attracted the attention of men, yes, for her architecture and not her mind, but that was okay, since the world was one big zoo and all the critters had to get along, regardless of their programming. Despite their baser instincts, people were essentially *nice.*

This fairyland outlook changed for good the first time Marcus hit her.

He punched her straight in the face, four big knuckles permanently damaging the orbit of her left eye. During another "talk"—as in: *we have to talk*—he knocked out one of her lower incisors and dislocated her temporomandibular joint on the right side. Amidst profuse apologies for his temper he cheerfully paid the ophthalmologist and dentist, offered supermarket-bought flowers, and signed off with his signature phrase: "So we're okay, right?"

The first argument had been catalyzed by Daisy leaving a pair of her shoes too near the front door of their apartment. The shoes themselves were not the crime, merely a front for a whole unspoken bill of lading—toothpaste caps, the status of dirty dishes, leaving the TV on the "wrong" channel, all amassing in tiny increments like a slow pipe clog, no individual affront having the power to provoke violence by itself. Collectively, however, they piled up in deep sighs and rolled eyes. Even a watched pot boils eventually.

Marcus Quantrill had rolled into Las Cruces on behalf of his father's construction firm during the demolition of a shopping mall, which was replaced by a cluster of big-box stores that all needed to be built from the parking lot up. It was a fat, two-year gig. Daisy had begun an unfulfilling period of employment as a paralegal, grinding paychecks and becoming accustomed to the idea of a life where she was responsible for her own roof, meals and amenities. This was virtually a slap in the face to her family's entire dynamic, an old-school, very Catholic, aggressively Latino way of life that saw no problem housing several generations in a one-bedroom apartment where the kids slept on the floor because they were kids. Daisy was expected to run the typical user manual for humans: Graduate, "catch a man" by means fair or foul, and commence reproducing. None of this seemed like a particularly bright future to her—more like a lock-stepped sentence mandating unwanted pregnancy and a lifetime of denial where *she* would wind up in the same crowded living room as the other moms and grandmoms, bitching about the men who had betrayed or abandoned them, and waiting for someone else in the family to die in order to have something to talk about. As a result of her rebellion, her father had not spoken to her for three years...and her mother voiced her opinion at such length that it was a healthy idea to abjure "innocent" conversation altogether.

What did you do today? Mm-hm.

Daisy and Marcus met in a tavern called the Horned Toad Bar & Grill, whose signature cocktail, the Horny Toad, was a red vodka concoction in honor of the ability of *Phrynosoma*'s ability to shoot blood out of its eyes as a response to danger. Or so the story went, as told by patrons and barkeeps unaware that the horned toad was neither a toad nor a frog.

Marcus was four years older than Daisy, newly divorced from a stick-in-the-mud wife (his term) who had been content to let him support her as she increased in size at an exponential rate and diligently watched endless TV talk shows from which she collected hot-button phrases to bash him whenever she felt stagnant. The consumer items they should have, the notions to which the ladies on the talk shows all agreed they should aspire. The life they ought to be leading, according to all the experts. Her job, she said, was to be a homemaker and bear his children. Since she was not pregnant and not disposed to housekeeping, this left her very little to do. Several times she had tossed the relationship dice on an accidental impregnation, forgetting her pills, pinning his rubbers, even fishing used condoms out of the trash, before he started flushing them. Marcus did not want children. Marcus wanted sex. Marcus would soon be trapped onto the correct path, given time.

Marcus advanced the clock before she could adequately prepare a new host. As far as he knew, that night in the Horned Toad, his ex was still billeted at her parents' house. Daisy sympathized.

She surprised him by splitting their tab, something Marcus had never seen the women of his accustomed caste do. They had sweaty, cinematic sex.

But they were not married; never had been. Daisy had lied to David Vollmand to that extent. There had been no tragic miscarried pregnancy, except for its use as a conversational tool to garner a quick nod of silent agreement—it was a detail nearly universal in its sadness, and so could provide handy armor against unwanted questions.

Marcus gradually turned into his own ex-wife once he and Daisy moved in together. In keeping with his father's connections, their condo was superb. Marcus became a supervisor, gained seventy pounds, and started to sulk daily about his lack of free-range sexual attractiveness until it decayed into a monotone backbeat to almost every conversation, the kind of talk designed to beg superficial reassurance that could then be attacked for sounding patronizing. He urged Daisy to quit her job since he was making more money. He disliked it when she was not home when he returned. He pressured her to marry him the first time she accused him of cheating on her.

Daisy sensed which demands would come next. She had enjoyed the security features of the condo when it was new, but now she saw this love nest as a cage designed to isolate her.

Controlled substances do not interact well with such tension.

First came Marcus' self-loathing, the balm for which was kind words, followed by sloppy-sorrowful drunk interludes. Then came the increasing pressure to wed, leavened by bleary protestations of true love. Then came something new: a fist in the face, since Daisy had been so unreasonable.

"You simple bitch," he had said when he hit her.

Daisy stormed out. Marcus won her back. This naughty-then-nice pendulum swung back and forth for nearly two months. Outsiders who advise "just leave" rarely have any conception of your own special complexities, the reasons you don't just leave. Even that guy who cut off his own arm in the Utah mountains had to work his way up to the act. You wait to see if things will improve. You strive to avoid the provocative move that will tear your life off what moorings it has left, even if those bonds are shabby and illusory. If you think you're immune to this kind of hopeful self-delusion, then you're superhuman. And sometimes, if you doggedly persevere, an unexpected option drops right out of the trees.

Daisy met Alma.

Alma offered Daisy a surprising piece of advice.

"Let him hit you one more time," Alma had said.

Alma had been there the next time Marcus went caveman, and yelled in Daisy's face that she was a "dumbass spic" before splitting her lip. He was getting better at his own rage cycle, the pump-up, the insults that justified and fed the first blow as an appetizer for a second. It had become a routine. Daisy still had a faint scar from where her own teeth had bitten through.

Alma destroyed a terra cotta vase on the back of Marcus' head as he was stomping around, knocking things off tables, generating fresh steam. When Marcus woke up, Alma was straddling him with a gun in his mouth.

"Say you're sorry," Alma said.

"Fuck you," Marcus said. *Fugg Yahhou.*

Alma blew the back of his head off. Daisy was unprepared for the mess, and vomited. That's natural, Alma told her, the first time.

It was Marcus' pistol, a nickel-plated Taurus .9mm loaded with hollow points. Alma had worn latex gloves. Marcus had therefore committed suicide.

Daisy was paralyzed. Simple murder was not part of her worldview, no matter how justified. Alma cleaned up the puke, so as not to leave a puzzle for investigators.

"What the hell am I gonna *do*?" Daisy cried, over and over.

"Don't sweat this *puto*," Alma said. "I have a plan."

Alma's plan was breathtaking in its simplicity, and outrageous in its import.

"In order to live a new life," Alma said, "you have to erase the old life. No baggage; I mean zero."

"You mean move away, change my name," Daisy said, dully.

"Move away and change your name *after* you've flushed everybody who ever hurt you." Alma's eyes went metallic and definitive. "And by flush, I mean erase, totally. None of that AA shit about making amends. People hurt you big and hurt you small, and they need to not be using up our air anymore."

Breathtaking, outrageous? More horrifying.

"It's easier than you think," said Alma. "I'll help you. Show you how not to trip over your own laces. Over eighty thousand people vanish without a trace in the U.S. alone, every single goddamned year, and you can't tell me they've all joined cults, lost their minds, or been abducted. Like, give me a name."

Daisy was convulsively shaking her head *no*. "You can't just…"

"I can," said Alma. "I have. Give me a name. Somebody who hurt you."

It took a while but Daisy finally told Alma the story of how super-jock Quentin Farrier had taken her heart and rent it to flinders with two simple words, a million years ago when she was a high school teenager. Daisy never inquired as to the doings of her former classmates. She had, without thinking about it, already begun the erasure process, to better her life.

Alma provided Daisy with a little black book. Inscribed on the first page were the names of Marcus Quantrill, Quentin Farrier, and Glenda Subiron—all crossed out in red.

"Remember them," Alma said. "Remember every single person who caused you the kind of harm that could trap you into the wrong life. And write them in here. And when they're dealt with, cross them out and forget about them."

But as an exercise, the list-making could be cleansing, like an inflammatory letter you write to vent your anger, but never mail. Daisy started the list with a bunch of names from her old high school. And quite to her surprise, the more she thought about it, the more the list grew. Erase them all. Start fresh. Begin again as a whole new person. Figure out the traits you desire and *become* that person, willfully, by grand design.

Alma was scary-good at this. So good, Daisy thought, that she could almost turn pro.

It wasn't such a crazy idea after all.

Within the next two weeks, Quentin Farrier was dead. So was his pig wife, Glenda, formerly Subiron, formerly living. And no one had noticed or cared, beyond the usual pro forma family expressions of grief and lost potential, last week's dull news.

Alma's idea was a keeper, all right. Daisy could almost (but not quite) believe she had defanged the disruption power old names held over her life simply by writing those names in the book Alma had supplied. The act got those people out of your head and stashed them someplace neutral.

Daisy was dismayed by how many of her emotional pitfalls had been seeded by minor acts, the casual brutalities and innocent meanness of people who had "grown up" little better than children themselves. She was mildly shocked to find the bones of her personality had been set so young, and more shocked to realize the smallest offense at an early age can establish a destructive pattern for an entire lifetime. If you did not wish to be completely defined by your defensive reactions to people— even children—who for one stupid reason or another had harmed you inside or out, you had to give their harm back to them.

Alma found those people and literally shoved them out of the world. Homicide was a downside. But they were three deep already and the world, if anything, was thankful for the regained space. You could make a demise look less premeditated by carefully building fictions about robbery, accident or suicide. Learn the habits of your prey, and weaknesses will be revealed that could provide the best story to use.

Your life, ultimately, is only the story you tell to others.

But what did Alma get out of it?

"Listen, babe," Alma said. "In my business, you don't deal in motive. You don't keep souvenirs and you don't get personal. You make one kind of point with a fictional narrative, like an arranged car crash for a drunk driver, or you make another kind of point with a bullet, for the benefit of the people who will ask, *who would want to shoot that guy?*"

"So for you it's like bagging groceries," said Daisy. "Or plumbing."

"It's a service. It's a business. It's a growth industry in a depressed economy. You obviously have more trouble sleeping at night than I do, so I'd say you're the one with the problem. What do I get? I get the knowledge that you've learned how to stop being life's victim. One more like you in the world means I'm not alone."

"Why me?"

"Why *not* you?"

Daisy really did not have a comeback for that one.

And the list of crossed out names in the book grew.

Until a guy named Derek David Vollmand had stumbled across Daisy's old yearbook picture, attached to a locator search engine, and pressed SEND.

Alma had become furious. "And *what* was this bullshit with this Dave guy? He's a connection to your past! I can't believe you were so fucking weak."

"I wasn't weak," said Daisy, bristling at the idea that Alma thought she owned her, like a dog. "He was. I was...curious."

"The new you can't be curious about the old you," said Alma.

"You're not my mother." Daisy's voice and gaze had both gone flat. "I had a mother. She died, and I don't need another one. You're not my boss, or my keeper." She had an uncomfortable twinge, as though her mouth was setting her up for another roundhouse from Marcus, after all this time.

"Oh, and I should just butt out and let you chase some misty vision of romance? For a random factor, he's got you pretty lubed up."

"What are you talking about? He's just a guy. Some guy I barely spoke to in school. He remembered me."

"That's what I'm talking about," said Alma. "Crap from the past. Erase it, or be dragged backward."

"It's not what you think." Daisy was aware how lame this sounded even as she said it.

"No? You sure?" Alma let the silence gouge Daisy for a moment before swooping in for the finish. "He fucked up a colleague of mine. Killed him, in fact. Killed him like he knew how. He killed an expert in killing, on his first try. Is that the guy you had a nice latte with?"

There was no reason for Daisy to know the complex map of switchbacks that had inadvertently led to Bryan Silver's death. First Bryan had been outfoxed and waylaid. Then he had been finished off in the hospital. The first took skill, maybe luck, but the second required sheer determination as ice-cold as liquid nitrogen. This phantom from Daisy's distant past did not fit with the story he had presented to the world—the boring job, the heartstring-tugging detail of his dog, his mundane life in front of a bunch of screens.

Daisy's voice was quiet but solid: "Let me handle this one."

In 2007 the information was spread out on the Internet like a happy whore, willing to indulge all comers:

SAN ANDRES HIGH SCHOOL
CLASS OF 1987
!!! 20-YEAR REUNION !!!

And for every year thereafter, it remained available to anybody who could Google it.

Daisy Villareal had clicked on it, way back then. So had Derek David Vollmand. They each cracked open the vault door to the past for a peek, strictly as lurkers, even though that click-thru left a footprint forever, or at least until the servers crashed or some faraway mystery cache got collaterally negated by a wily digital terrorist in pursuit of informational anarchy.

Neither Daisy nor David had grown into the sort of people who could enjoy that kind of bathetic wallow. The suggestion was that the passage of years could be magically reversed by bunting, balloons, punch and an embarrassed DJ fatalistically cueing his laptop to one embalmed zombie hit after another—Journey, Guns 'N Roses, 'Gasm, Phil Collins, the eternal damnation that was the Steve Miller Band, the deadly inevitability of the one-hit wonders like the Vapors' "Turning Japanese," the Waitresses' "I Know What Boys Like," or, Bog help us all, Timbuk 3's "The Future's So Bright, I Gotta Wear Shades." Name your vapidity, from "Papa Don't Preach" to "Funkytown," from XTC to Vixen, from Bruce Willis to Don Johnson…it all sucked.

Just like the high skool daze you were expected to warmly re-embrace.

The only really interesting news was finding out who died.

The real agenda was a lottery-tumbler stir of decomposed status quo: Who succeeded or failed, who got out or got trapped, who grew and who shrank. The rest was a carnival whirl of sagging paunches, lost hair, inebriated misremembrance, and desperate longing that could have made a terrible opera. The forced flash of billboard teeth gave way to an almost vulpine hunger for anything different, anything better, any other could-have-been life. The successful people, the happy ones, never came back to bob for such poison apples. They stayed away, more cunning than wise, to let their former victims and inferiors dish about them.

Daisy and David harbored no such delusions of betterment. The simple necessity of remaining unseen and unremarked took precedence as a matter of emotional survival. Dangerous enough, it was, to risk a glimpse and hope not to be nailed doing it. That way, you could continue to kid yourself that your formative years did not cripple you to this day.

How come nobody ever brought an AK-47 to one of these soirees?

Daisy and David has been fewer than twenty miles apart when they had both stumbled across the website link for the reunion banner. Roughly seven hundred miles to the east, the repository of their shared past lives was about to be crudely exhumed, beyond their control or endorsement, which unfair circumstance seemed to demand a corrective reaction. That was what hunters counted on—the innate compulsion of prey to rise to bait.

Better to stay forgotten, a background player, and hope your name was forgotten. *What was her name again? Remember that one guy in Quill & Scroll, Daniel, Devon something?*

You never knew who might be trying to keep track of you.

David Kemp's half-forgotten name wasn't even in her little black book.

This was all long before deceptively free social media hookups trumped the feared Big Brother paradigm with a phenomenon that came to be called "the tyranny of attention."

Daisy, in her place, was relieved that no such site harbored a timeline of everything she had ever done. David, in his place, separately, felt the same relief, as transient and illusory as it was.

The creatures of the pit do not like having light shined on them. Prod them, and they will retaliate.

Rolf & Max

The man sitting across from Rolf Dettrick looked barely out of high school himself. Five-seven in overpriced clothes and sporting a platinum Tag Heuer Monaco wristwatch he checked a little too often. Maintaining a mild coke jones, from his bustle and jitter. Lifts in his Ferragamo loafers. Prematurely balding at twenty-five, but with the same muddy brown gaze and bold black eyebrows of his father, he reminded Rolf of the sort of intense-looking Middle Eastern college student whose face surprises no one when it turns up on a terrorist mugshot.

This was Maximillian Wilsoni, second son of the late Aristede, and heir to whatever bounty his older brother, Augustus, deemed suitable to dispense as current chairman of the Wilsoni businesses in Florida. Augustus had sent little brother Max to represent the family. This bestowal of new responsibilities was recent. It was time for Max to step up. Rolf knew this, just as he knew that when he spoke to Max, he was speaking to August by proxy. Max would want to make an impression and demonstrate his worthiness, so the whole tribe could go on fleecing and screwing each other inside a higher fiscal bracket.

The bodyguards had probably belonged to the patriarch, Aristede, since way-back-when. They wore their weary combat experience in the same ill-cut way they wore their too-tight suits, in the manner of soldiers forced to stand at ease for hours as punishment. That they were armed was no great distress to Rolf, who knew he could outgun such drones.

Max Wilsoni slurped his espresso like a slumming Cuban. His hooded eyes had skimmed the history in the folder Rolf had provided, now and then hitching onto some stray morsel of data that was news. Rolf had counted upon Max knowing most of the backstory already.

"David Kemp supposedly died in a car crash nearly ten years ago," said Rolf. "This Bureau file was compiled by an agent named Stanton Weeks, who died in 2002. As you can see—"

"Fucker didn't die," said Max. "Not for real." His eyes assumed a reptilian flatness. "So, where is he?"

"He was flushed out by a freelancer. And now he's on the run, topside. Which presents a very limited window of opportunity, should you care to take advantage of it."

"What do you get out of it?" Max seemed to be reading from a teleprompter deep inside his coffee cup.

"Kemp, or Vollmand if you prefer, became a minor administrative problem for CHASE," said Rolf.

Max gave a mildly stoned grin. "You want me to clean him up for you."

"Not exactly. I do not have his precise location yet. But when I find out, I thought it might be useful to let you know privately."

"Lemme see if I track this," Max said. "After all this time, you come up with this fucking guy, David, whatever." He pronounced it Da-*veed*, with a Latin inflection. "But you give him to me, for what? For free?" In Max's universe, nothing came free without a hidden, hideous tariff.

This was exactly the trajectory Rolf had hoped for, knowing all along that he could not deal straight with criminals.

"CHASE isn't all that different from the Bureau," Rolf said. "Or for that matter, the board of directors of a drugstore chain. Advancement is strictly by the numbers, with no imagination. I only want this man tangentially. I was thinking you might want him more urgently. If so, and you think this information is worthy of some kind of reward, I leave that to you—but only *after* his file is closed, if you get my meaning."

"Yeah, real generous." Max worked his mouth around as though his jaw wasn't seating properly. "Look, man, my father was kind of a dick. He was all up in that underworld crap. I'm a legitimate businessman."

"Absolutely." Rolf smiled his best grassroots-candidate smile, tamping down the urge to shoot this moronic peon in the forehead.

"My brother runs most of the business," Max said. "But he don't run all of it."

"I'm not talking to your brother, Max. I'm talking to you."

"Yeah, points for that. Let's say I was interested in this guy. Y'know, for argument's sake. What do you want from me?"

"A simple exchange of information. If I find him, I'll tell you. If you find him, tell me. It would not do to have two collection operations stepping on each other. If this person was to disappear from the face of the earth, that would be fine because technically, he doesn't exist. But if he does vanish, and I'm not responsible, I need to know about it in complete confidentiality."

"Plus you want some kind of payoff for ratting him out."

"That's entirely up to you. See, CHASE doesn't have a retirement program. No benefits, no Social Security, no 401K."

"Ahee." Max emitted a congested laugh. He thought he understood.

The avarice in his face was a bigger challenge to hide, though, and Rolf was reading it accurately. This punk was still working out how to accrue favor with his big brother by dealing with old familial blood-debts. He was wriggling on the hook, thinking he had command of the ocean.

CHASE Alpha, whose name could not possibly have been James Smith for real, had granted Rolf temporary carte blanche in the matter of resolving Alma Acevedo, a former CHASE operative who had recently assassinated a CHASE asset, Morgan Deane of Mount Olympus. Rolf now recognized the job as a typical swap: the Deane hit had been handed to Alma by the recently deceased Bryan Silver (who sometimes posed as a fake FBI dude named Lester Buttram). In return, Bryan had assumed the responsibility for whacking the former David Kemp, now Vollmand, and failed. Aristede Wilsoni's heirs would be very interested to know that the man who had precipitated their patriarch's downfall was still breathing air as a beneficiary of witness protection, instead of deep-fried to a golden black in a long-ago car wreck. All Rolf had to do was whistle, and a CHASE cleanup squad would be at his disposal within half an hour. But that wasn't impressive enough. Rolf wanted to demonstrate a scorched-earth attitude to James Smith, his superior, cure his own bureaucratic fumble (letting Alma get away from CHASE alive) and reap the rewards of fealty. It was a field decision to bring in Maximillian Wilsoni, and once Rolf had taken Max's measure, he felt secure his call had been a good one.

Max would pretend languid indifference, but he wasn't that good an actor. Max would rally an army of thugs and bonebreakers to make what remained of David Vollmand's life into an overwound guitar string about to snap. Ever watch a squirrel eat? They exist in a perfect state of complete panic all the time. That's what Rolf wanted for David Vollmand. And when Vollmand cracked like a egg, he would lead to Alma, and the merciless jungle food chain would yield, at the very least, a fat CHASE promotion for Rolf.

Maybe even the Alpha slot.

He would kill Alma himself, and it would be beautiful.

But first he wanted to put a CHASE team on Vollmand, in addition to the harassment value of Max's boys, who frequently ignored the gameplay of cover or alibis. You never knew—Max's crew might find Vollmand first. Either way, Rolf would get the credit.

Max had accepted Rolf the way Rolf intended, as a functionary out of his depth in the bold strokes of street-level warfare. A certain amount of attitude had to be processed when dealing with lowlifes of Max's ilk. The bonus, in this case, was the high possibility that Rolf could fob off the wetwork to Max and his killer munchkins, thereby demonstrating his frugality with CHASE assets.

Let Max think what he wished, insofar as he could think. He was on Rolf's hook, and as disposable as most bait.

"You give me the guy," said Max, "and I'll make some moves. We get him, I'll make sure you get some kinda compensation. That the kinda deal you looking at?"

Fucking amateur, thought Rolf.

"We are speaking the same language exactly," said Rolf, cutting loose another of his vote-winning smiles.

Alma & Hood

Hood was Alma Acevedo's job broker. No other name; just Hood.

Beyond the encrypted contacts and identity firewalls, Hood was the man who distributed work dossiers and cash payments, treating both with schooled disdain that exemplified just how long he had made a living at hastening strangers to their death. The details of any individual file were of marginal interest to him. The money did not hypnotize him. Money was something to be salted around in order to achieve objectives and balance the books. He disliked disorder and held emotional flamboyance in contempt.

Alma had heard the scuttle that Hood had come to America from the former Soviet Union following the collapse of the Berlin Wall. He was a pale, muscular man in his mid-50s with a crewcut scrub of sandy hair and eyebrows to match. He never wore a wristwatch or jewelry and only begrudgingly deferred to slim bifocals for close work. What Alma had seen of his face and hands offered no details of distinction. No scars. Nothing to render his face more memorable than a vinyl blank, stamped out of a mold of thousands just like it. She had heard he had a couple of tattoos removed. Like every other available piece of information about Hood, this was mostly hearsay.

Alma had no idea what Hood did, when he wasn't briefing her, or paying her. And Hood almost never called you. You made regular contact and Hood would leave messages outlining drops and meeting places. Stats for special equipment or circumstances were given in person. Rarely did Hood repeat himself.

Almost never. Rarely. Both of those conditions had changed today. Hood had called Alma for a face-to-face. During this, he said things more than once. He had not brought a dossier for her. It was clear that he was agitated.

"You're lit up like a neon sign," Hood told her, in the midst of a noisy bistro called Anti-Café on Melrose—the part of Melrose just prior to the Beverly Center on La Cienega, where the storefronts still had a heartbeat. Further east, every second and third display window was vacant. A lot of enterprises had cleared out during the last recession, lending a ghost town ambience to the formerly vital area whose pall extended all the way past Highland Avenue. Here, in the district of the still-living emporia, the customer clatter was sufficient to mask out any attempt to eavesdrop by dish or mike.

"Bryan Silver was terminated in the hospital as a result of the job you handed off to him," Hood said. "A job not on our roster. I accept that these trades sometimes happen. But this was not a contract of any sort, was it?"

"No," Alma said, sipping her café crème, eyes elsewhere.

"You thought this assignment up on your own, for reasons of your own?"

"Yes."

"The Morgan Deane job—the legitimately-contracted job that Bryan gave to you in trade—was performed up to specs. But. It has aroused the attention of your old employers at CHASE, and you know how CHASE deals with loose ends."

She did.

"I am now down one worker, which is a nuisance. But he is no longer able to collect his pay for the job you did in his stead." Hood tipped back a triple espresso all at once. "I propose to pay you for that job."

"But?" Alma said.

"But your sudden visibility as a CHASE target means I am now down *two* workers." Was that a hint of pique she read in his colorless gaze?

"What do you want me to do?"

"I confess I fail to understand why you needed to subcontract a job, but it seems that job—even though it was compromised—did not conflict with any job on my books. Was it personal?"

"Yes."

Alma knew what this admission might make Hood think. That she had let a private issue intrude into her professional life. That perhaps she had spun out to hit the wall of usefulness. That her judgment had become impaired. But better to tell Hood the truth than try to confect a story he would surely dismantle. He let these implications sink in with no further comment.

The saving grace was that Hood would not care about the *why*.

"What I think you need to do is go under, deep. Consider an identity reset, and I don't mean a cheap one, which is why I have chosen to pay you for Deane. All I care about in that regard is that the contractor was pleased."

Hood was not talking about fake IDs and a phony credit card. He was implying complete erasure, plastic surgery, maybe permanent relocation to a foreign country, five or six steps beyond what Alma had done in order to stop being someone named Lily Tamario, years ago.

"How did this happen?" she said.

"Morgan Deane had an apron-string to CHASE. He was beholden to them for reasons I have not yet uncovered. But that connection extends to CHASE wanting to demonstrate their absolute accountability. If they look after their own, it looks good to their other clients. That puts you in a world of hurt, until the hacks at CHASE are convinced you don't exist any more."

Alma was stung by the abrupt thought that Hood could easily kill her, and give her to CHASE for bonus points.

No, Hood wouldn't do that. He'd hire someone. An equal opposite, like Bryan Silver or any one of a half-dozen other independents.

Or all of them. Make it payback for Silver, to balance the scales on behalf of one of their own breed.

She tried to read his intent and had to admit she was doing a lousy job.

"What if CHASE took out Bryan?" she said.

"Unknown," said Hood. "That is a possibility."

"It stinks like a setup. To force you to retaliate."

"I've considered that."

Typically for Hood, he illuminated no further. She was going to have to twist in the wind on her own.

"Payment for the Deane job will be delivered to the mail drop in two business days," Hood said.

Great. If it was an ambush, she would die when she went to grab money she needed, which probably would not be there to begin with.

"I have to go," Hood said. "You understand that we are not related until the entire situation is cleaned up, yes?"

That meant don't call, don't text, a vacuum of contact. Alma was now technically one of the unemployed.

Alma sat for nearly twenty minutes after Hood left, looking for answers in the bottom of an empty coffee cup, rousing the ire of the wait staff for using up a table during peak hours. Safer in here, for the moment, than outside.

Once she walked out that door, the whole world was going to view her differently.

Dave & Daisy

"Slow down, Dave, goddammit. You sound like you've been tweaking or something."

Hayden's voice never sounded so far away as it did buzzing from the earpiece of one of the last standing outdoor payphones in Los Angeles, a carrel rooted to the restroom side of a Mobil station on Saticoy, deep in the Valley sprawl of car dealerships and porn studios. Stickered, grimy, post-apocalyptic, with a bottomless appetite for coins.

"Excuse the hell out of me," I said, fighting a constant urge to keep my back to the nearest wall. "You saw the apartment."

"Yeah, and I checked on Kingi. Who is fine, by the way. What sociopath would want to Tase your dog? I was thinking hot prowl—you know, when robbers come in not expecting to find occupants. That was before I saw all the blood."

"Not mine," I said. "I shot the guy. Not fatally, I don't think."

"Which was why you naturally scrammed out at lightspeed, to avoid the cops—"

I overrode his oncoming lecture. "Just listen. The guy had an iPhone with Daisy's picture on it. Hayden, I think she might be some kind of target. Don't ask me why or how. But I have to see her—and you—before I do anything else. This isn't just a foiled burglary. It's something larger, and I can't dish on it over the phone. I'll let you know where to meet me."

"You're not making a whole hell of a lot of sen—"

I hung up, the victim of seeing too many films that gave time specs for a trace. Past Daisy and Hayden, I wanted to see my dog, to verify with my own eyes that Kingi was okay.

The Tropical Paradise Motel was anything but. It had last been painted circa the Nixon administration and its main design scheme seemed rendered in "soot." None of the neon on the signage functioned. It was so lacking in character that it appeared almost too perfect, as though a set designer had grunged it up. Third-hand thrift store furnishings, carpeting more akin to a dust caul. Sputtering tube TV. Swaybacked bed with dysfunctional Magic Fingers, deflated pillows, linens smelling vaguely between bleach and mildew. The door lock was loose. It jiggled. Every door in this dive had been kicked in more than once. Ancient dead insects were grouped in tiny, long-term graveyards on the windowsills, so old even the spiders wouldn't eat them. The curtains hung mismatched and flaccid, the same way scavenged clothing hangs on a homeless person. It was perfect. It was forty bucks a night. It was on Woodman, right around the corner from the gas station. I was a ten-minute drive away from my now-compromised apartment.

Where David Kemp had lived as David Vollmand, safely, up until now.

My FBI sponsor, Stanton Weeks, had retired in 2009. Part of my covenant with WitSec included an emergency number for Weeks…which no longer functioned. After a certain period under a new identity, your handlers tend to move on to new problems. I could get assistance from a federal agency, but that would take time I did not have right now. It would have to go through channels. Some of those channels were part of the riverwork of departments that maybe—just maybe—could have unknowingly helped a gunman come looking for me. Schmuck to the last, your call for help is what gets you killed.

I naturally thought of my old nemesis, Aristede Wilsoni…who had been dead for eight years, killed by his competitors or creditors. Why now?

I had a sliver under eight hundred bucks in cash and a trunk full of pistols. In my mad-hare dash from the apartment I had risked one pit stop at an ATM. I would not be revisiting that option. Likewise the credit cards—I used them once and once only, to board Kingi at the vet's. I accomplished this in the first twenty minutes after running out the back door.

Now I was eyeballing cars at the gas station, looking for an over-nighter so I could swap plates.

I was a fugitive. It was mildly unnerving how easily the old paranoid mindset resurged. I had spent years trying to lie myself happy. It turned out that the fear matrix, my mental catalogue of caution, had merely gone dormant until it reactivated at full strength.

In his allotted lag time, Hayden had mentioned seeing Kingi at the vet's. My open-ended charge was good for the limit of the credit card—about four grand—and I had no idea how fast that would be eaten up. It didn't matter. I wanted to see my dog but there was no reason for Kingi to go on the run with me, as amusing as he might have found the diversion. Kingi was a symbol of normalcy, something I needed to work my way back toward while trying to stay alive to figure out who needed to erase me.

Next stop: Starbucks.

The vibe was similar to Espresso mi Historia, but here the Losers on Laptops seemed more strung out and hopeless, the pathology of the Internet a barrier of fog between them and their devices. They leaned forward and squinted close as though seeking clarification in an unknown language, or validation from a mystery soup of undecoded intel. They appeared rudderless and lost. One latte later I managed to scoot away with two cellphones—older Nokias, for calls and messages, not all-encompassing devices, ergo, idle. A Bluetooth or iPhone is per-petually lit up, demanding attention to the point where Beverly Hills cosmetologists were now recommending Botox injections to stave off the wrinkles formed by interminable peering and texting.

David J. Schow

Most coffeehouses operate on the classic GIGO theory—garbage in, garbage out—requiring you to earn the honor of toilet privileges by purchasing a beverage. In the Starbucks unisex bathroom I used one phone to text Daisy and the other to text Hayden with simple directives for what I hoped was a secret meet-up. Then I wiped down the phones and left them in the loo on top of the toilet tank. I know how annoying it is to lose your phone.

Proposing a favorite restaurant or bar, or any place predictable, was asking for grief. Best bet was to find a rendez where, under normal circumstances, I would never be seen. It had to be public. It had to be near a lot of main artery streets and the freeway. Just in case.

Mango Joy was a vegan eatery that had risen from the ashes of a busted art gallery near Vineland and Moorpark, between a Pizza Hut and the Medical Arts Pharmacy, perilously close to my former neighborhood, but with plenty of get-out roads. I stashed my car almost two blocks distant, around a residential corner. Permit parking was beginning to seep even into this neighborhood.

The front windows of the restaurant had been replaced with leaded stained glass, below a large plywood sign festooned with hand-painted clouds and rainbows. Vomit. I braced myself for the olfactory assault of patchouli oil.

A jaunty brass bell over the door jingled to announce my entry. Inside, three tables out of twelve were occupied. About half the flora was fake and a lot of bamboo had been added for atmosphere. It was set up bistro-style with a nominal bar at the deep end. Past that, down the narrow corridor to the kitchen, would be restrooms and an open back door. It was still July, and humid at night.

Framing the bar were more handpainted signs extolling the geo-friendly wonderment of meatless, organic, gluten-free living. The joint smelled like saffron and cinnamon, not unpleasantly. The woman behind the bar was looking at me as though she'd dealt with my type before. She set up a shot before I was all the way to her.

"Tip that back," she said. "Wheat grass. It'll make your day better, I promise. On the house."

She had a haircut of almost Marine severity, dyed platinum. Many vivid tattoos of aquatic creatures on her bare arms. She was wearing a nicely worn-in denim vest and a couple of embroidered thongs around one wrist. Her eyes were so blue and alive they pained me; she was not reedy and desiccated as I had expected, but vibrant and alert. She practically glowed. She was her own best advertisement.

"That tastes very...clean," I finally said, setting the empty shot glass down next to a jar full of hash oil lollipops.

"It's a powerful detoxifier," she said. "Stimulates the thyroid, cleanses the blood. It's actually very similar to blood—the chlorophyll carries oxygen the same way hemoglobin does. I bet you didn't want to know any of that shit, right?"

"It's good to know," I allowed.

"Yeah, you have that virgin look. Relax. Everything in here will make you feel better. Take any one of those tables. Yell if you need things."

"Yell for Mango Joy?" I actually felt healthier for a moment.

"Just Joy. That's me. Joy. It's a name."

I shook my head as though missing an obvious punchline. Joy, right.

Joy had very petite breasts, like a French model. She had no need of a brassiere and I was grateful she had chosen not to wear one. Her bold nipples were pierced with simple posts that glinted from the depths of her vest. Breasts are called boobs because that's what they turn most men into.

Over the course of the next ten minutes, I learned that most hard alcohol was vegan by definition, excluding a subset that might be polluted with egg whites or fish-derived clarifiers. Joy set me up with an aperitif she called Monkey Beer: pepper-infused vodka, pure pineapple juice, lime, and ginger beer—no animal or nut byproducts; vegan friendly but not kosher, weirdly enough. It certainly could soften the edges of a rough day.

Up from sleep, there is a brief phase during wake-up where your mind pauses to reassure yourself you are still living. Only when alertness returns do you remember all the reasons you dread the coming day, mostly leftover garbage from the previous day. This moment was like that.

Then the urgency elbowed all other moods aside. I had to come clean to Hayden. I had to warn Daisy. After that I had my own fate to figure out.

Then the little brass bell jingled again and Daisy walked in, looking as harried as I felt.

She rushed right over without ceremony and half-sat on the edge of the seat across from me, as though ready to bolt to show she was not fully committed to sitting down or lingering, despite Joy's coercive spiel.

"We have to get out of here," she said. "Did you text anyone else?"

"Hayden," I said. "Are you okay?"

"Then we *really* have to get out of here," she said, scanning all around.

I was supposed to be looking at Daisy the way I had the first time— face, tits, legs, repeat—but one of her hands was out of sight, wrangling a soft calfskin shoulder bag. The sort of bag that provided a fold-over pocket so you could reach inside to unobtrusively grasp a firearm.

Silly woman. She should have just tucked a gun into the butt of her pants, like I had.

My trusty Beretta, all the way from the Kemp saga in Florida, was hidden by my untucked shirt and the back of the chair. It was gorged on a 20-round factory mag (totally illegal in California) which caused the heel of the clip to jut out less than an inch. This forced me into straighter posture when standing, to obscure the bulge, and by now was as warm as I was. I reviewed Daisy's ensemble. Still with the skintight jeans and low-heeled boots—so she could sprint if she had to. It wasn't coat weather, and there was no way she could have finessed a spine hide.

"Is that Hayden?" she said, cranking around toward the door. Her back was to it. I had stationed myself so I could monitor both access points, front and rear.

The little brass bell jingled.

"Hey," said Hayden, all hale-fellow-well-met.

Then Daisy stood up and started shooting.

This was not how I had envisioned my dream date.

Daisy smiles, says hello, and opens my brains to the air with what looked like a .45 semiauto. *Sucker, hah-hah, you get the twist ending.*

Back in Florida, Aristede Wilsoni's soldiers had tried twice to take me in public, first in the lobby of the New Neon Palms Hotel (where I had badgered up the same way I was doing now, at the Tropical Paradise), then in sunlight, right on the sidewalk, backstops and collateral casualties be damned. The first attempt in Florida had been at my apartment, too. The second time, I was able to return fire but stopped an incoming slug with my right leg. Third time, same deal, I caught another bullet in my back. I still had the scars, and a resultant pre-arthritic condition in my leg. The old wounds were now buzzing loudly with sense memory. I was time-traveling. The pattern was repeating.

Six dozen things happened simultaneously.

Daisy jerked straight up as though yanked, the gun appearing in her hand like close-up magic. She fired right toward my face, near enough for me to feel the heat of the muzzle flash. She fired more than one time.

Joy did an inelegant backward sprawl behind the bar. She had just been walking toward us to greet Daisy but a fusillade of gunfire from the rear corridor dissuaded her. Perhaps she had been robbed before, at this location, and developed reflexes.

The front door glass shattered as I fumbled the chair, trying to reach around for my Beretta. The little brass bell was still jingling.

Daisy wasn't shooting at me, but past me. Toward the back.

I landed hard on my right knee. The musculature near my old bullet wound hollered, and I went off-balance.

Another shooter had crept in through the back about the time Hayden had made his entrance. I was *supposed* to look Hayden's way instead of monitoring my own six. The narrow hallway plus the salvo from Daisy caused the shooter to skew target so the first few slugs flew Hayden's way.

From under the table edge I could see Hayden hugging the wall as bamboo splintered apart near his face, hazing him.

Hayden had whipped out a gun. He was trying to center me, and he didn't look like he was joking.

Mango Joy—the place, not the person—started coming apart one bullet at a time.

The threesome seated closest to the front entry were all moving. A nice lady in a paisley frock and sandals let out a yelp as a nail-hole of blood blossomed at her collarbone. The velocity of the exiting slug twisted her to fall against Hayden, spoiling his aim, and she sank down as though deflating.

One of the two men with the nice lady collided with his dinner and rebounded through the stained glass, which had already been holed by several stray shots from the rear. His table spilled and crockery disintegrated. When he went backward through the colored panels, street traffic could be seen outside.

The other guy tried his best to compress himself into a hedgehog ball on the floor, spattered with airborne food. The other customers, I couldn't say.

All I could discern in the rear hallway was a shadow making gunfire, so I started unloading the Beretta in that direction. Twenty rounds is a lot of trigger pulls.

Daisy pivoted and stepped over me. I was right between her legs. The air was swimming with eddies of discharge smoke.

She put two rounds into Hayden as though swatting a cockroach. Hayden's body chose to stop playing tough, and collapsed. Dishes and frags were making a jukebox of residual noise.

The back hallway was vacant.

Daisy and I sighted on each other at the same time; me on the floor aiming up, her standing over me aiming down.

There came that elongated second of combat time, where you swear you can hear individual breathing, clocks ticking, the little brass bell—now on the floor—emitting one last clink as it rolled to a stop.

Daisy and I continued to point our guns at each other. That seemed to absorb about a week of waiting.

Then she grabbed my hand and pulled me to my feet. As she had said, we had to get out of here. Because unlike the dust-up at my apartment, what happened at Mango Joy would make the news.

Hayden, Before

When Hayden Mathis returned to his Sherman Oaks apartment after seeing Dave Vollmand's wrecked place firsthand and confirming that Dave's dog, Kingi, was laid up at the veterinary on Ventura, he had not been expecting to be greeted by the sight of a man sitting on his own couch, aiming a pistol at him.

"I'll be damned," Hayden said. "Rolf. Don't tell me you've come to cap my ass in my own living room."

Rolf Dettrick rolled his eyes and placed the gun on the table, bore averted. The man displayed textbook muzzle awareness. "Long story, amigo. I helped myself to one of your beers. Why don't you crack one too, and I'll catch you up."

This was mildly pleasant. Hayden had not seen Rolf for the better part of half a decade.

About the time Rolf had been recruited to CHASE, Hayden Mathis was fresh off a clandestine Middle Eastern deployment, having made the career decision to stop ducking bullets and go for something a bit more domestic and tactical; less wildfire. Some people got addicted to battleground pressure, spiking higher highs until they lost limbs, their lives, or worse, degenerated into PTSD zombies who could only mainline hazard. The FBI liked Hayden's jacket, ironically assigning him as a field independent to California, where surveys had proven some drive-time commuters suffered greater stress than fighter pilots in war zones.

Hayden could just as easily have become part of the CHASE family, but liked to nurture the delusion that since he was still only in his mid-thirties, his options could remain wide open. He enjoyed being an on-call jack-of-all-trades; you never knew what odd, special gig might drop out of the mix and require unique skills. Popular media advised that people Hayden's age should already be deep into what they called a mid-life crisis. Of course popular media was mostly for general audiences, who had been culturally sucker-punched into comic book dimwittery.

One of his hobby projects, as Hayden called them, was a job handed down by a Bureau agent named Stanton Weeks, to keep a cultivating eye on a WitSec asset named Dave Vollmand, who in the years since his rebirth had settled unobtrusively into his revised life. In the parlance, Vollmand had gone dormant, gradually requiring less and less watch-dogging by the Bureau that had used him to advantage some criminal clusterfuck back in Florida. Time passed, witnesses died, and the heat receded by degrees.

Hayden liked Dave Vollmand, whoever he really was. They were both maintaining secret lives. They easily became hang-out buddies. Hayden never mentioned his own genesis, and Vollmand never spoke of his own. Their relationship built valuable new backstory.

When Rolf Dettrick spotted Hayden's name in Dave Vollmand's sealed FBI file, he felt the welcome *click* of disparate pieces falling into place for new play. Rolf sought Alma Acevedo, who for some berserk reason had invented a wholly unauthorized contract hit on Vollmand.

Inquiries, as they say, were initiated.

Vollmand's recent activity had seemed so boring and mundane that it almost had to be a cover story. It was *too* unprovocative, yet its edges revealed premeditation—such as the DVD job that kept him inside quiet walls for much of his waking time. His insulation from the world of the walking dead was not hermetic or suspicious, but it functioned excellently.

"How'd you get the file?" said Hayden. He busied himself with some pointless, superficial cleanup in the kitchen.

"Called in a favor at the Bureau," said Rolf. "It was still classified, but no longer red-tagged. Its urgency index had depreciated. And it was a complete accident that your buddy's name came up. What I can't figure out is why, all of a sudden, an ex-CHASE operative needs to kill your pet witness."

"Yeah, that's weird. Because Dave Vollmand doesn't *do* anything except his job, and walk the dog I set him up with as a contingency."

"You placed the dog?"

"I thought it was a good idea," said Hayden. "And I had access to a decommissioned K9 that had been hurt. You know, if anything hairy went down, I thought Dave would take the dog with him. But the guy who breached his apartment Tasered the dog...and fried the tracking chip I implanted after Dave brought Kingi back from recovery."

"Luck sucks. You didn't tag anything else?" Rolf refused to indulge the despair of hope. His mental model cross-pollinated optimist with pessimist to yield a practical hybrid—the realist. Reckless optimism only won you self-denial. Similar pessimism won you self-defeat. Realism brought confidence and courage. Something's lost and something's gained in every living day, as Joni Mitchell had observed. *Christ,* Rolf chided himself; *get a grip.*

"Not necessary," said Hayden, rummaging around the fridge spoilage for another beer. "He wasn't flagged for surveillance. He wasn't in any kind of danger until your girl brought him some. Besides, I thought the dog was a good idea. A passive trace, in case I needed it, or got sidetracked onto some other job."

Rolf closed his eyes for fifteen seconds. "Okay. The dude who Tased the dog was one of Alma Acevedo's co-workers."

"Freelance?"

"Correct. In return, Alma neutralized a CHASE asset her guy had tried to hit once before."

"So to prevent exposure, he handed off the job to Alma?"

"Yeah. But we don't know who contracted the Morgan Deane hit. I'm beginning to think it was something random; somebody Deane just pissed off for one reason or another."

"That still doesn't explain why Alma would manufacture a hit on Dave Vollmand."

"I *know*; I know!" Rolf banged his bottle for emphasis and slopped a bit of foam. "And you have no idea where he'd run?"

"Zero," said Hayden. "He left the dog on account at the vet's, got all the cash he could from the bank, didn't show up at work, and went under...almost like he *knew* how to do it."

"Plus he patched a professional sent to shoot him," said Rolf. "That guy was completely outplayed." He omitted the detail that he had murdered Bryan Silver at the hospital—let Vollmand take the heat on that one. "Did you know Vollmand had guns?"

"If he did, I never saw them."

"Well, he did. More than one. And we have to assume he's got warpower with him. What about his car?"

"Black Infiniti, about seven years old. Not at the apartment. A rental would require plastic, again. It's been less than a day. He's probably still driving it around, if he's driving it anywhere and isn't just holed up." Hayden checked a file on his laptop for the plate number, which was listed along with registration and VIN, Vollmand's Social Security number, his bank routing information, the skinny on his charge cards, and assorted Internet handles and passwords that were no longer useful—all in a maintenance folder.

"Is he smart enough to change the plates?" said Rolf.

"I guess yes," said Hayden. "Let's err on the side of caution."

"Copy that." The whole maze was making Rolf weary. "Listen...I was hoping to resolve this without activating a whole CHASE team, but I can have them if I want them. I got a fallback plan behind that, too. But right now, I need to know if you'll give up your boy."

Hayden raked his fingers through the one-day stubble on his cheeks and chin. "Sure," he said. He stripped his glasses to polish them. "I mean, he's a nice enough guy and everything, but all he knows about me is the story I gave him—you know, divorced, odd jobs, the usual shrug. He thinks I do DVD art; digital design, because I knew that would appeal toward his current wage job."

The designs to sell movies had arrived in regular packet files on Hayden's computer as needed. Some faceless Art Center student did them for a couple hundred bucks a throw, plus nondisclosure. The Bureau had the kid by the shorts on defaulted loans plus a couple of misdemeanors that could easily be ramped into felonies if he didn't behave. And the work actually was used on commercial releases.

Rolf was direct. "How would you feel if we had to put him down?"

Hayden thought this over honestly. "Sad but not outta the park."

Humanity is a teeming sea with an imaginary barrier cutting right through the middle. On one side are ordinary citizens. On the other are the people who puppeteer them via distraction, staging phony coups, rigging elections, dictating fashion, pumping dogma, defining normalcy. Telling credible stories. The first side supplies the taxes and other such tributes spent by the other side. The first side needs to remain grazing, fat, happy or stunned to accomplish the goals of their masters, who perpetuate the myth of equal opportunity because the biggest lies yield the biggest dividends. Often, you could choose your side of the divide. Hayden did not wish to become one with the mass he saw as deluded pawns. He preferred his shadow existence, and relied upon his ability to slip through the cracks. Occasionally, to persevere, you had to acknowledge there were bigger dogs in the yard than little old you.

"He called me," Hayden said. "From some payphone. I think he took the iPhone of the guy who broke into his place. But I don't have any way to determine mobile positioning. No roaming tag; no multiateration. If he's smart, he won't have it for long anyway. There's this old flame he found, from high school. He said her picture was on the guy's phone."

Rolf almost smacked his forehead. "This is making less and less sense. He contacted somebody from, what, twenty-thirty *years* ago?"

"I know—not consistent with low profile," said Hayden. "It was just an unrequited girlfriend thing. You must have one, right? The one that got away?"

Everybody did.

"Did he say anything else?"

Hayden shook his head. His beer had disappeared from the bottle without him noticing. "Just that he'd be in touch."

At that moment, Hayden's personal iPhone buzzed with a new text message from *DV*.

Hayden raked his hands in the air, his fingers clawlike. "Every time I get out, they *pull me back in* again."

Rolf didn't get the reference, and didn't laugh.

They found Dave Vollmand's Infiniti parked a block and a half away from the Mango Joy restaurant. Sure enough—boosted plates. Vollmand had tucked his ride into Landale Street, northeast of the target, around a corner.

Hayden had unboxed a fairly pristine, two-tone Browning Hi-Power Practical with fixed sights and a ring hammer. It had probably left the factory in 1995, the only evident wear being some holster skids on the top left side of the slide. It was chambered for .40 caliber Smith & Wesson ammo, which Hayden had loaded into two steel-matte clips. He stuck the gun into a belt scabbard under the tails of a loose, open shirt.

Rolf came packing one of Gaston Glock's bad boys, a fourth-generation Model 21, its large grip due to the double column of .45 cartridges. A floorplate mod had added four extra rounds to the magazine's original capacity of thirteen, plus one already in the pipe. His backup piece was a Charter Arms Bulldog in .357 caliber with a five-round cylinder.

Under active conditions, that was twenty-three useful shots prior to the first reload. If you couldn't solve your problem with that much spinning lead, you needed a bigger gun or a smaller problem.

"You shouldn't even have to draw down," said Rolf as they approached the restaurant. "I've got this."

"If you start blasting away at norms, make sure I'm not one of them," said Hayden. Norms were called "dumbfucks" in CHASE argot.

From range drills, Rolf knew he could deliver his entire magazine of eighteen Black Talons in just over four seconds with minimum stray. These Winchester rounds were jacketed hollow points engineered to flower with sharp edges upon contact with what was euphemistically called "wet media." Stop 'em and drop 'em, norms and dumbfucks both, because when an op went above a certain budget level, the spoilage cost to civilians was factored in. It was cheaper and often cleaner to shoot through a hostage to pay off a target, for example. Nobody missed dumbfucks for long. They congested the world, cut you off in traffic, outraged you with their pastoral stupidity, and you have already wished them dead a million times. Norm policemen cost slightly more to smooth over but even they weren't immune. All the rest was merely bullshit you jump-scanned past on TiVO.

"You enter frontally," Rolf told Hayden as they did an oblique approach. "You're the good pal come to the rescue. He spooks, or tries to bolt out the rear, I've got him."

Hayden nodded once, his talk time expired, and they split paths.

Coming up on the portals of Mango Joy, Hayden caught a look at the mysterious Daisy—a total deluxe package—and felt a little grind of envy. His own high school heartthrob, Lola Wiseman, had sprawled into a bible belt breeder, the kind he saw mocked on the *People of WalMart* website, usually from the rear, in photos barely sufficient to contain them. If this was Daisy, she had her back to the door but was twisted halfway to see his entrance. Her lips said the words *is that Hayden?* as a tiny bell above the door tinkled.

"Hey," Hayden said, ready to be introduced.

That was when Rolf opened fire from the rear corridor, and the interior of Mango Joy turned into a freestyle shooting competition. Whoever scores the most points wins.

Daisy was bolt upright, shooting without blinking.

Dave hit the floor and then *he* came up with *another* gun.

The waitress, owner, whatever, disappeared behind a counter as though the rug had been yanked from beneath her feet. Dave and Daisy were both in motion, and Rolf's pattern screamed tracking fire—toward Hayden. So much for the backstop. Hayden flattened himself against the nearest wall as fake bamboo chaffed into dust, inches from his face.

Hayden was still trying to scramble his weapon into play. Lost Dave, the primary target. A pity.

But as he sighted, Daisy rotated with nearly supernatural precision and gave him two shots, center mass.

Hayden's body stopped cooperating with his brain, and he fell. He could not feel his own gun, or know if it was still in his grasp.

It was over in less than ten seconds.

Rolf had found a guy in cook's whites goldbricking with a cigarette near the rear trash haul-away, and kissed him with the butt of the Glock to keep him quiet. He found the back door open and edged into the corridor so the light would not bounce off him.

He wanted to question this Dave Vollmand guy about Alma Acevedo, but to do that properly, he and Hayden would have to Jody-step Dave out of the public eye. He took stock of the room, the patrons, placement, and avenues of potential movement. Then he caught a little fist of intake breath that jammed in his esophagus and nearly made him cough.

Alma Acevedo was *sitting right there*, talking to David Vollmand.

Which surprise caused Rolf to jigger his first few shots, as the mission parameter in his head suddenly flipped upside-down. It took a millisecond for the new imperative to shove to the head of the line and lock in: *Kill everyone in this place if you have to, but get her. Now.*

It was all the time Alma needed to answer his gunfire with her own, and she would be as direct and unforgiving as her reputation.

Worse, Hayden's pal Dave was also packing. This was expected. But under stress he was a better shot than Rolf had anticipated.

Hayden went down.

It was time to retreat and rethink. Countermeasures had already been taken.

Rolf had found his long-lost student.

Where you are in Los Angeles when you call 911 will determine who responds, most often LAPD or county sheriffs. Mango Joy was in the gray zone between North Hollywood and Studio City, and the nearest rolling uniforms had come from the NoHo station, to answer a frantic multiple reports of shots fired in the vicinity of an automobile collision. First to the scene were the patrol duo of Fernando Duarte, a Grade I probie, and his field trainer, Officer "Bulka," short for Albulkasem Gibani. They found four wrecked cars blocking the street, two with bullet holes that had caused them to crash into the other two. About fifty pedestrians had come out of nowhere to mill around, and none had witnessed a thing. It was all over before any of them noticed or grabbed their cellphone.

There were two corpses—Arthur Caudill, who had dumped through the front window after being shot, and an unidentified man, mid-30s, from whom the only gun found on scene was recovered. The shooter carried no ID.

Joy Templeton, owner of the restaurant, had sustained a gunshot wound to her left side, where a bullet had zipped between her ribs to bury itself deep within her macrobiotically-cleansed innards. Gunshot trauma had set in and EMTs had to whisk her to St. Joe's for treatment. Another ambulance arrived to take away Joy's cook, Hector Villanueva, who was bleeding profusely from concussion and what turned out to be a hairline fracture in his skull. Another customer, Violet Daws, had also stopped a bullet in addition to numerous lacerations caused by flying glass. By the time detectives and news cameras showed up, most of the talking was done by a survivor named Glendon Ellis, a friend of Violet and Arthur's who had been dining with them.

Glendon maintained that the event had been a drive-by shooting, even though none of the cars outside had been the cause. Shortly afterward, Officer Duarte made Grade II.

When the whole mess rated sixty seconds on the eleven o'clock news, it appeared under the screamer banner *Gang Violence.*

Dave, After

Her body was pressed hard against mine, in the dark, in an airway between two buildings away from the light of the street. It was barely two feet wide. It stank of urine and pulverized cement.

"Now is not the time," she said quietly. Even calmly.

She said this because I was pointing my Beretta directly at her—just as she had responded by drawing down on me, in a standoff—just after I had asked, in so many words rendered vaporous by sheer panic, what the hell was going on.

I will always believe that if Daisy had, for some unfathomable reason, come to kill me, she would have done it at that moment. Instead, the flash tension elongated until it was ridiculous. We both continued breathing.

"Okay," she said. "Hammers down together. On three. Okay?"

She counted off and we decocked simultaneously. If she was as relieved as I was, she didn't show it. If there were stories to be spun, the what-why-when-where-how of good journalism, we had to survive to make them up.

"Car," I said, pointing. She nodded.

We dashed for it like teenagers ducking police spotlights. I didn't want to have to explain any of this to a bunch of surly uniforms yet, and apparently she felt the same way.

As part of my DVD job, I had seen plenty of action sequences. As part of my other life, my previous life, I had experienced just enough violence firsthand to know that reality does not play out as overwrought hyperbole—most often, your brain cannot process all that is happening while it occurs. Extravagant explosions and slow-motion kung-fu were attempts to dissect fury into digestible bits made glittery and attractive by a lot of empty showoff and fetishistic over-detail. In violence, the most pertinent bits were made up by your own brain in hindsight to impose order on chaos. The same went for dreams.

Or car chases. Something about their shape compels the eye to skip them wholly, because they don't provide any information. It's a time-out of which your mind now says, *okay, here comes the action sequence,* and the story will resume once all the fire and thunder is dispensed. The dream sequence. The fight sequence. The sex sequence. Nothing really happens; nothing fundamental changes during the combat scene, the sex fugue, or the psychedelic pageant. When you can read the first paragraph line of some bloated, best-selling beach paperback—thereby denying yourself a bunch of *sequences* that were filler anyway—and still track a rudimentary story, you'll understand the difference between actual reading, and junk that flies in one eye and out the other. Or try listening to a movie instead of watching it, to see what is gained or superfluous. I have.

Most padding in shiny entertainment can be short-formed as a repeated one-liner, like that crazy guy in that haunted hotel movie typing "all work and no play" over and over. The snappy phrase that lodged in my head for such occasions had come from a really old Firesign Theatre routine. Nick Danger, Third Eye.

"I felt like I was being kicked in the head by the whole chorus line at Minsky's."

I call it a Minsky's Moment. The section of movie you fast-forward through because you know it's all a digital cartoon. The part of the barbarian epic where the physics-defying sword fight begins. The text you skip because you know it's all fluff. Try it, whenever your mind can only view events as a *sequence* sometime. The Minsky's Moment plugs in anywhere, and saves a lot of bother.

The plunging unreality of blink-and-you'll-miss-it physical jeopardy is the reason that bystanders and witnesses talk the way they do on the bits of news generated by the aftermath. "I don't believe this happened," they say. "I can't believe this just happened." Because they really cannot; they're unable to. They are *disabled.* They haven't had the time to make up stories that seek to decant logic from happenstance. The suspension of disbelief necessary to most fiction has become too weighty to hoist, when the imagination has atrophied.

Blunted by comic books and video games, toys and sports, and a 140-character limit that eliminates the possibility of paying "strict attention" to anything, many modern humanoids of our momentous 21st Century have traded the experiential for the observational, becoming sideline looky-loos consuming the experience of others, keeping their distance and staying safely uninvolved. Nonetheless, they slow down to do the vulture-gawk at accident scenes because they, too, need their little fictions—especially the ones that reassure them that if they behave, nothing bad will ever befall them.

My mortgage sucks, but at least my kid isn't possessed by a real demon.

I hate my job, but as long as I stay in the city, I won't get eaten by a giant snake or a clan of cannibal hillbillies.

My life is loveless, but at least I won't be burned and heartbroken.

Sex, drugs, rock 'n roll and the limitless midway of diversions beckons. It's all popcorn fun and plot twists until it falls on top of you.

"Why did you bring a gun?" I tried to ask that of Daisy with the proper gravity once we were inside my Inifiniti and moving, but my voice cracked right in the middle of the sentence.

"Why did you?" she said, watching behind us. "Just get us out of here, please."

Okay, put a pin in that thought for later.

"Why is your picture on the iPhone of the guy who tried to kill me?"

Her head jerked around. "Tell me you didn't keep the phone."

"No. No cells. No prepaid phones for more than one call. I've been followed before."

"What about this car?" she said. "Lojack, Ravelco, Street Eagle, anything like that?"

"No. I switched the plates."

"Where's your dog? Kingi?"

"Boarded at the vet's. The man who came into my place Tased him."

"Sorry about that," she said, as though she was somehow responsible. "Goddamned *Rolf.* It figures."

"Rolf?" Was she imitating a dog's bark?

"The man shooting at us in the dark. He turned your friend Hayden, or Hayden was a plant, which was why he had a gun, too. Rolf was shooting at me. Hayden's reaction said Hayden had no idea what was really going down, but he was in on the surface details, which means that at some level, he was playing you."

"What about the other people in the restaurant?"

"Irrelevant," Daisy said. "Rolf Dettrick came for me. Somewhere, a tire blew, and it has something to do with the reason you're packing a gun."

"That's a really long story," I sighed.

"Well, as long as you don't shoot me and I don't shoot you, we might be able to figure it out together."

Charmingly, she left out the part where she said *that's the only reason you're still alive.*

Tropical Paradise

"I like it," Daisy said of the motel room. "Downscale, forsaken, off the path. You didn't use a credit card?"

I unnecessarily made sure the door was locked, again—not that the Masonite barricade would stand up to a slingshot. "Cash only, no questions asked."

"How do you know it?" She was eyeballing every nook in the room.

"Random," I said.

"It's not like a pattern?" she said, ever-wary. "Patterns are bad."

"You mean a pattern, like I treat all my dates this royally?" I shook my head. "No, tonight was extra-special. I wanted you to feel pampered."

"Pretty sure of yourself." She stretched full length atop the pill-furred comforter atop on the sagging bed. I heard her tendons crackle. Suddenly she rolled off, peered beneath the frame, and dragged out my bag of guns.

"Oh, my," she said. "You really know how to gear up for a party." Then, one by one, she extracted the weapons and checked them professionally. She worked the actions to test the resistance of the slide springs. She thumbed the hammers to get an idea of alignment and trigger travel for each. She popped magazines and examined the loads, nodding. She could probably name every single cartridge.

"I've got some beer and Doritos," I said.

"Sold. No porn?"

"I didn't really have time to check." I pulled two Amber Bocks out of the trashcan full of half-melted ice.

"I don't get porn, anyway," she mused. "Watching actors have sex doesn't help me have sex. If I'm alone I'd rather just close my eyes and use my imagination."

"You're doing it again," I said. Her eyebrows went up. *Who, me?* "That deflection mechanism. The body language, the tease, the big pheromonal assault to misdirect, like sleight-of-hand. I already think you're attractive, Daisy. You've been in the back of my mind for years, and when you walked into that coffeehouse the first time, you were the stuff dreams are made of. But don't play me. Please. I've been racheted around enough for one lifetime, today."

She pursed her lips and looked at the floor. "Y'know...that might be the nicest thing anyone has ever said to me." She destroyed most of her brew in one long draught. "God. Thirsty."

"Stress dehydrates you. Wipes out B vitamins. Alcohol dehydrates you, too, but right now I don't give a shit." I snorted. "People are always finding excuses to give themselves little rewards. Like in the movies, characters freak out and grab the scotch, as medicine. Real people do it because they learned it from fictional people. You see a tragedy and you're supposed to make a certain face or the audience won't buy your grief. We're all playacting—you and me more than most, seems like."

"It's cover," she said. "Armor. It's necessary." Her face unscrewed into an abrupt *oh shit* expression. "Did you check your car?"

I was lagging behind. "My car?"

"Yeah, the car we just came here in! It's not out of the realm of possibility that Rolf tagged it before he came into the restaurant."

She meant Rolf had hung a leash on us. I saw her do the math.

"Hayden would know your car, right, even if you hid it?" She moved to check the view from the windows. "The make, the color?"

"Yeah, if they had bothered to walk six blocks in every direction around the restaurant before coming in," I said. "Oh. Shit."

Daisy moved sharp for the bed. "They're already here."

A long splinter jumped from the door as the drapes twitched and the window glass disintegrated. A team, using suppressors, keeping their distance, probing by fire.

On the door hit I went down to hands and knees.

Daisy emerged from the bathroom holding the lid to the toilet tank. "Here," she said. "Punch through the wall, there. Do it now!" She indicated the far side of the bed, which offered the best cover. She grabbed one of my bag guns in each hand, snapping the slides into battery and jamming the pistols down into her waistband, which was pretty miraculous considering how tight her jeans were. Then she grabbed two more guns. "They'll be waiting for us to fall out the bathroom window. We're not going to."

She positioned herself close to the window frame—more wood in the construction to hamper a bullet, there—and began feeding gunfire to give the invaders a focus for their attention. She fired accurately, two-handed.

I battered the wall with the corner of the toilet tank lid and the thin veneer easily gave way to old lath and plaster. No pipes blocking the way, as you'd find in the bathroom. I hit it again. On the third strike I penetrated into the next room. A peephole that had to be widened into a passageway.

*I felt kicked in the head by...*Jesus, I was living a Minsky's Moment, and it wasn't boring or superfluous *at all.*

I redoubled my efforts to widen the hole while Daisy laid down an uninterrupted fusillade of gunfire, to bring the noise and keep the attention of our attackers eyes-front, because any second now they would storm the bathroom window—the backside of the motel. The wall sundered pretty agreeably. I was breathing demolition dust from half a century ago, probably packed with mold spores. The tank lid was crude, but heavy and solid, and directly I could see into the unoccupied room next door. If anyone had been in there, they had lit off in a hurry when the maniac started coming through the wall.

Response fire tore up the front of the room as Daisy kept cover and I felt five or six hot lead bees zing past close enough for me to feel them vibrate. One spanged off the tank lid and nearly knocked it out of my hands.

"I think I hit at least one," said Daisy over her shoulder. "They're being *real* careful. Give me some good news."

"We're through!"

The hole in the wall was a ragged, lopsided, toothy maw, but big enough to squeeze through, if you enjoyed the thought of reenacting your own birth.

"Go!" Daisy said. "Right behind you!"

The next salvo all but collapsed the front wall of our ex-room with the weird, spitting sounds of incoming rounds with no bang-bang to herald them. The air was awash not with gunsmoke (unlikely) or cordite (outdated), but with a floating haze of pulverized building material.

My other guns were spent and lost. Daisy had the piece I'd seen her pull at Mango Joy, and I still had my Beretta. She practically fell on top of me as she skewed through the hole in the wall.

"That's a strike team out there," she said, wiping grit from her eyes with a pestered expression. "They have patterns, procedures that will delay them. They all look to their lead for the next move. We've got about ten seconds to outmaneuver them."

"How?"

"They'll come at the door in a V-shape, a wedge. You follow me, do what I do, and shoot until you're empty. I've only got this mag left."

She grabbed my hand, dragged me in her wake...

...flung back the door, and ran right out into the open in a low, fast crouch.

About one second for them to see us. They were concentrating on the next room over. Another half-second for them to react. During which Daisy and I laid down a spray of cover fire. Three-quarters of a second for the fireteam to alter trajectory and recommence shooting. Now I could see two men, bearing military rifles. Another man further back, seeing us just now, drawing a pistol, his teeth bared.

When the driver of the nearest car saw us coming, he hastily tried to shift gears up from idle and back away. But his window was open and within one hiccup of time, Daisy's sizzling hot muzzle was cooking the flesh of the man's neck before he could fish up a weapon of his own.

"Whoa, whoa, I *drive*, that's all!" the man protested. Meaning *don't kill me, please; I'm just the messenger.*

By then the first two fireteam shooters had turned to accommodate our unexpected flanking run while two more came running around from the back of the motel. They did not look fooled, outmaneuvered or embarrassed. Of each pair, one man was always firing while the other refreshed clips. Their choreography was impressive, but by then, we had the cover of the car—bulletproof shell, slug glass, nondeflating tires.

The team lead was screaming at his men, bellowing at the driver of the other car to block us. I watched the bullets from his pistol skim off the windshield a foot away from my face.

I dived into the backseat as Daisy shoved the driver over. By the time she slammed her door I threw a forearm around the driver's neck and dragged him uncomfortably back, to introduce his head to the bore of the Beretta. I had to keep him in close-up because I was out of ammo already.

Daisy threw the Buick Lucerne into reverse, attempting a spur-of-the-moment backup collision that might cripple the other nearly identical vehicle. She missed the "kneecap"—the critical spot at the wheelwell you need to smash in order compromise the tire.

She backed out of the motel lot at admirable speed.

"You, Mister Whoa," she shouted at the driver beside her, still in my grasp. "What's your name?"

"Uhhh, Fletcher!" he said, having nearly forgotten.

"Okay, Fletcher, what's your sidearm?"

"Just a Llama nine."

"All right, you're going to hand it to my partner behind you. Don't sweat it, Fletcher, you're doing real good so far."

"Whatever you say, ma'am," Fletcher said. He had neglected to breathe enough to get the whole sentence out without squeaking.

"Don't call me ma'am," said Daisy, driving backward and palavering all at once. "Makes me feel old."

The Lucerne jounced backward onto Woodman Avenue, snarling traffic.

Rolf Dettrick was in command of a standard-issue CHASE strike team. Two cars—each driver an experienced getaway jockey who could be brought into gunfire as a last resort, but whose general duty was to stay behind the wheel—plus four shooters (two per vehicle) in light body armor, wielding full-auto assault rifles augmented with combat rounds, night sights, M4-2000 silencers and flash suppressors. The rifles had been recently liberated from an "unguarded but secure" SWAT training facility in downtown L.A. by thieves who only had to use bolt cutters; final score: twenty-one submachine guns, nineteen semi-auto pistols and an "undisclosed" amount of ammunition. The covenant of the strike team was the fast grab or the fast kill, with all instrumental personnel instructed to do the second if the first could not be accomplished.

Everyone was radioed up, although Rolf knew the usual earbuds were of scant use during a melee. He needed to corral his targets, box them and take them, not obliterate them in a firefight. He need to *contain* them.

The late Hayden Mathis had watched while Rolf secreted a short-range tracker (all matte, no lights) in Dave Vollmand's Infiniti once they spotted it. Vollmand had picked a good speed hide around a residential corner (no lots, no curbside), but quick access from the restaurant had determined a limited radius. As it turned out, the homer had been a good idea. It came through loud and clear once everyone had fled Mango Joy. Hayden Mathis had not fared so well, but Rolf had gained a negotiative advantage—Alma Acevedo had just killed an FBI satellite.

Were Alma and Dave Vollmand still together? That seemed reckless and untoward. They should have split up immediately. On the possibility they had not, Rolf summoned the CHASE team just in case Alma was still hanging around. He was still within budget. Nail Alma, and CHASE could answer for the death of Morgan Deane, so Rolf knew James Smith (Chase Alpha) would approve. Neither Rolf nor CHASE was interested in Dave Vollmand except as a link to Alma, a hostage, a bargaining chip, or a fall guy. Hayden Mathis could be pinned on Vollmand to make the Bureau happy, Alma would be unplugged, and everyone could go back to biz as usual.

The team convened two blocks away from the Tropical Paradise Motel, not far from the 405 freeway, the Van Nuys Airport, and the L.A. River, that serpentine stone dragon that bisected the entire Valley. Rolf drew a fast job map in the dust on the hood of one of the Buick Lucernes CHASE had provided. Such combat-ready vehicles waited in rental lots all over America (hence the light coating of dust), unavailable to the general public, on standby until someone at CHASE clicked a mouse.

The layout of the Tropical Paradise Motel was a typical long-arm L-shape with a courtyard. The chase cars would bracket both sides of the empty swimming pool to prevent Dave Vollmand's Infiniti from haring away. Rolf drew little arrows, much akin to a football plan or a film director's markers for camera movement. Strike One to the left, Strike Two to the right.

That makes me Strike Three, Rolf thought with almost no humor.

David J. Schow

At the first action indicator, Alma Acevedo would most likely jettison herself through a rear bathroom window, so after buttoning up the motel manager and ascertaining that the subject room was occupied, Rolf planned to haze his targets frontally via salvo. Gunfire makes some people move fast and recklessly. It makes dumbfucks freeze. Almost immediately following the first salvo, the outside men on the pattern, one each from Strike One and Strike Two, would move to cover the rear of the building, careful not to cross their lines of fire with the men in front. The pattern was known as a "rat trap." Make your target run toward a destination where you already have sights on them.

The teams centered the motel room and converged, textbook, the silencers stuttering not much louder than drumming fingers on sheet metal.

Hell was unleashed back at them from the front window. No silencers, just a mechanistic delivery of a great amount of lead on two moving tangents that hampered both upfront shooters with hits to their Kevlar, even more textbook.

Terrific, thought Rolf. *Now we're gonna be on the news again.*

Even with body armor, a shooter's natural inclination is to seek hard cover if one has to deal with return fire. You don't just stand there like an invincible robot, because you are vulnerable to arm hits, leg hits, and that irksome gremlin of the field shield, armpit hits, not to mention the lucky headshot.

Then Alma jack-in-the-boxed unexpectedly out of the next room over with her charge in tow. Boyfriend, accomplice, whatever, it didn't matter because both of them were shooting handguns. The first two CHASE men were caught offsides.

"Upfront!" Rolf radioed to the two men assigned to cover the rear escape. "They're upfront, shoot to support!"

They weren't making a hopeless play for the Infiniti. They weren't reenacting the suicidal climax of *Butch Cassidy and the Sundance Kid*. They were going for the Strike Two car.

Rolf brought up his Glock and unloaded it in their direction. Distance and motion were both working against him. It is very difficult to hit a moving target with a handgun, even under optimum range conditions. You do your best under the circumstances; spray lead and hope someone falls down.

Just as the other two CHASE men ran around to join the fray, Rolf saw what was about to happen with slow, collapsing horror.

"Driver One!" he shouted, breaking into a low, loping run. "Driver One! Block Two! Block Two!"

Alma had selected the CHASE car with its butt toward the hotel driveway.

"Goddammit!"

Strike Two crunched Strike One's rear wheelwell, but it was a miss.

Now the whole bollixed operation was about to become, hilariously, a pursuit—that is to say, a chase.

Strike Three, though Rolf. *Yep—that one's gonna come back to bite my ass, for sure.*

<hr />

Careening in reverse, the Lucerne clipped the front of a lumbering food truck bearing the legend *Comidas Excellentes - Nueva Cocina*. The truck dropped onto its right front fender and bit into a parked SUV, setting off a (useless) car alarm. Behind the food truck, which lurched and settled like a beached yacht, a party girl in a weathered Benz stood on her brakes while waving both hands in the air around her head in an *omigod-omigod-omigod* gesture frequently observed in L.A. traffic. This took her hands off the wheel. The Benz nosed into the ass of the food truck at about thirty-five per. The landscaper behind the Benz ditz reacted well, even though he was exhausted from a full day of outdoor work in the July sun. He swerved. One more day of labor would have prized him with long-awaited new tires for his pickup, but his gods were not smiling. His bald left front blew like a cannon shot and his top-heavy load of mowers and blowers went into the street. Idiots congregated; shooting pictures with their phones while some of the southbound dolts on Woodman, clear of the mayhem, actually stopped their cars to catch a rearward look. This left a momentarily clear tunnel for the Lucerne, still catapulting backward, to jackknife ass-up over the median and interrupt traffic in the northbound lane as it crashed down hard enough to shatter the teeth in your mouth, throwing loose parts. Vile billows of vulcanized smoke erupted from the wheel wells as the car slammed into forward motion at last, pedal down.

Strike One—containing Rolf Dettrick, the wheelman, and the nearest shooter Rolf could grab before engaging his hot pursuit—had to negotiate stragglers, onlookers, the food truck, and assorted yard equipment, including a grimy gas lawnmower that rolled right into their path on its own, as though it had nothing better to do.

Three men had been left behind with no transpo. One of the Strike Two soldiers had stopped a bullet with his femur. Their orders were to divest weapons and call a prearranged CHASE number for extraction and medical. They did not need Rolf to babysit them.

Nor was the pursuit strictly necessary, under normal circumstances, since the Strike Two car could be easily tracked. But Alma would know that. She would dump the vehicle as soon as she was out of Rolf's line-of-sight.

"She's heading for the freeway," said the Strike One driver, a snake-eyed fellow named Oshuda.

"No, she's not," said Rolf. "She's heading for the reservoir."

"You mean the river."

Rolf snorted, with an out-of-towner's sense of disdain. "That's not a fucking *river.*"

The Los Angeles River is a man-made, fixed-course channel that bisects the San Fernando Valley, mouthed in the Simi Hills and Santa Monica Mountains. It is almost fifty miles long, eventually dumping in Long Beach. You've seen its runoff channels used in dozens of noir potboilers. It is the access point the giant, atomically mutated ants used to nest in the city storm drains in *Them!* (and if black-and-white films aren't your thing, think of the truck chase in *Terminator 2*— another special edition disc I vetted). It usually dwindles to a trickle in the dry season, the belly of the channel awash in flotsam, rock runoff, and garbage. There are homeless settlements beneath many of the bridges. Fornicating teenagers enjoy taking advantage of the fenced banks and darkness. The gaping flood control ports are ideal for a nefarious rendezvous—dope deal, mob hit, you name it. An amazing variety of mountain wildlife also call the bizarre "river" home. Birds, beavers, even bobcats. You can actually catch bass and catfish at some points.

I'd never actually experienced it, until Daisy drove us right into it. I'd discovered Kingi near one of its overpasses. It ran very near my former home. But now we were intimately close, cruising through puddles that blasted broad fans of dirty water upward, dodging tumbleweeds and boulders in the dark, running fast, headlights off.

I still had my neck-lock on Fletcher, the deposed driver, and I now had his own fully-loaded Llama 9mm to threaten him with. Daisy drove by instinct, almost heedlessly, like a skatepunk determined to beat a video game.

Lights teakettled down the slope behind us—two hot, glowing pinpoints that seemed to bounce (I thought of marbles cast into a dish), then firmed level and increased speed. Any second now some ghetto bird would fire up a searchlight and begin dogging us from above.

"Get ready to bail, Fletcher," Daisy said. She veered the car onto the wide slope and the whole car tilted heavily to the right.

"Yes ma'am," Fletcher said, compliant and slightly petrified.

"I said don't call me that. You're going to have to eat a little road rash." She cut speed a few degrees, fighting the wheel to keep the car oriented. "Now."

I turned Fletcher loose. He pulled the door handle. Gravity dropped the door open and he fell free.

Daisy pumped the brakes to slam the door behind him. Then she soared back down into the darkest part of the river, hydroplaning around an enormous stone column I realized was a bridge support only when we were past it. Dead branches tried to grab our car and failed.

I imagined Fletcher rolling down the incline trying not to break bones, a discard nobody wanted, a refugee from the Isle of Misfit Toys. With any luck, he would stagger to his feet and try to flag down the car pursuing us. Most likely, they would ignore him. But if they picked him up, or even slowed to consider him, that bought us running distance.

"Do you have any idea where we are?" I said from the backseat, too loudly. The last fifteen minutes or so seemed to mandate yelling. "Do you have any idea what the hell you're doing?"

"Yes," Daisy said, without looking back.

She had begun a drunken weaving pattern, up-down, side-to-side, to tempt the pursuit car to try copying. After a moment the headlights behind us, larger now due to the decreased lag, juddered up toward the sky. Metal shrieked as the chase car's speed ground down to nothing. The headlights angled off in the wrong direction, stuck.

"What happened?"

"The gutter," she said, turning one thumb down.

In the center of the Los Angeles River culvert is a boxy depression, the shape of an upside-down staple, a big squared-off divot. That's where you see most of the pallid feed from the viaduct dribbling along when the channel itself is arid. It was possible to fly your car's tires over it if you hit the gap fast enough, mostly at a right angle, though this is not recommended for the integrity of your chassis. Filled with water, it resembles a flat surface.

But if you try to drive right down the center of the channel and are not careful, your tires will fall into ambush and you'll be jammed like a skewed slot car.

Just in time, too, since an LAPD chopper had made its first pass overhead, searchlight tasting and sampling the topography.

Daisy halted the Lucerne in a side-skid, pluming up fat feather of water. We were in the shadows beneath the next bridge.

"Hurry." She was out of the car, having already popped the trunk.

Two or three desperate shots droned downriver, but at this distance it was hopeless, angry gunfire. Emotional punctuation.

Climbing out, I realized Daisy had spun our car to give us a barrier while we pillaged the trunk. Protection against a random lucky hit, even though the bad guys were almost a football field away.

The first thing she handed me was bottled water. "Take it." She had snatched up a small first aid kit.

The second thing she handed me was an AR-15 with a lot of jazz on the rails, a beefed up machine gun the same as those used by the raiders. It was Grim Reaper black; warm from its nap in the trunk.

She found a web vest with a few spare mags and threaded into it. Two baton flashlights, one for me. Among a spill of ammo cartons she turned up cartridges in 9mm (for my Beretta and Llama) and .45 caliber (for her own Smith). She inclined her chin, in silhouette, toward a yawning drainage tunnel a few steps away.

"Take my hand and move sharp," she said. "I'm hit."

━✦━

"Axle's busted," Oshuda confirmed to Rolf Dettrick as the police whirlybird thundered past above them. "Good trick."

Their car was wedged into the runoff gutter at a forty-five degree angle, engine steaming.

Rolf swore an acid stream of invective and fired uselessly into the night ahead of them until the slide of his Glock locked back. Failure to do this was an infamous Achilles heel of the Glock, blamed on everything from a dirty gun to weak ammo, from a worn follower or slide spring to the operator riding the release lever with his thumb while shooting right-handed or freestyle. Rolf kept his weapon optimum. He broke down and cleaned it after every session. The gun was not at fault. The operator was.

Strike Two, their third passenger, was CHASE loan-out named Bixler, who had flown into Burbank from Santa Barbara for this meet. Two of his fellows had been local talent; the fourth had checked in from San Diego. Bixler sighed capaciously as he un-Velcroed with ripping sounds.

"A whole strike team, butt-fucked by two people with handguns," Bixler said. "Jeez. Alpha's gonna be pissed."

"Yeah, testify," muttered Rolf.

"Alexander caught at least one hit back there," said Bixler. "Boss, it ain't my place, but I sure as hell hope you know what you're doing."

"Noted," said Rolf. *Yeah, tell me about it. James Smith is never going to rubber stamp another strike team. He's going to say, "You're over budget, Rolf." Then he's going to say, "You're on your own, Rolf, use your ingenuity and don't bother me again until this problem is resolved."*

He had wanted a simple, direct mop-up. In, out. It was not going to happen. He was his own Strike Three.

The black-and-white chopper circled overhead and hit them with the spotlight.

"We've got to go get Fletcher," said Oshuda.

"Copy that," said Bixler. "Plus now we've got the cops to grease up, too." Rolf's whisper-thin FBI card was about to get another workout.

By the time he could regroup, the targets would be impossible to catch up with, in the endless maze of L.A. County's flood control subterrane.

It was time for Rolf to fall back to Plan B.

Dave, Gone Under

The air was mildly sulfurous, though not specifically unpleasant. It smelled like rampant biology. Most people don't realize L.A.'s storm drain network is completely separate from the sewer system. We were not mucking about in the liquid effluvia of over ten million daily toilet users.

Daisy's lower left side was saturated with blood above the belt line. She had rucked up her shirt so we could examine the wound by flashlight. Her navel was an innie.

She reached for one of the assault rifles. The stretch made her grimace and fresher blood oozed out.

"We don't need that right now," I said. "We need to—"

"Quiet; I need to see the mag."

She released the clip and thumbed up a round, which I knew to be either 5.56 NATO or .223 Winchester—standard—but that's all I knew. I would not have known how to get the clip out of the gun.

"These are special ops M4A1 variants," she said, as though the recitation helped her focus. "See this?" She held up the cartridge between bloodstained fingers. "Hardball, full metal jacket. I think it went all the way through."

Watching her fight to lodge herself into a position that did not hurt was itself painful.

"I was afraid they were using those frangible rounds—you know, the extreme-shock stuff used for close-quarter battle? They explode inside you. Help me tape this up. There should be some Quickclot in there."

I found a packet of Celox in the first aid kit. Film bandages to seal out air. My own belt, to bind the wrap. There was no way to impede the blood flow to that part of her body.

"Sorry," I kept saying.

"Just give me a minute and don't let me pass out."

"This has happened before?"

"Twice." She gnashed her teeth and sucked air. "*Shit*, that hurts!"

She doubled and I saw a hook-shaped scar on her lower back. "Is that what this is?" This was not my ideal fantasy version of getting to see her naked skin.

"No, that's a knife wound." She made the hissing sound again. "Dagger. A double-edged stabber. Has to be five or six inches long to reach vital organs...listen, if you need to catalogue all my damage, we're going to be here about a month, and I'd really like to move."

"Sorry."

"Stop saying 'sorry.' You did really good. In the restaurant. On the run. Really good." She clamped her arm around her wounded side and laboriously levered up to her feet. We were standing in about four inches of water.

"You mean really well."

"Fuck you," she said, more breath than voice, but she did allow a tiny smile. "Give me an arm so I don't fall on my face." Spotting me slinging both of the assault rifles, she added, "Lose those. We're not going to need them."

"You sure?" Something ancient in me riled at the notion of discarding a perfectly good lethal weapon.

"Positive. If they'd'a chased us in here, we would have heard them by now. They're not coming in. Too many different ways to go. That means bigger teams. Visibility. Exposure. CHASE isn't going to want that."

"Who's Chase?" I said, slogging along, supporting her. "The guy, er, *chasing* us?"

"Long story."

"We appear to have a lot of time."

The tendons on her neck were bulging with the strain of clenching her teeth, barricading pain. "CHASE is not a person. CHASE is an organization. The person chasing us is named Rolf Dettrick. He's Chase Delta. He's from the past, which really *is* a long story, for later."

"And when am I supposed to ask about the guy with your picture on his phone?"

Her eyes rolled up. "Much later, different story, even longer, and thank you for leaving it on hold until we get out of here." Her mouth tightened into a grim, bloodless line. "We could have just shot each other, I guess."

"That means we're doing really well," I said, sounding lighter than I intended. "Getting along in a give-and-take social situation. Gradually sharing and becoming comfortable in each other's company."

Her eyes gave me the finger. "Oh, don't tell me—the bullet hole is foreplay and you're hard as a girder right now. *Please* don't tell me you want to fuck the bullet hole..."

"I hadn't even thought of that," I said, appearing honest strictly by omission. "What kind of sickos do you normally go out with?" I almost said *go to bed with,* and that would have bent my transparent innocence the wrong way.

"The frequently armed kind," she said. "One can never be too careful in today's confusing dating environment." She was mocking me, now. "And one should never, *ever,* set up face-to-face fantasy encounters based on Internet evidence; you're just setting yourself up for a bad fall, or worse, a scam like the story about the rich African prince who *needs your help* to transfer lots of money right now."

"True," I said. "But you showed up anyway."

"Point." She smiled. "Help me with this ladder thing." She had selected a point of ascension back into the Overworld. "You're going to have to go up first—I can't manage the manhole cover."

Just for a second, I wanted to stay down here. Surrounded by concrete, just another rat in the labyrinth. I felt this need pulsing off Daisy, too, but she was wounded and this was a seriously unsanitary hole-up. I wanted no one to care about us, to forget we existed, to let us go. I wanted to shuck our identities like snakeskin and emerge brand-new, without history, obligations or debts. One sure way to accomplish that was death. For the rest of us, the living, we had no alternative but to brace ourselves. Fight hard. Persevere.

For whatever reason, via unknowable machinations, we were together. We were an *us*, now.

Junkies. Tweakers. Drunks. Panhandling bums. Street-loosed lunatics. You've seen them all, limping along, ragged and forsaken, arguing with invisible enemies, incoherently bumming change, shouting for no external reason against the conflagrations inside their heads. On bus stops, packed in an entire bin's-worth of discard clothing, weaving back and forth. Filth-besmirched and snoring inside the jimmied gates of failed storefronts, the hot tar stench of their dysfunction a palpable thing, like an occult thundercloud of woeful damnation.

Daisy and I looked just like them. Sodden clothing, bloodstains, soiled madhouse rejects. If we stood still long enough, the police would tell us to move along. We had just emerged from a low-rent walk-in-clinic where Daisy was presented as the victim of a construction site mishap involving a spear of rusty rebar that went right through her side. The doctor, a guy named Darden, didn't buy the story for a moment. But like most of the inept pill-pushers in these joints, he could be rendered indifferent with a cash bonus. The ID Daisy used was fake, anyway, and it's not like this was the first time a clinic had been presented with spurious documentation.

That left me with less than a hundred bucks.

Nobody cares how bizarre you look if you ride the subway or bus in Los Angeles. On Hollywood Boulevard, we were merely another sideshow in the endless doo-dah parade.

"Hotel," she said. "Soon."

The Walk of the Stars was a riot of smoke shops, shitty clothing outlets and tchotchke hucksters. Only in movies does anyone see pimps and hookers on the Boulevard; you'd think scenarists and directors would know that by now. The pull of the mythic always prevails. That's why strangers come here to photograph the Hollywood sign on faraway Mount Lee. They think it's a ride or an "entertainment experience." It's something one *does*, an almost genetic coding that cannot be countered. Ask them, as they stand in the middle of Beachwood Drive, why they are shoving their children *into traffic* for the sake of a souvenir snap, and they won't be able to give you a sensible answer; in fact, they'll look at you as though you're the nutty one.

She directed me to one of the shops with instructions to procure large, un-bloodied sweatshirts that could hide our handguns. She handed me what appeared to be a credit card, an ironclad no-no in light of the kind of people who sought to detain or murder us.

Yes—a Visa card (for all intents) bearing the name Harold Simpson, with the proper embossing, holograms and mag stripe (for all purposes).

It was not, however, a Visa card.

"This is called a CC—carbon clone," she said. "You take it in there and use it to pay. It mirror-logs the last data sent through the card reader, PIN and all, if there is one. Or for gas stations, a zip code. The goofball at the counter almost never looks at the name on the card; they barely handle the cards at all, anymore, because everybody is so afraid of getting their identity ripped off."

"Yeah," I said. "You don't even have to sign, half the time, anymore." People whipped out plastic at Starbucks now, for god's sake.

"Next port of call, use the card again, it resets with new data. Like, at a hotel. Even if there's a problem with the card—if the last user is really on the button about charges that won't show up for several weeks—by the time you use it again, the information has changed. You say, 'oh, no worries, let me try another card.' The credit card companies don't call an alert because that data has already been locally used. And so on, leap-frogging. These are useful for staying off the grid. The only far-distant possibility is some keyboard jockey with too much leisure time, paying deep attention and knowing what patterns to look for. Never happens if you recycle fast. This is the closest you'll ever get to viability as an anonymous consumer."

She was right. The smiling Iranian gent behind the souvenir counter never batted an eyelash. He thanked me for choosing his shop. He never once glanced at the card or asked to see confirming ID.

Maybe this was one of the mystery reasons the L.A. County Jail had locked up and held hundreds of innocent people just last year in one of the biggest mistaken-identity gaffes you never heard about...because these poor slobs possessed the same *names* as legitimate suspects. Or— you guessed it—they had their digital identities thieved. Wrong place, wrong time, wrong *name*. The cops evaded prosecution because as far as they knew, they were acting on valid warrants.

Daisy and I made our way east and checked into a two-story travel lodge accustomed to transients and tourists, the Trailblazer Motor Hotel near Western, far from where the march of sidewalk celebrity stars ended on the Boulevard, downscale enough for family travelers to judge it dicey. It presented very little to the street and featured a large interior courtyard, with the usual amenities of a one-night-stand fuck pit. The crappy Wi-Fi was a plus clue for those very few guests afraid of being monitored from the air itself.

Daisy picked it. The burlesque squire in the back of my brain would have suggested the Roosevelt Hotel, still seeking to impress her. The blunt twin beds had a lingering tang of disinfectant. If your life has deposited you in certain circumstances—like jail—you know the smell. It wasn't a dealbreaker.

The door had a knob lock, a swing-bar latch, and a privacy chain. I put out the Do Not Disturb card and watched Daisy gingerly sit on one bed, then half-recline with pillows wadded behind her. She seemed to deflate.

"God," she said. "I want a shower but I can't move."

"Take your time." We had fresh dressings and antibiotics for her injury.

"Find a vending machine," she said, seeming sleepy. "Something with a lot of sugar and caffeine in it. And ice, lots of it. Please." She had placed her pistol on the nightstand. An hour or two ago, we had been pointing guns at each other.

I found deeply chilled Dr Peppers and filled a motel trashcan with ice, the same as I had for my beer at the Tropical Paradise.

"How did you know about the gutter thing?" I asked.

"I drove the aqueduct in a rented car, once," she said. "At night, no lights, same deal. To see. Just in case I ever needed to know."

"You mean in case something like this ever happened."

"Contingency," she said. "Is this what you thought it might be like? Our dream date?"

"I don't know." I sat down, careful of jostling the bed. "You think you might like to share with me what you're mixed up in?"

"You first," she said.

If a faceless cadre of bad guys had gone to such lengths to flush me, then it was a plan beyond my ability to countermand. In my position, I could only wait for the hammer to fall. I tried to twist it into some Hitchcockian predicament of mistaken identity, but only half-heartedly. Ultimately I gave Daisy my whole story, the short version.

She nodded as though a few stray details clicked. Then she told me a story of her own.

It was a tale of a little black book, and the elimination of everyone with any connection to her distant past. A book that, over the years, had added a name here and there—a new name that was quickly crossed out. In the past decade, the Internet had ballooned into a monstrous, sucking vortex of interconnectivity as a new generation of humans sought to record their every twitch and blink onto a soulless monolith of sheer data that could apparently storehouse even outdated facts forever. Most of the information was harmless day-to-day maundering—blogging, from "Web logging," a term that had already witnessed its own obsolescence in the accelerated jargon of net-speak.

I hate my parents.

I'm totally bored.

School sucks.

Somebody buy me this thing. WANT.

My cat is weird.

Most of the social reference online dated rather abruptly to the mid-1990s, but gradual inroads were being made further back, into the past, in the manner of erosion trails carved over long periods of time. That was one thing Daisy remained vigilant about, from behind a series of blind IDs and online switchbacks: anyone or anything that could betray her in the present day.

Such as a decades-old wannabe suitor checking up on what had become of Daisy Villareal of San Andres High School, strictly as the kind of lark intended to prove that Daisy, so attractive during the years of berserk hormones, was now the size of a refrigerator, with a litter of kids and several ex-manthings. Lesser men do the same thing with Playboy Playmates, every day.

Except that Daisy arranged for anyone who ever asked questions to never be able to ask them again. Problem solved, danger averted.

"Including me," I said, having almost lost my voice.

"Yeah." That was all she said. One syllable that brought down the whole fantasy in Hindenburg flames. She glanced at her gun but made no move for it.

"But, circumstances…" I petered out. I couldn't contain the idea.

"Yeah. Pretty much. Don't worry. Everything's changed. About time it did. Neither of us could just go on the way we were."

A transition had occurred. Like a distant star burning out, or a new one bursting to brilliant life.

Not so long ago, this woman had targeted me for death.

"I was under," I said, watching my feet, averting her gaze. "I was secure. I had a spasm of, I don't know what you'd call it. Not nostalgia, that's too easy. The people who remain perfect in your memory are the ones you never get to know, who you never develop any relationship with. They're perfect because they have no downside. They're idealizations."

"They're pure," she said. "I'm not."

"Yeah, you couldn't be; I mean, I know that. Me neither. But when you walked into that coffee shop, the first time…god, you were like fresh air. Too desirable. But that was a setup, too, wasn't it? It was the prologue to get me to do whatever you wanted, to line myself up for my own assassination."

"Initially, sure," she said as though it was standard operating procedure for dealing with dupes. "But very quickly, some of the things you said, the way you presented yourself, with your dog and all…it reminded me of that past, the way things were before life got complicated, when all our fuckups were still in front of us."

"Blazing youth," I said. "Those eternally optimistic high school folk."

"Look at it this way. Most people invest limited time in relationships and get antsy if things don't move *fast* enough to address their primal urges. 'Brad' makes a date with 'Muffy' to meet at some Chinese restaurant at eight sharp. The clock is ticking and both of them want to feel a *return* on their time investment—both crave payback for the valuable time taken away from their 9-to-5. Both are in a big hurry, so both micromanage, nitpick, split hairs, because they've made their potential relationship into a rising and falling stock that defines who they are. And investors always want more return, faster. That's why Brad and Muffy will cut and run. Their spoilage date is predetermined, and it's usually between milk and yoghurt. So at least you can't say I wasted your time."

She took my hand when she said this.

"You can go," she said. "The hacks at CHASE are hunting me, not you. You're an accident. Although Rolf Dettrick has probably implicated you in your friend's death at the restaurant, just for harassment value."

"Chase Delta," I said. "What if I was to stick with you until this thing is done?"

"Very dangerous. More of the same; what we got tonight."

"We did pretty good as a team."

"You're deluding yourself. These people play for keeps and they don't give out gold stars for fairness. No merit badges for being a righteous guy."

"My old life is gone, Daisy. Down the shredder. This is what I've got."

"I think under the circumstances you should probably start calling me Alma."

I shook my head. "I like Daisy better than Alma."

She appeared to ponder that for a moment, and find it worthy. She cracked the tiniest hint of a smile, her eyes raven in the incandescent gloom of the old bulbs in the room lamps. "Yeah, Alma can be a real bitch."

"Talented, though." Genuine ability earned some people the right to be monsters, or euphemistically, "eccentric."

"Lie down with me," she said.

My heart tried to leap directly through my ribcage. "No, I...I...*stink*; I need a shower..."

Outstanding. In bed with his dream girl, David Vollmand prevaricates.

"Don't be so nervous," she said. "I'm completely at your mercy." She was also in the twilight zone invoked by extremely good painkillers.

"Let me soak my head," I said. "Forgive me."

"It's you that needs to forgive me. Keep that in mind."

Like a coward, Dave Vollmand practically ran for the bathroom.

The pounding water was lukewarm but plentiful. I watched my day go down the drain in spirals of grime.

You wanted her. Now ask what's required for you to have her, or keep her. Ask whether it's up to you at all.

Ask why all hotel single-serve soaps smell the same.

Ask why you didn't bring one of your guns into the bathroom, just in case.

Fatigue continued to send its slow tentacles around my brain, my guts and heart, exerting steady pressure, gaining purchase. My legs began to vibrate just from standing in the shower; muscle spasms. I was running on the memory of fumes.

Redonning my wretched clothes seemed pointlessly chivalric, and as exhausted as I felt, that primordial DNA jelly in my hindbrain insisted that I *just wear the towel*, as a mating signal. No matter how civilized our behavior, it remains a mask and a lie. In public, we constantly size ourselves up against our competition. Who we'd fuck. Who we'd kill. Who we're better than. Every time, every single day.

Daisy had probably embraced sleep. She didn't seem like a TV watcher. My mission was to crawl into the opposite bed and try to dream.

Her clothes were discarded, inside-out, in a heap between the two beds, one of her boots standing stubbornly erect, the other drooped over. Balled athletic socks were strewn where they were pitched, like two white dumplings. The only light in the room now was a 40-watter on the nightstand. Everything was cast into deep, Expressionistic shadows. I had no idea what time it was.

I treaded like a cat burglar, trying not to disturb the air.

"Where do you think you're going?"

I stopped. Caught.

"Come here. There's plenty of room and I sort of have to stay on my right side."

She was under the sheet. The room cooler hummed on low. She held a corner of the sheet aloft so I could slide in next to her.

"Let me explain something," she said, as she yanked loose my damp towel and dropped it on the floor. "After a job, a mission, a gig—what we went through tonight—the blowback in your brain can get toxic. You think every move and event over and over until your eyes start burning because you can't close them, you can't sleep no matter how worn out you are. You dry-rev until your sanity starts to scorch."

"Guilty," I said, very aware that there was less than a foot of distance between her nakedness and mine.

"I need this," she said. "The skin contact. It's animal, it's primal. It's life-affirming. You understand?"

She put my hand on her belly and guided it up to one breast. On the way, my thumb traced over a hard graffito of scar tissue.

"Is that—?"

"Yeah, another bullet, like I said."

There was a stiff, shiny patch of skin about the breadth of my hand, covering most of her left shoulder blade. A burn, she told me, also work-related, from a job she almost did not survive.

I directed her attention to my old bullet wounds, right calf, upper right shoulder.

"Not the first time someone has tried to kill me," I said. "Someone with resources and intent. I don't have anything anyone would want, except my life."

"Did you kill anybody?" she asked.

"Directly? No. At least, I don't think so. I have shot back at men who were shooting at me."

"Indirectly is okay, then?" She really seemed to draw sustenance just by touching me. Her grasp grew more direct.

"It's the same thing, isn't it?"

"Mm-hm. And you only need to kill once, to be a killer."

She had gathered me up in one hand and guided my own fingers to her groin with her other. We were undercover, under covers.

"Like that," she said, relaxing into the rhythm. "We have to be careful. I don't want to spring a leak."

I lost my manly tumescence. I was concentrating on her. Meanwhile, no matter how aroused she became, surfing tactile waves, none of it diminished her awareness of the door, which she kept monitoring.

After an immeasurable time my fingers felt her vaginal ring contract sharply, seven or eight hard hits, totally out of control. She drifted down as though afloat, exhaling her peak, admonishing me not to move that hand, now, *at all.*

Her grip on my penis had gone as vague as, well, my penis had.

"Sorry," I whispered. "I think I'm a little overwhelmed."

"Come up here," she said, and the next thing I knew, I was in her mouth.

Things got somewhat difficult to track, after that.

Daisy revealed she had gotten her tubes tied as soon as she could find a physician who would not lecture her on the glories of reproduction. Her riposte was that too many people—even the modern, the realists, and the supposedly enlightened—still banked on the fairytale wish-fulfillment of the "accidental" pregnancy to chart the rest of their lives, because it was easier, it was God's will, it was what people did.

I had felt the same way when I had gotten my vasectomy, although to hit that point unduly might make it seem as though I was concocting artificial reinforcement for whatever bond we had. *Look, we're alike! Same tribe and everything!* I no longer needed to be that bald.

"Think we can get lost in a crowd of a hundred thousand?" she said, her voice right next to my ear. She was still on her right side. "That's the national average of people who vanish every year without a trace."

"Harder to do with no money," I said. "I got about eighty-seven dollars to my name right now."

"I've got money. Cash money, the cleanest kind. Putting my hands on it might be tough, though. If Rolf is any good, if CHASE is on the ball, he'll know about it."

"So this is the scene in the movie where the cash is in a sports bag, stashed in a locker at a bus terminal, and eight dozen cops are waiting for someone to stroll up with the right key."

"Pretty close," she said. "Hey, you *chose* this. "You're going to be changed by this. Welcome to the other side."

"Tell me what you're thinking," I said, and she did.

Rolf & Hood

Lily Tamario's first job for CHASE, in early 2005, was as a courier. Typically, it was a setup to gauge her reaction to unanticipated stress. The only warning Rolf Dettrick gave her was: "Your option is to go unarmed, but I wouldn't recommend it." That was all the hint she needed.

The assignment was a cash drop, a "simple" hand-off. Eighty thousand dollars, wrapped in a legal brief envelope, was to be conveyed to a contact thumbnailed as AG (for "Antonije Gligorijevic"), who in turn would parcel funds to assorted sub-contractees in return for minor maintenance services rendered.

AG looked more Arabic than Serbian. That was the first tell.

The meet was in an alley, not a public place. That was the second tell.

"It is code name," Anton told her. "Nobody uses real names."

"Tell me something, Anton," she said. "Do you know what this envelope is for?"

"Nobody tells me nothing," said Anton, licking his lips, eyeballing her. His nervousness was the third tell. "I am just messenger."

"A messenger with a revolver in his armpit. You should know where this money is going, Anton. Now I'm going to have to check on you." She shrugged.

"Please to just give it to me now, please," he said. His smile was evil.

"Afraid I can't do that." *Comme si, comme ça.* Her gesture put her hands in the air between them just as Anton reached for his weapon.

The dropped money bundle was already on its way to the ground. Inevitably, Anton's gaze followed it.

She grabbed his gun arm at the elbow and slammed upward with her free hand—the one that had been holding the envelope—to drive the weapon right into his face. In the next quarter second her fingertips found the nerve nexus in his wrist, and dug in while she stepped around to unhinge his knee with a heel sweep. Without his arms free to absorb impact, Anton hit the ground hard with her on top of him. She pinched his voicebox tight.

"You fail," she said.

The gun was a tarted up Colt Python .357, with Hogue grips and a ramped front sight that had knocked out one of Anton's incisors. She kept the weapon, remembering Rolf's advice, and came home with the package. Rolf assigned her the name Alma Acevedo and advised that her organizational designation was now Chase Lima.

Chase Lima was remanded to the Cube for basic training.

The Cube was a five-story building tucked into the Colorado Rockies that presented itself as a software development corporation, complete with phony lobby staff. It was not apparent from the exterior, but apart from the cosmetic entry point, every window or door aperture had been welded shut with plate steel. Ingress and egress was determined solely by the occupants of a control room, in charge of dozens of cameras and monitors within the facility. The Cube was so called because the interior of the structure could be almost infinitely reconfigured, akin to twisting the facets of a Rubik's Cube. Walls and floors could be jiggered at will. Horizontal could become vertical. Here, the preternatural "door in the floor" was easily achieved. There was a dial on one of the control panels that some wag had labeled "infinite undulate" with a Post-It. The stress analyst in charge was named Deka Van Cline, who had once told Rolf, "We put a serial killer into the Cube and he lasted fifteen minutes. Mass murderer—nothing. They just don't have the combat skills."

Imagine trying to negotiate a shape-shifting maze of rooms while someone is shooting at you, in the dark. Imagine elimination heats in such an arena.

Out of Chase Alpha's earshot, personnel called the Cube a Clusterfucked Heads-up Ass-backward Stress Emporium.

The Cube forced subjects to evolve, most pointedly in regard to stress diffusion, improvisational skills under duress, reaction time, proximity sense (or "skin radar"), enhancement of the kill drive, escape/ evasion, "next-stepping" (or anticipating precisely what your opponent will do and getting there three steps ahead of him or her), and especially what Van Cline called "rippling."

"Picture your thoughts and reactions as ripples in a pond," she once said. "Everything makes ripples. Every ripple affects every other ripple. Your task is to cultivate a mental state in which, instantaneously, you can shut down every single ripple and restore the surface of the pond to complete calm. Most people's thoughts and emotions pollute their ability to react immediately. You shall have no such handicap."

Honed by the Cube, Chase Lima became as hot as a Saturday Night Special. Alma was Rolf's 50-cal round—the kind that hits harder from fifteen hundred yards than a .44 Magnum at point blank range.

Then, after nearly three years of spotless field performance, Alma had refused to terminate a whistle-blowing corporate toiler named Efram Obermeyer, who had abused his top-security clearance by going public with a shopping list of clients for several defense contractors, then publishing a thinly-veiled roman à clef bestseller—*Chum for the Big Sharks*, by the pseudonymous "Clive Bricklin"—that made the pseudonymous culprits even more obvious, to the joy of a whole battalion of attorneys. At a private summit—in civilian parlance, a blowjob smoker where a gang of stiff-necked hawks got shitfaced enough to broach revenge scenarios—several military and dumbfuck indictees pooled their private treasure into a fund to insure that Obermeyer evaporated forever...and indeed, that is what basically happened. Alma had helped the guy *escape*.

"Why?" Rolf had said.

"I couldn't do it," she had told him at the time. "I saw his place, his family. Who love him, by the way. I saw his paintings. They're good. He changed people's lives for the better, Rolf, what goddamned *difference* does it make? As far as the uniforms at the Pentagon know, he's dead and unrecoverable. That's what they wanted."

"And when they find out that you cheated, my phone is going to become uncomfortably hot," Rolf said. "Obermeyer will leak. Somehow, some way, some day."

"Not if he does what I told him to do. This guy, this target, was not one of the usual drones or scumbags we take down." She vised her head, aware of the sludge pot she had stirred up. Her words divulged that she had seen her *target* as a *guy*, her worst misstep. "He mattered. He wasn't hurting anyone except the golden parachute brigade."

"Ethics are not our call. You know that. Artistic temperament doesn't count for sour owl shit. Smith is going to want at least one of my balls."

"Blame it on me, then," said Alma.

"Chain of command," he reminded her. "My responsibility. Feces descends. Obermeyer will surface and a CHASE team will finish the job. That's clunky but at least there's closure. Where did you squirrel him?"

"I forgot."

Hallelujah. That was the beginning of the end for Alma at CHASE. What was Rolf supposed to do, weigh the good citizenship variables of every target? That had nothing to do with reliable service. The personal lives of marks should not be permitted to factor in unless those details helped expedite the job. *Feelings* about dumbfucks were not allowed.

Feelings about your personal 50-cal round, however...

Rolf never betrayed Alma's role, and to this day, Efram Obermeyer was still dead as of 2008. Rolf had groomed Alma, trained her, and watched her run like a superstar, only to be brought low by some personal motivation so buried in her deepest self that he would probably never find out what it had been. It was almost as if Alma's internal gyros had forced her away from CHASE before she could flame out or get killed on the job...like the destiny of most other ex-CHASE worker bees.

Another aspect that stayed Rolf's punitive hand was the idea that maybe Alma was on to something, emotionally, as a human being. Something he might be able to utilize for his future survival.

Like maybe right now, as James Smith spit-roasted Rolf's scrotum by secure phone link. Stern boss metes out discipline.

"Assuaging the FBI and local law enforcement is costly," said Smith. "Most often it is simpler to barter return considerations, but those too cost money. You're no doubt aware of the current economy. It is not a fat time. It is a low-carb time for the organism. Every action must be beneficial. Gambling is discouraged."

If CHASE needed to diet, thought Rolf, it could start by cutting the doubletalk. But Smith was the successor to Henry Hawker Seligman, and politics commanded a certain trickle-down of affectation. Rolf understood how the game worked but was increasingly frustrated by its side rules, special codicils, and time-wasting blather—the Charnel House Androids' Stupefying Exclamations.

Or Cheap Hardcases Always Servicing Expenses. Things had to be dire for Smith to cite finances, though Rolf suspected the issue was a stalking horse for some larger bureaucratic threat to which he was not privy...at least, not at his current status. Where before, Rolf had kidded himself that he had no designs on the power chair at Chase, he had to admit the magnetism of the Chase Alpha slot now had a lot to do with the temptation to forge bold, vigorous change by his own will.

But first he had to clean up Alma, whatever her name was, now. Maybe, in the process, she would finally give up the long-lost Efram Obermeyer and thus earn Rolf a plump gold star for effort.

Or perhaps he should bail, and join the fugitives who somehow lived in a world without CHASE. Not bloody likely. Not yet.

It took Rolf ten minutes to triangulate the location of the Llama pistol belonging to Fletcher, the driver of the Strike Two car. The gun had one of Rolf's passive transponders riding piggyback inside the grip. If you are the architect of an innovation, you tend to stand by the concept whether your superiors keep exploiting it or not, and Rolf had insured that everyone on the strike team had weapons that were leashed with his microdevices, because he was nearly certain—going up against Alma—that somebody would get their firearm captured, almost a statistical inevitability. On Rolf's iPad screen the weapon showed as a green radiant dot, hovering in non-space above a grid map of Los Angeles County. The dot had been stable for several hours. Now it was moving.

"Crap," he muttered. Alma had realized the gun was tagged. This move was laden with the stink of diversion.

What interested Rolf was the gun's prior coordinates, where it had sat still for several hours before migrating. Another fleabag motel. That's where his targets had been before they made the gun. Perhaps they were still holed up there, or had left clues.

On CHASE-paid medical break were Fletcher, the now-gunless wheelman (abrasions, from his tumble down the concrete of the L.A. River), and the Strike shooters named Lambeen (fractured femur from bullet wound) and Alexander (high hit outside body armor). Rolf would not be hearing from James Smith again for a while.

Rolf had whistled up Max Wilsoni, and Max delivered a posse of roughnecks, a bent-nose brigade in ill-fitting tropical suits who seemed to have fallen out of a timewarp from Vegas in the 1950s. Along with these squires and seconds, Rolf was currently interviewing Alma Acevedo's job broker—a sterile, frigid, obliquely Scandinavian man named Mr. Hood.

Professional courtesy was not a major part of the exchange.

"We've had to ramp up our inquiry," Rolf said, just after Hood's nose had been splattered all over the left side of his face by a fist with a contact surface the size of a paperback book. "It's important for you to understand that you have no one to protect. Alma is already dead; she is merely still moving around. Now, I need to know what you know about where she will go next, yes?"

The Wilsoni man stepped in, enormous, displacing air in the room. His name was Franchi and he wore leather driving gloves to beat people up. When he clenched his fist, the calfskin crackled. At Rolf's direction, Franchi punched Hood very hard in the right temple, the kind of mean impact that could somersault your brain inside your skull. Hood's right eye began to occlude with blood.

"Stop," said Hood, desperately trying to swallow. "I saw her."

"You told me that already," said Rolf. "Franchi, don't hit him in the head any more. Work his guts."

"Wait, wait!" Hood's breath blew his own misted blood into the air in front of his face. "Cash drop. For Deane. Setup. In case I had to take her out myself."

Rolf stayed Franchi's eager hand. "You were going to pay her for Morgan Deane?"

"Because she completed the job." When Hood exhaled, one of his front teeth moved like a door ajar in a light breeze. "If retaliation was needed for Bryan Silver, then Alma would be in the crosshairs at a specific time." He could not enunciate; his speech was mushy and turbid.

Rolf saw no need to share the news that he had taken out Bryan Silver personally, back at St. Joe's in Burbank.

Alma on the run would need money.

"Where?" said Rolf.

"Go fuck yourself," Hood hissed. "What would I gain?"

"A little inter-agency cooperation," said Rolf. "It might serve you well."

"Bullshit. You'd sell your own people out in half a heartbeat. Those ex-military burnouts and psychos. These thugs, here. Get on with it."

Again, Rolf insisted: "Where?" Franchi gave Hood a piledriver just beneath the sternum—two inches higher might have killed too quickly.

Hood went fetal and husked more ensanguined air. Rolf waved Franchi off until Hood could recover his breath.

"Alma's gone under," said Hood. "Like a submarine…not what you're thinking…" He tried to laugh but it came out as a clotted cough. "She'll come up out of nowhere and sink your battleship."

"And you'll never be anything more than a mom and pop shop," said Rolf. "Aim higher. Save yourself. Where did you set her up?"

"Call your keeper." Hood smiled hideously, his face a mask of meat and crimson. "Call Chase Alpha. Who has power. Who can make guarantees. I want to hear the words from him, not from you, you fucking guard dog."

Hollywood Mailbox Associates was a mail drop and Xerox dive on the east side of Wilcox Avenue in Hollywood, cater-corner to the imposing Art Deco behemoth of the U.S. Post Office station, which had been sitting there in defiance of urban renewal since its construction in 1937 (the groundbreaking had actually been at the hands of infamous movie censor Will B. Hayes). HMA was the sort of place you run to get that last-minute passport photo; a convenience market for tape and cardboard boxes and shipping needs, forever displaying that one forlorn shelf of yellowed greeting cards and old Wite-Out nobody ever seems to browse.

Sandwiched between a low-profile sound studio and a parking lot, the layout of Hollywood Mailbox Associates was typical railroad shotgun with minimal street profile on the lower floor of an old two-story building with apartments above, accessed from the rear. The honeycomb of rental mailboxes was fed from a tiny cubicle behind while patrons used keys to get to their mail from the front. After business hours entry could be made via keypad and a rolling gate secured the rest of the enterprise to the rear where you could see it but not touch it. The box units were in plain sight through the front window, well-lit.

There were security cameras. The front window was masked in a variety of logos and flyers, which made direct surveillance of the box units cluttered, but not impossible.

The owner/managers of this establishment were a gay Korean couple who did not live on site. It was exactly two running blocks from the Hollywood Division of the LAPD.

Rolf set up a pair of two-man spy teams, one on the roof of the Hollywood postal station, the other in an apartment off Selma Avenue with line-of-sight to the rear of the mailbox building. Their job was to observe, not engage. Rolf and a Wilsoni man named Kurland visited Hollywood Mailbox Associates during business hours to assess the make of security cameras used, and whether their feed could be unobtrusively tapped. As expected, the cameras were more than a decade old, and hardwired to ancient videotape recorders. There was no broadcast to pluck out of the air. Given time, a transmitter could be piggy-backed onto the array to give Rolf eyes inside, but Rolf honestly did not know how much prep time there was to be had.

Hood's envelope, sealed up with tape and stickered as a Customs-cleared delivery from England, was sitting less than two feet away from Rolf as he went through the diversionary motions of having one of the Koreans make photocopies. Per Hood's admission, the envelope contained $50,000 in clean cash. Almost as though he had X-ray vision, Rolf could *see* the damned thing behind the metal door of box number 770, waiting.

But Rolf was not interested in the money.

What if she was to walk in here, right now, during my recon?

That might be messy.

What if Dave Vollmand showed up instead? He'd have to find a box he had never seen, and pretend he belonged—all hesitation factors.

Broad daylight or middle of the night?

Rolf detested variables, which were not the CHASE way. But to break pattern with CHASE methodology was the procedure needed now. Playing by the CHASE book earlier had won him nothing, and James Smith had practically disowned Rolf to clean up his own spill. Rather than augmenting his dossier for promotion, Rolf was now fighting to hang onto his Chase Delta status. Smith made this clear when Hood was on the horn. Hood wanted guarantees from the top man himself, and got them.

That was the absolute last favor Smith was going to cut Rolf. When Rolf took the secure cellphone back from Hood's pulverized ear, the line was already dead.

Bullying the Koreans and appropriating the money would not work as leverage. Alma would just fade. The false security of the setup was needed intact so that it could function as a mousetrap. Hence, two more Wilsoni men were in charge of making sure Hood spent his time healing, and not making phone calls. They had free permission to terminate Hood if he made the smallest suspect move. Nobody normal would miss Hood, in the world.

Grabbing Dave Vollmand as a hostage would not work, either. Alma was smart enough to cut such pawns loose.

Killing dumbfucks for the sake of convenience was distracting, but Rolf had done so plenty of times, just to circumvent the bother, and it had always been cleaner. Now he wanted to kill Dave Vollmand, who had nothing to do with anything, simply for the sake of personal satisfaction—payback for all the trouble he had perhaps not caused directly, but nonetheless remained responsible for.

Just beyond his ring of surveillance, Rolf and the rest of the Wilsoni men were on standby, ready to constrict the noose. The rest was the living hell of waiting, coffee and bathroom trips, time parceled out in ounces of stomach acid. Sitting in a work car with Kurland, Rolf popped a Prilosec and chased it with a hit of methedrine.

Four minutes past midnight, less than thirty-six hours following the events at the Tropical Paradise, the voice of one of the men on top of the post office crackled over the walkie:

"I think we've got movement inside the store."

The Drop

For the record, I have never in my life seen a cloud "scud." They roil, they billow, mass, ebb and swell. By the same token, shots from gunfire do not "ring out," no matter what nitwit newscasters say on programs you should not be watching anyway, just to preserve your sense of reality. Gunfire punches the air out of a space spherically. Ignition and launch of a projectile—bullet—absorbs an infinitesimal slice of a single second. If it is near your head the sensation is like being slapped on the ear with a ruler. You feel the report inside your vitals like the pluck of a bass guitar string under heavy amplification. Your head might "ring" afterward, because unsilenced gunfire is deafening to the unprotected ear, but as for the shots themselves ringing out—no.

The past day and a half had put paid to that myth.

"Goddammit," Daisy said in a growl from the back of her throat. "I *knew* it."

She had disassembled the Llama pistol I had taken from Fletcher, our temporary guest during our pulse-pounding vehicular pursuit.

"Knew what?"

"This pistol is tagged. It's probably transmitting."

"So dunk it in water."

"No. We have to assume it has given away this position. Better to put it in motion. Rolf might follow it instead of us."

"I am really beginning to hate this guy Rolf," I said.

David J. Schow

"He's persistent."

Using the carbon clone, I had obtained wrapped sandwiches, deli sushi, snack food and more medical supplies from a Ralph's supermarket a couple of blocks away. Now Daisy dumped out a full bag of chips—Linden Farms Oven-Baked Potato Slices—and stashed the pistol inside the bag.

"The foil messes up the signal," she explained. "Like in the good old days when you could use a Doritos bag to sneak DVDs past a scanner."

"Add shoplifting to our résumé of criminal skills," I said.

"Just dispose of this," she said. "Creatively."

It was hilarious, to amble out in public bearing a homing device that might as well have been a sandwich board reading SHOOT ME, with a potato chip bag as my only armor. I threw the pistol into the dump bay of a wandering municipal garbage truck. The truck roared like a prehistoric beast. I watched it lumber away for a long beat.

I kept the bag; folded it up and put it in my pocket. You never know.

When I returned, Daisy had sketched out the basics of the mailbox drop where her payoff waited, about a mile west of our current location.

"Just to be safe," she said, "we have to get out of this motel. We've had the gun too long and the gun has been talking. Unless you want to replay what happened at the Tropical Paradise."

"No thanks," I said. "So where do we go? Another motel?"

"That's a pattern. Rolf will canvass every similar place in the area. We could go really far out, but I want to grab this cash first."

"I don't think it would be a great idea to stroll around in public right now," I offered.

"We're not," she said. "We're going camping."

I had no idea Daisy was talking about taking hostages.

The mail drop was across the street from the Hollywood Post Office.

186

We were half a block away, facing the rear of the building that housed her mailbox drop.

"I don't think there's a cordon yet," she said. She described circles in the air with a finger. "Rings of surveillance. They let you in but not out."

"How do we know for sure?"

"We walk in the back door, there, and see if anybody shoots at us."

Swell.

The back of the building opened onto a small permit parking lot (street parking is hard to come by in Hollywood) and featured a fire escape that looked rusted into obsolescence. The second floor of the structure appeared to have been subdivided from larger, loft-style apartments into smaller ones on either side of a central corridor that ran front to back. The entry was locked by a single deadbolt to which tenants had a pass key. There was a grimy callbox and buzzer setup whose lightbulb had failed. Six units.

Daisy snagged the drop-down ladder on the fire escape.

"You sure you're okay to climb?"

"I have to be," she said. "Don't worry about me."

We used the ladder to move one floor up. The hallway windows were open here, for ventilation, since it was the middle of summer. No window bars.

"Take your pick," she said of the apartments.

We walked heel-and-toe down the corridor, listening for a vacancy. Number Five was alive with children's voices, television, and lower grownup tones in stern reprimand. Number Four was alive with the rhythm thrum of Quiet Riot's "Metal Health," a song I have always hated. Probably some big hair monkey from the Guitar Institute of Technology not cognizant that the acronym for his school was GIT. By Number Three we became aware that the entire hallway smelled like a stale microwave burrito. The carpeting was so old it was developing tool use and a philosophy.

Then the door to Number Two opened, and made our decision for us. The guy who boiled out had a lot of tats and piercings and an inadequately landscaped Mohawk. He reeked of skunkweed and was wearing a sleeveless T-shirt that read HATE ME in bloodspatter red. His stoner-pink eyes got a load of Daisy and he grinned.

"Hey, gorgeous," he said. "What up, *mija?*"

Daisy put her .45 under his chin and backed him up the way he had come.

"How many inside?" she said.

"Aww, shit! This is some fuckin home invasion shit, dude, like Manson Family bullshit!" His eyes were wide with imagined mayhem.

She tapped him with the muzzle to keep his attention. "Who else?"

"Aww, just Florelinda, dude, she's in the *shower...*shit!"

Daisy waved me inside and I shut the door.

"Then let her finish her shower," she said. "We don't want to hurt you. We've just come to rent a little bit of your time."

Life was happening too fast for our new friend. "What...?" He sat down hard in an abused recliner covered with a tissue-thin bedsheet.

"We need to hang out with you a little while. We will pay you for your trouble." To me, she said: "Pay him. And put your gun away." Then she turned back, staying on the subject, pressing him ahead. "So this is not a whole lot of trouble, correct? It's not like you had a lot of plans going on, right—what's your name?"

"Uh...Boris. Boris. Really." He was trying to look downward through his own flesh to see the weapon that jeopardized him. The angle was impossible and that boosted his distress.

"Well, I suppose somewhere in the world there has to be somebody who's not a Russian politician whose name is legitimately Boris, right?"

Boris tried to nod enthusiastically but his chin kept hitting the muzzle. His eyes got wider when I stashed my Beretta and dug out all the remaining cash I had—four twenties and assorted change.

She let Boris hold the money. "See? Just relax. Now, Boris, does this building have a trash chute, or a laundry chute, or an old elevator, anything like that?"

188

"*Nuh*-no," Boris said. "Oh, *god...*"

I was awaiting further instructions when Florelinda emerged from the bedroom (and presumably the bathroom beyond) wearing a towel, but only on her head. She was otherwise gloriously naked and supremely vulnerable. She had as many tattoos as Boris, scattered randomly. Vines and cherry blossoms. Some poorly-inspired Celtic hash. A dragon that had been inked in outline but not colored yet. Her hand went to her mouth in a classic what-the-fuck gesture she had probably learned from watching actors pretend to be shocked in movies, but she was mildly stoned, too, and her dismay did not register completely. Her pubic hair was shaved into a thin arrow that pointed downward. Large aureolae around large nipples, both run through with stainless steel hex-top barbells. Her navel piercing featured a tiny ceramic broken heart.

"Sit down, Flor," said Daisy. "Right next to Boris, here."

She shuffled over meekly, leaving humid footprints on the wood floor. "We don't have any money," she said. "We don't have anything worth a shit."

"We don't want anything from you, Flor, except your time, which we can pay for." Daisy looked to me, then back to Flor more pointedly. "Flor, are you a junkie?"

Florelinda glanced skittishly at Boris. "Was," she said. "Not now. I got a job."

"Good," said Daisy. "Don't lie about that to any of us, especially Boris. I find cooking shit in there, it's not going to go well. Understand?"

Flor nodded. She seemed about to burst into tears.

The apartment was a typical post-adolescent rathole; Boris and Flor had never actually bought a piece of furniture in their short lives. A lot of strewn clothing in the bedroom. Box spring on the floor; many posters to cover wall cracks and water damage. Several season's worth of holiday string lighting in place of genuine illumination. A ragged orange tabby named Lucifer, who hid the entire time. A couple of dirty, ornate bongs flanked a mammoth flatscreen TV.

"Watch them and keep them quiet," Daisy told me. "Be right back." Boris was already showing Flor the money they were earning by doing nothing.

"You guys are like Bonnie and Clyde, right?" babbled Boris. "That's rad, I mean, we're not gonna call cops or nothing, like, hey, I got my own—"

"Stop talking now, Boris," I said.

Boris was moving as many parts of his body as he could while remaining seated. He crossed his legs. He uncrossed them. He gnawed his fingernails, pinky-ed out his ears, found new nuggets of crust in his eyes and vibrated as though he was sailing on crystal.

"Okay, right, I gotcha, that's totally cool, like, do you, um, mind if we smoke a bowl?"

"Sit still. Shut up. Smoke a bowl later."

Flor glared at him as though he had just murdered the cat. "You were staring at her," she said, sotto voce.

"What?" He whispered back as though they were in a foxhole.

"I'm naked and you were staring at *her*."

"I never *seen* her before!"

"You let her in."

The entire history of male-female disagreement was about to spill all over me in a stream of emotional vomit. He would thrust; she would parry. He would stridently profess innocence and she would vociferously affirm his guilt. And repeat. And repeat. He did not find her sexy anymore. Oh yes he did. They were going nowhere, scraping by on rent and dreading their thirties. You looked at her the way you look at those TV women; you want them. Yeah, but I live with you. And repeat. All this turbulence, for some foggy crime that was more a matter of DNA than will. I might have to shoot them both to keep this contretemps from blooming into a fullblown domestic call.

It was all about punishment, payback, and the assignment of blame through which people rationalize their unfulfillment.

It's not my fault. It's someone else's. Whammo—human congress.

Boris and Flor were the latest players to use a very old script.

Fortunately, Daisy returned. "Got it," she said. "Interior stairwell, at the end of the hall. Door's nailed shut. Boris, have you got any tools?"

Boris pondered this as he would a challenging trigonometry function. "Oh—you mean, like, *tools?*"

"Exactly. A prybar. A claw hammer."

"You're not gonna like hurt Flor, are you? I mean, I'll do whatever you want." His first utterance was designed to curry favor with Flor; man-as-protector and all that. But his second made Flor narrow her spiteful gaze again, because she knew in her soul that this female invader wanted to fuck her boyfriend, just to make her feel worse about herself.

"Show me."

Boris checked around to see if getting up was permitted, then conducted Daisy to the kitchenette after telling me, of Flor, "Don't like rape her, okay?"

Yeah, you never knew when I might lose control and go on a lust rampage, running loose with a gun and a never-ending hard-on.

Daisy returned, behind Boris, with a corrosion-pitted crowbar, and equally sad hammer, a dispenser of Scotch tape, and a roll of filament packing tape. We used the last two to bind Boris and Flor together at the wrists and ankles. If you use enough winds of Scotch tape, it'll hold anything. We trussed them to the bed with a jaunty lightstring of Day of the Dead skulls and, most importantly, gagged them with assorted stray clothing. Improvisation was key. They could probably wrestle their way free by dawn to continue their argument.

Then smoke that bowl.

David J. Schow

The old stairwell was populated mostly by a variety of spiders. One grand dame of a black widow had multiple hashmarks on her abdomen, as though she had earned a chevron for every five humans killed. There were empty, caved-in cardboard boxes containing nothing and several decades of dust—so much that you could slip on it.

The access had probably been sealed off to deter squatters, once the lower floor had turned to commercial use. The ground-floor door seemed solid and immobile. It turned out to have three-quarter-inch plywood bolted into the molding from the obverse side. The door itself was a heavy, four-panel job dating from the 1960s. Daisy knocked a slat out of the topmost panel at eye level and went to work gouging the plywood.

"Probably an interior wall, now," she said. Using a keychain flashlight (also obtained from Boris and Flor), we peered through the splintery hole she had made.

We were looking into the dim recess at the rear of the mailbox store. The layout was contiguous with the upper floor, if you imagined the apartment level with fewer hollow-core walls. The stairwell we had used was original to the building, that is, it predated the addition of the fire escape.

"Security?" I said.

"Probably old, probably fuzzy, but no problem," Daisy said. "We own it. Help me shove one corner of this wood out so we can get a grip."

The barrier was well done and had held solid for years, waiting for us to come along and violate it. At least it hadn't revealed itself as a brick wall.

The first thing we encountered inside the rear of the store was a former closet pressed into service as a bay for the security monitor and a lot of jackstrawed cleaning junk. Feeds from three cameras led directly to two actual VHS recorders, one of which was powered down or not working. Its partner was grinding tape. This was peripherally amazing—I hadn't seen a working VHS machine in nearly a decade, although, sure, I supposed people still used them. Daisy ejected the only

192

tape to be had and handed it off to me. Then she bent and pulled the single plug that juiced the whole array.

"Alarm?"

"Not on this gear, not in a place like this," she said, more confident than me. "Works to our advantage. A higher tech system, Rolf would be able to glean the signal."

"He knows about this place?" We were both speaking in hushed whispers.

"He does if he's any good," she admitted. "He'll have gotten to Hood by now."

"And Hood is...? Never mind."

"Give me the light."

She moved carefully inside the chamber for the mailboxes, leading with one shoulder, walking sideways. She quickly located her objective and collected it. She had to rip the envelope open on the spot and verify that it was not padded with junk paper instead of hard cash. Multiple greenback portraits stared back at her—the only fellow emblazoned on our nation's currency who was never a U.S. President.

But she wasn't staring at good old Benjamin. Her gaze was on the floor. Then she was shoving me.

"We're made. Let's get out of here!"

The two gangster hardasses on the roof of the post office were named Giorgio and DuFleck. At forty-seven, Giorgio had worked for Aristede Wilsoni back in the day, making threats and breaking selected bone groups, and could still dimly remember the tenure-rattling shakeup caused by his boss' exposure in the press back in the Aughts. DuFleck was next-generation, hired by Wilsoni's elder son Augustus and deployed by little brother Max. So mostly, they swapped war stories while waiting for something to happen at Hollywood Mailbox Associates, across the street. Giorgio had been at the meeting between Max Wilsoni and the mysterious black ops fellow, who had not given a name Giorgio could recall. This watchdog gig had been one yield of that meeting and Giorgio was glad to be back on the clock. DuFleck was more impatient, and wanted to kill something, already.

They had snacks, radios, binocs, a laser locator, sidearms, and just for fun, a Barrett MRAD sniper's rifle in .338 Lapua Magnum, a long-range hunter-killer customized for a suppressor, with night optics on the upper rail. The polymer magazine held ten rounds, just in case. The Barrett had been DuFleck's idea, since the front window of the mailbox joint was maybe forty yards distant. Giorgio preferred closer encounters, where you could taste the fear you manufactured and witness it in your target's eyes as you re-explained the universe to him. Or her.

To Giorgio, the Barrett resembled some kind of sci-fi weapon. It seemed cumbersome.

"That's just it," said DuFleck, who himself resembled a showbiz agent who had figured out how to survive in prison. "This is the perfect compromise between your standard military field issue gun, which only shoots NATO-sized rounds, and the humungous Barretts that shoot fifty-cal. It's like a big-buck hunting rifle redesigned by the Army."

"For hunting people," said Giorgio as he drained a juice box. His experience of people-hunting favored the trusty blade, or bare hands.

"This will penetrate most body armor at a thousand meters. Put a bullet right into the engine block of a car, if you want. I'll show you, if we have to wait around here much longer. Stop it deader than flyshit."

"Would it kill, like, a rhinoceros?" said Giorgio, who only knew rhinos existed from watching television.

"You'd probably need a slightly bigger gun for that. Elephant, hippo. Maybe we'll get to take off a head. I'll show you; it's awesome."

DuFleck knew his tech, but he didn't know enough not to eat crunchy snacks while on a stakeout. Giorgio thought mildly about cutting his throat, though not in an angry way—it was just something he always thought about.

"We've got movement inside."

Giorgio dutifully repeated this into his radio.

DuFleck had the laser sighting device pressed to his eyes and was making tick-adjustments with his index finger. "Oh, man, this is too easy." He immediately hoisted the stock of the Barrett, tilting it forward onto its bipod. The first round was already chambered.

"Sit tight until 'go,'" Giorgio cautioned him.

"Fuck that," said DuFleck, as he squeezed the trigger. *Boom.*

The hinged door to Box #770 coughed itself a wide metallic hole as Daisy roughhoused me away by the arm. No shot "rang out." The slug tore into a desk behind us, briefly tipping it up onto its rearward legs from the sheer velocity. Paperwork and rickrack drop-kicked into the air. It was four minutes after midnight.

The second shot came in precisely two feet to the left of the first, augering downward as though the delivery vantage was high. Which made the floor the worst place to be. The bullet destroyed another portion of the mailbox bank as though sailing through paper. The shooter was guessing most likely retreat angles and firing to cover them, and he was a very good guesser. The store had been mapped.

Daisy shoved me in front of her, back the way we had come.

Rushed into the comparative security of the abandoned stairwell, she caught me up: "Laser tracking dot. On the floor. Remember the cordon? We're going to have to find another way out. Be ready to shoot. This way."

They let you in but not out, she had said. That meant the rings of surveillance were now constricting around the building.

"Roof," she said.

Rolf's coffee hit the floorboard of the work car the instant Giorgio reported movement inside the store.

"Goddammit, who's firing?" he shouted into his comm as he levered free of the car, weapon up.

Gunshots might attract blue knights. They were two blocks from the police station, for christ's sake.

"Runners on the roof," reported Weaver, from the rearward post. He was East, on another rooftop with a guy named Palermo. DuFleck and Giorgio were West. Kurland and Rolf were North, on ground level, parked in front of two utility shooters in another vehicle. South, covering the parking lot, were two more Wilsoni men named Babcoq and Hickey. The snap-shut was designed so they could converge from all directions at once, each man covering his partner the way Kurland had Rolf's back, now.

That plan was shot to hell.

"Rooftops," Rolf transmitted. "Hold if you can see them up top. They're not going anywhere."

"Shoot 'em?" said Weaver from East.

"Shoot 'em."

"Copy," said Giorgio, West. *"Can't see 'em. There's an air conditioner in the way."*

"I don't have visual," confirmed Weaver, East. *"They either hit the deck or went back inside."*

"This is Babcoq, South, I have the rear entry in sight."

"Nothing coming out the front," said Giorgio, from the top of the post office.

"Rooftops, hold your positions," said Rolf. "Brooks and Fanelli, close the rear. Babcoq, Hickey, move to cover the southwest corner by the street."

The two backup men brought their car into the parking lot from the north, to cover the back door while Weaver and Palermo covered them.

Now, if only they had a target...

Alma was drawing them closer, tightening the knot herself. This would force them to enter the building, to search room by room. To subdivide. It was a tactic straight out of CHASE 101.

"All right," Rolf said. "Now we go messy. South, prepare for a frontal breach with West's cover. Brooks, Fanelli, breach the rear with West's cover. Anything questionable, kill it."

Where they hell were they?

I thought Daisy had said "roll on me," when in fact what she said was "Roll. On me." Meaning I should follow her lead.

We were spreadeagled on the tarpaper roof of the building housing the mailbox place. One floor below us, somewhere, Boris and Flor were still trussed up in their apartment, dreaming of freedom and marijuana. Rolf Dettrick had eyes and guns on our roof, but there was a parapet barrier about a foot and a half high, plus a lot of ductwork. The ambient light from the street lent us a lot of shadow in which to crawl. I was pretty sure that if either of us stuck up our heads to reconnoiter, it would instantly show up in some shooter's reticle and we'd win the worst kind of barbering.

I got thoroughly studded with asphalt flecks as we rolled, clumsily, laterally, snaking around pipes and vent supports. There was a lot of trash up here—fast-food garbage and blown leaves mulched to muck—and agitation of any of it might provide an untoward signal.

"Okay," Daisy said. "About five feet to your right there's a drop-off. A space between the buildings about two feet wide. We go down, we've got two exits on street level. But everything's covered, so we have to bias our hunters. Hope you're up for a little mountaineering."

I didn't bother to ask how she knew about the gap.

She was peering through a runoff port for a rain gutter, to the east.

"Shooters on the roof, over there," she said. "Closer than the ones on top of the post office. If there's a doorway below us, they control it already. They're coming up. Jesus, they must have ten guys, or more."

"More than the motel," I said, distantly proud that we merited such manpower.

"Just press your back against the wall when I tell you, and scoot down. Let gravity help you. It's just like rock climbing."

I had never been rock climbing.

"Go!"

She rose to present minimal profile and dealt five fast shots in the direction of the watchdogs to the east. This would galvanize everyone—the eastward team would be grabbing cover, the westward team would be looking for muzzle flashes, trying to track a target, and everybody below would hesitate for a few seconds while the action sorted itself out. If all our opponents were keyed to Rolf's lead, they would want new orders. The gunshots echoed brackishly, resounding off all the concrete. There is no urban sound like it, and if you have heard this noise in the middle of the night, you, too, have frozen in place for just an instant, asking yourself if that was what you *really* heard, then waiting for more. Seasoned Californians dealt with earthquakes the same way.

The brick walls I was wedged between were treacherous with moist grime, thanks to the offshore flows that dew up Los Angeles in the summertime. Everything smelled like tar and rotting bodies. I skidded and fell several feet before mashing myself stable, like a fat cat stuck behind a sofa. Daisy was above me and to the left. She held fast in counter-tension and then let herself drop. The ground was only about twenty feet below. The danger was that in bending your knees to absorb impact, you'd bash your head into the wall.

I slid further down with all the grace of a toilet clog coming free, and crash-landed into something soft and wet, with a furious crackle of old trash bags. Something wickedly sharp and splintered sank into my left side, snapping against a rib. There was a very good chance I had landed on some homeless dude, squatting in this rank space. It was abrim with more garbage.

I bit into my own forearm to keep from making noise, at being punctured. Whatever purchase my feet had found—it was black as the inside of Satan's asshole down here, remember—disassembled and dumped me heavily onto my left side, my face scraping paint chips off brick all the way down.

Daisy grabbed my hand. No chatter.

Pointed eastward, she began to burrow *under* all the garbage piled up in the airway. I remembered a group of Dumpsters one door to the left of where we had entered the building earlier. Like POWs belaying dirtpiles in *The Great Escape*, like rogue platelets infiltrating a narrow vein, we wormed in, her ass right in my face, her feet pushing off against my own shoulders.

You can imagine.

And this wasn't *new* garbage, oh no. This was the accumulated shit that fell out of the Dumpsters months ago. The smell was utterly unique.

A startled rat about the size of a terrier decided to make a getaway across my back. I hoped it did not whiff the fresh blood coursing from my side—I could feel it dripping—and opt to grab a sample.

We were an undulating, composite being, moving deeply, carefully, and quietly into a purgatorial, reeking mass we could not see. I felt the trash close over my legs from behind. We were swallowed. My face kissed some gelid crap that stayed stuck like Crisco. Or dog diarrhea. Or spoiled viscera.

No Beretta in my waistband. I had lost it during the drop, or on the roof.

"Hold still!" Daisy hissed at me from the darkness ahead. We were totally cocooned in garbage.

All the other side had to do was secure the exits, sweep the building, discover the interstitial space from the roof, and begin shooting down into it. Daisy was waiting for them to summon the backups to join the search once they believed they controlled the building. They would waste time in the old stairwell, the store, and certainly in the apartments, where they might discover Boris and Flor tied up, and that would delay them more for a short interview session.

They would expect us to vacate in haste instead of hanging close.

Just ahead of me, Daisy probably went into some Zen sniper other-world, maybe even grabbed a crap-nap. Me, I could smell every elapsed second, and could not quit myself of the gnawing need to *get out*.

She knew this, of course, which was why she went first—to block my bolt into the open, where crosshairs waited.

My life had become the world's worst zombie movie: Run, hole up, and battle. Run and battle, then hole up. Battle, hole up again, then run. There was no reference copy or printed continuity to check against. It did nothing more than *happen*, with extravagant sloppiness and illogic.

Part of me craved the comfort of my old routine, vetting 6.1 loss-less audio, checking for decent sync, sniffing out blooms in contrast or bad color handling, reviewing opticals for fade, or whether dupe footage was "transparent" to the original. What was happening to me now, *as* it was happening, was *exhausting*.

Five friends on spring break...

Yeah, as if they were studious academics or worthwhile human beings before they met the sharks or chainsaw hillbillies. No, they were jagoffs who back-doored their way into medical degrees, like that pill-pushing robot of pharmacology Daisy and I had bribed.

There's just ONE problem...

Problem: the movie sucks.

This was no action-packed thrill ride, glorious hyperkinetic shootouts in exotic locations, the ole bullet ballet. This was dirty and damned near post-apocalyptic. The minute-to-minute stress would eat you alive and suck the marrow from your bones.

Sex and violence is soft-soaped as "romance and adventure" in American culture; in short, the downside is blurred to make it seem a desirable alternative to the mundane. Believe me, you wouldn't last five minutes—bloodied, sleepless, drained dry.

Run, hole up, battle.

Not Internet. Not a movie. Real. Happening now. No sage or wizard elder or Magic Negro to explain the plot twists or provide a handy, just-in-the-nick-of-time salvation.

There was just one problem.

The way those zombie movies usually ended was when the last member of the cast of plucky human specimens finally succumbed. Almost never was there a turnaround, a restoration of order. Nope. They ended when the last man or woman standing got eaten. Over and out.

If we got out of this spot, then what?

The simplest solution would be for Daisy to put a bullet in my head and move on. Or Daisy would get knocked off the board and I would be remanded to humorless functionaries with all the time in the cosmos. Who would then probably kill me, after an eternity of torture.

It was almost too much for my skull to contain. Definitely a Minsky's Moment. A kick to the head by the entire chorus line.

"Hey." Daisy's foot nudged me.

I had squirmed around to cradle my forehead against my folded arms, my nose an inch away from something that stank so eye-wateringly that if it wasn't vomit, I'd be oddly disappointed.

It was after two o'clock in the morning.

People shouting. Car doors slamming. The red-blue bounce of police flashbars.

Her feet wormed forward, and I followed her.

There was a tiny demon poking a fondue fork into Sgt. Larry Pipps' guts. Pipps had a peptic ulcer, for which he drank buttermilk before bedtime,

David J. Schow

among other palliatives. He had decided to take the shots-fired call five minutes before officially going off shift. What the hell, it was right by the Hollywood station, right? And now he had an FBI anus all up in his biz, droning about jurisdiction.

"Agent Collins," he began, as a gas bubble oozed up from his nethers.

"*Special* Agent Collins," the suit corrected him, flashing his ID a second unnecessary time. Prick.

"You're supposed to clear operations with local PD. Sir."

"There was no time, Officer Phipps."

"Pipps. *Sergeant.*" Couldn't this deskboy see the stripes?

"My apologies, Sergeant."

It was the even-handed, fake courtesy that cheesed Pipps the most. Pipps was a doer. And he could wallop these Bureau guys with their own attitude. Everything these suits said came from some seminar on how to control, coerce, and convince.

"Look, Mr. Collins, we can waste all night out here comparing length and girth, or—"

"Agreed," Collins said smoothly. "Fact is, Sergeant, it was a hostage situation and we had to move quickly. Before we could even alert your men, we had gunfire."

A nearby patrol officer, Lupita Mendoza, bristled at the "your men" but Pipps waved her off.

"The perps are under warrant for interstate flight. I have their jackets with me."

These were spiffy and utterly damning want/warrant printouts that one of Wilsoni's men had whomped together in less than half an hour, using completely credible FBI letterhead and the Bureau's own digital template. The photos were the best part; neither Alma Acevedo or David Vollmand looked very happy.

"As you can see, they've got about a dozen aliases each," Rolf said, as Collins.

"Hostages?" said Pipps.

202

"Second floor. We found them trussed up with packing tape. Some drug paraphernalia; nothing exciting." (Later, just to stir the stew, these two victims would describe their assailants as a pair of black men wearing Raiders hoodies.) "We recovered an unpapered Beretta in the trash between the two buildings in the breezeway right there." He held up Dave Vollmand's gun in a plastic bag for Pipps' approval. "You can run it but it won't tell us anything we don't already know."

"Hostages for what?" said Pipps, squinting one eye as though the thought pained him. His eyebrows were bushy-white. He was pushing the speed limit at age fifty-five. He had seen military service on foreign soil. He had seen hostages in war zones, and what happened to them, for real.

"That's a debriefing question," Rolf-as-Collins said, arrogantly skipping past the skinny. "The good news is that there are no bodies to pick up."

"So what happened to your perps? How'd they get clear?"

"Unknown."

For that brief instant, Pipps could see how hungry Collins was to collar his prospects. It was one small quality he could appreciate in this otherwise-prick.

"They were in the building. They were on the roof. They opened fire and a couple of my agents returned fire. Then they must have scooted down the breezeway, there, somehow got past us, and blended into the local wildlife. Although how they got past my spotters is anybody's call."

Best not to add the detail about the snipers.

Pipps scanned the scene. His uniforms were unreeling cordon tape. "Nice to know the Bureau is fallible, sometimes."

"Bad night for everybody," Collins mused. "Now I've got to go prepare a briefing for your department—*way* too early in the morning."

Pipps was not going to get anything else out of this guy. He had left his patrol cruiser blockading Selma Avenue at Wilcox, within sight of a cordon officer who had been laying street flares. It was one of the newer LAPD vehicles without a shotgun mount up front, either on the cage or the dash. Pipps missed the presence of the dash clamp and the reassuring nearness of a handy 12-gauge. Now the "shoutguns," as he called them, were exiled to trunk storage by modernization, airbags, and "officer safety"—this last being one of the reasons street-sweepers were maintained with a full tube but an empty chamber... because too many of L.A.'s finest had blown holes in the roofs of their cop cars.

Pipps was flying solo tonight, looking forward to a couple of wind-down Jack & Cokes and whatever bounty Netflix had brought to his mailbox.

The acid in his stomach trebled when Pipps returned to his cruiser's parking spot and found it had been moved.

As in *re*moved. Gone.

As in stolen.

THE
STRESS-STRAIN
CURVE

Bumblebee

"Hey, hot pants, I think I spy with my little eye...your boner." The old woman in the hot-room bed coughed out a pallid laugh. One syllable—*hah*.

James Smith, Chase Alpha, had come to see if Bumblebee—Carlotta Elsinore—had gained any clarity in the past few days. She had issued a veiled warning about pursuing the former Alma Acevedo—the former Chase Lima—and now the caution seemed to be yielding rotten fruit. No fewer than *three* skirmishes in Los Angeles, none productive, and Smith was beginning to doubt the efficacy of his chosen avatar, Chase Delta—Rolf Dettrick.

It will be the end of you, Carlotta had said.

But which path was the deadly one, if Carlotta was right? Terminate the pursuit and cut Alma free, or cut to the chase (so to speak) and terminate Alma? Neither option seemed fraught with imminent catastrophe for CHASE as an entity. Smith resented the mere concept that anyone who had endured CHASE training could simply quit and work elsewhere, true. Yet erasing one more assassin in a universe full of them did not seem personally threatening, either. It was business, the conduction of which incurred casualties. It was a small job in the scheme of things, sub-radar, non-public, a simple fix that should have been a checkmark on a to-do list in a daybook. Now Rolf Dettrick was delivering less than optimum performance. Was Alma that slippery, or was Rolf beginning to lose his edge?

Smith was at a loss for answers, which was why he had capitulated to another consultation with Bumblebee. She was detritus from the old guard at CHASE, and her continued presence here—caretaken, fed and watered until her eventual death—was a covenant Smith had undertaken long ago, to honor the wishes of CHASE founder Henry Hawker Seligman, Smith's mentor. This, despite the snickers and whispers from underlings that there was still a crazy old psychic on the premises.

The new CHASE—the next generation of the organization—was edging up on Smith's tail, heel-nipping. Rolf Dettrick was to have been the bridge that would steward the next evolution.

But the shootout at the Mango Joy restaurant had incurred a costly amount of smoothing over; ditto the shootout at the Tropical Paradise Motel. Two mismanaged kills at the first, including a Bureau satellite named Hayden Mathis, and an attention-getting vehicular pursuit at the second, no kills, but wounded soldiers and lots of noise. Then Dettrick had gone totally rogue for a third attempt, using imported gangsters when his CHASE budget ran out—more noise, more exposure, but at least that one had not piled new bodies into the red. Maybe there was a pattern to it. Perhaps Dettrick was finding his stride. According to the watchwords of CHASE, he had *improvised* and *adapted*, but had yet to *overcome*.

"I thought I told you already," Carlotta croaked from the center of her web of hoses and monitors. "This is sexual harassment."

"I was thinking of the early seventies," said Smith. "When you first joined us." Carlotta had to be led into her epiphanies. It was like sculpting, or piloting a powerful car on a challenging roadway.

"Ancient fucking history, limpy."

"You impressed Seligman back then. I was wondering whether you still had anything, or if you just enjoy delivering hot air."

Keep the dare mild.

This was why Smith had established a strict weapons protocol for anyone entering Carlotta's hothouse chamber. No guns or blades. No needles unless administered by a med tech with a wingman to oversee. It was feasible that Carlotta might try to take her own life, although certainly that was within even her tepid power without tools. The real hazard was that Carlotta might be able to gain enough of a grip on someone's mind to use weapons by proxy. It had never happened, but Smith's slightly superstitious nature was merely being thorough.

One baleful blue eye rolled to fix him. "Seligman was a closet queen. Easy to dazzle. Want proof? He hired you. What a circle-jerk."

"Seligman provided for you," said Smith. He became aware that his perspiration was not merely from the greenhouse humidity in Carlotta's chamber. He was nervous. His skin alarms were sounding. This was not the first time this had happened in Carlotta's presence. Something about her, even withered and impotent, had the power to upset and derail, in the manner of a whistle beyond human hearing. He was thankful for the UV eyecups, so Carlotta could not probe his gaze.

"Provided?" Carlotta gave back a snort of contempt. "He provided this torture chamber so you could keep me alive, and sneak in here to finger my twat when I'm all doped up."

"You wish." It was a strange sensation for Smith to say that—like telling his own mother to fuck off and die in the middle of a nice slice of pie.

"Archangel, you prick," Carlotta said. "Look it up."

She was talking about a time before instant access. Somewhere in this very building, entry-level CHASE keyboard monkeys were still transferring old files to a central database. Typos and misdirected attention necessitated another crew just to proofread what the first group typed. It was a common problem with universities attempting to port their libraries into digital reference. One misstroke on an old Dewey Decimal number, and a book could be lost for decades in the system. It was a bottleneck that hampered even the Library of Congress to this day.

Project Archangel had been a program to cultivate future CHASE assets from childhood. Smith had heard Seligman mention it once or twice as a write-off for R&D.

"You kidnapped my future." Carlotta scowled. "I hope you die of cancer of the dick."

Smith knew that Seligman had leveraged Carlotta's early cooperation in CHASE using Carlotta's daughter, Ingrid. But Ingrid Elsinore's file had been closed in the late seventies, and Smith was fairly certain that Ingrid had died or been decommissioned, which in CHASE amounted to the same thing. Yet the Bee was still staring at him.

"Oh. *Oh.* Lights coming on, are they?"

"You have to be more specific, Carlotta."

"I'm ninety-six fucking years old, you syphilitic. And you want me to do your fucking job for you. Fuck you. Earn a dime, for once."

Smith flashed back to the long-distance call that had come from Rolf Dettrick when Rolf had sequestered a lead named Hood—some West Coast cockroach involved in the whole Morgan Deane screwup. For control of the moment and intel needed by Dettrick, Smith had compromised his own principles by assuring Hood no further harm would befall him, when what the guy needed was a simple two in the chest and one in the brain pan. Smith dismissed the exchange as strictly negotiative; sometimes, even CHASE had to give a little in order to get a lot.

And despite that concession, Alma Acevedo was still at large.

Despite deployment of otherwise-reliable CHASE resources, Alma was still on the loose, almost as if she had a fairy godmother on the inside.

"Don't you decide to die on me, Carlotta," Smith said as the urgent need to get out of the room crept across his flesh. "I'm going to need you."

"Jerk off for me," she rasped. "Spill your curdled seed on the floor where I can watch it dry, because that's another little part of you I can watch die. My eggs aren't any good to you any more. Let's pull 'em out and fry 'em up, over easy. I need the cholesterol."

"Don't go anywhere," Smith said, as he turned.

"Suck my toes. Learn what death tastes like. You want to jam a barb into me, do it like a man."

"Sure thing, Carlotta."

Hood, After

Another isometric hospital bed, in another hospital. As a shortform reference to privileged individuals in the know, the place was called St. Burke's, although there was no Saint Burke. Less than a mile from where Bryan Silver had been murdered at St. Joseph's (legit hospital; real saint), St. Burke's was an offshoot of a two-bedroom, post-war saltbox in Burbank, a town named after a dentist, though few modern-day residents knew this.

The housing boom of the mid-1990s had allowed for Burbank's proliferation of so-called "McMansions," whose selling point was that a modest one-story cottage on a modest lot could be replaced by a sprawling, cheaply-built, multi-story behemoth on exactly the same parcel of land. Small houses that at best could be termed quaint were supplanted by hyperthyroidal tract homes apparently beamed to Burbank from some failed mega-development out in the desert, and never mind that the new structures frequently butted up against each other right on the property lines.

St. Burke's presented a run-down fifties face to the residential street on which it was located, but behind the original house there was a two-story addition extending back some seventy feet, of completely nondescript white stucco, and lacking windows. This was a place where certain specific credentials and a considerable amount of cash could get you through the front door, in order to be checked in as a special patient

211

in the back. Its principal boutique clientele consisted of people needing professional medical care without the annoying delay of due process, forms, or the undue attention of law enforcement.

Had David and Daisy been on the other side of the mountain from Hollywood, they might have retreated to St. Burke's after their adventure in the storm drains…except that would have been predictable. Dave had suggested somehow utilizing the veterinarian where Kingi the dog was boarded, but that, too, had been too far away and again, predictable.

Presently it was where Alma Acevedo's job broker, Hood, was recuperating after getting most of his life bludgeoned out by Rolf Dettrick and the Wilsoni thugs. He was a guest of St. Burke's under the name Farrington, an emergency alias that was also known to Alma Acevedo.

Hood had been battered by a seasoned sadist. Nearly his entire head was bandaged and he was locked into a neck brace. If the wires were any clue, he had a broken jaw. His gray eyes, holed up in little caverns of gauze, were bloodshot, but Daisy only had to see one of them to verify his identity.

This was after she had put down the pair of Wilsoni men assigned by Rolf Dettrick to watchdog Hood—another predictability that worked to her advantage.

"You've seen cops on hospital duty," she had told David. "Working the magazine, working the coffee. The guys Rolf will have left will feel insulted by the scut duty, and they'll be itching to prove how tough they are. At the same time, they don't feel they're on the front lines."

"So it's easy to be brave when the danger isn't likely," David said.

"A minute or two will tell me all I need to know from Hood. You have to be able to control the room for that period of time."

This was after they had ditched the police car, a mere six blocks or so away from Hollywood Mailbox Associates.

Los Angeles was in the process of phasing out its Crown Vics in favor of newer Chevy PPVs (for Police Patrol Vehicle), in sum an upgunned version of the Caprice, still in classic cop-car black and white. The cruiser had its own WiFi, Ethernet, and a wireless-mesh multi-hop bundle in the trunk. The backseat even featured a cutout to better accommodate handcuffed suspects.

"This is the first time I've ever ridden in the front seat of one of these," Dave had noted.

"This is the first time I've ever driven one," Daisy said.

And they both had the same feeling at the same time. With police-band scanners right in front of them, next to screens that promised all the information technology they could possibly need, behind bullet-proof glass, inside a weaponized automobile with a jacked-up six-liter V8 offering 355 horses, they both knew they were cocooned in relative safety for only a few moments, since this car had to be abandoned as well. David wanted to curl up in the seat and go to sleep. But Daisy was right; they had to lose the ride, as tempting as it was. It put sacrificing a rental into perspective.

The streetsweeper in the trunk was as new as the vehicle—not the expected Remington 870 or Ithaca pump shotgun, but a Benelli M4 Super 90 semi-auto 12-gauge. The trunk also offered another Medikit and a box of .45 caliber rounds. More regret, as they had to leave the body armor behind.

They ditched the squad car near De Longpre Park—Charles Bukowski's old 'hood—leaving the doors open so the homeless could mess with the car and thereby hamper immediate pursuit.

With the shotgun wrapped in a blanket and their meager new possessions slung, they hopped a cab for Burbank. Modern vagabonds.

The two Wilsoni soldiers were easy to pick out. David guessed correctly, but Daisy had made them straightaway as though they were wearing nametags. Somehow she had just known they would be outside, smoking. She waited until they could be corralled together, her striding boldly forth with a winning smile and a *hiya boys*, whereupon her weapon was up before their hands could touch gunmetal. Only then did they see David covering with the shotgun, the shrouded Benelli at an angle that excluded Daisy. Smart enough to know they had been outmaneuvered, they remained nameless. Neither had been part of the Hollywood fracas, and neither retained much idea of what Daisy or David looked like. Their loss. They were gagged and trussed together behind a Dumpster of medical waste. Daisy was pretty sure this residential sector was not zoned for that kind of disposal.

But St. Burke's was a secret, to everyone except those with the need to know.

Hood was fifth bed on the upper ward, where there were only two other people convalescing. One was watching a raucous game show on some cable channel that never stopped playing them, ever. Old ones, new ones, vintage repeats. Answer the question and win a prize. You could win a whole new life by knowing your bible trivia or the capital of Chile.

"I'm sorry for the trouble," Daisy told Hood's unblinking eye. "But you should have been straight with me. You should have paid me when I saw you, not tried to play both ends against the middle. CHASE hates games."

Hood exhaled a long, congested sigh of loss. It was less painful than trying to nod his head. The metal brace in Hood's mouth made his speech slushy. "I got immunity," he said. "From Chase Alpha."

"And I got the money."

Even a polite editorial chuckle would have been a bad health move for Hood. "You call this even?"

"You don't sell out your people. But they probably didn't leave you much choice."

"Did this," said Hood. "Not CHASE. Their big dog wants you...but... the rest of them want *him*."

David and Daisy traded incomprehension. This news flash was why they had come, why they had risked exposure at a predictable stop.

"The rest of them?"

"Not CHASE," Hood said again.

"Rolf has gone outside CHASE," Daisy said. "This is worse than I thought."

Under ordinary circumstances, the checks, balances and bureaucracy of CHASE would allow them wasted time and loopholes. Bargains could be struck. No sin was above all-American dealmaking. But now Rolf Dettrick had assembled another team. Now he was no longer a representative of a larger concern to which he was answerable. Now it had gotten personal. Now he was hunting.

David and Daisy's "minute or two" with Hood was all used up.

"We have to keep moving," she told David as they tried to exit as unobtrusively as possible.

"Another cheap motel?" David said, with forced brightness that came out all wrong.

It was another shortfall demonstrating the difference between the real and the reel. In countless in-yo-face adrenalin-overdose action movies, nobody ever stopped to rest, eat, or hit the bathroom. A scene-to-scene cut could make bloodstains magically fade on your clothing. Even gigantic guns never ran dry of ammo—there was always another magazine handy. Since David had to checklist many movies of similar disposition, he experimented once with the timeline of a Blu-Ray thriller called *Forced Pursuit* (2001). He skipped the cartoonish CGI and its violations of the laws of car-chase physics. He disqualified the stunts that were frankly impossible in Earth gravity. Against a copy of the script continuity, using day-versus-night shifts, he determined the time the action onscreen was supposed to have absorbed, during which the main characters got no sleep, took no stimulants, and resorted only to first aid of the rip-up-your-blouse caliber. They never ate a meal, not even a snack, and were only seen drinking once—beer, not water. David worked up a little chart to account for the off-screen time during which some of these more basic human needs might have been serviced, and it did not amount to much. Onscreen, the protagonists—the people being pursued forcefully—were not only wily and physically fit, but evidenced bottomless inner resources when it came to weapons handling and kung-fu skills. One fight scene absorbed five minutes of screen time, not counting slo-mo. The male half of the boy-girl team-up was pounded upon by some steroidal wrestler in a battle that destroyed masonry walls and a lot of furniture, after disarming each other in the aftermath of a gunfire exchange that expended several thousand rounds with no casualties apart from auxiliary bad guys, stuntmen who would reappear three scenes later to die yet again. From his own limited personal experience, David knew that most face-to-face fights were academic after the first few landed blows. The vision blurs from head trauma. See how fast you can rally when a champagne bottle is broken against the side of your head. Champagne bottles are very thick. Even if you fall down properly (as Hayden Mathis had demonstrated), what if you whack your occipital against a brass rail? And so on. One big reveal of *Forced Pursuit* was the female lead's completely unexpected ability to pilot a helicopter, presented as a deus ex machina third-act save. Even if you flew combat duty in war, it did not mean you would immediately comprehend the control panels of a Bell JetRanger stolen from a news crew. Think of the hesitation you experience when presented with an unfamiliar rental car; even if it is only a few moments of orientation, it counts for elapsed time. That sort of delay didn't exist in *Forced Pursuit*.

No one in movies was ever unsure for longer than it took to jump-cut.

According to David's calculations, the *Forced Pursuit* action took place over the course of approximately a day and a half from first engagement, this time being compressed into the final forty minutes of the film.

David and Daisy had cleared out of St. Burke's a little bit over ninety-six hours from David's last paid workday at Starburst Post. In the past four days—which felt like a month or more—David had gotten involved in three gunfights, one brain-rattling vehicular pursuit, and several automobile thefts. He had dove through a table, battered through a wall, gotten as drainpiped as a wharf rat, and spent several relaxing hours buried in decomposing garbage. He had shot at least one man—Bryan Silver—and shot *at* many more. Most likely he had plugged his turncoat best friend, Hayden Mathis, too. He had stuck a gun in the ear of Fletcher, the CHASE driver, and snarled cinematic threats. He had stolen goods from a hijacked police car. He had drawn down on people in a hospital. He had taken hostages. He had helped dress Daisy's gunshot wound. He had taken exactly one shower.

Impossible, he would have said, had this been part of a movie.

Alpha / Chicago

Another night, another job, another bail-out banker. They were servicing each other these days, as army ants deprived of prey will readily
cannibalize their own. Kill a golden parachutist, and few investigators
ever stuck with the case long enough to find out where all the money
went. There was so much class resentment in play that even if the job
profiled as a suicide instead of a murder, the underpaid police and
wage-adjusted detectives were thinking the same thing as the general
public: *He got what he deserved.*

Virginia Stark had a ritual she enjoyed.

"Place the glass in the center of your forehead if you want to live longer."

It was summertime in Evanston, Illinois. More open windows at
night. Jeremy Piven and John Cusack had homes here. Best not to rile the
celebrities. Therefore, Ginny needed a suppressor, and she packed a good
one—a boxy SilencerCo Osprey. At eleven ounces, it actually improved
the balance of her host firearm even though it resembled a squared-off
candy bar hanging off the muzzle of her Nitron-finished Sig P220. Ginny
was a Sig gal all the way, if brand loyalty counted for anything.

She had "pre-staged" the Osprey with wire-pulling gel so it could
be fired "wet" for a nearly thousand percent noise reduction, paring
the blast of a subsonic .45 caliber round down to a loud handclap or
door slam. Water was better as a dampening medium, but could leak
or dribble out if the weapon drifted off dead level. You had to be ready

for speckles—the gel would vaporize and blow back as mist, leaving the weapon steaming like a cigar. She'd heard Chase Delta preferred the Hartcoat can. In gun fetishism, there was very little spread between the effete and the elite.

No ear protection was needed, because there would be no "sonic crack."

The dumbfuck was named Milton Breast. Yeah, really. He was a large, lumpen man who stood quavering in his state-of-the-art chef's kitchen, surrounded by stainless steel that rarely captured his own fingerprints. The same could not be said for his spectacles, which were thickly smudged. His eyes sought answers through occluded lenses. His lips were loose, slack and wet as he tried to parse an escape strategy. His dentures were yellowed. He did as he was told and placed the shot glass against his forehead firmly enough to leave an imprint ring, the same as a tiny target.

The shot glass sported a jaunty painted logo: *Stolen from Mustang Ranch, Nevada!* It featured a big-bosomed, cartoon cowboy honey.

It disintegrated spectacularly when Ginny fired through it from six feet away. Her gun range taste ran to targets that *demonstrated* a positive hit; glass, colored water, certain big types of fruit. Simply holing a mark and watching him cease brain function and fall down like a dropped doll was somehow anticlimactic.

She had not lied to Milton. He had lived nearly a minute longer because of the shot glass thing.

Ginny had ghosted away and wrapped up her current bill of lading when the message appeared on her phone: *Call home.* It was nearly 3:00 A.M., but she responded promptly, even though it meant getting her ass to New York as expeditiously as possible.

Of mixed Euro stock, Virginia Stark stood five-six barefoot, and privately thought herself a bit too hippy, although it gave her great bikini curves. Her stance was wide, on short tiger-paw feet that enhanced her spatial relationship with complete balance, dancer-sure. Privately she hated her feet, which she judged "snubbed." Her hands were a pleasant aberration, with tapered pianist fingers; man-sized hands. Cute as the proverbial button in childhood, she had never totally shed the baby-fat look, which made her cheeky as an adult. Strangers always underestimated her age. She was the sort of woman who would get carded well into her forties, although she had not yet cleared that hurdle of ego. Her hair was black and curly, shot through with threads of pure white ever since her nineteenth birthday. She maintained it in an unruly cloud about her head; she liked to feel air moving through it. Although her eyesight was a dead-solid 20/20, she usually wore tinted glasses to conceal her most striking feature—a partial *heterochromia iridum* in her left eye, which resulted in a pie-slice wedge of hazel interrupting the cornflower blue in the three to five o'clock sector. This sort of thing was much more common in cats and dogs. In a job where one needed to blend or vanish, and have witnesses *not* remember your face, it was a handicap that drove her to excel in other areas she *could* control.

Ginny so disliked her designation that she was the only operative in the history of CHASE to successfully petition James Smith for a name change. She hated "Chase Charlie"—too tomboy—and so defaulted to the old Western Union phonetic alphabet, where C stood for "Chicago."

And now Chase Alpha desired an audience with Chase Chicago in the dead of the ayem.

Ginny was second-generation CHASE. Her mother, Chase Tango, had fielded under Henry Hawker Seligman's administration. Ginny was admirably free of political ambition when it came to CHASE, particularly since the news that Chase Foxtrot—Mindy Zayden—had been summarily erased, and another piece of old news, the former Chase Lima, had gone rogue. Ginny had no desire to wrestle with the serpents swallowing each other in the pit of policy. Her talents were focused on job excellence; to become the best version of herself possible. She had only recently joined "Club Five-0"—the unofficial cognomen for operatives who had successfully cleared fifty contracts.

Having completed job number fifty-two—ironically, in Chicago—
she had her best face on when she went to answer James Smith's
summons, secretly hoping this meet was not disciplinary. Everyone at
CHASE could feel the tremors of the past few days. Things were unset-
tled, and every worker was taking extra-special pains to insure their
personal jackets were flawless. Maybe it was the economy. Nobody
wanted to think about what layoffs at CHASE might be like.

Which was why Ginny concentrated on that very idea. The best way
to cull assassins was to point them at each other. Which made every
meeting, every conversation a potential trap.

"What do you remember about your mother?" James Smith asked her.

"Chase Tango," Ginny said, crisply. "Seconded to Project Archangel."

"You're one of the few living human beings on the planet who knows
that, you know."

"Selective breeding is not popular in America unless it gets people better hamburgers," said Ginny. "I got complete disclosure from the
beginning. Actually, that sense of being chosen—adopted, if you will—
has been of immeasurable benefit to my own development. I don't mean
to recite the specs like a robot, sir, but I'm proud of it. Unlike others."

"Unlike...?"

"I'm talking about Chase Lima, sir. She rebelled. She quit. If that is
a concern insofar as my own position at CHASE, I would urge you not to
worry. I'm in. I'm solid."

"Well, then, we can put your mind at ease on that score," said Smith,
his thin lips going taut and white—his version of a smile. "Although it
is because of the former Chase Lima that I called you in. Sit down,
won't you?"

Ginny had been standing, knees locked, preparing to field hits.
Uncharacteristically, there was a waiting chair on her side of Smith's naked,
glass-topped desk. She realized Smith must have put the chair there himself. Gone out, found it, moved it, parked it. This was serious. The chair
was anything but comfortable. Ginny felt a brief flashback twinge to the

seat used for Bus Stop training inside the Cube. To be seated in a meeting, generally, was to place your eyeline below that of your superior in a passive act of submission. But now her gaze was dead-level with Smith's.

"My fear," said Smith, "is that Chase Delta has permitted old personal issues to hamper his collection and erasure of the former Chase Lima. That since Rolf Dettrick trained Alma Acevedo, he has somehow handicapped himself when it comes to eliminating her. Three tries so far, and nothing. There is a possibility that he is helping her, perhaps even unconsciously. But there is another possibility I now am forced to admit. Do you know the history of Bumblebee at CHASE?"

"Old school psychic," Ginny said. "From the seventies. I didn't know she was still alive."

"Not kicking, but her synapses are still firing, and believe it or not, she is still useful. Her daughter was named Ingrid. Ingrid knew your mother, Veronica. What can you conclude from this?"

Data unspooled quickly across Ginny's memory. "That Ingrid was part of Project Archangel?"

"Exactly. The same way your mother was. You are the only product of Project Archangel still vital to CHASE. The only other one is running around free-range, on the loose, with a man of Rolf Dettrick's talents unable to sequester her."

"You believe Alma is in contact with Bumblebee?" Ginny wanted to say "in psychic contact," but it would just sound too ridiculous.

"She might not even be aware of it," said Smith. "But if it leaks, it has to be plugged, yes?"

"Terminate Bumblebee," Ginny said quickly. "Sir."

"I haven't decided that yet. It could be like a two-way stream of intel, you see. If true, then it has value we never suspected. It might turn out that the Archangel team was on to something, way back when. You see the dilemma?"

"Yes, sir." *Here it comes*, thought Ginny. *The chance to ramp up my own personal best.*

"I want you to concentrate your...um, meditative attention toward both Bumblebee and Alma. And get ready to travel. I am going to resolve this one myself, personally."

"Yes, sir," Ginny said. "I'll do my best."

It was historic. It was monumental. James Smith was going to place himself back in the game, with Ginny at his side. It was the sort of rush dumbfucks got from receiving a huge check or experiencing a record orgasm. Ginny fought to keep her vision from plunging, or displaying any external clue of the excitement rushing up within her.

"I'm ready now," Ginny said.

Safari

The Safari Inn on Olive Avenue in Burbank was noteworthy mostly for its retro spear-and-shield neon sign, which suggested Technicolor tiki adventures in the heart of what Burbank called its "media district," within striking range of several movie studios and the NBC monolith. Open-faced to street traffic, its walls were thin and its appointments had apparently been in use since the mid-1960s, which qualified it for historical landmark status. You've probably seen the structure in films. For me it was a game to name check movies that had used the joint as a location. *True Romance, Apollo 13, Coach Carter.* You could easily have stumped me on TV shows.

It was a motel; it served that single purpose. For the undiscriminating or the desperate, it was enough. For walking-wounded fugitives, it was ideal.

Daisy filled the bathroom with steam while I collapsed on the gaudy comforter. She took nearly an hour, inspecting her damage, patching her wounds, washing away our immediate past.

Another clothing swap, courtesy of a nearby sporting goods store. The police Medikit was well-appointed and there was no need to scope out a drugstore. Food. Shelter. Respite.

She practically dragged me on top of her.

So quickly, did I recognize the pattern: she used sex to erase and reset.

For me, it was the payoff to the fantasy. Less arousing, when you know how you are being used. More predictable, when your glands succumb to the animal and don't care about the backstory. I was sure she thought I was disinterested or unattracted, neither of which was true. With the objections and nitpicks and excuses flushed aside, we hit a rhythm as two creatures trying to meld into one.

But beyond the physical gratification served by good, honest coupling, there waited the more dangerous specter of talk in the dark—that exchange that sandtraps you when someone you value says "we need to talk." I was dreading it. At least trapped coyotes had the option of gnawing off their own leg.

"Mobility, motility," said Daisy. "That was one of the CHASE mantras. Stay moving, stay flexible to make death parameters less rigid."

"This is more than a little bit crazy," I told her. "You're positing layer upon layer of assassins—so many that they've begun to feed on each other, to the detriment of innocent bystanders, backstops and collateral damage everywhere. Listen to yourself—'death parameters.' Jesus."

"I'm still waiting for you to tell me I've lost touch with reality," she said.

"Well, you're really patient about it."

"But you don't need to hear the sermon about how no one is innocent anymore, brave new world and all that. Things like CHASE are as real as it gets, and the public at large turns a blind eye at their peril. CHASE and the organizations like it are natural selection in action. They're not superhuman and don't have occult powers. They are an inevitable development of our civilization." She was on her side, facing me, to baby her bullet wound.

"You mean a byproduct," I said. "Like pollution. A mosquito immune to insecticide. A new species equipped to survive what ordinary people can't."

"Tell me I'm wrong. Consider your recent reality and tell me I've lost touch with mine." She sipped straight scotch gingerly. Just a hint of rocket fuel to level her system. She knew, as the most skilled drinkers do, that you had to keep the liquor happy. She smelled sumptuous. I visualized pheromones streaming from the even surface of her skin. After a meditative sigh, she went on:

"The people you call 'ordinary' have always chosen blissful ignorance over hard truth—just look how they crack up at the slightest pressure. A bank scams them, they keep their accounts. A relative dies and they smash into the death wall, going completely inert in blubbering grief. People want smooth sailing with no bumps, and that is abnormal for any thinking creature. So they stop thinking; they stay shitfaced to ease their perceived pain because they're terrified of opening the door to *real* pain. They develop 'conditions' that excuse them from having to cope. The whole culture is built on excuses, a mass of slackers and incompetents being towed by a few who aren't necessarily smarter or better, just more cunning. And what does that get you? It gets you a culture where the law of the jungle has been superseded by a society that allows its excess baggage to survive. The rich and the poor are exactly the same in their petty wants and needs, and as people—as human beings—they're not good for much beyond grind-stoning, reproducing, hoping for better and constantly trying to find a way to cheat."

Now try to remember your worst breakup, ever. The emotional catastrophe that scraped your soul raw and left you skinless. Liberation from a toxic parasite or abandonment by someone you thought you could trust. The clear-blue, outta-nowhere wallop to your worldview. The one that made you feel as though you were drowning. Or the one that made you feel as though you could finally breathe again.

Everybody has at least one. Even those who lack them *make them up* so they'll have a romantic tale of woe to share. The cicatrized damage meant to explain the personality quirk. The big excuse, or lie, for the Google map of your life.

That's a lot of storytelling listeners are supposed to take on faith. It follows that if you massage the narrative—bias the report on your past—you can handily manipulate the listener. Frequently it is emotional terrorism by some cowardly bully whose life is someone else's fault, always. It gets them what they want: sympathy, attention, sanctuary, a defender or a fresh fall guy.

Sometimes, less often, it is simply armor.

Even more rarely, it is the plain truth.

"I'm trying my best to understand it all," I said.

"You're better equipped than most." She was gazing at the ceiling in the dark as traffic lights splayed through the curtains. "You know it can't go on forever, but it could get worse at any moment. I won't say 'trust me' because that would sound too manipulative."

"I already trust you."

"You shouldn't." Another sip, another long, drawn-out breath of pain being determinedly aerated. "But I don't want to mislead you. CHASE had this thing called the Cube. A training building. They water-boarded me in there. I did three straight days on Bus Stop."

As Daisy outlined it, Bus Stop was an endurance run of Inquisitional elegance. It consisted of a single folding metal chair and a rotating shift of overseers. You sat on the chair, not restrained in any way. Your guardians ensured that you never fell asleep, ate, took a break, or did *anything* except sit upright on the chair. After ten hours it was maddening. After a day, pooled in your own excreta, muscles howling, it was purgatorial.

Three days...

"Why are you telling me this?" I said, feeling her old torment at the edges of my perception, even now.

"Because you want to hear the tale of childhood abuse. The pedophile stepdad keeping our 'special secret' from the alcoholic mom. The firebombed happy family that 'made me this way.' If I told you that story, it would be a lie. It's what you want to hear, though, so you can parse me in your view of things. You're doing it right now—excusing me so I fit into a romantic vision of soul-mates on the run. And I am so-conveniently telling you things to reinforce that illusion. Why?"

"Keep your friends close, your enemies closer...and your targets, closest of all."

"You're trying to make me into Daisy—your Daisy—and she's not around much, anymore."

"Alma is?"

"You can't survive on a single personality. Everybody does it—different faces for different relationship values, depending on what you need."

"Yeah, but not everybody is a professional at it."

"It takes practice and experience to be anything but an amateur."

"And you *hate* being thought of as an amateur anything," I said. "What you're talking about is no different from 'operant conditioning.' Dog training."

"Jesus," she said, imitating my tone from earlier in order to throw my own words back at me. "*You* listen to yourself, why don't you? You read that in a book somewhere?"

You should be a librarian, long-ago Daisy had told long-lost me back in high school. *I mean, you like books and all of that stuff.*

I had, in fact, discovered the phrase in a handbook one night while trying to deduce Kingi's own backstory. Now I wanted to match Daisy term-for-term in the lingo sweepstakes, but she was too fast for me. Her frank gaze made sure she had my attention before she said:

"Deny that I've been saying exactly what you want to hear."

"But if that's true, isn't this heartfelt disclosure part of the script, too? You come clean, expecting me to trust you in return. Part of me does. Part of me doesn't. I think I've had enough honesty for one day." I helped myself to the scotch, feeling I'd earned a jolt. "On the run from hitmen. Secret clubs of killers. Cripes."

"Everyone on the planet has someone who wants to kill them," she said. "Most are too afraid to indulge the animal dynamic. They lack ethics but they fear reprisal. Lose that social incentive, and you wind up in a situation like we have. The people after us have more reasons to see us dead than I do, for targeting you in the first place. Did." She tried to look as forthright as she could, engaging my gaze. "I am not going to kill you."

"Which is exactly what I wanted to hear. Interesting that you didn't say you weren't going to *hurt* me, though."

"You want a guarantee, buy a toaster oven." At least she cracked a smile at that one. She was stroking my leg. More skin contact.

"How much of anything you've told me is true? CHASE, the contracts, the Cube, the Bus Stop, your hit list?"

"How much of it matters? CHASE is self-evident. The rest is... encouragement. You'll see as much truth as you need to. The truth is, we *need* the conspirators and plotters, the secret shadow masters of everything. Because the alternative—the truth—is more frightening, and the truth is that nobody's in charge. We're all just hanging on to our illusions. Right now I'm hoping your illusions don't get you killed."

"Then by implication, you know how this ends." I rolled to make sure I had her attention. "What comes after we run, hole up, battle, then do it all over again. My whole life has become a Minsky's Moment."

Her forehead formed the sweetest worry line, at my blather.

"Never mind," I said. "Old cliché. What I'm saying is, instead of running any more, we force their agenda. We cut to the climax before they're ready. Instead of letting them bait us, we bait them."

She could not mask her instant interest. "How?"

"We load up for bear, confront them, and make them do something besides shoot at us. We let them think they're ahead of us, when we're lurking right behind them."

"I'm not following you."

"We let them trap us. But it's our trap."

"I'm sorry, David—I must be groggy or something. You intend to do this how?"

"By you and me not doing what they want. By me doing what I want."

"And that would be—?"

"I want to go get my dog back."

"Yes," she said without hesitation. "That seems correct. Do the unlikely thing."

She concurred too quickly, and that made my naked flesh horripilate with alarm. I had not had my emotions surgically removed by secret masters. I wasn't a good enough rookie superspy to sideline my own tells. Cold sweat abruptly sheeted me and I could see my own chest pulsing in the semi-dark as my heart thudded. I was acutely aware of my own breathing. I was, in fact, going into mild shock.

Because a whole pile of disarrayed alphabet blocks in my brain had suddenly aligned to form the word *setup*. This possibility hurled together a passel of observations about my own past few days.

Such as Daisy's uncanny prescience during the point-and-shoot at Mango Joy. Her sixth sense at the Tropical Paradise; the way she seemed to know in advance how to escape. Her whole mousetrap ride in the L.A. River basin. Her unqualified certainty that Hayden Mathis had been a plant, which now looked to be brutally true. The oh-so-convenient reveal of the carbon clone card. Her definitive reaction time during the ambush at Hollywood Mailbox Associates.

Was she leading me, following a predetermined scenario, like a script? Was that how she had stayed ahead of the game, by biasing what I saw?

To hide my distress was impossible, and she noticed right away.

"What is it?" she said. "You just went pale."

"Daisy, how do you know what's going to happen? I mean, like, every time so far?" I nearly lost my voice, saying the words out loud.

"I don't," she said, her own voice divulging the perfect amount of uncertainty. "Some of it is instinct and training. Some of it, I can't account for; I just *know*. Does that sound weird?"

"All this is not random," I said rather lamely. I was edging ever-closer to grabbing for the nearest tinfoil hat.

"It bothers me, too. I feel like a rat in a maze, playing someone else's game. The maze is tough, but at exactly the right moment, little arrows appear that say *this way to the cheese, stupid.* I can't explain how I know. I just know. And you sound like a man who thinks he's being played. For whatever it's worth, that's not true."

She folded her hands together across her tummy to emphasize she was on standby. She did not clasp my hand meaningfully, or begin by saying my name—the way parents do when you're about to be dressed down. Either of those moves would have made her earnestness artificial. She could have aimed low and grabbed my dick again, going glandular to fog the issue. Cheap theatrics.

"Intuition?" I finally said.

"It's all I've got, right now."

And she was all I had, right now. She had told me repeatedly to just cut loose, and let the administrative dust settle, yet we were still a duo on the lam. This was a truck chase in an action movie. The driver gets punched out. The hero shoots through the roof and scuttles under the speeding vehicle, always in motion. The accelerator is always pedal-down. It never occurs to anyone in an action flick to just *stop the truck.* That would never do; then there would be no stunt sequence.

"Let's say we go for my dog," I said. "Tell me how it works."

Kingi

"You're not gonna believe this, but I think we got a hit on the vet."

Marco Franchi, the Wilsoni man who had not been part of the button-down balls-up at the mailbox joint, had been monitoring the assorted wiretaps Rolf Dettrick had emplaced shortly prior to the mess he made in Hollywood. Bugging people was easy and simple; what Franchi could not readily understand was the rationale behind some of Dettrick's choices. Franchi preferred direct action, such as punching holes in that guy Hood until he spewed the proper information to save his own wretched life. Franchi meat-shopped the dude until he was breathing his own blood…then Dettrick said not to kill him, based on orders from a higher authority. That was a shame. Franchi enjoyed the coup de grace. He was a basically simple, direct sort of killer.

But now one of Dettrick's odd targets had pinged.

"All right," said Dettrick, who had enjoyed the luxury of a shower and shave. He already had a map of the layout—the blueprint for the veterinary on Ventura Boulevard, the parking lot, the adjacent businesses. He pointed out notations made in red marker. "Cordon team, here, here, and here. Franchi, I want you as my number two on this one."

That was encouraging news.

"But no shooting unless I shoot first."

That was a letdown.

"A#1 target is the woman," Dettrick continued as he addressed the larger squad, composed mostly of men who had been at the mailbox debacle except for DuFleck, the idiot who had fired prematurely. He had been punched out by his older partner, Giorgio, to neutralize his enthusiasm, and was currently nursing a fractured jaw. "Alive if at all possible, but dead if not, and this time you will *all* wait for my go. The string has played too long, gentlemen. Neither your superior nor mine has infinite patience, so this *will* end tonight."

"All due respect," said Giorgio, "but according to Max Wilsoni, our target is not your ladyfriend, but the guy she's running with. We don't have the luxury of alive-or-dead. Mr. Wilsoni wants the guy alive, period."

"All the more reason for no capricious gunfire," said Dettrick. "Where there's one, there's the other. I have no idea why, but it works out for all of us, yes?"

"Excuse *me*," said Palermo, a short, sturdy man with heavy brows and exceedingly hairy arms. "But that bitch *shot* at us." He and his eastern surveillance partner, Weaver, had suffered Alma's hazing fire from the roof. "If it hadn't'a been suppressing fire, we'd both be fuckin dead if your girl is as good as you say she is. So is she good, or lucky, or what?"

General murmurs of assent, all around.

"Scared of a little gunfire, Mr. Palermo?" said Dettrick.

"No *sir*." Palermo dealt Rolf's attitude back with the ease of checking a bet in poker. "But as long as you're straight with us, as long as you don't talk to us like we're some kinda Mob goons out of a TV show, we can deliver as good or better than your highpants gang of assassins with all the right paperwork. Am I right or am I right?"

"He's right," Giorgio said. "This is what you call your interdepartmental cooperation, Mr. Dettrick. We're not a plastic bag full of Army men and we're not disposable because we're not in your club. We answer to the Wilsoni Brothers. You want us to answer to you, you earn that respect by giving us certain guarantees, just like you did with that tubesteak Franchi tenderized for you."

How about I guarantee CHASE *doesn't open a work file on you, you fucking shaved ape?* Rolf thought. They were muscle, all of them, iron-pumping martial arts showoffs. Under normal circumstances he could have them all killed as easily as Egyptian high priests murdered their burial contingents to keep sites sacred and secret. But they were all he had to work with right now. They were making noises as though they wanted to call a strike and haul in union reps. It was a typical bargaining gambit for men of their caste.

"Okay, first guarantee," said Rolf. "Your boss will get David Vollmand, alive and intact, to dispose of whatever way he wishes. Second guarantee: You men are strictly backup. That means no gunfire, but I need you as a fist I can close. What else?"

"We know about CHASE," said Palermo. "Some of us want in."

Giorgio did, definitely. So did Kurland, Rolf's second from the mailbox gig, and Hickey, one of the parking lot watchdogs. Plus Palermo. The rest of them were not sold yet. Rolf could see from their eyes they were trying to weigh Wilsoni loyalty versus job opportunity. Four men pre-sold out of ten, with the rest ping-ponging and Franchi trying to figure out whether Rolf's choice of him as a second, right now, was a good sign or not. Franchi's eyes said he would swing with the majority... as though this was some kind of democracy.

"Then consider this an audition," said Rolf, who had no such latitude to offer, and no time to curry these thugs individually.

"Bonuses," said Weaver, from the rear. "For performance. You remember who helped you and reward them accordingly."

It was natural for these men to view CHASE as a pot of slush-funded gold, because they didn't know any better. Another lie would not harm them or help them any more.

"Naturally," said Rolf, with just the right tone of dismissiveness. "I need to point out, gentlemen, that we incurred zero casualties in Hollywood. The same goes for this op."

Giorgio moved closer to Rolf's map. "Then show us your plan."

Rolf's gambit was to neutralize the veterinary staff and stake out the office for the arrival of David, or Alma, or both. Either way he could get what he wanted, satisfy Max Wilsoni, and bring James Smith a trophy. The sole random factor would be the accidental intrusion of some citizen with a bona fide late-night pet emergency, who could be kept at bay by the buzzer-locked door, standard procedure for after-hours. Rolf could have his perimeter crew collect such stragglers in the parking lot.

Franchi was holding an empty pet carrier as Rolf buzzed the intercom. Female voice: *"Sherman Oaks PetCare."*

Rolf segued into his rattled-citizen voice: "Uh, hi there, yeah, I've got a raccoon here, it bit my little girl, it was in the garbage can—"

"Slow down, sir."

His intention was to sound panicked enough to encourage a swift entry. Employees like this disliked babblers and usually rushed to calm them, mostly to shut them up.

"Yeah, right, anyway, it bit her—I think—but it might have, like, rabies, y'know? I got it. I shot it with a .22. My daughter is in the hospital at Sherman Oaks Medical but I thought I should bring this thing right away, because—well, rabies is serious, right, and we need to know—"

The door buzzed.

"We're in," Rolf said into his comm. He felt twitchy, with minor shakes akin to someone experiencing hypoxia psychosis, which required extra effort to conceal. He hadn't worked out in days and had been hitting the speed a bit too liberally. Most of all, he wanted to stride in and shoot something. Anything to scotch this goddamned endless hide-and-seek.

The entrance to Sherman Oaks PetCare was a double glass door from the parking lot. The office presented no observable profile to Ventura Boulevard. The lobby consisted of a long, tri-cornered counter—people and their pets and problems used up a lot of lateral room—that presented a subtle barrier at chest height, higher than a bar or desk. The blueprint had given the layout as a long, fat-bottomed L-shape, past the counter. Angled hallways with consultation cubicles on both sides, leading to a larger rear room with garage-door access for bigger jobs, storage, and general work area with a soundproofed side door that led directly to a indoor kennel run.

The woman at the counter wore a string-tied floral jersey, halfway between an apron and a smock. Her hair was pinned back.

But it was Alma, all right. She already had a pistol leveled at Franchi.

Then something hit Rolf in the back of the neck like a red-hot meteor, and Rolf fell down, dropping his own gun, with no time to do anything at all except wet his pants and groove on the lightning bolts inside his eyelids.

"What you are suggesting is completely unethical and illegal," Dr. Marion Fuller told David.

He and Daisy were behind closed doors in Fuller's office at the pet clinic. It was shortly before dinnertime. That meant an evening rush of commuters unable to address their pet needs in person any other time. Upfront, Beatrice had her hands full with phone duties and a fellow with a sick iguana in a cardboard box who did not yet understand that Sherman Oaks PetCare did not deal with "exotics"—basically reptiles, since they allowed wiggle room for rats and ferrets—and a referral to a specialty hospital was needed for the best care. Another ranch hand named Kim was busy sequestering two cats from two owners, while a leashed Jack Russell terrier in the outer office barked steadily, almost metronomically. Its determined quest for attention was muted by Dr. Fuller's door.

Kingi was still stashed in the kennel run, completely energetic and happy to assert his dogness against the other prisoners. David and Daisy had given no advance notice of their visit, and requested a moment of private time not to threaten the staff or make demands, but merely to inform the doctor as to what was about to happen in her place of business and healing.

"I understand, Doctor, and believe me I'm not slamming down an ultimatum," said David. "But the second you enter that Kingi is billed and released on a computer, this place is going to be surrounded by very dangerous people who have no compunction about mowing down bystanders. This *will* happen. And in a sense, it's bigger than any of us."

"Plus, we'd be happy to provide ten thousand dollars to the clinic for all the trouble," Daisy said. She was standing behind David in a casual-enforcer position, and looked serious enough. A better inducement was the cash, right there, live and in color, in an envelope now on Fuller's desk next to a sno-globe of a howling wolf.

Fuller tapped a pencil against a schedule book on her desk. She was a very fit middle-fifties with glasses on a necklace. "Is the money stolen?"

"No."

"We've been jacked several times," Fuller said. "Junkies after Phenobarbital, smash-and-grabbers after whatever wasn't bolted down. That's why the meds are in a special lockdown vault now, and that's why the security system is brand new. It broadcasts to a secure server so the discs can't be compromised here."

"I don't want anything here," said David, "except my dog."

"Call the police," said Fuller. She dug into the bridge of her nose to avert a migraine spike.

"These people have the power to neutralize the police," said Daisy. "You are perfectly free to call them yourself, but the result will be the same. You'll be gag-ordered by men who don't blink their eyes, and who will have sterling silver credentials."

"Tell them we forced you. Tell them we took you hostage," said David. "It won't matter because they'll spin it that way, anyhow. We just want the use of the building for a few hours in the dead of night, and the only reason I'm telling you this is to keep you and your people safe. Honest. Please."

"We get emergency calls in the dead of night," said Fuller.

"Yes, and until we give you an all-clear, you can port them to other vets," said Daisy. "Send them to Beverly Oaks—they're eight blocks away."

"You've really done your homework," said Fuller. "Why would I send my own customers down the street?"

"You can claim a family emergency."

"So you've decided that already, hm?"

"No," said David. "We're throwing ourselves on your mercy."

Beatrice—the larger of the two assistants—tapped once on the office door and peeked in. "Doc? Mrs. Delacorte is here with her Persian again; says there's blood in the urine."

Outside the Jack Russell was still barking.

"He stepped in broken glass," said Beatrice.

"Godammit," Fuller whispered, her eyes in abstract focus.

"And we've got preps in Two and Five—one of those is to euthanize."

This took more time—you had to be brisk and firm, yet sympathetic to owners who were frequently paralyzed with grief.

Murder occurred nearly every day at Sherman Oaks PetCare.

"Give the put-down to Ernest," said Fuller. "He's got to leave at seven."

Ernest was another of the six doctors in the group, and the only other one on office hours this night—truncated due to some personal issue to which neither David nor Daisy were privy.

Dr. Fuller's shoulders sagged as though they had gained a hundred-weight burden. "Unethical, like I said. Illegal. I should be whistling up the cops right now. But according to what you say, something bad is going to happen whether I like it or not, and the police will just shine me on if I ask them what's really going on."

Think of the last time you saw police cars sealing off a city block. Hazard tape and stern warnings. You assumed anything requiring such mobilization would be newsworthy, and you would discover what had transpired later, most likely on television...and there was never a mention of any action. Inquiry won you a stone wall. Thus, nothing happened. It was none of your business. You stayed in the dark, and law enforcement likes it that way.

"You brought that dog in here," Fuller continued, "when someone else had thrown him out like garbage. You were not a pet owner yet you took the responsibility. You stashed him here so he would be safe when you got in trouble. That counts for a lot in my book. I guess it was inevitable that your trouble would come back here. None of what you say makes this right or preferable. But."

"But?" David remained as hopeful as Daisy stood stoic.

Fuller placed her fingers on the envelope. "But we need the money."

It was 8:00 P.M. when David Vollmand's billing for services rendered cleared, knocking the available limit on his credit card down to pocket change. Marco Franchi read it within five minutes of the transaction, and alerted Rolf Dettrick.

Rolf's cordon team had the perimeter sewn up by 8:15.

Rolf entered Sherman Oaks PetCare at 8:17, with Franchi right behind him. Franchi was in mid-draw on a sawed-off shotgun concealed inside a pet carrier.

Rolf's face bounced off the floor of the veterinary lobby at approximately 8:17:14. The first thing he saw upon regaining his motor functions was a large wall clock behind the reception desk. It was 9:02 P.M.

He was securely duct-taped to a chair in the waiting room—part of a multi-seat row that was bolted to the floor and out-of-eyeline from the door. His crotch was damp and humid; he had pissed himself.

Duct-taped right next to him was Marco Franchi, sporting a large-caliber bullet hole in the center of his forehead. The cinder-block wall behind him was rained in blood and exit matter. It resembled one of those abstract paintings done by that monkey, the kind of art rich morons bought as a sociological joke, this one being from the simian's red period. The placement of clotted hair was sublime. Runoff had pooled on the floor tiles.

"Fancy meeting you here," Alma said. "You come to make a donation to the dog and cat fund?"

She was still wearing the medical drawstring scrub pants and tunic that had caused Rolf to hesitate, just for an oversplit second, to ID her.

Standing near was David Vollmand, wearing a dark blue shirt smock and pointing Rolf's own Glock 21 at him, Hartcoat silencer and all. The pocket of the smock was gravid with Rolf's backup piece, the Charter Arms Bulldog. Franchi's jack-in-the-box piece, a cut-down Benelli smooth-bore shorty, was on the counter next to what looked like a police nightstick, plus Franchi's carry gun, a Taurus Tracker revolver in .44 Magnum overpowered enough to stop a grizzly bear.

Rolf's throat felt jammed with salt and steel wool.

"Usually in the movies," said David, "when you see a veterinarian's office, it's shorthand for a criminal getting a meatball patch on a gunshot wound. They make a big deal out of all the on-site narcotics, but you know what? None of the drugs in here will put you out like a stoplight on an intramuscular injection—that's TV shit. Even etrophine hydrochloride. A single drop can kill you, and it needs an antidote. But it's a morphine derivative. Takes time to cycle through the body. Nope." He picked up the baton from the counter. "Shockstick works better."

David had been standing atop the back of the chair group to which Rolf was currently secured, up high so as not to present a lurking body profile to Rolf's peripheral vision when he entered. By the time he dropped the stunner on Rolf's neck, giving him 800,000 volts, Daisy had Franchi squared in the sights of her Smith.

They sat Franchi down first while Rolf spasmed on the floor. When he was taped up, Daisy said:

"You're the one that did Hood." She cocked her head like a curious puppy. "You *enjoyed* it."

Franchi was about to say, *"eat me, puta"* but Daisy shot him in the head before he could get the first vowels out.

Rolf did not need to ask what happened. He was the star of the aftermath.

"What now?" he said. It was an effort. His whole body wanted to take a long nap in a foreign country.

"Why?" said Daisy.

"Morgan Deane. He was one of Chase Alpha's tools." Rolf tried to spit but couldn't work up the saliva; his lips were numb. "Your method gave you away."

"Dammit." Daisy shook her head. "What about him?" She meant David.

"Conduit to you. That's all."

David looked askance at Rolf. "I don't believe it."

"There's a bunch of fellows outside who would really like to meet you," said Rolf, finding his iron again. "The name Max Wilsoni ring any bells?"

"You're full of shit."

"If you think so, then walk out the door. You're a free man."

"Give us a personal moment," Daisy said to David.

"Right. I'll get the dog."

Daisy ignored the collected firepower on the counter but kept her Smith with her as she squatted right in front of Rolf. He was helpless, immobilized, and she did not fear him.

David entered the kennel run and there was Kingi—alive, awake, alert and sassy. The dog's tail went out of control when he spotted David, and their reunion was about as messy as could be imagined.

Franchi's blood was all over Rolf's right shoulder. Rolf was the *man in charge*, dammit, and no matter how compromised his position or how turbid his nerve endings, former subordinates just...plain...didn't treat him this way.

"You're no longer the man in charge," Daisy said.

His lip tried to curl into a sneer and made it about halfway. *"You,"* he said. "You're highballing. You need a runoff ramp. You're playing Efram Obermeyer all over again. Your job is not to *save* people." Air seethed past his clenched teeth, making little bubbles. "What is this dumbfuck to you? Some fling, some tragic soul, some wayward puppy? He's nobody."

"That's not for you to determine," Daisy told him. "You no longer get to say what my job is."

"I will when there's a roomful of guys with a shotgun up the ass of your stupid charity case."

"Not going to happen," she said. "Because I've got you. I outplayed you. Your problem, right now, is to get out of this with your skin still on. No doubt you've got a cordon around this place. You will tell them to withdraw. You will tell me just what the hell it is you really want—why all this fuss? Or I'm going to set you on fire. Nothing personal."

"Sorry, kiddo," Dave told the dog. "Sorry about the trouble. Sorry about the apartment—I know it's too small. I'm just glad you're okay."

Kingi looked great. A bit put off at being kenneled, this more than overwhelmed by his reunion with his human. He had been not only treated, but bathed. Even his teeth looked cleaner. His batwing ears were upright and alert.

"Bet you're itching for a little action, huh?" David sniffed; their re-bonding after the past few excoriating days was choking him up unexpectedly. "Well, we've got plenty of that. Too much."

Slurp.

Their heads cranked sharply, as one. Someone had fired a gun in the outer office.

The last thing James Smith expected to see when he and Ginny Stark back-doored the veterinarian's was Rolf Dettrick, duct taped to a chair and apparently drugged, next to another guy who had soldier scribbled all over him in the bloodspatter of his own death.

They came in hot, guns up in hi-lo cover. A separate CHASE team under Smith's command already had control of Rolf's outer ring of backup guys—one ring had closed on the other. Smith wanted this encounter up close, personal, and unpopulated.

And Alma Acevedo, the former Chase Lima now name-tagged as Daisy Villareal, was *crouching right there* with her back to their guns, with no draw time. She was wearing a nurse's smock. Such a bald catch could only mean another trap, so Smith and Ginny maintained three-sixty peripheral awareness.

Smith nodded to Ginny. *Shoot her.* No parley, no exposition. They could clean up after every threat was dead.

Ginny put her green laser sight on Alma's back and fired.

But Alma had seen Rolf trying to hold stiff and pretend he had not seen the two new players enter. She could see movement behind her in his eyes. She flattened, rolling to bring up her own weapon for a response as Ginny's slug plowed into Rolf's ribcage.

Standard procedure would have had Ginny tracking her moving target with a hectoring fan of bullets. But a new tableau had unfolded.

Ginny spun. Her peripheral awareness was as uncanny as rumored. She centered the laser dot right on David's forehead just as David got the drop on James Smith at point blank range with Franchi's .44.

Ginny had David dead to rights. David had Smith. And Daisy had Ginny.

"Okay, okay, everybody hold!" said Smith, flustered at last. "No shooting."

"Shoot him," said Rolf in a thin gasp. Meaning Smith. This stranger who had fucked up David's life now wanted him to kill some other stranger.

"Ginny, you know how this works," said Daisy, who apparently knew the other woman. "You and me, the slightest trigger indicator, the other one of us is firing already. Forget the competition." It was all in a tensing of posture, a narrowing of the eyes, the preparation to shoot. Each of them could read the other the way house flies could use air currents and skin tautness to evade a swat. Micro-indicators of which ordinary people were unaware.

"Shoot him," Rolf said again, unsuccessfully trying to see his newest bullet wound as his metabolism started freaking out.

"Let us go," said David.

"Done," said Smith, the back of his neck scaring up at the closeness of the pistol in David's grasp.

"*Don't listen to him!*" Rolf said. "This whole thing—*his* orders."

"And you're just going to let us skate?" said Daisy, holding firm on Ginny, whom she knew to be the most dangerous shooter in the room...after herself. "Somehow I doubt that. It's personal for you now, Rolf."

If everybody fired at once, Rolf would become the new head of CHASE. If he lived. If Daisy didn't execute him on the spot.

"Ginny," Rolf said. "Bravo."

This caused Ginny's gaze to flicker toward Smith, who was now mightily pissed off. "You pusillanimous little traitor," he whispered, meaning Rolf.

Then, in a fingersnap as Ginny's trigger finger moved back one fiftieth of a millimeter, it was all academic.

Because out of nowhere, a huge German Shepherd with a black face bulleted in to chomp on her gun arm. The dog attacked from below eye level, springing from a stalking crouch, surprising everybody with its stealth and silence.

Ginny's shot skinned flesh off David's head above his right ear as the dog took her down before the echo died. David was not even aware of his own reflexive trigger pull, or the sound of the Taurus announcing serious pain.

Smith crashed to his knees and spun onto one side, his own wild shot at Daisy missing by a yard. His neck was gone. His head was barely held on by one scrap of flesh, like a hank of Scotch tape on the hinge of a broken watermelon.

Ginny had already wrestled her Sig around to blow the dog's head into casserole. David kicked the gun from her grasp. It was what she wanted—to lure him near enough to grab. Daisy would try to center her, but not at the risk of holing her partner. Ginny booted the dog backward, dumped David with a leg spill, wrapped her legs around him from behind, and got him in a textbook larynx lock. She could rip out his voicebox and show it to him as he died. Her gun was within easy collection distance. Daisy didn't have a shot.

So she recentered her muzzle attention on Rolf.

"Enough of this shit!" Ginny said. "You're no longer relevant! You're no longer CHASE. Why don't you just fuck off!?"

"Yeah," David said, his voice strangulated. "Fuck off. I've got this. Get your ass out the back, they way they came in. Now. Do it."

"No!" The hammer was back on her Sig, ready to send Rolf to hell.

"I just promoted this guy!" David said. "He's not going to kill me."

"Listen to him," said Rolf. "I am not going to kill him. I am not going to allow Ginny to kill him. But you have to get out, now, before the cordons close. This place is a heartbeat away from filling up with gunmen, and none of them are officers of the law. We all most likely die. I can fix it. If I don't pass out first."

"Go, Daisy, get out of here!" David shouted. "You go, I stay—this ends with me, goddammit!"

Ginny cocked one eye at her captive. Who the hell was "Daisy?"

Dave

Nothing focuses your attention like getting the crap beaten out of you. Especially by seasoned men of violence who know how to dole out hurt in measured doses, avoid serious turning-point damage, and keep you awake for every elongated instant. My whole face felt like a ripe tumor, my guts were scrapple, and my extremities were on fire with nerve alerts, the bad kind. They say no one uses phone books anymore. Not true. Ever since the days of the old sweat-down in the police interrogation cells of countless films noir, a big fat phone book had remained ideal for smashing people about the head.

Wham. My Minsky's Moment was all mine, now. I owned it. Kicked in the head by the whole chorus line, et cetera. *Wham.*

The sole beneficial effect came from the very first blow (the one you dread while it is incoming)—it cleared the snot-blocks in my sinuses before I passed out. Sadly, I woke up.

Daisy left me. *Wham.* I told her to, and she did it. *Splat.*

Something told me she would hesitate and try to bargain our way out of the standoff at Sherman Oaks PetCare. It would be more run, hide, and battle, just like in the worst zombie flicks; we would repeat the pattern over and over if we stayed together.

I did not know any of the names or designations of the people currently engaged in pulping me. They circled and traded jibes among themselves, shadow figures, crude sketches of bad guys. They did not seek information from me or withhold pain to coerce cooperation. My role was to sit, restrained, and absorb blows, period.

I saw a row of theater seats, some occupied by bulky enforcers, others laden with strips of plywood or defrocked, dusty fixtures. The guys sitting down had their legs draped over armrests or their feet chocked against seat-backs. They needed an usher to chide their disrespect. Half of them were slurping coffee beverages, ridiculous high-caloric shit with dome lids and whipped cream. Were we waiting for the rest of the audience to show up?

One of them said, "This asshole got Franchi killed. He *owes*."

Punch, to the GI tract.

Another said, "Killing him is not our call."

Wham. Wonderful—I would get to live through more of this.

I saw reluctance skirt Daisy's expression when I had told her to get out, get clear. That was all I wanted, to see her in conflict about leaving me. This pounding was the payoff I was volunteering to endure in return for a glimpse that she cared, that our adventure had meant something, that I was more than just another demoted target. It was what we had agreed to back at the Safari Inn: if the situation goes sour, split up. Give them two targets instead of one. Divide, conquer, evade, harass.

I figured it out later. My recollect was scattered worse than a spilled bucket of crushed ice. Somebody blew cigar smoke into my face and then roundhoused me in the side of the head. My world lurched into a Dutch angle, the kind of tilted point of view meant to confer hallucinations or dreams.

I had been remanded to the good graces of the Wilsoni family. I had no idea they had twigged to my existence, which had remained secret for the better part of a decade. My past-due bill was for my part in the destruction of the patriarch, Aristede. I had tried to hide from retribution, and in the end I rushed to embrace it just to break the stranglehold of the run-hide-battle cycle.

As Rolf Dettrick had said, the pet hospital filled up with gunmen, and none of them were blue knights. Rolf wanted to preserve me as an asset for recapturing Daisy—his objective—but was too far gone from his gunshot wound to make much sense. The command decision fell to his number two, the new Chase Bravo, the woman whom Daisy had called "Ginny." Of the two groups of enforcers outside, one was CHASE, and one was Wilsoni, all in deep conflict about the next course of action, because Sherman Oaks PetCare had become a hot zone they needed to evacuate. To placate the Wilsoni men, Ginny gave them me, because she had bigger headaches to process, such as keeping Rolf alive. From what I had seen, she had no desire to be the point person for a hydra like CHASE. That was now Rolf's job, and whatever fiction they cared to concoct about how James Smith had checked out would be just fine.

Apparently we were inside a closed moviehouse. There is nothing like the ambience of an auditorium full of padded seats, so the acoustics were a big clue. I guessed there was no hurry to clear out before the next show. I was the feature event.

I had no idea what day it was. What time. "Break time" is a funny expression. It can mean recess. It can mean time to break things, like me.

Even funnier: I no longer cared. The outer limits of my own pain threshold were becoming as familiar as the breakers and eddies. Daisy got out, got clear. And I got to put an end to my own fear.

This was the part of the movie where trouble piled ever more thickly onto the head of the protagonist. Daisy just running away was not logical; audiences would hate that. Unless they understood it from my point of view: the only way to set her free was to make a sacrifice.

Wham.

"What a fucking piece of work. You shoulda taken ole Rolf *hostage*, man, pay for play, bargained your way out. Instead, he gets a ree-ward, and you get a big splintery stick shoved up your ass."

David J. Schow

The speaker was a short dude, Latino or Middle Eastern, in drug dealer flash. He looked fifteen. Pattern baldness. Max Wilsoni. Still a child when I had written about his father. I knew he had an older brother, Augustus. Maybe his part in this came later, but Max was like a cartoon version of his dad, grossly obvious, all surface.

"You're an idiot," I said. Loose teeth, swollen gums, my tongue like a badger stuffed into my mouth.

Somebody hit me, for insulting the royalty.

"Look like you're the idiot, you dumb fuck."

Dumbfuck was what CHASE called citizens, a bit of argot for which little Max was not in the loop.

"You're being set up," I managed to say without fainting. "CHASE gave you what you wanted—me. CHASE wants their woman back, their hitter. She will come for me and CHASE knows it. I'm bait." I admit I was just making this up as I went along. "But by keeping me, you're turning yourself into bait, too."

"How you figure that?" Max said in a patronizing tone. "She your *girlfriend* or something?"

"No. High school crush."

"Aww, don't fuck with me. She ain't gonna fall for anything so obvious. She ain't gonna risk it. Shit, dude, I've got twenty guys here. You don't know it because your brain is Jell-O, but we've moved you twice. She'd break her cover for *your* sorry ass, all heroic and shit? Right. You don't know much about women."

Why wasn't I dead already? It was not just Max's pocket sadism and schoolyard tyrant approach that kept me breathing. He was talking tough but out of his depth. His men could whale on me until I was comatose, deceased, or a retard, but what would be the jackpot for that? Busted up as I was, it was still a display—I had no information to leak. If I did not die on the spot, so what? Max was waiting for clearance, instructions. He needed permission from on high, which meant either CHASE or his brother had to tell him what to do next.

250

"Think about it, Max. Why would CHASE let you have me?"

"Part of our deal," he said, but the uncertainty was coming out of his pores.

"Why would Rolf give me up to *you?*"

"He used my soldiers. He found you for us. Even trade."

"No. He's hanging back so that when Daisy comes out of the wood-work, all the casualties will be yours...don't you get it?"

At least this colloquy was delaying my next wallop to the head.

"Ole Rolf is in no position to hang on anything," Max said. "He's in the hospital because his own chick shot him in the guts. Painful. You should be thinking about that, eh?"

It was part of the goad, the caveman display, the pump-up to the next round of violence. It was Max's way of asserting himself in front of his crew. It was a diversion.

"You got Franchi killed."

"I didn't kill him."

"You owe for my father," Max said, sullen, still clutching for new reasons to bash me.

"I didn't kill him, either."

Boom. Another impact jarred my teeth and crossed my eyes. I bit my tongue—not for the first time—and my mouth was rich with the hot sauce of my own blood.

But I *had* killed James Smith, by sheer autoreflexion or not. It was not self-defense. It was fright and startlement that caused my finger to snap the trigger on the pistol at the back of his neck. I had taken his life. As Daisy had said, you only need to kill once, to be a killer.

Another killer, one blissfully free of compunction or moral conflict, was steaming up to hit me again on Max's behalf.

"Wait, wait," I said. Getting words out was an effort when my entire body wanted to shut down, but these words were worth the struggle. "Rolf had CHASE but he uses *your* guys? Doesn't that tell you something?"

David J. Schow

"Yeah, stupid—my guys are better."

"Max—Rolf has left the reservation. He's off the chain. His own boss had him shot. Think."

Watching Max attempt thought would have been amusing, in any other context. He froze like a laptop trying to load a huge file.

"And if Rolf is the boss now, you think he's going to give a damn about you or what you want, for free?"

404—ERROR, PLEASE RESTART.

A big man holding a canvas tube filled with powdered lead was standing right behind Max, ready to move in for a new session. I think his name was Hickey. He worked and twisted the tube as though choking a Freudian snake in a bad dream. He was massaging a metaphorical hard-on.

"Wait," Max said.

Daisy

Kingi stared at Daisy. Daisy stared back, as though the dog was accusing her.

"*What,*" she said.

The Shep did not provide any clues. He had stayed on her six as though by direct order, all the way through the layers of security surrounding Sherman Oaks PetCare, scooting out a mere ninety seconds before the web constricted. En route, she had put down three men nonlethally, although one of them, who stank of Chase, would have to breathe orally for about a month. She shock-sticked the second, and ramrodded the third to hang him up on a low barbed wire fence.

The tacit agreement she had made with David was to split up in case of imminent trouble. That seemed inadequate and cold now, since she was the one who had gotten away. Or, if you counted the dog, two-thirds of their team. The teams aligned against them had ten, twenty warm bodies each. On any other day the escape would have been a brag-worthy achievement.

But how had she divined the exact route James Smith and Ginny Stark had used for ingress? How had she known the first guard she encountered was a Chase operative, and the other two were...different, like the men who had tried to ambush her at the mailbox joint?

The same way she knew that *right now* had been the time for her to bail and get away. Her instinct, or intuition, compelled her the moment

David had insisted she leave. The unspoken and most important part was her surety that if she had stayed, if she and David were still together...

She would be dead now.

That was the deal David had made with himself: to face his faceless tormentors, at whatever risk, to interrupt what had become a cruel game for them. To sacrifice himself to deal her free, and perhaps lose his own life to know what was going on. To stop wriggling on the hook, running, fighting, hiding, then doing it all over again.

Alma would have handled things differently: *Go for the guaranteed kill—James Smith. Put him down as rabid. This defangs David's threat potential and lumbers Ginny with the choice of either shooting David (who now lacked a target) or re-sighting to shoot Alma. Use that delay to sight and shoot Ginny, which would probably not be a kill on the first round, because Ginny would already be moving. Track her and kill her, with or without David's help. Then shoot Rolf Dettrick, who was offered up as help- lessly as a buffet. Then let the CHASE and Wilsoni men button up the scene, temporarily leaderless and itching for a malefactor to kill. Give them David.*

Because it had not happened that way, Daisy realized that Alma had died tonight.

This left Daisy with two options: Break character and go completely under, as Hood had advised, or continue fighting. She could go for David. She could go directly for Rolf Dettrick. Both were predictable, neither would end without more casualties. Rolf had come after her, specifically, on orders from Chase Alpha. She did not know every single detail, but she knew that if Rolf survived, he could spin the events to assure that he would become the new director of CHASE. That was the deal in his mind when he offered Ginny the Bravo slot. Was that enough to clear her debt for quitting the organization? Or would the newly-empowered Rolf redouble his efforts to eliminate her, with the whole club now eager to do his bidding and curry his favor?

And if David was already dead, what was the point of exposing herself even more? Killing everyone in CHASE would not level the scales, then.

He had traded his freedom for hers. Not by accident.

And now the damned dog was staring her down, waiting for her to make a decision.

Smith had brought Ginny because Ginny had hunches, acted on non-physical clues, got gut feelings that proved out. Ginny's mother, Veronica Stark—Chase Tango—was one of the very few sanctioned "CHASE inactives."

In CHASE-speak, Veronica was retired, yet still living. That alone was a rarity.

In plain language, Ginny's blood-wired bio-connection to the source (or amplifier) of her strange premonitions was still alive, hence the vitality of her run-and-gun attenuated senses.

It was one of the reasons Ginny and Alma Acevedo could not be opponents in combat. During training, each had demonstrated an uncanny knack for leap-frogging the other in the mental race toward a trigger pull or precipitous leap. Some evidence had suggested the presence of one might be able to block or fog the abilities of the other.

Ginny Stark and Alma Acevedo had both been products of Project Archangel.

But Ingrid (no last name given), Alma's mother, had been dead for twelve years.

Kingi watched Daisy, his eyes patient and hopeful.

The news came in a fiery flash, like a Doomsday premonition or a sulfur match igniting against her inner eyelids: *Your grandmother, Carlotta, is still alive. The woman once known in CHASE as Bumblebee.*

Carlotta had to be the conduit for Daisy's "feelings." Weak, intermittent, most often vague in detail, not comprehensive, but still...

...still good enough to account for every presagement Daisy's vitals had registered as true.

Daisy's vision spotted briefly with heliographic circles, a feeling akin to an imminent swoon. David was not dead. Her gut instinct told her so.

Daisy had never felt any sense of connection with the boy toys and rental bodies she routinely used to relieve post-job sexual stress. But David had been inside her, and their minds had touched, however faintly. Some nonphysical engine was blinking green inside her brain, telling her that David had not been executed, not yet.

And the dog was looking at her like it was the most obvious conclusion in the universe. *Duh, took you long enough, girl genius.*

Dr. Ernest DiFalco had phoned Dr. Marion Fuller at three o'clock in the morning to inform her that Sherman Oaks PetCare had been robbed sometime during the night, that there was very little damage, no missing inventory to speak of, and that she could expect to answer to investigators when she showed up for work the next day.

The break-in would not even rate as minor news. This sort of crap happened all the time; Marion had even told David and Daisy as much.

"What *happened* in here?" Marion asked Daisy.

Daisy stared somewhat disbelievingly at the wall where Franchi had drawn his final breath. CHASE janitorial had worked a cleanup miracle in record time.

"There was some violence," Daisy said. "Mostly a lot of saber-rattling."

Marion looked at her dourly. "I know—none of my beeswax, right?"

Daisy's advantage was that it would never occur to either CHASE or the Wilsoni men to return to the scene expecting to find her. She was supposed to give the veterinary a wide berth, per the rule of non-repeating patterns, to never use the same path for entrance and exit, all those cautions.

"I brought another donation," Daisy confided to the doctor. "And all you need to do this time is let me access your tracking records for pets with chips."

"Don't tell me you lost *another* dog?"

"Something like that."

Prior to the time the bad guys had shown up, while David and Daisy were busy outfitting themselves in the uniforms of the clinic, David had spotted the pistol grip of the pneumatic hypo used to implant the newest iteration of tracking chips. Its dermal needle was about two millimeters in diameter, or about the width of the edge of a nickel; scary enough, and wince-worthy.

There was a booklet to go with it.

The unique-identity RFID homer chips were somewhat beefier than the standard tagging chips, which needed to pass within several yards of a scanner. These Gen-4 devices were more properly transponders requiring challenge-response authentications, usually under encryption, not dissimilar to the chip that can reveal the coordinates of your mobile device to anyone with the ability to scan for it...from much greater distances.

Or the doodad Rolf uses to track CHASE's guns, thought Daisy.

David and Daisy had injected each other, inner thigh. The corresponding files were logged as *Spot* and *Fido*.

"Nobody uses those names anymore," said Marion, who disliked the marginalization of animals through the use of cutie-pie names. Daisy was searching for Fido. The speed with which she located him was a testament to the efficiency of the entire program.

The program even supplied a grid map.

Rolf

"...without immediate surgical assistance, he could have been dead in fifteen minutes. Abdominal trauma almost always involves the penetration or rupture of the intestines, the colon, major organs. He was amazingly lucky. The bullet we dug out of him was a nasty piece of business indeed—designed to flange and shred, using his own tissue to cause more hydrostatic damage..."

The words washed over Rolf Dettrick. He was only murkily aware of their passage. He had no idea who was speaking or where he was. Somebody had thought he was awake and capable of processing information. Maybe it was the medical chatter of a TV show, seeping into his brain. Somebody had seen his eyes crack open and recklessly assumed Rolf was conscious.

Fine, thought Rolf. *Let them take my pulse and shine lights in my eyes. My pupils don't dilate unless I order them to.*

Voice #1 spieled onward: "Small bowel is one of the most common injuries in GSW. This was what we call visceral/vascular. He took twenty units of blood. Organ failure is not a danger here but sepsis was. As you can see, we performed a laparotomy and were able to close the skin."

"I don't think he can hear you," said Voice #2.

"He's aware," said Voice #1. "Maybe you can talk to him."

Ginny moved up on the starboard side of the hospital bed. It was a private room at St. Joe's in Burbank, with two CHASE men right outside the door—Bixler, the import from Santa Barbara, and Kolascheck, the

259

other uninjured shooter from the fracas at the Tropical Paradise Motel. Both men were eager and overcompensatory; they were the palace guards for the new head of CHASE, after all. The hows and whys of the new order interested them no more than another bogus Presidential election. What prompted their fealty was their recent battle experience alongside Rolf, which they hoped would be noted and rewarded in due time.

Long live the King.

Other CHASE men were on the corridors, the lobby, the elevators. They had been fully briefed by Ginny as acting point. Should Alma Acevedo waltz in, there would be no misidentification, no hesitation, and no screwups.

The cover story had swum together as follows: Alma had taken Rolf hostage at Sherman Oaks PetCare and murdered James Smith after killing a Wilsoni man, Marco Franchi. Ginny had rescued Rolf. Alma escaped during the ensuing exchange, sacrificing her accomplice, David Vollmand, who was a wanted man by the Wilsoni group. Ginny gave them Vollmand to cure the loss of Franchi and fulfill the side deal Rolf had made with Max Wilsoni.

It was a crackerjack story because it was nearly ninety percent true.

"Where are they?" Rolf said from deep within his pool of medication and dressage.

"Alma has slipped the grid," Ginny said. "Vollmand belongs to Wilsoni, now."

"Good." To expel a word was an effort, but Rolf was a fighter.

"Thank you for choosing me as Chase Bravo, sir."

"You earned it. And if you didn't, you will."

"What do you want to do?"

Rolf inhaled slowly, nasally, then swallowed. "Nothing."

"Sir?" She had already assigned a crew to watch Wilsoni's men, hoping her nemesis might blunder into a pointless grab for David Vollmand, an asset who no longer had any value except as a lure for her rematch with Alma.

"You don't have to prove you're better than her," Rolf said.

"I'm already better than her. Would you object if I took her out on my own?"

"No. It would be a relief. Any other recommendations?"

"Terminate Bumblebee, sir. When James Smith asked for a recommendation, that was the one I made."

"Why?"

"Project Archangel. It needs to be un-created."

"No objection there, either. CHASE is going to change big, Ginny. You sure you don't want a larger role?"

"I'd prefer you to be the exec. You have the skill to upgun the entire organization. I don't do well with politics or admin."

"But your operational choices, while I'm laid up here like a steak slowly spoiling, have been excellent."

"I prefer the field. Sir."

"You prefer to be my hammer. My bulldozer. Being a loyalist is easy. Being competent is much harder, and being excellent is rare. I need smart doers, not yes men or women."

With some labor Rolf was able to minutely rearrange his position on the hated bed, in anticipation of a meal he did not want to eat, but would consume per doctor's orders to resurrect himself as quickly as he could.

"Where did Max's men take Vollmand?"

"Someplace called the Falcon," said Ginny. "So our spotters say. I think it's an old movie theater west of here. Shut down or abandoned or condemned."

Here came an orderly with a dinner tray. Both were equally nondescript.

"Update me whenever I'm conscious," Rolf half-joked.

"Roger that," Ginny said.

They had no way of knowing that everyone at the Falcon was already dead.

A Night at the Cinema

True conspiratorial thinking requires four conditions:

1: Belief that an agency is covering up facts.

2: Belief that those facts can be hidden successfully, even in an age of transparency, full disclosure, and a populace that loves betraying secrets.

3: Belief that whatever agency is involved in a coverup is itself culpable—that the coverup is in their own self-interest.

4: Belief that the truth is invisible to "lesser" people, thus requiring individuals with special perceptions to tell everyone else what is really going on, no matter how illogical.

The human need for drama is key, more so than evidence. Most people are predisposed to believe dramatic events have equally dramatic triggers. This makes for a more emotionally satisfying quest. Just ask Don Quixote. Ask any UFOlogist. It's why people love happy endings.

It's why people watch movies—not as I did, to scrutinize the technical presentation, but to reaffirm their worldview by willingly allowing their emotions to be manipulated by fictional contrivances.

It's all popcorn fun and plot twists until it happens to you. That was catchy and pithy and I had probably said it already, failing to divert any captor with my pluck.

Between beatings I learned we were inside the husk of the old Falcon movie theater on Vineland, near Victory Boulevard, another neighborhood cinema that had fallen to the juggernaut of multiplexes and had been awaiting some kind of rebirth since 2009. The former Studio Theatre, on Ventura in Studio City, had become a Bookstar, of all things—one dying business replaced by another. At least they kept the marquee. I wasn't all that far from what was left of Mango Joy, or for that matter, my apartment.

The big, lifeless screen had a large diagonal rip leading from the upper left corner. The curtains were reeled back and shrouded in dust. The floor was littered with the detritus of some half-assed deconstruction and several of the rearward rows of seats had been removed. Wilsoni's men had bound me down front row center. When my view was not engorged with leering faces (silhouetted due to the work lights shadowing them) or incoming fists or implements, all I could see was that vast white expanse of dirty, wounded movie screen. It sagged unsung and unmourned, awaiting the day it would be finally shoved aside for something better. No one needed it any more.

In my fugue I wondered if it could feel pain.

The Falcon had opened its doors in 1940 during the Second World War as a neighborhood theater to serve the booming suburbia of the San Fernando Valley. Still years away from the threat of television, the Falcon had been a social nexus during the period when "a night at the cinema" meant just that—most of an evening, absorbed by newsreels, cartoons, double features and even singalongs and raffles. Today, we all lived in the future and all the socializing you might want or need could be held in the palm of your hand.

Or so others told us, as they encouraged us to buy more glittery toys so we could all participate in our own self-destruction, front row.

Reduced into proper consuming clusters based on the obsolete model of the nuclear family, people fretted about issues beyond their psychology—faith, ego, the *why am I here?* game—while jailing themselves into double-locked bastilles from which their worldly desires could be obtained by clicking an icon. People were more isolated from one another than ever before; their shared experience demoted to images on someone else's iPhone. Look at any dinner table and see how many people are staring at a screen instead of each other, lobotomized into narcotic dependence on a device. The only phase our corporate masters had overlooked was the actual transorbital psychosurgery.

Thanks to the new century's smokescreen of terrorism, which flattened human rights in the name of some wraithlike common good that never once revealed itself, the idea of electronic implants at birth for positive ID had been mooted more than once. As Daisy had said, the ordinary citizen's job was to keep grind-stoning, reproducing, and hoping for better...because the only way to affect genuine change was to jeopardize someone else's fourth-quarter profits.

Enter the conspirators, always a step ahead of the conspiracy theorists they always managed to regularly discredit via ridicule. Enter CHASE, and the dozens of organizations like it.

And what had Daisy and I done? We had embraced the future, leashing ourselves to transponders, no different from nervous teens seeking a justice of the peace with a fluid conception of legal age.

Contemporary film theory held that the modern trend toward "chaos cinema" was a natural evolution, an outgrowth of "classic cinema" filtered through "intensified continuity" to become dragster fuel espresso instead of watery java. The product became too fast, too loud, hyperactive, overstuffed with 3D and computer-generated ridiculum, assaultive with promiscuous cutting and shaky-cam, allowing its attention-deficit audience to sense action but not experience it. Chaos cinema was an event, like a bullet train collision, instead of a narrative, like a story.

Chaos cinema bullied you until you gave up. My Minsky's Moment had been expanded to feature length.

Americans were said to love competition. What that really meant was they loved reductive list-making. Your favorite songs, your top ten movies, your "likes," followed by a winnow-down of your chosen

David J. Schow

three out of five, always with the goal of pinpointing a Number One that somehow defined your tastes and personality. Who won the Super Bowl, the Oscar or the Nobel. These completely arbitrary or corrupt gold standards were then compared to your picks in order to determine where you fit in among your fellow ground pounders.

Two men—actually little more than two phantom voices in my congested perception—were debating who was the sexiest woman in pop culture this year. Their opinionation had brought them to another cherished benchmark in low thought, the idea of an ultimate battle royale. One thing versus another thing—who would win?—which could yield a new champion to depose. Superman versus Mighty Mouse. Beatles versus Stones. Stockings versus pantyhose. Coke versus Pepsi. And so on, unto mundane insanity.

The current contenders were two hotties apparently named Jowly and Anus Ton, which hit my ear like a bad translation of Japanese movie monster names, the way Gojira had become Godzilla, which I knew because I had worked on that DVD about the big fire-breathing city-stomper. Assorted fornicatory attributes were duly attacked and defended with colorfully specific crudities. The assessments were very much like one of those conversations you can't help overhearing by drunks at the next table, the kind that makes you reconsider suicide versus homicide.

Good tits. Not so good. No ass to speak of. I'd do her. Nah, she's had like how many babies? I'd still do both of 'em. I'd fuck her till her holes connect.

This junk mail drifted through my ears in snatches (you should pardon the expression), fragmented and distorted, looping back on itself like print-through on a bad soundtrack. It was the language of my delirium, the only target that could distract from the waves of pain.

There is a minor endorphin release in the human brain associated with the cessation of an irritant. The oncoming firetruck siren stops wailing, the baby stops crying, the alarm clock clicks to SNOOZE, and your brain goes *ahhh.*

The two guys stopped talking entirely. My mind was a whipped cat hiding deep in a closet, balled up and waiting to die, so the silence took an eon to register.

Nobody in the Falcon Theater was talking anymore.

The CD player had come from a pawnshop. It was a decade and a half out of style and resembled the head of a robot or a big mechanical fly, whose "eyes" were the convex screens over the bass kickers, a boombox extra cued by flipping a toggle marked MEGABASS.

The CD in the player dish had been burned from downloaded music files. First up was thirty seconds of silence. Next came a blistering Christmas carol by a band called Peen, "Ho, Ho, Holocaust"—a six-minute firebomb of sludge featuring a lot of screaming. It segued into Honey Hole's "Pull My Finger" just in case extra time was required.

The smoke packets were homemade, the old but venerable way: sugar, potassium nitrate (from the fertilizer aisle of a hardware store) and baking soda. The fuses were toilet paper strips marinated in the slurry scraped from the heads of strike-anywhere matches.

The Molotov cocktail was homemade, too, containing a slush of gasoline and shredded Styrofoam, which equaled hillbilly napalm.

The cellular blocker box had come from a "spyveillance" store on Magnolia Avenue called Gadget Supershop. Powered by a stepped-up 9-volt battery similar to the voltage magnifiers used in stun guns, the box could obliterate any cell-based communications signal within a 100-foot radius. Fifty-five bucks. This sort of toy was illegal to own in California, but easy to obtain. It was compact, practical, and way too much fun, and if you did not believe that, you had not tried one in a restaurant.

Or a movie theater.

Daisy had secreted the CD player in the back of the Falcon, where the rows of seats had been removed. There had been no time to configure elaborate radio detonators for multiple timed ignition, so she had to rely on her ability to scuttle unobtrusively between the rows of remaining theater seats, lighting her one-minute fuses and leaving smoke packets in a strategic scatter. By the time the smoke from the fuses themselves was seen or smelled, it would already be too late to do anything about them.

She knew CHASE had eyes on the Falcon, but getting past that outer ring of passive surveillance had been elementary, as in grade school. If there were no CHASE people inside, then the spyboys with binoculars would not be authorized to intercede. They were there to watch, and Daisy had her ingress and egress planned to bypass their notice.

She moved in darkness, against blackness, sleeved in nonreflective midnight from head to toe, less visible than her own shadow, only her eyes exposed, her boots tightly-bound to her legs. Stick-on foam cushions—the kind you insert to relieve foot pain—were attached upside-down to her soles and matted out. Her second-skin fabric gloves featured neoprene-nubbled palms for tactile positivity. The index fingers were shorn for better trigger control. The wristlets were rubber-banded tight.

Her darkbound hand arched up from the sea of seats like a languid, curious cobra, holding the remote control for the CD player. She pressed PLAY.

In the remaining thirty seconds, she distributed the rest of the smoke packets, always moving.

"Ho, Ho, Holocaust" went off like a thermobaric attack, attracting the immediate notice of the group of men near the stage who were busy torturing David Vollmand.

"What the fuck is this happy horseshit?" said Hickey, who had to shout to be heard.

"It's Max, he's fuckin with us," said Palermo, the short, simian-looking one.

"Giorgio—find that and kill it!"

Giorgio already had his gun out, and huffed up the aisle with a pained parental expression. *You kids turn that shit down.*

When the first packet began to emit clouds of thick white smoke, Daisy flamed the center of the auditorium with the Molotov. The blocker box was switched on and left behind.

The cartridges in both her .45 autopistols—one Smith for each hand—were Buffalo Bore 230-grain flat-points so powerful they required a swap-out of the recoil springs to 22-pounders (from the pistol's normal factory eighteen). There was no such thing as a "one shot stop" or a mystical magic bullet that could compensate for training, experience and placement. The .45 cartridge relied on frontal mass and caliber for effectiveness, not velocity or bullet expansion. The Buffalos were also packed with low-flash powder that could help preserve your night sight. They were hot, devastating loads.

Because Daisy would be working close-quarter.

Somebody shouted *"Fire!"* needlessly. The only two extinguishers in the Falcon had been used and not refilled years ago, their needles stalled at zero.

Daisy shot Giorgio in the side of the head. He vanished into a fog-bank and did not reappear.

A few panic shots, as the men below tried to rally. Daisy was already scooting across to the other aisle. There were seven men she had to track. Six, less Giorgio. She could not have known of Max Wilsoni's earlier boast of having "twenty guys here," nor that the head count was distributed over rotating shifts, which decreased in manpower as David Vollmand proved less a tempting lure and more a line of inquiry that was not going to pan out. Plus, Max had other business to transact while in the City of Angels, and needed his own tour support. Barring a surprise—some loaf walking in with coffee for the rest, or an extra gunman hidden like a spare tire—Daisy's running count was accurate. Seven minus one.

The first four were easy, in all the smoke and confusion. Headshots all around, with Daisy as a jack-in-the-box Grim Reaper. That one shot stop myth pertained to body mass, not to a projectile that would blow a hole in your skull as fat as a beer can and burst out the far side in a geyser of brain and bone.

The final two tough guys were a bit cagier. They went back-to-back, one of them targeting David.

"Stop or he dies," said the man, yelling into uncertain space. The threat was empty; if they had been authorized to kill David Vollmand, it would have already happened, either by overzealousness or "mistake." Their eyes were watering from the smoke. The whole place was eagerly catching fire and the light had turned stroboscopic.

"Ho, Ho, Holocaust" kept playing even as the boombox cooked.

Daisy was eight feet away from them.

She fired both pistols at once on a intersecting vector. The man who had shouted lost his mind. Lost everything, in fact, from the collarbones up, as the two incoming slugs crossed the X mark above his soft palate. His head blew apart like a dandelion, ceasing to exist so quickly there was no time for an autonomic trigger pull. The concussion knocked his partner off true. The second man spun and tried to fire at the source, but Daisy had already moved again. He was staggered by the gore from his buddy's neck, which was still pattering down as he turned. His buddy got into his eyes.

Daisy fired a little too quickly, hitting the second man only in the chest. He fell down anyway. Daisy vaulted the final row of seats and put a bonus round into his head. Seven, all tolled.

Before reinforcements. Before backup. Before outside interference. But for the noise, no alert had been raised. Even if one of the unlucky seven had called for help, his cellphone would have given him a sad display of no bars.

"Hey," David said, on another planet somewhere, pummeled and mis-tracking. "Now I *know* I must be dreaming…"

He was so limp when Daisy sliced him free that she knew she would have to laundry-sack him out. He was well and fully marinated but had sustained no broken bones, per the torturer's craft.

The whole massacre made the news as *Mob Drug Deal Gone Bad.*

The Ides
of August

Rolf Dettrick stepped out of the scalding multidirectional shower stall, feeling...*refreshed* was not quite the right word, but *stable*. He was proud he had managed a light, low-impact workout without blowing a seam. No burnouts, not yet. The bullet pucker scarring his chest resembled an auxiliary navel. In the past four weeks its color had become less angry, the danger of infection tamped down by a Big Gulp of antibiotics. When Rolf strode he could still feel an ominous interior "pull" on his right side, a stiffness that became more pronounced if he was fatigued.

More gray, at his temples, there in the steam-speckled mirror. Was that possible, in so brief a time?

Christ, he was only thirty-five when James Smith had assigned him to sweep up Alma Acevedo, and he was *still* thirty-five—his next birthday was seven months distant. He felt ninety. The stress was bleaching his hair.

He had seen his protégé comport herself exceptionally, when aligned against him. A source of cold pride, yes, but also a nagging blinker of undone wetwork. Seated in an ergonomic chair at Smith's sterile glass desk, Rolf knew he owed his former boss closure. CHASE no longer cared about Alma Acevedo, Lily Tamario, or Daisy Villareal. CHASE had new mosquitoes to squash, courtesy of a Fed contract that had sanctioned the expungement of a phalanx of Internet troublemakers who just would not shut up about the current economic downturn. Daisy—ex-Chase Lima—was a hangnail; yesterday's crisis. James Smith had gone active once again, after years at this very desk, just to take her out. It had cost him his life. It had won Rolf the Alpha position.

Rolf knew he couldn't let the issue go. Smith would not have. So Ginny Stark, the new Chase Bravo, had received a text: *Call Home.*

"You're looking fit," Ginny said as she entered the inner sanctum.

"I feel rusty," Rolf admitted.

"The desk suits you."

Constrictive clothing was still a minor bother. Rolf was wearing track gear and running shoes, hoping to steal another treadmill hour. He seemed to go through drinking water by the gallon and was thirsty all the time, now.

"So, Alma." Ginny cut right to the main course, arms folded almost as if she was that cocksure.

"Stop reading my mind."

"I can't, you know." She offered him a conciliatory smile. "I get impressions, that's all. It's swarming around you like a neon cocoon."

"Great. I might as well make a video and put it on YouTube."

"Something like, 'Please come home, all is forgiven, we love you honey, now stand right there so we can shoot you'?"

Rolf puzzled his lips together, enjoying the dalliance. "Hey, that might work."

"Anything?"

"Nothing. Zero hits. Bupkis. What the hell, she never existed in the first place, right?"

"Nothing," Ginny repeated, as though something vital yet elusive had been overlooked. "All this time, you've been waiting for her to come back here and clean house."

"And I realized that was escalation thinking," said Rolf. "Like in some movie where the bad guy headquarters has to blow up, or there's nothing an audience can recognize as an ending."

274

"She wanted out, she got out, and she wants to stay out. But sooner or later, her method will betray her again, just like it did the first time. If CHASE notices or cares, we play the whole game all over again. But I think *you* think the greater danger is that she will eventually join up with some other club whose interests are not CHASE-friendly, and there we are, back again."

"She can't *not* be who she is," said Rolf, steepling his fingers.

"No more than me," Ginny said. "She just obfuscates by creating additional identities. At our core, we're the same."

"That's why I called you in. You and me. We stamp this done. I'm not a hundred percent, but I'm good to go."

Ginny experienced a weird flashback to her first meet with James Smith, regarding Alma. "I'm ready now," she said.

"Then let's go retire Project Archangel together."

"Smells like Limburger dick," said Carlotta from her bed as Rolf and Ginny approached. "Same cheese, different pig."

The Bee had her oral prosthetic in place, which seemed a lewd joke all by itself. Her pallor was livid, as though she was decomposing already, had cyanosis, or had been mistreated with silver nitrate tincture. She resembled a shrunken blue-gray alien slowly sinking into a bog of sheets.

"Carlotta," Rolf said by way of introduction, "meet Ginny." Per Smith's antediluvian weapons protocol, neither of them were armed in Carlotta's presence.

"Oh, the *other* one. Enough sweet talk. Which one of you fucked Johnnie to death? Did you both do him, lips and hips?"

"Smith," Rolf clarified, for Ginny's benefit.

"Ole Johnnie bit the big weenie and ate his own poop on Hawaiian rolls all the way to hell," Carlotta cackled. "No need to tell me *that*. You should have gotten me a thank-you card."

"We have James Smith to thank for having you as our guest all these years," Rolf said. How had Smith ever feigned respect for this woman?

"He tried to fuck me for nearly forty years. I *told* that asshole that chasing after that Alma's pretty pink pussy would be the end of him. Did he listen? *Noooo.* He yanked his own peepee until it ripped off. Now *you're* here. What're you, the new cock on the block?" Her hand pawed around for a call button. "I want my goddamned morphine."

Rolf gently moved the call stick out of range. "We need you clear, Carlotta. Ginny needs to ask you a question."

"What's wrong with your eye?" said Carlotta, her own blues rotating to consider Ginny.

"Defect in the iris," Ginny said, even as she realized that thanks to the UV eyecups she and Rolf were wearing, Carlotta could not *see* her eyes. By then Carlotta had reached to grab her hand.

"Well, shit on me," Carlotta said. "You're *her.* The rest of Archangel. I knew your mother. Veronica."

"And she knew your daughter, Ingrid."

It was an internal hit that made all of Bumblebee's ninety-six years surface on her face. Suddenly her frailty was exposed and obvious. The sclera of her eyes seemed to turn ochre as Rolf watched, the aftertint of a bad bruise.

"She's dead," Carlotta said, her gaze indicting Rolf now, since Smith was no longer available.

Ginny kept hold of Carlotta's withered claw. "I need you to tell me where Alma is. An impression. Anything."

Carlotta seemed to lose her bearings, the sharpness in her wizened gaze going vague. "Beautiful," she said.

Rolf let Ginny take the reins. "Yes, she was beautiful."

"Not was. Is."

Ginny moved close enough to take the old woman's face in her hands, gently. "And she loved you."

"Loves me," Carlotta said, her eyes blurring with tears.

"I'm right here, Grandma," Ginny said. "I still love you."

Ginny was smiling warmly. Carlotta, confused, sought answers in this younger woman's face. It was then that Rolf saw something unprecedented—a ghost of hope in Carlotta's features, an echo of something long-lost.

Ginny's thumbs wiped teardrops from the corners of Carlotta's eyes. "Where?" she said.

"This is a trick." Carlotta's vision swept toward Rolf.

"Where?" Ginny said. Her thumbs moved over Carlotta's eyes and began to press down. "Tell me."

Ginny's thumbnails were more than well-manicured. They were sharp enough to kill; nobody would X-ray her hands when boarding a commercial flight.

"*No...*" Carlotta wheezed. She was hardly capable of struggle.

Ginny's thumbnails sank into the upper orbits of Carlotta's eyes. Thin crescents of blood appeared but did not flow.

"Concentrate," Ginny said.

Carlotta's repertoire of sexual taunts was so insignificant that they would never merit mention in her file, not even as a scribbled one-liner about what a batty, cantankerous old lady she could be. She was nerve-dead by the time Ginny's thumbs were embedded knuckle-deep. Rolf heard the death rattle, which was too weak for the video monitors to record. Ginny blotted the goop on her hands using Carlotta's own sheet. Her face was flushed, in the manner of a leech after a good feed.

"Alma is up in the mountains."

"The last time we had this conversation," said Max Wilsoni on the speakerphone, "I lost men. My brother practically left me in a ditch with my balls in my mouth."

"All the more reason," said Rolf, happy that he did not have to deal with this cokehead weasel face-to-face. He knew the names of each of the Wilsoni casualties Alma had racked up in California, starting with Marco Franchi. Then Kurland, Giorgio, Weaver, Palermo, Hickey, Brooks, Fanelli—all killed at the Falcon Theater while Max had absented himself for cocktails and fellatio. The only surviving Wilsoni men had been the sniper, Mario DuFleck (who had been hospitalized by Giorgio for shooting too soon), and a participant in the Hollywood Mailbox Associates stakeout named Babcoq, first name Moses, who had reported the Falcon blaze to Max.

Rolf knew the names because both DuFleck and Babcoq seemed like good CHASE prospects, as he had promised under duress.

"The playing field has changed," Rolf continued. "I got the intel and now I'm giving it to you. We are narrowing in on both the woman who killed your men, and the man who brought down your father. If you don't think that's important enough, I should talk to your brother Augustus."

"No." The speaker voice buzzed coldly. "You should talk to *me*."

"As far as DuFleck and Babcoq are concerned, it is strictly elective. But you are their superior. I come to you first."

"I want Vollmand," Max said. "You bet both your ass cheeks I want him. The bitch, too. I want to put a gun in their mouth and blow the backs of their heads off and then piss in the hole. How many guys you need?"

"Now let me tell you what I want," said Rolf. "We've incurred casualties, too. Would you men object to seconding to CHASE?"

"What, you mean like, follow your guy's orders? Shit, dude, I'll *order* 'em to do that. One thing, though."

"Name it."

"I'm going, too. And we're takin pictures. That I can show to my brother."

"Snapshots make wonderful souvenirs."

"Fuckin A. My guys gotta *see* me there, in charge. Not like at that fuckin movie theater. You want the job done, call Max Wilsoni, that's what people will say. Goddamned right, I'm in. If you don't want their heads, I'll take 'em."

Max Wilsoni was still a pissant loudmouth out of his depth, which was what Rolf had counted on. All bristled up and ready to rumble. Equally ready to be disposed of. Hell, Rolf might even have DuFleck or Babcoq execute Max as an entree to CHASE.

"We are speaking the same language exactly," Rolf said.

Sylvanweir

If you want the homey small-town fakeness of a postcard mountain retreat, clean crisp high-altitude air, hiking paths, spas and craft shows, you go to Idyllwild to recharge your inner nature child. If you want privacy and can muster a fair level of luck versus persistence—and know the right people to ask—you may chance across an authentic hideaway like Sylvanweir. Both are buried high in the San Jacinto mountains southwest of Palm Springs. Idyllwild is accessed via the junction of Route 243 (the Banning-Idyllwild Panoramic Highway) with the 74 (the Idyllwild National Forest Highway); abundant you-can't-miss-it signage roads with names like Idyllwild Pine Cove and Idyllwild National Forest Highway.

Sylvanweir has no such markers, brochures, publicity, or bike rentals. There is no Chamber of Commerce, no traffic lights or crosswalks. In fact, there are no sidewalks. It has little public signage, a single barebones inn, and a coffee shop attached to a gas station. The staff at these enterprises is all local.

There is no sign proclaiming that you are now entering Sylvanweir, or any indicator that you have just left it.

The San Bernardino National Forest has many truck trails that spur from the 243 (renamed the Esperanza Firefighters Memorial Highway in 2007) to access smaller towns such as Pine Cove. The fork that leads to Sylvanweir has always been unmarked, because Sylvanweir never incorporated. It dropped off most maps around 1959, considered to be another wannabe township that died, hence, a ghost town.

Residences exist, mostly log cabin-style homes that tend to blend with the foliage, built back in gullies or shrouded by forest. What portions remain most visible to the passing eye are notably unwelcoming. The café features a "C" health certification prominently displayed in its front window. The inn advises *No Vacancies*. The gas station evokes the last-chancers from chainsaw massacre movies, the kind where you'd be likely to find a timber rattler coiled in the restroom's empty towel dispenser. The rest resembles frontier false-front flats erected for some Western shoot, then abandoned to the weather, ingloriously bunched on one side of the access road as though broomed there, a spasm of clapboard that never endured long enough to become census-designated.

Sylvanweir rejects the eye. *Honey, can we stop somewhere else? I can hold it. Idyllwild is less than an hour away...*

"Sylvan" means pastoral, abounding in trees. A "weir" is a small overflow dam used to alter the flow characteristics of a river or stream—a barrier.

After civil twilight the temperature could plunge into the twenties, but it was too early yet for snow, which locked Sylvanweir into isolation from October through March. The mountaintops were often fogged in with low cloud cover, and as each year died the precipitation made the roads icy and impassable. It was in mountain passes such as these that Westward Expansion settlers had perished, slowly freezing to death, breaking their wagons up for firewood and starving until they ate each other.

There were no charming rustics congregated around pot-bellied stoves here, no visitor guides to local points of interest because there weren't any, and an absolute zero Celsius sense of welcome.

And Daisy liked it that way.

Her stride was back and she no longer had to hitch to compensate for her gunshot wound. That could throw your spine out of whack and cause back problems. Sylvanweir was so quiet that it made you aware of all the noise you could make by merely existing. You could hear your clothing rustle and your own breathing commanded your attention, even when the wind was haunting the trees and the aural backdrop of flowing water provided a consistent form of white noise.

The very few adventurers who happened upon Sylvanweir by accident never lingered long enough to actually *look* at it.

She could hear every breath Kingi took as the dog trotted along beside her in perfect leash discipline. Every inquisitive whine, every fart.

People anxious to find somewhere more interesting than Sylvanweir would never notice how well the main swath of road was paved. They would never blunder deep enough into the uncharted forest to stumble across the rather sophisticated satellite dish array camouflaged there.

The vehicle that had brought Daisy here was clean of tracking devices, its GPS destroyed, its LoJack disabled, its gutwork swept for bugs. She had stolen the characterless white Jetta from a Toluca Lake pub, early on a Saturday night, and swapped out the plates for currently-stickered tags boosted from the holding corral of a North Hollywood collision shop. The Jetta was stashed in a barn well back from the roadway that led to the inn, under camo netting and padlock.

The trusty S&W .45, one of the pair she had used for the Falcon Theater turkey shoot, was warm against her hipbone inside her coat. Her rucksack contained groceries and medical supplies, the latter obtained from a local character named Doc Taylor, although that was not the woman's real name.

Nobody in Sylvanweir went by their former, real-world handle. The name Daisy had chosen for herself, from a Xeroxed list of the most common names in America, had been Maria Miller—the "Maria" in deference to her gene pool, the "Miller" seeming a better choice than "Brown," which struck her too much like a backhanded ethnic joke. In a supreme irony, the place did not boast a single "Smith."

Just to screw up the symmetry, "David" was number six on the list, but Sylvanweir already had a David—Dave Wilson, barkeep at the inn, a gruff sonofabitch indeed—so David Vollmand had transformed into Donald Martin at Daisy's behest.

Their transition was very smooth, since Maria Miller and Donald Martin had been sponsored by a local resident, Charles Johnson.

Kingi sidetracked to whizz on a conifer stump. Good thing they had stopped the Scrabble of names before they got around to re-christening the Shep, too.

"What is it with all the pissing?" Daisy asked the dog, who paid attention as though he might voice a reply. "You piss little squirts everywhere, like you're portioning out single-serves from a storage tank, then as soon as you're back inside you slurp up *exactly* as much as you just pissed out. So, in theory, you should never have to go out."

Kingi waited this out. Then he discovered something else, invisible to Daisy, that smelled *fascinating*.

About the only thing that could get you arrested or ejected from Sylvanweir—by Sheriff Bill Thompson—was talking about your past. This was contrary to human nature, especially if you were undistinguished. Think of the way the idiot ahead of you in the checkout line sprays personal information around like a puppy marking hydrants. They roll their eyes, flirt with the cashier, and emit bon mots designed to entertain and sympathize with the other mooks stranded in line, little observations about current affairs and everyone else's groceries intended to elicit a fleeting commonality. *We're all in this together and ain't things weird, neighbor?* They say their phone number out loud, in front of strangers, when their club card fails to process. They wonder how their personal information gets hijacked after leaving their mail on a countertop or flashing their MasterCard in plain view. They create mind-numbingly simplistic passwords and PIN numbers. They misplace their keys with astonishing regularity. They're even worse when they drink.

"Hey," said Linda Moore, on her way to fire up the grill at the inn's coffee shop. Linda was still in her mid-thirties but Daisy knew she had been a Sylvanweir resident for almost nine years. Petite, cute, blonde, a nerd girl who had been an anorexic as a teenager. She was at good heft now, and always appeared studious, as though cramming for an exam. "What a beautiful dog." She checked out Kingi's package. "I mean, what a handsome boy!"

"Yeah, he's a pistol."

Kingi abandoned the smear of crud on the road to commence sniffing Linda in earnest. A dog's nose has 220 million olfactory receptors, over forty times more than humans, plus an additional scent-processing bundle called Jacobsen's Organ. Sniffing behavior is actually a conscious disruption of the dog's normal breathing pattern. Data was conveyed to a proportionately large olfactory lobe of the brain. Recently it had been discovered that dogs could whiff out certain types of tumors in human beings. Daisy wondered what kind of pictures were formed by smells inside Kingi's coffin head.

"You're a good boy, aren't you?" said Linda, ruffling him.

Kingi flopped out his foot-long tongue to agree that yes, he was in fact a very good boy.

"Come on by for pot roast if you don't have anything special planned," said Linda. "No microwave shit, I promise."

What sort of plans would anyone have in Sylvanweir? Drag races, the opera, a Shriner's meeting? There was nothing here.

You could discuss anything you wanted with the other people living in Sylvanweir, except for your backstory. Where you were from and what you had done—anything that could be construed as evidence—were verboten. Over the years, there had been a few residents unenamored of the program.

But they had all been buried, deep in the enchanted forest.

Just Call Me Don

I watched more satellite TV in four weeks than I would have thought tolerable, even with 500 channels of crap to sort. I spent more time staring at a screen now than I ever had in perusing the same DVDs, over and over. Some of the fare was actually material I had vetted, such as a horror "threequel" in the *Piece by Piece* series, subtitled *The Choicest Cut.*

Five MORE friends on YET ANOTHER spring break...

The jock, the slut, the rich asshole, the fifth wheel and the nice girl who Rambos up to become the Last Woman Standing, or, in horror film parlance, the Final Girl. Whose survival enables the fourquel, or whose ancestors can provide the fodder for what had charmingly become known as a "premake."

Piece by Piece also occupied the cinematic subset of the "found footage" movie, meaning that most of the presentation was of the shaky-cam variety, with little concern for lighting, framing, continuity, or coherence. This trend skyrocketed when *The Blair Witch Project*, in 1999, returned nearly a quarter of a billion dollars on a budget skirting sixty grand, all-in. The spunky independent movie galvanized legitimate studios top-heavy with waste, perks, and bloated flops and ushered in the present day wisdom that films "needed" to be shot for less than a million...or *over* a hundred million. Anything in between was chum. This sort of business acumen wouldn't play even in a nuthouse, but it was

287

still gospel to many Hollywood types who by normal standards would never be considered insane or irrational.

Add the impingement of chaos cinema, and the whole circus became a three-ring cluster migraine.

My life had dwindled down to other people's programming.

There was plenty of time for me to run the entire gamut of Type II trauma—the cycles of shock, guilt, depression, terror, anxiety, irritability and hostility; self-blame, loss of control, stress, deep denial, flashbacks, and just a tiny sliver of substance abuse, courtesy of pills and alcohol. My face was still puffy and looked as if it had been used to sand a table. It reminded me of a Bondoed car after a wreck, not stronger at the broken points (as Hemingway had suggested, but then, look how he turned out), but spackled, deceptive in its patched-up wholeness. The immediate pain had subsided into a symphony of rainbow bruising, muscle and joint agony, and spasms of fitful sleep that were more akin to hallucinogenic coma. Smarter people than me had specified stages for what was called "macrotrauma."

Stage One was the first seventy-two hours following the damage. Inflammation, pain, swelling, redness, the whole menu. I had no specific memory of this part.

Stage Two was the "regeneration" phase, when fibroblasts begin to synthesize scar tissue. Collagen forms. Wounds contract. Capillaries begin to link up again via "budding." I dimly remembered seeing a car interior from a ninety-degree angle, prone on the backseat. Daisy had been driving the car.

Stage Two could take anywhere from two days to six weeks. Stage Three demanded even more downtime, as muscle tissue is notoriously slow to repair. Myogenesis and fibrosis are dangers. This is called the "remodeling" phase. Under ideal conditions, another three weeks to a year, and you carry the twitches and pings with you for the rest of your life.

We had embarked on some bizarre variety of vacation. Log cabins. Hushed conferences. A lady doctor prodding and palpating. Medicines, dressings, dope and disinfectant. Horrific, jolting wakeups. Night sweats. The TV as my babysitter. I had always wondered why Alex Trebek was never a contestant on *Jeopardy*, himself. Maybe he didn't really know so much, but he sure talked like he did.

The sliced-and-diced teen hotties of *Piece by Piece* had no problem with trauma. They were above it, or beyond feeling it. They kept running and fighting until confirmed on-camera kill by farm implement. I envied their apparent ability to compartmentalize pain.

Max Wilsoni's men, true to specs, had not broken any of my bones. What they had accomplished was an extended physical pounding almost elegant in its boundaries. It had come in phases, itself, and absorbed hours until Daisy somehow got me clear. I thought of the waterboarding spell she had mentioned, and wondered if it had been better or worse. The Cube—more or less painful?

Her whole life: how much trauma had she processed, how long had it taken, and is any such hurt ever truly repaired?

"What's up, Don?"

That was me, now; my secret club code-name.

Daisy entered the cabin with a backpack full of forage.

"You just missed my benchpress," I said. "Four hundred pounds, clean. I think I'll go for the Olympics." I had lifted one finger a quarter of an inch to acknowledge her entrance.

"Doc's stopping by later," she said. "On her rounds."

That was good. I liked Doc Taylor. She had a safecracker's touch and a wild thundercloud of curly white hair she tried to tame by yanking back into a billowy horsetail. Calm gray eyes. Dentures. Short, compact. Healthy front porch. Anywhere from a weathered late forties to a robust mid-sixties. I'm pretty sure she had seen me naked at least twice. She had excavated the pet chips from my leg, and Daisy's, before they could travel too far astray in the fat tissue of the inner thigh. She popped them out like pimentos. Devices such as tracking chips were a big no-no in Sylvanweir. Fido and Spot had been crushed underheel long before I regained any sort of coherence. That was okay; Fido and Spot had done their jobs.

In the lobby of the inn, a fair distance from the first of the cabins, I remembered a painting on the wall, lit as to convey significance. It was an impasto oil study of an old hand-plow, rusted and sundered, its wood split, half-buried in a trove of winter snow. It seemed very forlorn, that disused chunk of equipment. It wanted to tell stories, like the sunbeaten faces of Native American grandfathers. It hinted that it could still turn a field if it really had to. Some of the peaks of pigment on the canvas were as thick as whipped cream; it was an original. The artist's signature was a tiny O with a sprig bisecting the right side, like a tipped-over letter Q. It was barely perceptible, rendered a half-shade darker than the rest of the background.

I recalled Daisy saying "look at that," some days or weeks earlier.

The proprietor of the inn, a burly Gothic Santa named Will Green, was engaged in telling Daisy about his "show room" while I stayed in my collapsible wheelchair and stared at the painting, wanting to walk into it and become lost. Apparently the show room was a dire tenement shithole intended to deter passing looky-loos from lingering in Sylvanweir longer than it took to turn their cars around. The real accommodations—the cabins—were for "real" guests.

Inside my head, I was in the same place as that forsaken farm implement, which would never know the glory of silencing a squawking teen cliché in some movie.

Daisy shaved my face with an electric razor to prevent my follicles from becoming ingrown where sterilization and meds needed regular application. It was somewhat like the old pasha fantasy; handmaidens grooming you...but no sex, at least not until I was capable of walking across the room under my own power without caving in or passing out.

"Where are we, again?" I must have asked that two dozen times, and the answer was always the same.

"Safe."

There are many inflections you can lend a single one-syllable word. The tone of Daisy saying "safe" had altered subtly over the past week, as though she was withholding information or was less certain of our security. The sound of the word had not become ominous, not yet.

She watched me like a mama hawk as I stumped to the bathroom on crutches. My insides were so tender that a basic human exercise such as sitting on the toilet became a pageant of grimaces. To be less precious about it, I was afraid I might shit my own intestines in a spill of ruptured, inside-out hosework, every time. At least my urine was finally clear of blood.

The first time, Daisy had to clean me up, no differently from an infant.

"Is this what you thought it might be like? Our dream date?" she had said, back in the storm drains, so long ago.

I couldn't help falling in love with her, which scared and sobered me because I knew I could not possibly keep her. There was no happily-ever-after to this scenario, no cheat to make it real.

Daisy was the single most screwed up human being I had ever encountered, and she was too good for me.

Said the potty philosopher, unable to wipe his own ass...

It was still daylight when Doc Taylor dropped by to read my vital signs and adjudge my progress.

I instantly broke the unwritten rule again by asking, "Doctor, can *you* explain this place to me?"

She smiled and I wished I could read her mind. "You're safe here, Mr. Martin." She released the blood pressure cuff on my arm.

"Okay, how about this," I said. "Are you a real doctor?"

Again the smile, to roadblock the true answer. "Yes."

"Sorry. I'm still learning not to pry."

She met my eyes. "Good."

A mote of light in her gaze caught the rest of her thought:...*because outsiders are not welcome here. Especially inquisitive ones.*

David J. Schow

"I mean, your blood pressure is good," she said. "White cells, good. Hematocrit, good—you're no longer bleeding inside."

What if everybody in Sylvanweir had a story like mine and Daisy's? That would explain the bland names, the low profile, the resolute rejection of passersby. What was I going to do...write an exposé?

Hell, no—I was one of them, now.

That's when I noticed, for the first conscious time, that Doc Taylor was wearing a sidearm.

Sheriff Bill Thompson was always packing, too—a race-gunned Kimber Gold Combat II in stainless steel. Two of them, in fact, one on each hip like an ex-biker turned fire chief turned gunslinger, the match-grade .45s reposing in a hand-tooled steerhide belt with double buckles. Sheriff Bill was about the size of a Coke machine, three hundred pounds easy, mostly above the belt without a whisper of flab, his blouse skin-tight to display his shoulders and biceps. Dark, almost Indian features; condor eyes. Gold earring. A jaw you could use to shatter block ice.

"Looks like you're patching up nicely," Sheriff Bill said, working a moist toothpick and sucking lifeforce from a can of Mountain Dew. Whenever he moved, it seemed to displace air in the room.

Kingi the dog never took his gaze off Sheriff Bill for the duration.

"Doc Taylor threatened that I might actually live," I said. That won me a concession in the form of a tight smile, lips together, one side twitching up as though jerked on a string.

"She's pulled many a man back from the brink," Sheriff Bill said, with a nod to Daisy. "Ladies, too. Mountain air helps."

"How long have you been here, Sheriff?"

The toothpick slid from one side of his mouth to the other. He actually seemed to consider answering the question. "Awhile."

"Sorry. I'm still trying to figure out how to be less nosy."

"Your business is to get better," Bill said. He looked at his empty can as though someone else had drunk it, then looked around for a replacement, which Daisy handed him. "I'm sure this is a little strange for you. Caginess is second nature up here. Better for you to risk asking than to pretend not to notice."

"He's surrounded by benefactors," said Daisy. She was outfitted in denim, hiking boots and a down vest over a cowl top, sipping microwave cocoa. "Think back, Bill—remember how you were, at first."

That pulled a modest laugh out of Sheriff Bill.

"Yeah. What do you think, Maria? Can I trust ole Don here, just a tiny bit?"

She looked in my direction, making the classic zipped-lips, cross your heart gesture.

"People love stories," said Bill. "If you don't give 'em a story, they make one up anywhoo. I'll tell you a story. Made up, not true. Like a parable, you might say. Once upon a time there was this dude who ate some really bad trouble with two forks. He gorged himself on the wrong. Landed here with three bullets in him and a broken leg. He weren't no good for the outside world anymore; too many evil men were too interested in seeing him dead. So he died to make them happy. In his place there came a new man, new name, clean slate, no worries. Ta-da."

Sheriff Bill was his own best magic trick.

"How long has Sylvanweir been...um, the place it is?"

"Hah!" This genuinely amused the big man. "Awhile. Listen, Don, you just do what you're doing. Hole up, heal up. You look like a man I might like to have a drink with, when you're capable."

"Linda's got pot roast tonight," offered Daisy. "Maybe me and the dog will take her up on it. Donald has turned into a sofa spud."

"Hah!" The Mountain Dew can pinged. Bill's fingers were incapable of holding the can without putting little dents in it as he drank.

"I have been sitting here for a couple of weeks now," I said, shifting around in search of a more comfortable position in my chair, which was a fool's quest. "Thinking too much. So you'll forgive me, I hope, for wondering about how the local economy works. This isn't a tourist town, that's obvious. There might as well be a huge sign on the border that reads *Go Away*."

In fact, there was no sign announcing Sylvanweir, anywhere.

"And from what I've seen, all the locals are armed. Not just packing. Extravagantly armed. You're wearing over four thousand dollars worth of handgun there, not counting the mods."

"Can't fault you for noticing," said Bill. "It's okay to carry, here. I say so. To dance around your question a bit, let's just say that everything is paid for."

"Okay, I'm going to stop apologizing, now."

"Hah! No you ain't." He seemed honestly taken with me. "Son, *everybody* here's got the same questions, but we live quite well without chapter and verse on the answers, if you know what I mean."

"I can keep my big trap shut."

"That's sorta the question I came here to ask you, and you just answered it. No harm, no foul, right? Plus you got Maria here to vouch for you. She's like family."

Daisy rolled her eyes. "Gee, thanks, *dad*."

"She's a world-beater, that girl. You two make a good couple. That is, when your face ain't all hamburgered. I'm assuming, and you know what they say."

"When you assume you make an *ass* out of *u* and *me* both."

"Hah! You've got it."

Sheriff Bill rolled out amidst much creaking of cowhide, his big roughout boots shaking the floorboards.

"That man is immense," I said. "Senior class, compared to the fifth graders who beat me up."

"He does cut a swath," said Daisy. "Same with the Doc. Same with everyone here. They blend to present the profile of rustics, but their old personalities can't help but peek through."

"I didn't want to mention it in front of him, but..." I stopped, my brain wide open in search of the correct words. "You've been here before. Otherwise, how did you set this up so fast? How did you know where to land?"

"Courtesy of a gentleman named Charlie Johnson," she said. "You'll be meeting him today, too. It's rather like holding court, isn't it?"

"Nobody's kissed my ring, yet."

"That's unsanitary. But you look well enough that maybe kissing your scepter might not be out of the question."

Admit it: Sex is the terminus of every infatuation.

You're walking down the street, working the statistical curve of copulation. Who you would, who you wouldn't, who you might, from the teeming mass of humanity on the hoof. The conversations, the encounters, the dinners and cocktails, the mindless banter, the callbacks and gestures, every available weapon in the arsenal is aimed at the goal of intromission, thanks to the timeless genetic mandate to reproduce.

Eat, excrete, make more of yourself...then kill.

Sex was designed to be pleasurable, so it would always seem imperative. Wily viruses that we are, we discovered ways to circumvent the encumbrance of parenthood in order to pursue sex for the goal of pleasure. Which, according to some doomsayers, was the beginning of the end of civilization. In post-feminist, 21st Century terms, in a world where alpha males were mostly immature punks, was a man more in control of himself actually attractive to women sexually, or was he merely a "beta" to be used and discarded?

There's just one problem...

Erection was no problem, not given Daisy's skill. Sitting still was the problem, because any kind of vigorous motion was a source of fresh pain. Humping, thrusting, standing up, breathing. She turned around and backed slowly onto me, seating well but not putting her weight in my lap. This was slow and sinuous, not frantic and brain-bursting. My penis was eager; the rest of me was on lockdown. She moved tidally for a long while. If you are fortunate in life, there are some people of whom you will always think, *he or she is a perfect fit for me*—even if they left you, vanished, died or changed into someone else. The sense memory of your personal ballistics never fades.

I felt the bungee-plunge of contractions commence as her hands reached backward to grab something, anything to hold onto, finally gripping the arms of the chair. She was doing her damndest not to slam down on me.

I supposed it was adequately personal—if she only needed a hard thing to rub against, Sylvanweir could probably supply a more athletic candidate.

Then again, maybe this was just part of Doc Taylor's prescription for healing.

I didn't spring any leaks, have a seizure, or burst any internal plumbing.

Freud or Jung or somebody said that climax obliterates the ego.

"Is this what you thought it might be like? Our dream date?"

Kingi generously minded his own dog biz, staying curled up by the hearth.

I felt better. And worse, at the same time. Infatuation can be like that.

Charlie Johnson embraced Daisy warmly. This was a reunion, not a social gesture. They had history.

A professorial man; I'd guess late fifties. Square jaw, furrowed forehead, precise eyewear, healthy but receding hair, bushy-white. Capable, knotty hands like a powerful jeweler. He seemed on the thin side, as though he had pared off too much weight; his trousers seemed bunched at the waist. One of those reedy men who is almost all leg. Looking down to his boot I saw the aluminum clamp of an orthopedic brace on his right foot.

He doffed his coat and then unstrapped the semiauto pistol nestled in his armpit. I saw RUGER stamped on the grip and guessed it to be a .40 or .45.

"So you're the guy who's brought her back to us," Charlie said as he shook my hand.

"She brought me," I said. "I don't even remember the trip."

He cast a knowing eye toward Daisy. "God, where have I heard *this* one before?"

"Shut up," she said happily, like a chiding sibling.

I had to proceed cautiously. I was being tested and I knew it.

"I'm a big admirer of your work," I told Charlie.

I had read Clive Bricklin's book *Chum for the Big Sharks* back in '09. A scalding indictment of the abuses wreaked on taxpayers by U.S. defense contractors, it ranked right up there with Jeremy Scahill's *Blackwater* and Richard Ney's *The Wall Street Jungle*, and like Ney, Bricklin had been an insider, which translated as whistleblower, traitor, pariah and target, in that order. He displeased a lot of suits and uniforms, who all rat-packed together in denial, because Bricklin had blessed them with painfully obvious aliases. "Clive Bricklin" was itself a pseudonym. The jacket photo had depicted a rangy blond chap in aviator shades, a little too leading-man to be real. The author had used a stand-in.

Nothing like the man before me now.

"He means the painting," Daisy clarified.

"Oh," said Charlie. "*Oh*...yes. It seems that all painters, even mediocre ones, eventually succumb to the magnetism of Western art. It's the American shorthand for legitimacy, I suppose."

Very much like the man before me now had been a gent named Efram Obermeyer, late of the DeltaMax international armaments conglomerate. No mustache now, less hair, but still banded with rancher sinew. I recalled him from the very beginning of the arms scandal. Obermeyer had been the man behind the Clive Bricklin pen-name, and the suits knew it. It was child's play to leverage agents, editors and publishers, especially when you threatened to kill their families.

The suits got him.

Watch the news: Every time there's a crisis—civil unrest, a budget calamity, amber alert, hostage standoff, imminent war—right after the juicy shots designed to get your attention, there always follows a direct cut to a wood-paneled room full of people in suits. I recognized the pattern from too many melodramas. Officials were always seen to be working on the problem at hand, as though they had a clue, when in fact it was those selfsame suits who were usually responsible for fucking everything up. These people gave themselves *raises*; do you really think they would voluntarily un-employ themselves?

Back in early 2008, a bunch of suits got CHASE on the horn and purchased the death of Efram Obermeyer, a.k.a. "Clive Bricklin." And they nailed him. He died.

And thanks to Daisy's intercession, "Charles Johnson" was born. He was her turning point, after which Alma Acevedo could no longer work for CHASE.

He was standing right in front of me, talking about folk art. He still signed his paintings with an iconographic O.

"Do you have family, Charlie?"

"I did. They're not in the picture now."

"Did you love them?"

"Yes. And I know they're okay. And now I spend a lot of time in reflection. The painting helps. I'm not supposed to ask, of course, but I take it you might have had some similar trouble?"

"Not now," I said.

Kingi yawned cavernously. People sure *jawed* a lot.

"You thinking about staying?" asked Charlie.

"Awhile," I said.

"I let him go," said Daisy, by firelight now since the sun had waned. "And Rolf Dettrick let me go—that is, he covered for me, even though I parted company with CHASE. As far as the world was concerned, Efram Obermeyer had died right on schedule."

"Why?" My painkillers were starting to kick my butt, warmly.

"Because he wasn't a suit," said Daisy, about three double shots of Jack into her comfort zone. "His family wasn't the usual hateful catastrophe. He was an artist, like you were a writer. None of that was supposed to matter, and it usually didn't, when you had to deal with some polished turd, some fat cat or corporate tool. We had complete jackets on targets. You had to get inside their lives and know their thoughts, in order to service them. The files were always full of cheating, spousal abuse, privilege, racketeering, you name it. Always bad; always malignant."

"Until Efram, Clive, and Charlie."

"He wasn't hurting anyone except parasites. I told Rolf that."

"And that was bye-bye, CHASE?"

"Rolf always assumed he would clean it up later and nobody would be the wiser. It didn't happen that way." She sipped, running old tapes in her mind. Wait long enough, and the format becomes obsolete, and everyone forgets. Try accessing your old files on floppy disc, sometime.

"Efram Obermeyer was Rolf's dirty little secret. The one slip that could jeopardize him at CHASE."

"Mm-hm." She sipped again. "Until Rolf himself becomes the head of the organization. Now he can rewrite that ancient history any way he pleases."

Wait long enough, and the old format becomes obsolete. Similarly, Daisy had changed. There was more of her in the room now; less of Alma or Lily or Chase Lima.

The phone in the cabin rang.

All the phones in Sylvanweir were routed through a central switchboard at the inn, a closed-loop system for communication with the rest of the town. No long distance calls were permitted, and cellphones were frowned upon unless they were tailless and encrypted. Far past the cabin group in the woods was an enormous, camouflaged dish array, not cheap. It allowed Internet access and satellite feeds for TV, and I did not need to be told it was utterly secure, too.

Kingi's ears shot to full parade attention.

"Probably the Doc," Daisy said, rising to answer.

Somebody started thumping furiously on the door. Kingi let loose a series of warning barks.

"I can get it," I said. "I can manage."

Daisy lifted the receiver and all she heard was a steady peeping, in groups of three, like Morse code, as though a number button was being pressed three times, then paused, then repeated.

"Open up, goddammit!" Sheriff Bill Thompson shouted from outside.

At the sight of my open hand, Kingi clammed up. He did not even draw breath. He stayed on point and waited for the revelation of the door.

"Shit," said Daisy at the phone. "It's a 1-1-1."

I hauled the doorway open. Sheriff Bill filled it, almost comically. Kingi stood down.

"Lock and load," he said. "Visitors."

He wasn't talking about lost tourists.

Versus

"Jesus H.," said Rolf Dettrick. "What a rinkydink setup. Not even a wide spot in the road." He glassed the inn with night optics from about a hundred yards out, in the bushes, off the pavement.

"Good hide," said Ginny, behind him.

"I hate this chicken-fried country bullshit," said Max. The hayseeds in this 'ville had probably never seen a pair of Ferragamo shoes. Pop a magnum of Cristal and these rednecks would probably dump the bubbly on their heads. For a city boy, this was a *Petticoat Junction* nightmare.

The only way in and the only way out were bottlenecked.

Rolf commanded two CHASE teams similar to the single deployed at the Tropical Paradise Motel—twelve men, variously tasked, this time carrying special armament. First team lead was Kolascheck, from the previous job; second was the healed-up-and-good-to-go Lambeen, itching for compensation for the bullet he had stopped from Daisy's hazing fire. Their teammate Bixler had won himself a CHASE designation, as Chase Hotel in Rolf's new regime, and Bixler was the go-to point man if Rolf got compromised. The CHASE men were radioed up and kitted out with enough gear to turn a pocket skirmish into an all-out war.

Max Wilsoni had contributed an additional crew of ten nut-busters, including Mario DuFleck, the sniper from the mailbox gig, and Moses Babcoq, who had missed out on the slaughter at the Falcon Theater over a month ago. They brought their own favored sidearms and ordnance. Max's men disdained the SWAT pretensions of their CHASE co-workers, and had all come in their street clothes, adjusted, of course, to eliminate loud colors.

Somebody must have cleaned a Ross Superstore out of black turtlenecks, Rolf thought.

The agreement was that Max commanded Max's men, off cues from Rolf if practical. Rolf expected that whole program to nosedive as soon as there was active weapons engagement, but that was okay in a scenario he wanted to result in maximum destruction. He interspersed Max's men with his own on the cordons, so they could gain a nodding acquaintance and not draw down on each other. Among other goals, this was a prime opportunity for some of Max's guys to audition for CHASE.

"This is a tactical sweep and clear, gentlemen," Rolf had told the group. "What used to be called search and destroy before the language got all polite. There are two primary targets and zero secondaries. You have all been briefed. I want the two primes alive. Any cracker dumbfuck gets in your way, put them down hard. Mr. DuFleck and Mr. Babcoq, I know you and the rest of your guys want some payback for what happened to Franchi and the rest. Your opportunity is now. Mr. Bixler and Mr. Lambeen, I don't have to tell you that the primes would happily kill your asses just on general principles. Mr. Bixler will be our Number Two should we divide to conquer. Our principle is choke-hold, boys and girls, so on go, start squeezing."

Now, bunkered in the bushes like a commando, Rolf tapped Max on the shoulder. "Mr. Wilsoni, the go is yours."

Brilliantly, Rolf had given Max the honor of dropping the flag.

Just as Max was inhaling to give the command, someone started calling Rolf's name from the middle of the street.

They had rallied at the inn, about a quarter of the population of Sylvanweir. Introductions were quickly exchanged but I couldn't track half of them; they truly were invisible names. Susan White, Paul Davis, Mike Jackson. *Michael Jackson?* It was inevitable, I guessed, in the Chinese menu mix-and-match of prosaic nomenclature.

"Call me Mick," Jackson said behind a firm how-do-you-do.

Great. That made him the singer of "Blame it on the Boogie," the author of *The Underground Man*, or maybe the director of *The Bodyguard* and *Volcano*. Much lower profile, thanks...and in a world with no history, who would care?

Then Tom Jones introduced himself. The sheer banality took some getting used to. What's in a name? Thank Zeus there was no "Wayne John."

The people here all lived under the kind of names used by lazy American writers to evoke a phony baseline of domestic commonality, a whitebread shorthand for just-plain Everypersons: *Harold Simpson ignored the warnings about buying the old Vrolak mansion...* The only thing missing was the finger quotations.

1-1-1 was Sylvanweir's version of red alert.

"Where's everybody else?" I said.

"Out," said Sheriff Bill. "Deployed, you might say." Bill Thompson was concentrating on the CB and shortwave array housed inside a roll-top desk in Will Green's office. It crackled and a voice came through with better than digital clarity.

"Sheriff Bill, Babs has got a Humvee-looking thing blocking the road to the north, over."

Daisy whispered back to me, "Barbara Simmons."

Bill keyed the mike. "Joe Anderson, come back."

A second voice reported, *"Confirming Babs, Bill. Guy's got a heavy gun and can't stop playing with it. Looks like a military SAW, over."*

"Light machine gun," said Bill. "Everybody wants to be Sly Stallone."

"Rambo used an M60," I said to Daisy. The M249 Squad Auto Weapon was lighter, but the M60 packed heavier caliber. The SAW shot the same ammo as the M16 and all its offspring.

"Sheriff Bill, this is Fred Sanders on the south road. Same-same. Confirming one Humvee and one heavy gun on this end, too, over."

Bill kept the mike hot. "Mark Williams, tell me you've got their air, over."

"Affirmative," came Williams' voice. *"Hostiles. We're talking twenty, maybe thirty strong, and everything about their moves screams 'containment.' They want two primes—guess who—and every other warm body in this place is expendable, over."*

"Who's hot is who's new," said Paul Davis, staring at me.

I gave his glare right back. I was past apologizing.

"Knock it off, Paul," said Sheriff Bill. "Nobody *takes* anybody out of here. That's always been our rule. For you, for him, for me. It's how we live."

Mortified, Paul made his peace. "Sorry, man," he said to me as though he had just been reminded of scripture by the Almighty. He shook his head. *Silly; don't know what came over me.*

Daisy nodded at me, her own confirmation. I needed no deeper explanation or endorsement.

Abruptly, everyone gathered at the inn was spot-checking loads on their carry guns. Actions snapped, cylinders racheted, safeties became irrelevant. A little old lady I had met as Liz Christopher had produced a Ruger Redhawk half as big as she was. Daisy authorized both her Smiths and handed one of them to me.

"Mark Williams is our technical wizard," Bill said as he sleeved himself into battle-grade Kevlar. From a closet near the radio setup he withdrew a Bushmaster carbine with a birdcage flash hider and seated a fat mag of 6.8mm Remington—thirty rounds. This type of gun was called the Black ORC; the acronym had something to do with optics readiness, but I didn't see any special jazz mounted on the rail.

"Okay, then," said Sheriff Bill. "Gimme the bullhorn."

Buck Tichnor swept the road view past the gunsight of his SAW. A whole lot of nothing, in either direction. Not one vehicle had appeared for him to challenge in the two hours he had been posted. He was on his eighth cigarette and his mouth tasted close to owlshit.

He sat in the Humvee. He got out of the Humvee. He got back into the Humvee. Waiting was the gig. He was pulling his smokes down about halfway before grinding them out. He lit another. At this rate, he'd run dry in half an hour.

His M249 was a special-purpose variant that was just begging to be fired, with a 100-round soft-pak magazine belting the combo of one tracer to every four ball cartridges, total 'ville-chomping wipeout.

His touched his throat mike. "Tichnor, south, no activity." Five minutes from now, he'd do it all over again.

His glowing cigarette cherry was an almost perfect indicator, and he was totally unaware of the green laser sighting dot than came and went on the back of his neck.

Ernesto Mori wasn't exactly a "sneakerhead," but he did love his $600 Micropacers enough to become distressed when he stepped into a rancid pile of shit that appeared to have come from a dinosaur. A large dinosaur.

"Goddammit to hell," he muttered, while searching in the dark for a stick to start scraping. This woodsy nature crap was for farmers and retards. He did not speak loudly enough to interrupt radio crosstalk or expose his position; he was a pro, or liked to think so.

The CHASE man on his flank, Louis Somebodyorother, held up.

"What is it?"

"A whole lotta animal shit, is what it is. Louie, right?"

"What, you step in a pie?"

Ernesto held up his foot. It had gained several pounds.

"That is gross. What do you think, are there grizzly bears here?"

"Walk it off," advised Louis. "Stay tight. Consider it camouflage." He swept the space before them with the six-power autogated nite-sight mounted on his personal weapon, a left-handed Stag Arms 3G developed for three-gun competitions (hence the "3G"). At nearly four thousand dollars, the optics cost twice as much as the gun and Louis did not like the added weight, although he admired the package—the whole system ran off two AA batteries. He and Ernesto were supposed to emerge into something close to civilization, but all he could see in the amber-on-green reticle was more woods and more trees, where, potentially, more big shit-pies were lying in wait like snares.

He and Ernesto and others like them were slowly, gradually closing the perimeter noose. Louis preferred range conditions for gunfire and did not enjoy the idea of spraying ammo uselessly into the night with no spotters to appreciate his aim and speed, or tick off score boxes in his favor. This wasn't a competition, this was a round-up.

As Ernesto plied the poop off his shoes, a Sylvanweir resident named Robert Baker watched from a distance, using a matted-down, nonreflective monogoggle. Rob preferred this handy "spyglass" to the head-mounted variety. He could have attached it to his Springfield 30.06, but thought that would only look goofy and pretentious.

He only moved when the pair ahead of him moved. He did not step in the mass he recognized right away as elk feces.

Dan Hall had eyes on what he was pretty sure was the command trio, two men and a woman. He was too close to them to risk breaking radio.

The lead guy was an executive type, suited up in tac gear. The other guy was a subordinate or flunky, a city boy out of his element. The woman was the most interesting, her movements more surefooted and capable. Sidearms only; none bore rifles.

Dan had come to Sylvanweir as Specialist-6 Mallory Jeter, straight from a balls-up in Afghanistan that left a lot of good Rangers and Delta Force guys dead in the dirt. It turned out to be one of those dreaded max-deniability ops that was supposed to leave no living, contrary participants, and after hell-holing his way out of country on his own— starving, two bullets left for his sidearm (which had taken a hit itself and was less than reliable)—he stowed away on a petro tanker where he was discovered and conscripted to the lowest duties imaginable. Back in the U.S., as soon as he alerted his superiors, he found himself a hunted man in his own home country, where private contractors competed for the price on his head. Crap, man, he had worked side-by-side with those mercs in the 'Stan!

Currently he oversaw the rudimentary gas station in Sylvanweir, and had become a pretty good wrench. He kept the local vehicles tip-top, and had embraced the Zen of motor maintenance.

Seeing all the martial gear brought by the newcomers caused an unexpected pang of nostalgia in Dan. All that lovely, expensive hardware; lubed actions, exploding bullets, death-raining up-to-the-minute tech. American overkill had not worked very well in combat theaters since Vietnam, but the irresistible pull of the gadgetry still seeded a lot of cultural arrogance.

Once he caught sight of a new face in town—Daisy, walking her dog—he immediately wondered if she was, you know, available for dating. But Sheriff Bill had told him she was beavered up with some guy she'd brought with her. Hell, maybe the dude was a cripple; maybe she'd get bored. At least she was fresh fantasy fuel. Time had a way of bringing your desires to Sylvanweir, and Dan had learned infinite patience. If not, he could always go back to banging Linda Moore, whose lust for being spanked would forever remain a puzzlement. Linda loved superficial punishment, and Dan's schooling had been in punishment-for-real, punishment to damage, so it was a learning curve for both of them. Still, to lose all the dom/sub foolery would be refreshing.

He sized up the woman again, among the interloping trio. Good curves, a little short for Dan's optimum specs, but the shorter ones were always more limber. You never can tell until the clothes hit the floor. Maybe this one would be a capture. Maybe she would be offered illusory freedom in barter for a bit of hostage affection. Prisoners tried all kinds of tricks to keep on living.

But Dan knew one thing for sure: if these were hostiles, impinging on the security of Sylvanweir, none of them would walk out alive. That was the way it had to be.

Still...

Stan Bixler could see the gas station from his treeline. No activity there, either. He was beginning to wonder if Rolf's complex plan had been worth all the effort of staging and run-throughs. But Stan was newly minted as Chase Hotel, and tonight might be the crucible of his worthiness.

"Kolascheck," he whispered into his throat mike.

"On your four o'clock," Kolascheck came back.

"Move up." Bixler knew that Lambeen would slide into Kolascheck's vacated position.

Air movement told him that Kolascheck had married up.

"Have you seen anyone? I mean, any single person, since we started?"

"Negative." Kolascheck said it right into Bixler's ear. They were hunkered down, shadows among other shadows.

"I thought we were going to have to cut through collateral," said Bixler, almost subaurally. "This place seems deserted." It was 8:06 P.M. by his watch.

"They sure roll up the sidewalks." Kolascheck had gone full gonzo for the hunt, painting his face with a Rothco jungle stick, reliving some past military triumph. He was wearing a freakin' *helmet*, for christ's sake.

"I wish Alpha would call the fucking ball, already," said Bixler. "I mean, I'd like to shoot someone before break time."

"Like you're shooting off your mouth, now?"

That was unexpectedly harsh. Bixler was Chase Hotel now, and there was chain of command to consider. Perhaps Kolascheck had some unvoiced resentment he needed to vent, and if that was the case, Bixler decided to shut the guy down, pronto. Fist up his shirt and get in his face. It was probably attributable to battle stress, but Rolf Dettrick would not want such an infraction ignored.

Bixler turned to confront Kolascheck. All he saw was the oncoming buttstock, hissing through the air at the end of a home-run swing to pancake his nose and liberate his front teeth as it hit him dead bang between the eyes. Bixler went down like a folding chair with the bolts removed. In the silent quarter-second before his brain shut down, Bixler saw that the man who had coldcocked him was not Kolascheck at all, but someone else wearing Kolascheck's gear, striped in Kolascheck's face paint, listening to Kolascheck's radio, wielding Kolascheck's weapon...

Seating Kolascheck's CRKT blade deep into the nougat center of his heart. The CRKT stood for Columbia River Knife & Tool.

Bixler's gaze set and glazed over. His last thought was that if he was dead, that meant not only Kolascheck, but Lambeen was already toast, too.

Mario DuFleck was one with his Barrett MRAD, not the twenty-nine-pound, .50-caliber Ferrari, but certainly a racy Porsche at a pert fifteen pounds. MRAD stood for "Multi-Role Adaptive Design," and this was the same rifle he'd used on top of the Hollywood Post Office before that dickstump Giorgio had broken his jaw, which was still wired together, making the new Mario a man of few words. It also made him a man of meals taken through straws for six weeks (less than two to go), but whatever doesn't kill you makes you stronger, right?

Dumbshit Giorgio had gotten his ticket punched at the Falcon Theater. Served him right, as far as DuFleck was concerned. That old wop fuck should have retired years ago. Mario DuFleck was *right now*, baby. Max Wilsoni had passed him a bonus in return for his wear and tear, and DuFleck had invested in a Vortex Viper scope with a day/night add-on.

Rolf Dettrick's containment plan would have required an extra thirty guys to completely encircle Sylvanweir, so the deployment was engineered as a sweeping arc, a scythe. If you pictured the layout as a horizontally bisected O (not dissimilar to the way the former Efram Obermeyer signed his paintings, but with the line all the way through), the lower half was the woods, the line was the roadway, and the upper half was where the structures were. DuFleck was above the split, approximately a hundred and fifty yards past the rear of the gas station, watching the backside of the inn. If the game flushed, they'd come right into his sight picture.

Fifty yards to DuFleck's west, Moses Babcoq manned a similar post in a scissor crossfire.

Southeast, the CHASE and Wilsoni teams were bottling up the woods. Forest creatures made distant noises nothing like human passage.

And sure enough, other critters wearing clothes began to trickle from the back door of the inn, after they had extinguished the exterior lights.

Too tempting.

Shoot the first one and the others would scamper back inside. Let them form a little conga line and shoot the last one, and you could pick up two or three more downs in the ensuing bovine confusion. The kill zone was ten feet from the door before intermittent trees polluted the view. Okay, maybe lose the first one in order to reap the followers. Unless...

DuFleck dialed up his optics. He was under strict no-no orders insofar as terminating the two primes, but anyone else was fair game so he needed rock-solid ID on his shot choices. First out was an older man, baseball cap, definitely neither David Vollmand nor Alma Acevedo in disguise. Second: older woman, ditto. Good—they'd react more slowly.

Third and fourth: one figure helping another hump along, so at least one of them was impaired, which was wonderful. High collars, though, and their backs to his lens...best not to chance them, although Rolf would be eager to know about the handicap slowing down the other side. Perhaps one of them was wounded already.

But he was losing the first two. In a couple of seconds they would be obscured by cover. Still no go, from Rolf.

Fuck it. DuFleck was *right now*, baby. He squeezed the trigger, which he had tweaked because it was too light, originally.

One of the downsides of the MRAD was its recoil, which could honestly be compared to the kick of a small horse. The Thunder Beast titanium suppressor squished the report down to a handclap *crack* instead of an eye-popping explosion, thinned it out, in fact, to hobble anyone seeking the source of the shot. You still needed ear protection, though—hearing loss was a cumulative thing, and DuFleck was sensitive to any further damage that might befall his head. That was why he was earbudded, and why he didn't go for a full-on cheek weld with the stock before he fired; he knew the recoil would feel the same as walking his wired jaw right into a slammed door.

The guy in the hat flung his arms wide from a solid center mass hit.

DuFleck was deeply in love with the jargon of brand-name gun gear. Viper. Thunder Beast. The Grizzly Big Bore. He was a hardcore rock 'n roll animal, and he was here to remove life from the planet.

Before Hat-Man hit the ground, DuFleck had bolted another .338 Magnum round. The cartridges were bottlenecked, slightly over three and a half inches long, and could drop most of the hunter's Big Five of dangerous game (African elephant, black rhino, cape buffalo, leopard, and lion) from out to 1500 meters if used properly.

DuFleck's prey lacked tonnage, horns, fangs and claws. They had firearms much smaller than DuFleck's. He was able to collect the woman behind Hat-Man before the rest of his targets went to ground.

Because of the earbuds he missed some of the radio chatter. He dug out one plug in time to hear what sounded like a PA system, broadcasting from the street. He did not catch the gist, but it did not matter because seconds later, a lot of people opened fire.

The Ponderosa pine had a trunk nearly fifteen feet around and its plume crested at over a hundred meters from the ground. It had been growing in the same spot since the 19th Century and had been host to all kinds of lifeforms, from blister rust and bark-boring parasites to wildcats, bear cubs, and every rodent and bird known to the San Jacinto mountains.

With no breeze or earthquake tremor to prompt it, a wad of the tree detached itself and rappelled to the needle-carpeted forest floor.

The black nylon climbing line susurrated through Ed Kane's Cordex belaying gloves as controlled his descent. He was wearing his "tree suit," not quite a ghillie, but a confection he had whopped together from an olive coverall and available materials mere hours before, securing the pine sections with jute twine and fishing line. Even on the ground, this foliage-wear helped him blend and provided the necessary three-dimensional breakup, especially in the dark.

Ed sometimes buddied up with Mark Williams on electrical maintenance for the hamlet. He chopped and provided all Sylvanweir's firewood. He also made most of the supply runs, driving a flatbed truck down into the world, which was not a worry for him since he had changed his hair, his look, his glasses. He had done this many times before.

Ed's buy-in for Sylvanweir residency had been a hundred and fifty thousand dollars, cash. It was average, for an ante, and a bargain for Ed. Only he knew how unique he was among the other castaways, refugees, fugitives and runaways, because he was the only local who had arrived under false pretenses. No problem there, either—for the sake of his own survival, Ed had become a world-class yarn spinner. The man certainly could tell a convincing story.

He had gone by many names in the past, so assuming the mantle of "Edward Kane" had been slick and bumpless.

In Denver, where he had acquired much of the cash he used to buy a life in Sylvanweir, he was (to his knowledge) still being manhunted as "Rowan Woodward Crocker."

In Phoenix, police were still searching for a truck hijacker named "Foster Lawrence."

In Los Alamos he was still known as a *narcotraficante*—drug dealer—named "Gustavo Molina," a.k.a. "Rana Gutierrez," who had dealt down several of his competitors most brutally. Killed them with his bare hands, or any handy bludgeon. Killed heavily-armed men known to be fetishistic about their firepower (because, after all, they were dope traffickers)...by using no guns at all.

And authorities all the way up to the federal level, across five states, were still seeking the kidnapper, rapist and murderer who had been dubbed the Crossroads Killer, whose alleged victim tally stood at seventeen, all female, all teenagers, all blondes, except for Number 15, whose hair he had dyed so as not to disrupt the pattern.

Ed's special muffled carabiners made no noise as he came earthward. He was not packing a weapon of any sort. Weapons were items you acquired as you progressed through obstacles to a goal. When Sheriff Bill's 1-1-1 call came through, Ed grabbed his climbing gear and made for the trees at a dead run. That had been near dusk. Now the night was all around him, succoring him in its special embrace. He was a hunter who had just been granted free license and an open season, no bag limit.

At 7:55 P.M. Ed registered movement below him. The sounds of outsiders, unfamiliar with the terrain.

From his high vantage he could make out a staggered line in groups of two about twenty-five yards apart, closing in on the main road. Too loose to be a dragnet; it had to be a cordon. These men and women were not searching, they were narrowing a loop. No flashlights, many guns.

He flowed down from the trees, silent as a wolf spider.

Tac boots shuffled through the underbrush two feet away from Ed's face as he lay prone. Then—could he be seeing this right?—a pair of street shoes, the kind some tenderfoot would wear to a prom. Ed waited a beat. A formation like this always had a rear element.

Another pair of tac boots crunched twigs, about ten feet off to the north-northwest. There was no one behind this tail-watcher, who was talking, low and circumspect, either to himself or a radio.

Ed doubled a five-foot length of climbing rope (a shortie for securing things in a high hide) and used it to lasso the guy's leading foot, only jerking a little to make the man think he had tripped over a vine.

"Godammit to hell!" the fellow snarled, keeping his voice down. He went down hard on his left knee.

Ed sprang, a mutant bush come to life, and used the guy's own web vest to roll him so Ed landed on top, straddling him.

"Quiet!" Ed hissed.

Then Ed saw the expression he had been waiting for: the guy shut up obediently, thinking his ass had just been saved by an ally. By the time he got a better sight picture of Ed, the bushwhack was already done. Ed knuckle-punched the guy's Adam's apple through to the spine. He gargled blood and died.

Now Ed had a radio, and an acurized law enforcement grade AR-15 with too much junk on the rails—lasers and scopes, mostly.

Ed's monster had tasted first blood, and gently reminded Ed of its appetite. Sheriff Bill's usual bottom line was no kills prior to engagement, per his go, but if the evening got rowdy, nobody would know or care about Ed's preemptive strike.

He collared the mike about his own neck, happy that he had not accidentally smashed the commo. The weapon was cocked and locked with a 30-round mag. Dead Dude also provided a black-on-black knife, nearly seven inches of fixed tang carbon blade with a spear tip. Nope, definitely not a search party, but a party, nonetheless.

Ed flowed through the forest, serpentine.

His next guest was another tac hardcase, helmet and all. That helmet would be noteworthy swag, indeed. The monster flexed. Ed rose behind the man, silent as still air, and halved his throat. The soldier collapsed like a snipped clothesline. His face was tigered in camo paint as though he had been enacting some wargame wet dream. Ed rifled the corpse, found the tubes of Rothko paint that resembled big lipsticks, and quickly worked up his own visage. He did not need a mirror. With the face paint and the Kevlar lid on, he could be, well, anybody.

Ahead of him and to the left, another guy was scoping the street. A voice came over the radio:

"Kolascheck."

"On your four o'clock," Ed said, just raspy enough to be anybody.

"Move up."

Ed moved into a lurk behind the new contestant, who said over his shoulder, ""Have you seen anyone? I mean, any single person, since we started?"

"Negative," said Ed, feeling a twinge of guilt for lying, a trait beaten into him as a child. He moved up alongside the sentry and hunkered down. The man barely glanced at Ed's face, but did roll his eyes to indicate that there were still boundaries for overkill.

"I thought we were going to have to cut through collateral," said Bixler, almost subaurally. "This place seems deserted."

"They sure roll up the sidewalks," Ed said. Always appear to agree with the guys in charge. This one was clearly frustrated.

"I wish Alpha would call the fucking ball, already. I mean, I'd like to shoot someone before break time."

"Like you're shooting off your mouth, now?"

The surprised man turned, his mouth half-open, right into Ed's roundhouse swing of the buttstock. *Slam*—lights out, the same as that amateur-hour drug mule in New Mexico, four years ago.

The monster lunged forward then, almost impelling Ed into the roadway, insistent, its reptile view brimming with bloodlust. Ed swore he could feel his own ribs bow outward from the pressure.

Come on, Sheriff Bill, he screamed inside his own head. *Let's break the piñata and get this party started!*

A solid *chuff!* resounded from the far side of the road, somewhere back in the vicinity of the cabins, the report suppressed and wisping through the woods, a big gun pretending to be a fallen branch, but Ed knew the sound.

Finally! the monster bellowed. *Starting gun!*

You had to credit the sac on Sheriff Bill. The big man strode boldly into the center of the roadway, alone, real Western, his Bushmaster harnessed at high ready, trigger finger properly indexed. He raised a bullhorn. His stentorian voice echoed off the pavement.

"Rolf Dettrick. We are aware of your presence," Bill broadcast.

"How the fuck does Deputy Dawg know your *name?*" Max Wilsoni said from the treeline look-see where he had waited with Rolf and Ginny to shout out the green light.

"Bingo," affirmed Rolf.

"You are unauthorized and not, repeat, *not* welcome here. You will withdraw or the use of deadly force is approved. This is the only warning you will receive. You will stand down and depart immediately." Almost apologetically, he added, "Please."

"This is laughable," Ginny said to Rolf. "If you don't shoot him, I will."

"Shoot that *puto!*" Max shouted into the radio.

Off to their left a ten-round salvo lit up the evening and stitched a diagonal across Sheriff Bill from left hip to right shoulder. He avalanched down like a construction crane in a typhoon, one of those horrible news clips where you cannot believe something that big is caving in to meet the ground.

A funereal beat of silence, as Sheriff Bill remained motionless.

Then, gunfire. From twenty directions. Behind them.

Either the plan was going very well, or it had just seriously derailed.

Chaos Cinema

Between 8:07 and 8:09 P.M., once Sheriff Bill Thompson had been laid out flat in the middle of Sylvanweir's only street, the following things happened:

Robert Baker put a 30.06 round into the civilian, the guy with the shit on his shoes, who spun extravagantly as he went crashing down into the brush. His sidekick, the man with the more serious weapon, should have been the A-target, but Rob was lightning-fast on chambering another cartridge in his Springfield, and knew that in the time it took for his opponent (the chap with the Stag Arms rifle) to react, turn, and try to track the shot source for return fire, Rob could put three or four more rounds in the right place. He did.

Fred Sanders zeroed the Humvee gunner on the south road with his XADS laser sight and blew his hopes and dreams all over the side of the vehicle with a 739-grain .50-caliber round. Wartime snipers told tales of people literally rent in half by such bullets, which were powerful enough to behead a hippo. Freddy fired from less than twenty yards, using an Accuracy International AX50 with a free-floating stainless steel barrel. In the last heartbeat, he spitballed the shot; he was that close, and wanted to confirm his eyesight under pressure.

Moving in a lateral sweep based on his first position, Edward Kane plowed through five more invaders, stabbing them, crushing their skulls, and blasting them at point-blank range with their previous partner's weaponry. His monster was off the chain now, and happily gorging itself.

Daniel Hall saw the Latin-looking dude scream the go order into his radio, and presupposing this to be a point man, shot him in the back of the neck with a no-frills M4. The guy dropped as though through a trapdoor. Sheriff Bill was still down in the middle of the street.

Patricia Stevens, eighty feet away, fed her entire Addax Tactical clip of NATO hardball into three lurkers that had bunched up at the sound of the first shot.

From the roof of the inn, "Mick" Jackson crosshaired the silhouette that had opened fire on Sheriff Bill, and fed it an armor-piercing incendiary tracer from his bench-rested, bipodded LAR Grizzly Big Bore. The silhouette seemed to explode into smoke rings wafting around a brief spark of fire.

Brett Cochran, a Wilsoni soldier, was in the process of high-fiveing his buddy, Antonio Esparza, to toast their takedown of the sheriff, when Brett's chest caught fire and his lungs atomized in a cloud of impact that pitched him into the air. Esparza frantically tried to track a shot source, with his pal's fallout settling all over him. He died the same way, thanks to Mick Jackson.

Further north, at the sweep edge of Rolf's scythe move, several more CHASE/Wilsoni operatives were efficiently cut down from behind. There was an outer circle closing on the inner circle, the same pattern used against Rolf by James Smith at Studio City PetCare.

Soldiers were chancing out into the street now, distrustful of the forest behind them. One of the Humvees had broken post and was currently barreling in from the north.

Then Sheriff Bill sat up with a grunt, shaking his head no differently than a bear who had upset a beehive. Hostiles with sophisticated weapons were crossing the street twenty yards uphill. Bill's hand recovered his Bushmaster and he spat out a bee-swarm of his own. The poor saps on the road had nowhere to run. They tried to wave down the Humvee speeding toward them.

320

The Humvee veered, its run-flat mud radials making dinosaur sounds on the pavement, and juggernauted over the slowest man in the exposed group before nosing down to a dusty stop on the shoulder. It appeared to eat the guy, to suck him under with no leftovers in one skeleton-shattering gulp. Joe Anderson put a foot out of the cab for balance and cut up the stragglers with measured bursts from the captured SAW's century mag. Barbara "Babs" Simmons plunged from the passenger-side door, weed-whacking the treeline with an M4 on full rockin' auto.

Sheriff Bill rotated his fireline to the woods where Rolf, Ginny, and Max Wilsoni had been crouched with no thought of parley or palaver.

Enemy opposition seemed scattered, broken up and disorganized.

Fred Sanders brought the other Humvee in from the south.

Joe Anderson's SAW belt petered out. From behind him, a voice yelled, "Hey! Joe Sixpack! Yo, Joe-Bob!" He was cut to pieces and died thinking, *my name's not Joe-Bob...my name's not 'Joe' at all...*

Barbara Simmons tried to cap the shooter but was not sure if she had managed to hit anything.

Seeing Paul Davis on his nine o'clock with a rifle, Dan Hall signaled him to converge where Dan had holed the Latino-looking dude, Mr. Radiohead. But Max Wilsoni and his two accomplices, one male, one female, were gone. Joe Anderson was lying dead in the street.

Seeing movement, Sheriff Bill shot Paul Davis by accident.

David & Daisy, During

Dogs have better night vision than people. Their color-blindness is a myth; besides shades of gray, dogs can perceive well into the yellow and blue-violet spectra. Most dogs are nearsighted, hence the broad hand movements that accompany commands. I wished I could see as well as Kingi, since Daisy was marshaling me out the back door of the inn, toward the pathways that meandered toward various cabins.

Liz Christopher, the little old lady with the .44 Magnum, helped Daisy help me. A gent in an Orioles cap who had been quickly introduced as Sam Richards held the door for us. Sam and Liz interacted in a way that suggested they were a couple. Our hasty plan—per Sheriff Bill—was to fall back to a cabin and fortress up, fill all the windows with outbound gunpower, wait for friendlies to advance to be recognized, and shoot anyone else.

Sam doused the lights before we exited. I appreciated his caution and wondered how he had come to Sylvanweir. He resembled a psychology professor who had gone back to nature. Liz fit the misconception of a woman who read (or perhaps wrote) tea-cozy mysteries and drank a lot of Earl Grey. What had these innocuous people done, to land them here?

"This way," Sam said, just before he died.

Hit from behind, Sam's chest ruptured. His Orioles cap hit the dirt. His corpse lofted, blown completely out of his moccasins.

Daisy grabbed my arm at the elbow to force me down. It was a move I had seen bouncers use. Control the arm and you can make a body move any direction you wish.

Liz made the error of trying to rescue Sam as he fell, and it cost her life. I heard the moist thump of the second shot (silenced, for sure) speed in on the heels of the first, but could not figure a direction. Liz contracted around the hit and fell in a fetal clench.

"Crawl," Daisy said, leading the way. "There's probably more than one sniper."

I heard Sheriff Bill call out Rolf Dettrick by bullhorn, from the other side of the structure, stern and challenging, unflinching. We knew who they were.

That's another popular American misconception—that to expose a conspiracy is to eliminate it. It was a breaking point for a lot of badly thought-out thrillers. *Surprise—we've got you on tape, admitting your crimes.* In the real world, hard evidence was worthless against premium lawyers. Naming the guilty rarely deactivated them. The old Victorian concept of public shame had not made it across the pond to the New World. Americans love a winner. Even more so, they love a good bad guy.

Rolf Dettrick would not be weakened in any way by Sheriff Bill saying his name out loud.

Then, gunfire. *Twenty, maybe thirty strong*, Mark Williams had said on the radio, and it sounded as though all of them were shooting at once.

I dreaded the cramps. I had a whole-body muscle-ache as if I had run a twenty-mile marathon lugging a thirty-five pound training pack. My tendons had gone inelastic from recuperation. My blood surged to deliver a sledgehammer migraine. I needed cortisone, glucosamine, Synvek, steroids...air support, a bigger gun and a time machine...I needed a whole bottomless reserve of mad Korean mercenaries, like the ones Auric Goldfinger sent against James Bond in wave after wave.

I needed a brand new life, still sealed in a factory-fresh blister-pak, "mint in box," as collectors say. I wanted to flush old and buy new.

It took an agonizing eternity to belly-crawl to the cabin, where Kingi was barking inside. He wanted out to join the fray. I wanted in so I could hide under a blanket. Dumb dog.

"Snipers!" husked a voice from the darkness. "Don't shoot—it's Dan Hall!"

"Gas station?" I said to Daisy.

"Yeah. Dan, get over here! Stay low!"

Something about his movements told me that Dan Hall was ex-military, no lie. He had seen this kind of action before.

"I nailed one before Paul Davis got hit," he said breathlessly. "They're all over the place but pretty strung out. We totally bushwhacked them, but now we've got strays, I don't know how many."

"Paul got hit?" said Daisy.

"I couldn't help him. Alla sudden I had guys on three sides, not friendlies, and my mag is as dry as a sand sandwich. I need .556s or another gun."

"We barricade the cabin," said Daisy. "Let them come to us. I can't run and duck and jump and cover; David can't make it."

"Sounds good to me."

Inside, Kingi was still barking metronomically, like a bad novelty clock that just wouldn't stop, the same way that annoying Jack Russell had barked back at the vet's while Dave and Daisy were making their case. *Ark. Ark. Ark.*

"Get me in there so I can shut him up," I said.

Just as Daisy reached the door, a two-foot splinter of logwood gouted from the frame like a big switchblade snicking open. She belly-flopped as Dan and I scuttled inside, then kicked the door shut with her foot.

"About time you lost lambs showed up," said Rolf Dettrick.

We were all on the floor, staring in the wrong direction. Dan Hall, the guy from the gas station, made a courageous or foolhardy move to control the room by sweeping upward with his M4—empty, as he had said, but how were the interlopers to know?

Ginny Stark knew. She shot Dan in the chest with a Sig. Dan went face-down on the boards and stopped moving. Rolf covered Daisy and me with a big Glock in one hand and a similarly menacing autopistol in the other. Both he and Ginny were too far away to grab. Neither had suppressors; the time for those was long past.

Kingi was shackled by his own leash to the andirons in the fireplace, which were mortared into the firebrick. He lunged about and barked ferociously but was contained by the triple-braided leather (a selling point for mastery over larger dogs). Why hadn't Rolf or Ginny just killed him? Because then he wouldn't be barking, and I would have known something was wrong while still outside.

There was a third guest. Max Wilsoni was slumped haphazardly in my "sick chair," bleeding out from a hideous upper body bullet wound that had saturated his entire shirtfront in wet crimson. His head bobbed as though afloat in a tank and he had to fight to focus his vision. He resembled a junkie in sore need of a jolt. Even his teeth were outlined in blood. The last time I had seen him, he had been blowing Maduro smoke in my face.

Rolf crossed the Glock to capture Kingi. "Shut him up. I'd hate to shoot an animal."

"Kingi, *back-to-one!*" I shouted. The dog went instantly to his passive down-stay, head on forepaws, his eyebrows giving me a lacerating *WTF?*

My Minsky's Moment had rolled all the way home.

Options: Daisy and I could reach for our weapons and die instantly. That would have been too saccharine for her. Or, not even on our feet, we could stay where we were and listen. Because Rolf Dettrick would want to gloat; if not, we would already be collecting bullets with our flesh, the more the better, for the sake of suffering. Or...

Dammit, I was doing it again. Trying to impose logic on chaos. Waiting for the villain to declaim in a big monologue because that's what movie villains did when it was climax time. The whole enchilada— the reveal, the plot wrap to make sure the audience *gets it.* The Hollywood ending.

It didn't happen like that.

I was on my side. Daisy was crossed over me on one arm, halfway up, shielding me as she rose, her boots splaying to hoist her, her gun hand already full.

We all knew Mason Stone could *really* outrun a fireball only when he was Dash McChance, hero of *Short Fuse 2.*

All Rolf said was, "No."

Ginny's gaze flickered to Rolf as though he was nuts. That was the moment, right there. But we had all done this scene before.

New gunfire began to tear across the night, outside. People shouting. People shooting back at other people. Exterior madness to contrast interior tension.

Daisy and Ginny shot each other at exactly the same time, while I shot at Rolf Dettrick, and somebody else—I wasn't sure who—shot me.

Outside

Sheriff Bill Thompson, his chest throbbing from the slug strikes on his body armor (wind-stealers that made his head feel packed with vomit), macho'ed up enough to regroup elements of the Sylvanweir force in order to bracket the cabins. Mark Williams, a guy who resembled a 70s porn star gone to comfortable seed, brushy mustache and all, caught up, panting. He was packing a monolithic Desert Eagle pistol.

"Paul Davis has been shot," he reported.

"Killed?" said Sheriff Bill. Inhaling to give voice stabbed him with pain.

Williams nodded morosely. "Bob Baker nailed a couple of them; Ed Kane, too, I think."

"Did you see them?" asked

"Joe's gone," said Barbara Simmons, who had come in on the liberated Humvee with Joe and seen him die before dispatching his killers. "Haven't seen Ed or Dan Hall."

"Yeah," said Mick Jackson. "I saw Joe get hit. Liz and Sam are gone, too. There's a sniper in the trees out back."

"Goddammit," said Sheriff Bill. "I liked them old people. Liz never even got off a round from that howitzer of hers?"

"Sam dropped dead bang," said a saddened Mick. "Liz immediately after. But our newbie was smart enough to scoot."

"Dan Hall, come back," Sheriff Bill said into the radio. "Dan? Tell me you're out there."

"Sheriff Bill, this is Baker," came the response. *"Back of the gas station. Haven't seen Dan or Ed Kane. There's not one sniper out here—there's at least two, south of the cabins, over."*

"Mick, get back on the roof, see if you can spot 'em," said Bill.

"Maria and Don will go for the cabin," said Charles Johnson (Efram Obermeyer), meaning David and Daisy. "More defensible."

"Sheriff Bill, this is Pat Stevens, I've got three confirmed hostile downs. Joe ran over another one before they got him, over."

"Keep your radar high," Sheriff Bill sent back. "We've got snipers, copy?"

"Roger that, Sheriff Bill."

Dan Hall had still not checked in.

"Goddamn, that's what...*five* of us capped, at least?" said Will Green. "Five for one freakin guy we barely know?"

"Shut up, Will," said Charlie, sternly. "You know the code. We all do."

"That's right, Will," said Sheriff Bill. "We're family, and we go to the wire for each other. Not like out there." The sweep of his massive hand indicted the entire universe outside of Sylvanweir. "We'd all do it for you."

"That's right," said Linda Moore, mistress of the coffee shop and occasional bed-buddy to Daniel Hall, now MIA.

Will dipped his big bearded head, suddenly interested in a floorboard that he might need to treat for creaking, as master of the inn. "Just sayin. Sorry. I'm totally onboard. What do you want to do, Bill?"

"Babs, get yourself a wingman and go back out to that Humvee. Take it up the road and see if you can find their rally point. There's gotta be vans, SUVs, something parked not very far out. Mick can cover you from the roof of the inn."

"Got it," said Barbara Simmons, signaling for Charlie to accompany her. The notorious author and unknown artist made sure his AR-15 was "fed 'n ready."

"Will, Susan—with me. Mark Williams, on radio. The rest of you, we try to circle the cabins."

"Don't go out the back door," warned Mick Jackson as he hustled back to his rooftop post. "Bad guys out there."

Covered in ground sludge, his camo paint smeared with blood, Ed Kane eeled along the forest floor. He was the Crawling King Snake, just like in that John Lee Hooker song, but the voice in his head was Jim Morrison's, from the more famous cover version done by the Doors. He was moving victim to victim now, his monster riding the back of his skull and digging silver spurs into Ed's neck. *Giddyap.*

He had left captured guns in his wake, having gone completely to the blade. Instinct and the smell of death were his compass now. Surely did these guide him to where he was *supposed* to go.

"DuFleck, can you see the cabin?" came a soft voice from the brush ahead. Not even moonlit, it was a panorama of shadows against darker shadows. "Mario, this is Moses, repeat, can you see the cabin, over."

It was a lump of duff, a boulder that was speaking.

Ed's fingers closed firmly around the choils of Kolaschecks' black powder coated tac knife.

The sniper was prone and bagged, sighting a big gun on a bipod. His left elbow was perfectly positioned as a foundation point so the rifle's sling could transmit weight to the upper left arm in what was called the "triangle," to stabilize balance. Left leg extended parallel to the spine, toe pointed in. Right leg at a 45-degree angle, to control breathing, so his pulse beat could not disrupt steady sighting. Right hand grip on the rifle, firm but not tight.

Ed smothered the man's body with his own, no different from back-dooring a whore. The blade glided through the opening in the sniper's body armor, between the ribs, to pierce the heart as Ed suffocated the mouth with his blood-slicked Cordex glove. He twisted the seated blade, rupturing and calving the heart. Done.

Ed's monster had a raging erection.

Ed's monster smeared Moses Babcoq's blood on his face, adding it to his collection.

Too bad there weren't more women out here, so he could share.

Inside

Max Wilsoni realized he was checking out more with each drop of his blood that pattered to the floor. He had inhaled a great deal of cocaine to roadblock the pain, but it did not stop him from leaking. His glassy, dead-ahead stare was concerned with nothing other than David Vollmand. Ever so slowly, his numb fingers embraced his pistol, also shiny with his own blood, and the gun began to rise in supertime slo-mo, its hammer at full cock.

That was when it all tipped over. Daisy, Rolf, Ginny, David and Max were each a spinning plate in a circus act, gravitationally interdependent. One fall causes all to fall, breaking everything, and it was too clear to David that Max was going to skew and drop first.

Max's trigger lag was the microsecond Daisy needed to draw clear, and Ginny knew it.

The bore of Max's gun spit fire, thunder-clapping the air in the confines of the cabin.

Daisy brought her support arm up, causing her to fall across David as she fired.

Ginny let go with a volley that did not stop until the action on her Sig locked back. The gunfire merged into one long, continuous roar.

Rolf's big Glock joined the barrage as Ginny spun, her final round wasping into the ceiling timbers as she fell.

Daisy's sprawl jarred David's haphazard aim off Max, who sat in the chair drenched in his own blood, continuing fire even though he was no longer aiming at David, or anything. Again, like a metronome. The air blast from the close-quarter reports buffeted David's face, trying to make him shut his eyes. Daisy's spare Smith was a two-ton brick in his hand.

Instead of hitting Max, David's first and only shot strayed straight into Rolf's midsection. Daisy had only fired twice and was still on the floor, fighting to rise to hands and knees. She was hit.

So was David.

Max's sole aimed shot had stopped inside David's chest. He hadn't even felt it two seconds ago. Now it drowned his world in pain.

Ginny thrashed on the floor, her weapon forgotten, leaving a slug trail of her own blood behind Rolf.

Rolf's Glock clattered to the floorboards. His mouth was wide open. His hands were claws, crossed at the wrists in front of his stomach as he bent double. He had been gutshot back at the vet's and now he was gutshot again. His agony must have been incomparable.

Max Wilsoni's gaze had locked into infinity focus.

David tried to raise his left hand to steady his pistol but it would not obey. A wet divot had been blasted out of his biceps. A skim shot, taking meat and uncorking a lot of bloodflow, freshly frightening in its abundance.

The space swam and stank with ignited gunpowder, acrid and eye-burning; it tightened the air—no other smell is like it. Fools and romantics often cite the "smell of cordite" in bad films and worse books, even though cordite had not been manufactured for modern ammunition for over a century. Be careful to which clichés you succumb. This was no glorious, purifying gundown, the contestants' eyes blazing with righteousness as they placed bullets with marksman precision to soaring Ennio Morricone music. This was a shooting gallery of the confused and panicked; experts all, save David, yet people imbued in new terror for their very existence.

Rolf freefell to one knee hard enough to dislocate it. His expression stayed frozen in awe. He was a mighty fir, chainsawed at the root, and somebody had yelled timber. He unhinged with a leaden crash and his legs splayed.

Ginny found some interior reserve tank and stumbled wildly for the back door, yelping as her movements malfunctioned from the pain.

The front door came apart as the bolts broke free of the hasps under Sheriff Bill's boot. Others came in behind him, drawing down on Rolf, who had not budged but continued to emit a deep nasal whine.

David tried to get one leg beneath himself. He couldn't. Agony speared in and bent him.

A holocaust of warpower was zeroed on Rolf, who barely knew where he was now. Ginny was gone.

Her body bunched on the floor, Daisy lifted a hand to belay the guns. Her hand was coated in her own blood.

"Don't," she said.

If You Go Out in the Woods Tonight

Ginny Stark, the recently-minted Chase Bravo, was in bad shape. Her odd intuitive prowess had not extended to important larger details regarding her exchange of gunfire with the ex-Alma Acevedo. Having one of Daisy's flat-nosed Buffalos (the same rounds she had used at the Falcon Theater) stuck in her torso after shattering rib shards into one lung was bad enough. But Daisy had fired *twice*, with incredible speed and accuracy, the entry holes less than half an inch apart. No clean exit for either slug.

The scene replayed over and over in the proscenium arch of her mind. She had come for a simple execution and Rolf Dettrick had granted an unexpected reprieve the moment Max Wilsoni discharged his pistol, a filigreed little Cobra Patriot nine with crewelwork in 24-carat gold. As Ginny squeezed her own trigger, her brain knew she was already too far behind the curve. Then everyone joined the party. On autopilot, Ginny kept firing, target or no target, starving her Sig. Then the prime directive became *get out*, and she had to try to badger her uncooperative body toward self-preservation without the benefit of armament.

Dammit, she knew she should have forced Alma to get a shot glass. That was Ginny's signature, her flourish, and she had missed the moment. She had deviated from her ritual—the one that made all targets the same—and for the first time, she was carrying bullets inside her.

Ginny's entire left side had gone to sleep. She was exhaling pink, frothy lung blood. A jagged splinter of rib end had broken her flesh on impact. Her chest was swimming with hemorrhage. The "missile injury pattern" necessitated an emergency thoracotomy that was impossible and unattainable. Shock had sped in to fog her vision. Outgunned, flight had replaced fight, and she needed to keep moving, even as she could feel her own systems shutting down.

In all her fifty-plus gigs, Ginny had never been wounded by gunfire. She was that good, and that unlucky, because the distinction was what had given Alma—"Daisy"—the edge. Her Project Archangel sister was prepared to stop a bullet with her own body...from experience. Ginny, in the globally-expanded timeframe of her own trigger pull, had flinched infinitesimally, hesitant about eating lead on a pure, primal, animal level. It had nothing to do with duty or desire or depth of personal commitment. While she shot, some goblin in her hindbrain sabotaged her bold, steady stance by jigging her position *just so*, in order to present a negligibly smaller sight picture, because sometimes bullets could miss you by *that much*. It had thrown off Ginny's aim, and all the rest was the finish-line tear-up of betting stubs. She had hit Alma, surely. But Alma had hit her back in the same time—twice.

The entire exchange had used up less than five seconds.

She made it out the rear door of the cabin just as enemy forces breached the front. And now she had nowhere to go, in the middle of more nowhere. She crashed through underbrush no more silently than a stampeding beast. Her stealth was gone. Her life was going. At that moment, her genie wish, if it could have been granted, would have been for a extraction by chopper, a medevac back to civilization from this cruel outback. It was inelegant, this forced loss of control. It was the antithesis of all her training and skill. She had pissed herself.

"Oh, holy christ on a shitstick!" came a voice from the trees ahead of her. "Migod, girl, you're fucked up bad!"

Strong arms collected her.

338

"Jeezus, lemme look at you. Naw, that's serious, looks like you took on a killer shark and came second!"

"Help," she said, her voice effervescing. "Thank."

"Help you?" said the monster, speaking through the mouth of Ed Kane. "Girl, I been waiting to run into you *all night!*"

Mario DuFleck backed off his Viper scope and rubbed his eyes. No way he could be seeing what he *thought* he was seeing:

About fifty yards down and to his left, a man was vigorously raping a woman (apparently) prison-style (definitely). Had her bent over a tree trunk and was ramming her like a caveman trying to roll a boulder with his dick. A friendly? An enemy? Who could tell? The whole op had careened down into lunacy.

This sort of shit was deeply unprofessional.

The guy had her hair fisted up, pulling her head back all horsy, and installing a clear target in DuFleck's crosshairs.

DuFleck put a Magnum round through her head just to quell all the commotion. Mr. Love Machine sprang back as though he'd just penetrated a wall socket.

Quick as he was on the bolt, DuFleck did not get a second shot. The shadowman, cunning animal that *he* was, had already gone to ground.

"Babcoq, this is DuFleck, do you copy?"

Moses Babcoq was long gone. Operant chatter had settled to static. No, worse than static—dead air.

It was time to hare ass out of this shithole. Fall back to the rally point, twist off a beer, and find out who stood and who fell.

It was a forced march to the south of over a mile, through wicked terrain, DuFleck's progress hampered by the Barrett he could not bring himself to leave behind. The forest made haunted house noises all around him as he had to stop more than once to get his bearings. At last he used the nightscope to confirm the cluster of matte black SUVs that had brought in the teams. It was grouped in a row on the narrow shoulder of the roadway, and DuFleck could see people there, smoking, talking, waiting for new orders. But they were not CHASE soldiers, nor Wilsoni men.

It was the others, who nailed DuFleck as he walked toward them on the road.

David, After

This was a flashback. If not, my memory had been dumped into a blender on frappe. Always intriguing, to see what floats to the surface when you blend. The swirling orts and bits. The chunky stuff that can get caught between your teeth, or the vagrant details that trap themselves in the convolutions of your gray matter.

Same cabin, same convalescence easy chair—no, wait, it couldn't be, not with all the blood Max Wilsoni had voided into it. Okay; similar chair. Same Doc Taylor—Betty—hovering with that expression that said she was guarding eggs in a nest from predators. I expected to see the cabin all shot up, but that was wrong, too. Too many of the shots fired in here had hit something made out of flesh and bone.

Ceiling. Ahh, *there* it was! Max's last bullet, fired as he died. Little dark dot in the middle of the beam. Corona of fresher wood exposed to air by impact.

"Don't loll your head," said Doc Taylor. "You'll pass out."

Numb neverland of almost-pain, from good pharmaceuticals.

Time surfaced and submerged, shipwrecked but still ticking.

"This is the first time I seriously thought Sylvanweir was going to need an actual hospital," said Doc Taylor. "I've got enough dug-out bullets to braize together some sort of monument. People really need to learn to stop getting shot all the time."

"Daisy," I said.

"You mean Maria. She's right here, in the bedroom. She got hit bad but she'll live. The woman she shot, not so good. Will Green found her in the woods. A wolf, or several, had been chewing on her, post-mortem. She had been shot in the head *after* Maria shot her, by one of her own guys, they say. What a mess."

"Rolf." Aspects of the room presented themselves in colors not found in nature; I became aware that very possibly I was dreaming, or hallucinating, or perhaps simply waiting out the *sequence*.

The Minsky's chorus line had finally taken a break from kicking me in the head. Usually, breaks for dancers are infamously short.

"I presume you mean the fellow you shot in the breadbasket," said Doc Taylor, unrolling gauze. She could have been marinating a steak just below my sightline. Something juicy and bloody. Speckles of red wine on her clothing. Garlic and Worcestershire flecks; had to be. My stomach tried to heave.

"None of that," she cautioned. "No contractions, clenches, or violent movements for you. Hear me now: no fornicating. You could blow my artful stitching work." She smiled. "Sheriff Bill can give you the catch-up, later. You're high as a kite right now, and I probably look like some sex goddess to you."

"I love you," I said.

"No love allowed. You get an erection, it'll suck all the blood out of your brain and you'll die."

Something about her manner suggested she might be joking. Betty Taylor truly had lovely eyes. A vital, living blue, not arctic or metallic.

"Where's the dog?"

"Working. Since you're out of commission we had to use what we've got. Are you *sure* that dog wasn't hazard trained? Because Sheriff Bill used him as a cadaver dog—you know, to sniff out bodies? That puppy of yours went right to source, multiple times. Helped us clean up."

"How bad?"

Doc Taylor's gaze flattened. "Joe Anderson. Paul Davis. Poor old Sam and Liz, and Dan Hall, you know about. Carol Peterson was one of the last. Their rear element tried to pull out and she got surrounded. She took two of them with her, though. Brave lady."

"I didn't know Carol." This felt ineffably sad, that Carol Peterson and I had never met, or even exchanged meaningless cordialities. I wondered what her real name had been; how her story had gone.

"Paul was worst of all," she said. "Turns out Sheriff Bill shot him by accident. Bill's still beating himself up over it."

Paul Davis was the fellow who felt the invasion was my fault. He had almost braced me back at the inn, then backed down. Good man in battle—he knew which fights to pick, and had cut me slack. Without knowing him, either, I felt sorry for his death.

Sylvanweir had rallied to protect us, and lost at least six of its own. I had never experienced that kind of solidarity in my life, ever. Afterward, Sylvanweir had not lynched me in the lobby of the inn or run my nasty ass out of town on a rail. That whole expression suggests trains, but it came from Colonial times. It was the stage that usually followed tarring and feathering, which was exactly as horrible as you are imagining, especially considering *hot* tar. The "rail" was a fence rail or narrow post which you were made to straddle, usually naked (except for the tar and feathers) as your fellow citizens hoisted you high and joggled you as roughly as they could en route to dumping you at the town limits. Crotch damage was significant, and probably intentional.

I was still here. So were Daisy and Kingi. We were all alive.

My body wanted to sleep, but all my sleeping brain could do was replay old tapes. Wait long enough, and the format becomes obsolete, and everyone forgets...except you.

Sheriff Bill held his sheriff hat in his big sheriff hand. I had no idea whether he'd ever been in law enforcement for real.

"Your boy Dettrick?" he said, pacing and drinking Mountain Dew. "What a crackup. He asked if he could live here."

His movements were tender, even for such a large man. He was nursing some hurt.

I searched his expression for the punchline. "You didn't," I said.

Sheriff Bill released a chuckle that dove into a cough. "We don't let just *anybody* in here. But like good Americans, we were able to come to an arrangement. We made a deal."

"A deal..."

"Sylvanweir is a no-fly zone for CHASE." Yeah, Bill would have known about CHASE from Daisy. "Off limits, forever, no exceptions."

"What did Rolf get?"

"He got to live."

Wonderful. In less time than it took to bulk-CC an email, Daisy and I would be back on a generalized, kill-on-sight hit list.

"I know what you're thinking," said Sheriff Bill. "But you and Maria are part of the deal. 'The war stops here,' Dettrick said. Guess he thought he'd paid enough."

The old format had become obsolete. The new story had erased its predecessor. The new boss sat at the desk of the old boss...whom I had killed. I had helped pry Daisy out of obscurity and she had proven too much trouble to kill for the sake of old grudges. Augustus Wilsoni had no interest in pursuing some vendetta thought up by his idiot sibling, the wrongness of which had proven out in Max's death and the elimination of a bunch of old-guard tough guys who were holdovers from the outmoded regime, the gangster-think that flung everyone down the *Scarface* hole, as in Al Pacino, as in the zombie flicks that stop only when everybody is dead. Augustus did not feel his family blood howling for revenge the way Max had pretended to; he was a businessman... one seeking a way to deactivate his younger brother in family matters without having to pull the trigger on him personally, as it turned out. He was in the same position as Rolf Dettrick. Both were in charge now, determined to distinguish their dynasties by not repeating the mistakes of the past. They owed each other, in point of fact, which left the door wide open for the best kind of barter—the kind where both sides call it even.

Which left me bare-assed to the wind, with no guarantees. Which left me looking over my shoulder for the rest of my life, a quivering case-study in total paranoia realized, if I ever left Sylvanweir...or even if I stayed.

In the movies, when a character makes a joking reference to outrunning a fireball in the first act, he generally has to outrun a real explosion by the third act. No such closure, here. But in a metaphorical sense I had been outrunning a fireball for, well, *months*, now.

If Sheriff Bill spoke truthfully, and there was nothing to fear, that left the only alternative that was more dismaying: to return to some kind of mundane life, to sink back into the masses, and not be special any more.

Frankly, I could have died at that moment and been satisfied.

The day came when Daisy and I had mended to the point we were reasonably mobile, not so much whole as reconstructed.

A new face appeared in Sylvanweir, one Anthony Clark. In the weeks that followed came a second, Dorothy Scott. I was no longer the newbie.

Ed Kane, the new gas station guy, put me to work splitting rails, which was superior sweatwork for tone.

No killers came in the night.

Daisy and I had made love as best we could manage. The finality was palpable and she finally said, "I can't stay."

Silly of me, to think we'd spend the rest of our days changing each other's bandages.

"You can't go back out there," I said, knowing how lame it sounded. "Where would you go? Back to Hood? Cap off Rolf? For what?"

She was an assassin. For better or worse, it was her calling. And since the Invasion of Sylvanweir (as we came to call it), she had been running in neutral, using *up* time instead of using it. The excuse was recovery, and we could not stop our bodies from repairing, and so her time had come.

She held my head in her hands.

"God, you are such a dear," she said. "You bought the fantasy. You really did. But that fantasy doesn't exist. You made it up. There's just me. And *I* made me up."

She would take her leave that night, silently, while I was asleep, and I would never see her again.

Falcon

Rolf Dettrick reviewed his resurrected self in the mirror. Still more steel-gray than white wool, in his hair.

Six more months in a wheelchair, to accommodate his drainage bags and the fractured leg he had won in Sylvanweir. That time would cross his next birthday, his thirty-sixth. As an organization, CHASE was older than he was.

That was the problem, he realized. That was the solution. And he never would have had the epiphany without Chase Lima, a.k.a Lily Tomario, a.k.a. Alma Acevedo, a.k.a. Daisy. It was time to change the game itself, not the players.

Rolf consulted CHASE's primary financiers and power conduits. He presented a 104-page brief complete with flow charts. The suits and uniforms had paid attention. To them, Rolf was still a young man.

And now Rolf's finger hovered over a control key at James Smith's old glass-topped terminal. He had to be sure. There was no TAKE IT BACK key. He lingered over his decision, knowing there was absolutely no better way he could be using his time. That was rare: the realization that something momentous was happening in the moment, not afterward. It needed to be savored.

The late Mindy Zayden, the former Chase Foxtrot, had been right about one thing before Rolf had murdered her:

"The winds of change are gonna blow harsh and fierce. You and me, we're not obsolete equipment; we're seasoned pros. Do you want to wait for a guy like Smith to retire you?"

A wild card named David Vollmand had changed all that.

Too bad about Mindy. Too bad about Ginny Stark, too.

Rolf pushed SEND.

The new organization was called FALCON.

Present Tense

So I'm watching this movie called *High Speed Chase*, about a he and she on the run from shadow ops, where the main guy outwits a super-computer with a syllogism, somehow causing it to blow up. He & She have that Identikit look—He shaved and stubbled, She implanted and painted; both projecting that bland beauty that stamps them as this year's generic ideal. Without quips they have no personality beyond their "type." He & She sashay away in long shot, bowed but not broken, presumably to fuck their brains out now that they've "won" (finger quotes) by exposing the Big Bad Conspiracy during a conveniently live national television feed, during which they got pardoned by no less than the Prez himself.

Lies, humbug, bullshit.

I am back at Starburst Post, working my old job.

The excavation of bullets from my body by Doc Taylor in Sylvanweir has receded to a mushy and stilted memory, as though glimpsed out of order through a dirty aquarium.

I live in an unremarkable tract home, deeper in the Valley, because it has a generous yard that Kingi can run around like a berserk loon, chasing birds, woofing at nonexistent monsters, and augmenting his poop collection—it was something I had promised him. We go for long walks on hiking trails worn into the backside of undeveloped mountains. I read up on German Shepherds and learned the trait called "intelligent

David J. Schow

disobedience," by which Kingi had saved my life at the vet's office, what seems like a very long time ago.

No one is hunting either of us.

My name is still David Vollmand.

I stayed in Sylvanweir for several months following the "incident," as Sheriff Bill preferred to call it. Three weeks after Daisy left, I bid Sylvanweir adieu when it finally sank in that she was never coming back.

When I felt better and became more mobile, I visited the secret gravesite of Sylvanweir's dead. The enemy casualties of the action, numbering more than thirty CHASE and Wilsoni operatives, had been disposed of elsewhere, scattered throughout the uncharted wilderness, now dead unknowns. Ed Kane and Rob Baker had stacked corpses in their trusty pickup trucks like cordwood, gone out full and returned empty. Ed also disposed of the non-indigenous vehicles.

During this interim period, while I was still chopping wood for Ed Kane, Ed handed me a postcard addressed to Donald Martin, care of general delivery in Pine Cove, where there was a drop box for the collection of wayward snail mail. Rob Baker was the resident in charge of this infrequent and touchy form of communication. Sometimes, certain unassuming flecks and jots of outgoing mail had to be safely dispatched—such as Efram Obermeyer's rare messages to the rest of his family. His daughters were almost adults, now. Even more rarely, mail came back—coded, unassuming, superficially dull, dull, dull, so as not to encourage any notice of its passage. Rob collected the item and passed it to Ed, who gave it to me.

Nice guy, Ed Kane.

Fancy that—an actual piece of hand-to-hand mail with real Earthling writing on one side, no chips, no codes, no animation, no e-ddresses. The picture side featured Historic New Jersey (a night photo of the 1719 William Trent House). The postmark was from Trenton, four weeks earlier. On the message side of the card there was a single line written in block letters:

350

THE CHASE IS OVER, it read.

Had Rolf Dettrick been killed, deposed, replaced? Did she mean CHASE itself no longer existed? All I knew was that following the events at Sylvanweir, the crime consortium in Florida headed by Augustus Wilsoni had been placated in the matter of Max Wilsoni and a man Max sought for vendetta, mistakenly identified as David Vollmand. After much inquiry and loss of resources, it was determined on an official level that I was *not* the guy they were looking for. That had to have been Rolf Dettrick's doing.

Short version: I had no idea. My speculations were still trying to impose order on chaos.

Maybe the card wasn't even from Daisy.

There's a reason they call it a "crush." Youth is loud and the world goes on.

I tried every number, every email contact, all encryption levels. Tried blind guesswork. Tried to play Sherlock, to dope out the most obscure clue...which was not there. Nothing came back. Even the old online yearbook stuff from San Andres High School had evaporated, or rather, been subtly amended to exclude any mention of a Dalia Villareal, "Daisy" to her circle.

One user fail of the Internet is that viewers misinterpret the images they see on a screen as a kind of catalogue of their wants and desires. As though they can *have* any of the things they see, and the only real choice is selection, hence, "browsing." If most of your life is digital vapor instead of hard copy reality, reconsider your life, because it may not exist.

So far I have four guns stashed around my house—a Sig, one of Daisy's .45 Smiths, a Charter Arms .44 Bulldog, and an unpapered Mossberg.

The tale that made the rounds at Starburst Post was that I had experienced some sort of nervous breakdown, but was all better now—the kind of unsupported story that self-nourishes on the human mind's talent for re-sculpting incomplete facts into a palatable narrative. The faintest suggestion of any mental hiccup—indeed, any incapacity attached to the word "mental" at all—will drop both friends and acquaintances from your Exmas list, because they still believe intellectual dysfunction to be contagious, no differently than 14th Century hod carriers. I got the feeling that even Conchita, Starburst's warrior of reception, had dashed for the hand sanitizer as soon as she welcomed me back.

There was a FedEx envelope awaiting me at work. It contained refreshed ID (cards, licenses, passport) and a helpful, handy cheat sheet to cover my recent fall from the grid of human events. The cover story—and it was a good one—had me assisting the CIA in a zipped-lip investigation, and there were contacts for anyone who doubted my legitimacy to call. The package also contained $50,000 in cash. More of Rolf Dettrick's doing.

Unless...

Unless I had been given my life-packet back, whole and secure, sorry for the trouble, best wishes...in order to lure Daisy into the open once more. But that wasn't going to happen, even though I desperately wanted it to. Daisy made sure that could never happen again.

And while I understood, I could not accept her gift. So I accepted Rolf's.

Most people perceive themselves as passengers on a train, trapped there, staring out the windows at a world that speeds past their view, afraid to jump from the train—it's unstoppable—because, well, you know, you might be hurt or inconvenienced. Better to just ride the train and not cause any ruckus. And when you arrive at your destination, you're dead. Most people, even ordinary people, have this little hope, and essentially spend their lives waiting to die.

Hope drives life.

Not everyone is born with the capacity to love, like some kind of factory issue. Instead, Daisy had memory and invention. Each new person she became did not bear the burdens or obligations of the previous persona.

Every day I search, leaving digital footprints everywhere. Nothing of any interest ever zaps back. I can't muster much enthusiasm for online pursuits, not any more. This world makes you obsolete by the time you pass thirty-five, the age at which Mozart died. We've looped all the way 'round to our own pre-industrial period, where thirty-five years was considered longevity. We console ourselves with the idea that we are the last flame-tenders of our own vanishing antiquity.

Maybe I should become a librarian.

Acknowledgements

The Big Crush is the third book in a rough and unofficial trilogy of modern hardboiled stories set in Los Angeles, following *Internecine* and *Upgunned*. It is a sequel to neither; the loose idea was more like these three stories could be taking place at about the same time in the same city (the books can be read in any order and share a few common minor characters, as well). The concerns of the novel at hand, you'll notice, are set for the most part in the San Fernando Valley. It was interesting to experiment with ways books could be linked without having to resort to that scourge of modern crime fiction, the continuing character.

David Vollmand's rumination on conspiracy theory (p. 265) is drawn from Stephen Johnson's book *Silent Steel: The Mysterious Death of the Nuclear Attack Sub USS Scorpion* (Wiley & Sons, 2006). The citation of chaos cinema (page 267) is adapted from Matthias Stork's eponymous three-part video essay as run on the *Press Play* website (August, 2011). I shoplifted the "no fair" observation (p. 41) from my brother-in-arms, Michael Marshall Smith.

Due diligence demands I acknowledge the work of my betters, especially John Farris (for *The Fury*, in particular), James Crumley, and Rod Whitaker's pseudonymous novels about people named Hemlock and Hel.

David J. Schow

Credit also goes out to the Los Angeles Police K9 Fund, the Secret DJS Gun Lore Squad, and an old amigo, Darrell Huish, for providing a critical spark, completely inadvertently.

I can never thank my stalwart Subterranean crew enough, and you need to know that Bill Schafer, Geralyn Lance, Yanni Kuznia, Gail Cross & Gwenda Bond allow me to mess about with layout and design to an excruciating degree.

I also need to praise the madman members of Firesign Theatre during its glory days—Phil Austin, the late Peter Bergman, David Ossman and Philip Proctor—for many well-timed hours of aural (and deeply pollutive) gymnastics. They inspired Vollmand's "Minsky's Moment."

The stupendous Kerry Fitzmaurice is reading this right now, and knows I cite her with love—as always.

Our novel mascot is Muggsy—as always.

"Early adopter" and hardboiled brother Duane Swierczynski played a critical role in the process of getting this novel into *your* hot little hands, so thank him profusely and buy his books, please.

— **DJS** / 31 October 2018

356

To the memory of the man
variously known as:
Jean-Paul Morin
Nicholas Seare
Trevanian
Rodney Whitaker

All other characters and organizations
in this book lack any basis in reality—
although some of them do not realize that.